Apprenticeships

APPRENTICESHIPS

THE *BILDUNGSROMAN* FROM GOETHE TO SANTAYANA

BY

THOMAS L. JEFFERS

APPRENTICESHIPS
© Thomas L. Jeffers, 2005.

First published in 2005 by
PALGRAVE MACMILLAN™
175 Fifth Avenue, New York, N.Y. 10010 and
Houndmills, Basingstoke, Hampshire, England RG21 6XS
Companies and representatives throughout the world.

PALGRAVE MACMILLAN is the global academic imprint of the Palgrave Macmillan division of St. Martin's Press, LLC and of Palgrave Macmillan Ltd. Macmillan® is a registered trademark in the United States, United Kingdom and other countries. Palgrave is a registered trademark in the European Union and other countries.

ISBN 1–4039–6607–9

Library of Congress Cataloging-in-Publication Data

Jeffers, Thomas L., 1946–
    Apprenticeships : the Bildungsroman from Goethe to Santayana / Thomas L. Jeffers.
        p. cm.
    Includes bibliographical references and index.
    ISBN 1–4039–6607–9 (alk. paper)
        1. Bildungsromans—History and criticism. I. Title.

PN3448.B54J44 2005
809.3'9353—dc22   2004059990

A catalogue record for this book is available from the British Library.

Design by Newgen Imaging Systems (P) Ltd., Chennai, India.

First edition: April 2005

10 9 8 7 6 5 4 3 2 1

Printed in the United States of America.

In Memoriam, C.E.J. (1915–1975)

Contents

Acknowledgments

Early, often very different, versions of some sections of this book have appeared elsewhere as " 'We children were the in-betweens': Character (De)Formation in *Sons and Lovers*," *Texas Studies in Literature and Language* 43 (Summer 2000): 290–313; "Lawrence, *Sons and Lovers*, and the End of Sex," *The Hudson Review* 52 (Summer 1999): 191–204; "Forster's *The Longest Journey* and the Idea of Apprenticeship," *Texas Studies in Literature and Language* 30 (Summer 1988): 179–97; "Forms of Misprision: The Early- and Mid-Victorian Reception of Goethe's *Bildungsidee*," *University of Toronto Quarterly* 57 (Summer 1988): 501–15; and "Maisie's Moral Sense: Finding Out for Herself," *Nineteenth-Century Fiction* 34 (1979): 154–72. I thank the editors for permission to reprint this material.

I'm grateful also for a research year, too long ago, granted by the Harvard-Mellon Fellowship Program, and lately to my colleague and friend Milton Bates, who encouraged me to return to this project and vetted chapters as I wrote and revised them. The work was in many ways easier because my sons, Matthew and Adam, continuing their own apprenticeships, were off to college. To them, and to their mother and my wife, Pauli, I owe profound thanks.

Prologue

The German critic Walter Benjamin (1892–1940) once noted that the story, a short work descending from the fairy tales and fables of the oral tradition, typically offers us "counsel"—a moral, some practical advice, a proverb, or a maxim—which we can use in the conduct of our own lives. The novel, a long work dependent on print culture, rather more ambitiously tenders us "the meaning of life." Such a meaning, not reached until, and invariably summed up by, the moment of the hero's death, transcends any particular dilemma that counsel might give a solution to. A solution may be repeatable: the dilemma can come up again, and the principle underlying the solution—for example, that the gods favor a younger brother's risk-taking as often as they favor an elder brother's prudence—can have a validity for sisters as well as brothers, black folk as well as white, and so on. But a statement about the meaning of life takes an exceptionally long view, covering not only the hero's lifetime but also the lifetimes of people who resemble him. Further, the long view can in religious epochs go beyond temporality—the tick-tock of this world—to guess at the soul's condition in the eternal silence of the next.

All of which was beginning to sound quaint even in 1936, when in "The Storyteller" Benjamin was introducing the Russian Nikolai Leskov's tales to a German readership. As he fretted in another famous essay, an age of mechanical reproduction had little interest in the story's counsel or the novel's vision, partly because print was giving way to other media (phonographic, photographic, cinematic, etc.) and partly because the old beliefs about morality (risk-taking versus prudence, say) and eternality (which sort the divine favors) seemed as questionable as everything people had thought about military strategy, economics, diplomacy, and the value of the individual back before the assassination of Archduke Ferdinand in Sarajevo, and all the woe that followed. The Great War had literally and figuratively exploded the lot, and for a time both story and novel, in their traditional forms anyway, seemed as evolutionarily challenged as the cavalry charge, *laissez-faire* capitalism, balance-of-power political science, and the idea of the warrior champion.[1] Looking back, of course, we can see that *non*-traditional forms of narrative were emerging from the war with a brilliance that, if unable to command the nineteenth-century writers' large audiences (Charles Dickens and Fyodor Dostoevsky did not have to compete with the movies), was certainly able to represent the social and psychological realities of a new epoch. "On or about December 1910 human character changed," as Virginia Woolf histrionically put it—by August 1914 her contemporaries understood what she meant—and novels such as D. H. Lawrence's *Women in Love*, Marcel Proust's *In Search of Lost Time*, James Joyce's *Ulysses*, Thomas Mann's *The Magic Mountain*, F. Scott Fitzgerald's *The Great Gatsby*, or her own *To the Lighthouse* are evidence that writers with the requisite genius could yet bring us "news" of the event.

The narrative experiments of these high modernists between the world wars provoked some eminent scholars to trace the history of storytelling, and especially the novel, in order to understand where the modernists had come from. The greatest of these scholarly histories is undoubtedly Eric Auerbach's *Mimesis* (1946), written during World War II in Istanbul, but for my present purpose the most suggestive history—or sketch toward a history—is by the Russian critic M. M. Bakhtin (1895–1975). Equating "novel" with long narrative, he posits three important kinds—the novel of ordeal, the biographical novel, the family novel—that culminated in a fourth, the *Bildungsroman* or novel of self-cultivation, which is the subject of this study. The novel of ordeal derives from those epics of Gilgamesh, Achilles, Odysseus, or Aeneas, which, through rigorous tests, seek to determine whether the hero qualifies as a conqueror, lawmaker, lover, artistic genius, immoralist, or emancipator of an oppressed group. Nineteenth-century novels such as Stendhal's *Red and Black*, Balzac's *Lost Illusions*, Dostoevsky's *Crime and Punishment*, and George Meredith's *The Ordeal of Richard Feverel* are all of this kind. The biographical novel, descending from medieval saints' lives, may be instanced by Daniel Defoe's *Robinson Crusoe* or *Moll Flanders* or Samuel Richardson's *Pamela* or *Clarissa*, all careful to give the appearance of a tale grounded in what Woolf would call the "granite" of fact, but embellished and colored by the "rainbow" of art. In the later eighteenth century, the biographical merges with the family novel, of which Henry Fielding's *Tom Jones* or Christoph Martin Wieland's *The History of Agathon* are prototypes. Here the hero's life is situated in the context of the lives of parents, siblings, relatives, and wider community, the plot often leading to the formation of a family of his or her own. The heroes of the biographical or family novel are not mere "moving points," as they are in the travel or picaresque novel (another, less interesting kind), nor, like the hero of ordeal, are they just passing through a series of tests. They strive "for actual results," by which Bakhtin means some form of happiness, satisfaction, or maturity. Only, in their quest for results, these heroes don't undergo any important changes: even after conversions—Augustine's being the inescapable model—they remain themselves, only more so. Hence the breakthrough represented by the *Bildungsroman*, which was created in the second half of the eighteenth century. Its crucial theme is precisely change—physical, psychological, moral. The hero is no longer "*ready-made*" and, through all his shifts in fortune or social position, stable. He is what Bakhtin calls "the image of *man in the process of becoming*," whether through an idealized "idyllic time"—a sort of hypostatized Seven Ages of Man from the "Mewling and puking" infant to the youth "Seeking the bubble reputation" and so on—or through actual historical time. In the event-racked revolutionary years of the late eighteenth century, the emergence of the hero's character increasingly mirrored the emergence—socially, economically, politically, ideationally—of the world around him.[2]

The development of the *Bildungsroman* coincided with that of a particular educational ideal, articulated in France by Jean-Jacques Rousseau's *Émile* and in Germany by Friedrich Schiller's *Aesthetic Education*. Rousseau helped Europe realize that children were not miniature adults but creatures with their own peculiar needs and capacities, which parents and teachers had to honor. Schiller concentrated on how, in growing up, a child's needs and capacities might be shaped and directed. He thought of *Bildung* as the nurturing of an individual's many-sided potential—the development of the *uomo universale* (universal man: the Italian phrase bespoke the German adoration of Renaissance achievement).[3] His great friend Johann Wolfgang von Goethe, for his part, was more realistic. True, he had as a young man written to Johann Gottfried Herder of the importance of all-round, harmonious self-mastery, which he likened to Pindar's charioteer guiding his four horses in rhythm toward the goal. True, he himself had gone a long way toward becoming a *uomo universale*.[4] But he recognized that the achievements of modern civilization depended on specialization, his own being the writing of literary German, in which he had trained himself as he had not trained in drawing, building, or bureaucratic administration. Accordingly he gave his apprentice hero Wilhelm Meister the specific training, first in estate management and then in medicine, that his sentimental hero Werther had longed for but been denied. Only thus could Schiller's "aesthetic" sensibility—the individual's interest in all-roundedness—contribute to the common good. The desired universality would have to be attained through the aggregate of differentiated specialties—baker's work supplementing butcher's, builder's supplementing architect's, and so on.

Seen in the context of European history, this German humanism, culminating in eighteenth-century Weimar, appears as a late and largely fruitless flowering—"a purely intellectual preparation," in Georg Lukàcs' terms, "for a democratic revolution which never materialized, which never transformed the social structure as in France and England" (*Essays on Thomas Mann*, 95). Forced by his own political powerlessness to accommodate himself to the imperial state or principality, the German burgher had a worrisome tendency to confine his attention to the Schillerian self, and to let the organized Goethean aggregate go its own way. Caesar could render unto himself. Even Goethe, after all, had too often neglected Caesar's legitimate claims. In Part Two of his masterpiece *Faust*, the hero's quest for fresh opportunities to exploit his devil-heightened genius ultimately settles on a civil-engineering project in Holland, and Goethe's focus is less on the dike than on the complexly interesting mind of the man who designs it. In the *Wilhelm Meister* series, from the *Lehrjahre* (1795–1796) to the *Wanderjahre* (1829), the hero's several vocations seem but a quick answer to the "get a job" imperative. Politics, economics, sociology, and so on were important, yes, but Goethe's deeper preoccupations lay in questions about eros, parental responsibility, and freedom of choice.

Nevertheless, under his firm hand, *Wilhelm Meisters Lehrjahre* (*Wilhelm Meister's Apprenticeship*), like *Faust* (1808, 1832), maintains some kind of balance—call it 60/40—between inward and outward concerns. In the *Bildungsromane* that in Germany came after *Wilhelm Meister*, the ratio slipped to 70/30 or worse, as novelists fixed their attention ever more burningly, and resignedly, on the self: their heroes were wonderfully sensitive to ethico-religious matters, and appallingly obtuse to economic, political, and military matters, all emanating from the material power that protected, as well as exploited, their inwardness. Leaving material power to nobles, bureaucrats, and officers—the hereditary classes that for centuries had governed the nation—the burgher rarely tried, and was in any event never allowed, to become a self-governing citizen (or, as the West-facing liberal dissenters preferred to say, *citoyen*). As one such dissenter, Thomas Mann, later put it, the burgher complacently assumed that politics was a Machiavellian realm of "falsehood, murder, deceit, and violence," an attitude that by 1933 meant that he didn't want to think about politics at all. He wanted folk fairy tales, which Benjamin claimed was what fascism, with its "aestheticized" politics, offered.[5] Concentrated inward, most German novelists, like the Danish philosopher Søren Kierkegaard, may powerfully have equated truth and subjectivity, but their neglect of objectivity—the problem of how to arrange the human condition humanely—finally permitted the apotheosis of the impersonal state, and the isolation and submersion of the individual. In *Buddenbrooks*, *The Magic Mountain*, and *Doctor Faustus*, Mann, Goethe's twentieth-century successor, directed the art of fiction to tell this German story—to anatomize the nation's soul and state. His was a creative effort both plainly dangerous (the Nazis drove him into exile and almost certainly would have killed him if he had stayed home) and, it seemed amidst the rubble of World War II, utterly vain with regard to Germany itself. A darkness made visible by the luminous works of Goethe and Mann, but a darkness just the same.

In England and America the history of politics and the novel has been brighter. The idea of *Bildung* was translated by Thomas Carlyle, Ralph Waldo Emerson, Matthew Arnold, J. S. Mill, and Walter Pater into the idea of Culture, an idea concurrently and subsequently realized in fiction by Dickens, William Makepeace Thackeray, George Eliot, Meredith, Henry James, and (in the next century) by E. M. Forster, Theodore Dreiser, Woolf, George Santayana, Saul Bellow, Margaret Drabble, and other less remarkable authors. The liberal Anglo-American tradition—the relative openness and fluidity of the society, the Protestant interest in and respect for personal differences, the unfolding of the biographical and the family novel—helped these writers not only to sustain the Weimar classicists' case for the cultivation of the individual, but also to understand the problems of such cultivation in the context of vocation, courtship, and parent–child relations—always in crisis perhaps (no crisis, no novel), but always susceptible to analysis and to some measure of melioration. Among Anglo-American writers, soul-craft and statecraft, God and Caesar, inward and outward, have on average been kept in 50/50 balance. This equipoise may have made them (and us) less spiritually profound than Friedrich Hölderlin, Friedrich Nietzsche, or Rainer Maria Rilke in the Teutonic tradition, and less politically subtle and sage than Virgil, Dante, or Stendhal in the Latin. Still, we have reason to rejoice in the temperate, sensible-for-all-seasons nature of the *Bildungsromane* of the mixed Teutonic–Latin tradition that is our own—*Bildungsromane* that in telling ways epitomize our fiction as such. To go through such a novel is an occasion not only for a reader's individual cultivation (his vicarious growing up, or re-growing up) but for a generation of readers' collective cultivation (the coming of age of what Samuel Taylor Coleridge called "the clerisy," or simply the intellectuals, within a society). When the educated members of a generation read the early printings of *Wilhelm Meister* or Dickens's *David Copperfield*, for instance, their consciousness and conscience were, in the authentic Joycean sense, "forged." The novelist in question had helped to acculturate them, and if later readers make a good-faith effort, they will find that the novelist can acculturate *them*.

I don't carry the story of the German tradition of self-cultivation beyond *Wilhelm Meister*, since a generation ago W. H. Bruford and Michael Beddow, in brilliant complementary critiques, and most recently Michael Minden, with his gender-studies approach stressing themes of incest and inheritance from the Goethean to the Freudian era, have done so already. Within the Anglo-American tradition, preemption is a smaller problem, sometimes, as on Forster's *The Longest Journey* or Santayana's *The Last Puritan*, because very little outstanding criticism has ever been offered; sometimes, as on *Copperfield* or Lawrence's *Sons and Lovers*, because much of what over the last few decades has been offered in spades seems to me, whether as critic or teacher, so unhelpful. Jerome Buckley's *Season of Youth* (1974) offers a reliable definition of the *Bildungsroman* as a subgenre, but it ranges so widely that its treatment of individual novels is too thin, and in any case was even in 1974 too regardless of theory to seize the audience that could truly have profited from the author's good sense. Franco Moretti's *The Way of the World* (1987) is, if anything, over-regardful of theory, mostly Marxist, but his temperament is such that a love for Stendhal seems to exclude even a tolerance for Dickens. The upshot is, again, a study that makes Gallic readers glad to be Gallic but that makes Anglo-American readers feel, at best, defensive. I could not find a book about the *Bildungsroman* sufficiently conversant with theory to get at least a hearing from readers wedded to this -ism or that, yet also grounded, as Buckley was, in the immediate, pre-theoretic experience of encountering a work of art. Therefore I have written it myself, preferring, when I have had to choose, the report of my immediate experience over any theorizing afterthoughts. Which is to say I endorse Robert Warshow's dictum: "at the center of all truly successful criticism there is always a man reading a book, a man looking at a picture, a man watching a movie . . . and the critic must acknowledge that he is that man."[6]

In the face of the theory explosion of the past quarter century and the night-follows-dusk decay of literary studies, it is tempting to turn away altogether and just be "that man," stubbornly intent on the book, the picture, the movie. But pedagogically, with one's best students, to turn away is to abandon hope. Many of them, finding theory opaque or irrelevant, have adopted a principled know-nothing attitude, promising to read *Emma*, *Middlemarch*, or *Anna Karenina* every five years, but for the nonce emigrating from "English" into law, business, or medical school—an emigration that so far has done nothing to change the minds, or even catch the attention, of the theoreticians who now run literature departments. A high-dudgeon, know-nothing rejection of theorizing *in toto* won't give such students any reason to stay with literary studies, even in spirit. So in this book I try to offer a *via-media* know-something approach, taking the theoretic terms of my argument as much as possible from the novelists themselves and their immediate contemporaries,[7] while throughout addressing that mythic and indispensable person, the common reader, with whom Dr. Johnson rejoiced to ally himself.

Chapter 1, addressed primarily to an Anglophone not German audience, is about the foundational example of the *Bildungsroman*, Goethe's *Wilhelm Meister*, to which successors, even in English, pay at least tacit homage. Here the recurring preoccupations of novels about growing up—for example, the young person's affective development, from his relations with parents to those with friends of both sexes, or the development of his particular talents, which may help him decide what sort of work he will do in the wider world—are enfleshed if not for the first time then at the crucial time, the moment of the French Revolution. The commoner Wilhelm's claim to the right of self-cultivation chimed with the Third Estate's claim to the rights of liberty, equality, and fraternity. It was a revolutionary prelude to a century of liberal reform that would benefit the representative heroes of the *Bildungsromane* that followed.

Chapter 2 goes back to the origins of the idea of *Bildung* among the Weimar classicists, describes some nineteenth-century English culture-critics' assimilation of Goethe's *Bildungsidee* or idea of self-cultivation (thus establishing the intellectual background for the five representative Anglo-American novelists I then devote my attention to), and, with Goethe's example in mind, sketches a working definition of the *Bildungsroman* as a type of fiction.

The *Bildungsheld* (hero of self-cultivation) in Chapter 3 is David Copperfield, whose "autobiography" is as central to the Anglo-American tradition as Goethe's novel is to the German. Among the several themes that Dickens explores—love, work, the common boy's assertion of the right to take himself seriously—is that boy's fatherlessness, a factor in his memorable neglected-and-abused-child nightmare, of course, and emblematic of what seems to me a crisis of paternity throughout all the novels I consider, even Goethe's. If we can again learn how to read Dickens's 1850 book, pivotal in more than just a temporal sense to nineteenth-century English civilization, then we have good prospects for a fruitful reading or rereading of the novels I have left on the shelf.[8]

Chapter 4 mainly concerns James's small heroine in *What Maisie Knew* (1897), but also reaches back to Isabel Archer in *The Portrait of a Lady* (1881). Joining these figures, we can appreciate the American master's insights into the full cycle of development from childhood to girlhood to youth and beyond—insights especially into how the aesthetic sense contributes to the moral. These characters too are orphans, literally or figuratively, and must to a large extent find out things for themselves.

In chapter 5 the motherless, fatherless hero is Rickie Elliot of Forster's *The Longest Journey* (1907), a minor classic that, though the author's personal favorite, is usually passed over in favor of his bigger-themed *Howards End* and *Passage to India*. It deserves inclusion if only because of its exploration of same-sex affection. Without being an "out" queer propagandist, as he awkwardly is in *Maurice*, Forster enables us to think about the idea of brotherhood that was *there*, subtextually, in *David Copperfield* and would be there, explicitly, in Santayana's *The Last Puritan*.

Chapter 6, about Lawrence's *Sons and Lovers* (1913), is in one sense a more normal presentment of a hero's heterosexually oriented maturation, from mother to girlfriends, but in another sense it is a presentment, normal but not normative, of his being unable to break away from his loving mother, and this because his father is at best absently present. Lawrence brings the crisis of paternity into sharp focus, and does as much as any novelist to explain its social and economic causes.

The concluding chapter picks up *The Last Puritan* (1935) partly as a project in recuperation. I think it a noble achievement, self-consciously within the line of Goethe's *Bildungsroman* and a Mann-worthy novel of ideas, that was once exceptionally popular with general readers and ought to be so again. Santayana in any event expresses the philosophical dimension of what a psychologist would call identity formation, which enables us to describe the late- or post-Christian spiritual awareness not only of Oliver Alden, the (logically) last puritan, but of the earlier *Bildungshelden* too.

My epilogue celebrates these common tyros' labors to cultivate a self in the age of liberal reform; notes the imbalance between their affective and their vocational achievements (why are they better at loving than at working?); worries, effectively

I hope, about a major reason for this imbalance, namely the modern age's problematic life-without-father; and limns a historically informed but still somewhat platonic ideal of what the next great *Bildungsroman* might look like.

It could be objected that none of the heroes of these novels is a person of color, and only Maisie and Isabel Archer are female. There are studies available on the Latino/Latina, the Asian American, the African American, the cross-culturally female, and so forth *Bildungsroman*,[9] and my own purposes have seemed ambitious enough without trying to compass those occasionally heuristic though often overspecialized and hyphenated subsets. And in any event, youthful white males have come to seem like the segment of our society that one needs to worry about, and precisely because they constitute a large segment that—often fatherless, guilt-heaped, and feeling undervalued—tests lower, goes to college less often, and gets into legal trouble more than white females do.[10] But this is a sociological aside. The fact is that females are hardly a neglected focus in the *Bildungsromane* I have chosen to analyze: in addition to my Jamesian examples, there are prepotent femininities in *Wilhelm Meister*, *Copperfield*, and *Sons and Lovers*, indeed to the point of sometimes overwhelming the masculine leads, while in *The Longest Journey* and *The Last Puritan*, admittedly more homosocial stories, women are at least not uninterestingly present.

More pertinently it is fair to ask, very sweepingly, what these particular novels tell us about the fate of *Bildung* over the past two centuries. To anticipate, I suggest that an answer looks something like this: Goethe started out to see whether the life of a bright but fairly commonplace individual made any sense. Did it have a purpose, and if so, was that purpose bestowed from without, say by nature or by nature's God, or was it generated from within, by the person's own conscious choices and instinctive impulses? Or could it in some discernible way be the product of both, as in the Protestant concept of cooperative Grace? Goethe came to believe it *was* a product of both, and so, as the idea of *Bildung* was translated into the Anglo-American tradition, did Dickens and most of his contemporaries—Dickens himself along with Thackeray and Charlotte Brontë being more confident about the intervening solicitude of nature's God than Goethe could be, while George Eliot, Meredith, and Emily Brontë were typical of writers who, like Goethe, were confident only about the fortuity-plagued but still regulated selective processes of nature itself. How to define, describe, and regard "nature itself" was of course a contested question, and most of the mentioned writers were sometimes at odds with themselves, as well as with their peers, about the "how." Not that such philosophical inconsistencies mattered on every page; the novelistic tasks of dramatizing, narrating, and summarizing, or of notating the psychological goings-on of characters, were largely identical for the theistic Dickens, the agnostic Meredith or James, and the atheistic George Eliot—and ditto, half-a-century on, for the areligious Forster and the quasi-religious Lawrence. These Edwardian and Georgian novelists, intent like their Victorian forebears on their young heroes' relations with parents, siblings, friends, lovers, and the individuated strangers beyond, are recognizably Goethean, which is to say broadly romantic, insofar as they believe that a person's life has meaning. And this meaning, even if understood only retrospectively—grasping tomorrow what one is doing today—is cocreated by that person's particular choices, conscious or un-, and by the present but ineffable power that courses through all things. Human nature, in short, is for them no mere "social construct"; it is part of what in the poverty of speech we call nature itself, which, verbal poverty notwithstanding, is no "construct" either.

This passional conviction lifts our spirits at the serene close of *The Longest Journey* and even at the otherwise somber close of *Sons and Lovers*. The petering out of the hero of *The Last Puritan* seems, however, a more modernist kind of ending; his death in an auto accident shortly after the Armistice in 1918 being graver, more absurdly sad than, for example, the "good luck to you" valediction Mann gives Hans Castorp, charging amidst the exploding shells of 1914 at the end of *The Magic Mountain*. What had discouraged Santayana was more than the Great War, awful as that was; it was the feeling that, culturally, the times were out of joint either for the many-sided development of a bright though representative American youth, or for a productive integration of his specialization (it happens to be philosophy but could as well be painting, music, poetry, etc.) with the specializations of his compatriots (the business-men, engineers, lawyers, doctors, etc.). And this because the culture, not just American but English and European, hadn't yet arrived at a new philosophical synthesis to replace the exhausted romanticism for which, as poet and novelist, Goethe had been the supreme figure, and which Dickens, Forster, and Lawrence too had variously expressed. *The Last Puritan* can then be seen to belong at the end of the *Bildungsroman* tradition, and at the end of the romantic movement of which that sort of novel had been paradigmatic.

Chapter 1

Goethe's Classical *Bildungsroman*: Mastering the Art of Living

"[E]ach reader becomes his own Wilhelm Meister, an apprentice, a traveller, on his own account; and as his understanding is large or small, will Wilhelm and the whole work be real or the contrary." Thus to the young Henry James—he was only 22—was Goethe's *Wilhelm Meister's Apprenticeship* a high example of how a novelist could allow his hero to cultivate himself with wide open eyes and ears, and thereby could prompt us, his readers, to cultivate *our*selves. The larger our understanding, the better, obviously, but a certain receptive blankness won't be amiss either. Goethe has endowed Wilhelm with such intelligence, well enhanced by the people he meets, that in most cases however smart we are when we open the book, we will be even smarter when we close it.

It isn't, of course, a question of letting Wilhelm's—or even Goethe the narrator's—ideas dictate our own, especially since the latter's are often subtilized to the point of disappearance. Some of the earliest readers indeed worried that the author hadn't been intrusive enough in labeling vice and virtue—"artistic Atheism," Novalis called it, the ought-to-be God-spokesman Goethe dangerously stepping aside to let the readers judge for themselves.[1] But that, as George Eliot correctly argued, was precisely the point, and a decided novelistic strength.[2] We are meant to first perceive the world as Wilhelm does, then entertain his ideas as imaginative possibilities, and finally formulate critical ideas for ourselves. We grow up—all over again, quite possibly—as we double the hero's apprenticeship. This would be the desired readerly response to all the *Bildungsromane* fathered by Goethe's astonishing original. James thinks such a growing-up-with-the-hero experience particularly educative for young readers, who, as he tenderly says, "feel that it behooves them to attach a meaning to life." The lesson *Wilhelm Meister* teaches is—well, less how to *take in* life's meaning than to *give* it meaning: "how the experience of life may least be wasted, and best be turned to account."[3] Which, as in the "live all you can" preachments of James's own later novels (we look at two of them), is an ultimately anti-Calvinist matter of our seeing and knowing all we can, and not letting a too ascetic morality exclude the aesthetic, intellectual, and sensual pleasures that might be got along the way. Puritan readers may, James conceded, be foolish enough to detest Goethe's "moral economy," but they will be made less foolish by having something *"great"* to argue against.[4] I endeavor to define that greatness shortly, but first some preliminaries.

Background, Synopsis, and Plan

In this study I make some minimal assumptions about readers' knowledge of the lives of the novelists, and allude occasionally to salient episodes therein, but never, I hope, without a sufficient reminder as to what, when, and why. Beyond that, I advise readers as to the best biographies and get on to my chief business, which is the reading of the novels. These are classics, and I expect that my audience will have read them, if not recently than at some point in a busy lifetime. Which, I realize, is thoroughly unfair, for it is the expectation of all the works of criticism that I value highly, and I admit that I myself haven't always read every novel, poem, or play they discuss. Therefore I have determined to offer, near the beginning of each of my discussions of a novel, a short synopsis of its plot. The Anglophone audience I am positing will almost surely know enough about my English and American authors' careers to make sense of any biographical allusions I offer, or if necessary will have easy access to the *Oxford Companion to English* [and to American] *Literature*, or other standard reference works. With Goethe, however, a brief sketch of his life up to the years of composing *Wilhelm Meister* cannot be amiss.

Goethe (1749–1832) was born into a prosperous family in Frankfurt am Main, his father a retired lawyer who loved to travel and collect art, his mother the mayor's daughter connected with the city's patriciate. His happy childhood was marked by exceptional fondness for his sister (thence for pretty girls in general), Pietistic Christianity (thence for the Bible and religious music), and puppet shows (thence for the theater). Having been tutored at home, he went at age 16 to Leipzig to study law, but was soon occupied chiefly in letting the city's Parisian glamor remedy his provincial inadequacies. He committed himself to the theater—the best plays in Europe, mostly French, could be seen in Leipzig—and to reading, under the guidance of the poet and moralist Christian Fürchtegott Gellert, books by Englishmen such as Laurence Sterne and Samuel Richardson and by Germans such as Christoph Martin Wieland the novelist and Johann Joachim Winckelmann the art historian. Goethe began in Leipzig to write on his own—songs about wine and women in the Anacreonic mode and dramas in the Rococo—but in 1768 a serious illness forced him to return to Frankfurt, where he came under the influence of his mother's devout friend, Susanna von Klettenberg, whose life would be reflected in Book VI of *Wilhelm Meister*. Once recovered, Goethe went to Strasbourg, then part of France, where under Johann Gottfried von Herder's sway he began to discover, first, the primitive roots of literature—folk songs, the Hebrew Bible, Homer, Ossian—and second, the Gothic, whether in medieval cathedrals or in the poetry of Shakespeare. Germans were seizing on Shakespeare as an elemental, nonclassical, unregulated alternative to the French tradition of Racine and Corneille, and Goethe imitated him in *Götz von Berlichingen*, a prose play about an untamed sixteenth-century baron. He also began writing

Sturm und Drang (storm and stress) verse, a mood that ostensibly colored his first novel, *Die Leiden des jungen Werthers* (*The Sorrows* [more properly, the sufferings] *of Young Werther*, 1774), which famously started a European cult of suicide, prompted not merely by lovelornness but by *Weltschmerz*, a nameless discontent with the ways of the world. The author wasn't glorifying self-destruction; on the contrary, already beginning to distance himself from Gothic darkness, he was diagnosing the romantic source of the impulse to suicide and looking for a classical corrective.

Love affairs with various women—German students used to learn their names as medieval monks learned the stations of the cross—naturally inspired the creation of *Werther*, the storm-and-stress poems, and the serious plays, *Egmont* for instance. The latter was written in 1775, the year Goethe engaged himself to a patrician's daughter, Lili Schönemann, only to break off in the autumn when he accepted the young Duke Karl August's invitation to visit Weimar. It would remain his home for the rest of his life. The duke provided him ample opportunities to develop his talents on many fronts—from superintending mining and irrigation to issuing army uniforms and directing plays—while Charlotte von Stein, the formidable wife of a court official, taught him social graces and the value of platonic feminine stimulation. Eleven privileged years even of Weimar, however, could become routine, and in 1786 Goethe stole away to Italy, where for nearly two years he deliberately severed himself from his Gothic northern past and sought the archetypal world of Magna Graecia, the Hellenized Mediterranean culture before and beneath the Christian art of Venice, Florence, and Rome. The literary fruit of this journey, in addition to one of the best travel books ever written (*Die Italienische Reise* or *The Italian Journey*, not published till 1816–1818), were supreme dramas, *Torquato Tasso* and *Iphigenie auf Tauris*, and the *Römische Elegien* (*Roman Elegies*), verses that with classic Greek sensibility fuse eroticism and aestheticism.

Upon Goethe's return to Weimar in 1788, he began living with Christiane Vulpius, daughter of a lowly bureaucrat, to whom he was utterly devoted (she bore him several children, and in 1806 he married her). He also put aside most of his administrative duties in order to devote himself to science and literature, from which he was momentarily distracted when following his duke's counterrevolutionary army into France in 1792, an experience that, as a liberal anti-Jacobin, he soon recounted in memoirs, poems, and plays. The French Revolution would concentrate the mind of all Europe during the 1790s and beyond, but the key intellectual event in Goethe's life during these years was his friendship with Friedrich Schiller, who in a letter of 1794 characterized him as a consciously naïve poet—one who began in feeling, moved to abstract reflection, and then tellingly brought reflection back to feeling. Ideas, in short, were in Goethe's poems triumphantly embodied in things—natural objects, human speech and act. At this time Goethe began revising and extending the manu-script known as *Wilhelm Meisters theatralische Sendung* (*Wilhelm Meister's Theatrical Mission*), which dates from as early as 1773 (though not discovered and printed till 1910–1911) and which had petered out in 1786. The correspondence he had with Schiller about this new novel, *Wilhelm Meister's Apprenticeship*, is one of the most brilliant exchanges in German literary history.

This, omitting the final 36 years of Goethe's life, brings us to the plot of that novel, which is an unusual joining of realism and symbolism, the characters psychologically believable yet thematically grouped, as in a fable. The son of a successful businessman,

Wilhelm is in Book I much enamored of the theater and has an affair with the actress Mariana.[5] Having gotten her pregnant, he resolves that they should run away and join an acting troupe. In Book II, shocked by what he supposes to be Mariana's unfaithfulness, he burns his literary manuscripts and tries to do his father's bidding by going into business. But a meeting with the actors Laertes and the lively, alluring Philina scotches his business career—the sort of work his friend Werner is more suited to—and, along with the tightrope dancer Mignon and the mysterious Old Harper whom he has rescued from a circus, he joins Melina's theater company. Throughout these chapters there is much serious discussion of the history and function of drama, which continues in Book III when the company takes up residence at the drafty castle of a count interested in German (as against French) plays, especially ones written by himself. The actual life of actors, plagued by envy of one another and by disdain from their aristocratic patrons, is balanced by the ideal realm of drama on the page. Jarno, Wilhelm's intellectual mentor, opens up the possibility that Shakespeare is superior even to the towering Racine. In Book IV Wilhelm's study of Shakespeare suggests first a wild-oats-sowing Prince Hal model to emulate, then more soberly a Renaissance-man Prince Hamlet model. Such abstract speculations are interrupted by concrete misfortune when the company, having left the count's castle, is attacked by marauders; Wilhelm is wounded and then nursed by a lovely Amazonian woman, whose grace makes Philina seem cheap. The marauders have actually been lying in wait for this Amazonian and her friends, and Wilhelm has in effect taken the blow for her. In any event, he and the rest of Melina's company are now absorbed into one headed by Serlo, who with his sister Aurelia is a genuine actor—a perfect interlocutor for the Hamlet-obsessed Wilhelm, and a representative type of the performer personality (authentic on stage, inauthentic off). Book V describes the company's production of *Hamlet*, with Wilhelm, starring in the title role, offering his famous interpretation during rehearsal. On opening night the Ghost is played by a stranger who so resembles Wilhelm's recently deceased father that the young man's fright is quite genuine, the performance a success. He gets drunk during the cast party and ends up in bed with Philina, with Mignon jealously witnessing outside the door. The Harper, gone insane, sets the house on fire and must be committed to an asylum. Aurelia, like Ophelia jilted and driven mad by her lover Lothario, recklessly catches cold and dies—but not before reading the consolatory *Bekenntnisse einer schönen Seele* ("Confessions of a Fair Saint" or, as I will call her, a "Beautiful Soul"), which comprise Book VI.

The first five books have been a poeticizing, symbolizing expansion of the *Sendung*, and so are sometimes called the "*Theaterroman*." Book VI was an entirely new departure, a portrait of a religio-intellectual *Bildung* that Goethe honors in cases as special as the Beautiful Soul's. Book VII brings Wilhelm to the castle of Lothario, whom he intends to charge with perfidy toward Aurelia. Lothario, however, can responsibly justify his actions, and Wilhelm must acknowledge his own bit of sexual waywardness: the dead Mariana, he finds, is the mother of his son, the three-year-old Felix. Other women whom Lothario has known—Theresa and Lydia—are introduced, enabling Wilhelm to assess the full worth of that Amazonian beauty, now revealed to be Lothario's sister Natalia. Introduced too is the *Turmgesellschaft* (Society of the Tower), a secret organization that Lothario, Jarno, and various mysterious strangers in Wilhelm's life belong to, and that has been watching over his development. His initiation *à la* Mozart's *The Magic Flute*—a promotion from apprentice to master (*Meister*)—is at hand. That is the burden of Book VIII, the final part, along with a discussion of different theories of education, the initiate's purpose in life, the freedom of the will, and, with Mignon's death and funeral (it turns out she is the Harper's daughter, conceived incestuously), the proper attitude toward mortality. Scarcely believing his luck, Wilhelm marries Natalia, and is told he must now set out on his travels—the *Wanderjahre* of Goethe's last novel (*Wilhelm Meister's Years of Wandering* or *Travels*, 1821).

Those hitherto unfamiliar with *Wilhelm Meister* now have a rough knowledge of what is in it, but I don't expect any such person to want to read it—not till I have done my best to make it interesting. Those hitherto familiar with it already know it is interesting. Reading on, for them, will be a matter of remembering just how interesting it was when they first read it, and (I hope) how interesting in new ways it might be if they were to read it again.

A word in any case about method—the important question of how we engage with and then emerge from *Wilhelm Meister*. We get some valuable hints from the first critical reading the novel had, when Schiller went through the manuscript chapter by chapter and, as I have indicated, traded letters with the novelist. Events happen to Wilhelm, Schiller says of the recast chapters, "not actually *for his sake*" but for ours. Therefore Goethe, without seeming pushy, had to be sufficiently directive to bring the resistant reader at least into dialogue with his own ideas and if possible into agreement with them.[6] Concrete, lucid presentment of things, acts, speeches, and psychological goings-on will, as always, be the literary artist's principal duty—first make us *ap*prehend, then guide us to *com*prehend Wilhelm's world. But Goethe thinks we may need help—especially if we are young and inexperienced—disengaging ourselves from Wilhelm. Hence the coaching various members of the Tower offer him in the right way of viewing art. Jarno's advice on this subject is pertinent both for Wilhelm and for us. Wilhelm suffers from the common youthful tendency to overidentify with characters in books or on stage, most famously with Hamlet, the role his theatrical friends assign him. To see himself in Hamlet, or Hamlet in himself, is to get down on all fours with people who, in Jarno's words, bring "their conscience and their morals with them to the opera; . . . [or] bethink them of their loves and hatreds in contemplating a colonnade."[7] Of course a dramatic character is human and a colonnade isn't, but an aesthetic understanding of a play requires some of the detachment an architectural critic maintains toward a colonnade, asking how it is made, where it stands in relation to earlier works, and, with regard to the human content, how particular characters differ from as well as resemble one's peculiar self. That is salutary counsel for any (but especially any young) reader's approach to *Wilhelm Meister* and its successors. The characters are humanly lifelike, yes, but they aren't altogether identical with ourselves or our neighbors, and, like operas and colonnades, they are in every case inventions—constructs made of words.[8]

Enough prolegomenon. What follows in this chapter is the consideration of five issues clearly radiating in Goethe's mind from the central project of self-cultivation:

(1) the connection between the rise of the realistic novel, in Germany as in other nations, and the rise of individualism as such—the impulse toward self-determination that, encouraged by nature itself, prompts a youth at some point to resist his parents, especially his father;

(2) the upshot of Wilhelm's particular struggle-with-father, his supposed theatrical vocation, which isn't quite as disastrous as it seems;

(3) the several channels into which women, who in youth may also strike out against their parents, direct their energies, and what Wilhelm might learn from them;

(4) the corresponding channels for men's energies, among which Wilhelm must look for models ("What will I be when I grow up?"); and

(5) the philosophically complicated dialectic between (a) what Wilhelm must accept as necessary; (b) what he can freely choose to shape this way or that; and (c) the cooperation between his self-cultivating hand and the "higher hand" cultivating us all.

Realism, Individualism, and the "Natural" Struggle of Youth with Age

Goethe wrote *Wilhelm Meister* at the end of a century that had, so to speak, invented childhood. As Philippe Ariès' landmark *Centuries of Childhood* has demonstrated, the "young person" who in the Middle Ages *had* to be folded into the adult work force—death rates, poverty, and lack of social welfare systems required it—was in the wealthier and therefore healthier Enlightenment discovered to be something other than a miniature adult: to wit, a child. And writers from John Locke to Rousseau, William Blake to William Wordsworth, endeavored to define the child's special condition, to prescribe ways to nurture and educate it properly in order to bring it successfully through adolescence into adulthood. *Wilhelm Meister* was, in Nicholas Boyle's phrase, a "supremely uncourtly"—that is, a novelistic as against poetic or expository—contribution to this discussion.[9] But what does "novelistic" mean in this context?

In the beginning it wasn't a German notion at all. The realistic novel arose in early eighteenth-century England rather than on the Continent because, among several other factors,[10] the break with Catholicism and the commercial success of its liberated middle class had produced a society that was, in Francis Jeffrey's words (reviewing Carlyle's 1824 translation of Goethe's novel), already "free, sociable, discursive, reformed, [and] familiar" in Shakespeare's time, and by Defoe's time, when the gains of the Glorious Revolution were solidifying, was even more so. The late eighteenth-century bourgeois revolution in France brought analogous benefits to *its* society, such that by the 1830s Balzac in Paris could study what Dickens could in London, namely, the several classes mingled in the fascinatingly if cruelly competitive jostle of market capitalism. Germany had no such metropolitan center, and politically it was still stretching out of the feudal chrysalis, with a working class submissive and incurious, a burgher class small and self-protective, and a nobility far removed from them both. Goethe was a burgher, with little interest in the class below him, and with only a civil servant's access to the class above. (It is often essential, by the way, to insist on the term "burgher" in order to distinguish the mid-sector of German society—merchants, officers, university-educated professionals, the handful of intellectuals who wrote books and essays, and the lower ranks of the nobility—from its counterparts in French and English society, which should respectively be called the bourgeoisie and the middle-class.) In any event, Goethe would not have found much of interest among either the workers or the nobles. They were ingrown and narrow. His precursor burgher novelists had for these reasons been able to produce only self-reflexive Shandean sports such as Georg Christoph Lichtenberg's *The Waste Books* (or *Aphorisms*, 1765–1799), or ruminative *Bildungsromane* such as Wieland's *History of Agathon* (1766–1767). Novels like Wieland's, as T. J. Reed has said, were not just creations of an age concerned with education; they were a pis aller for writers for whom the social theme was as yet impossible.[11] In a representative eighteenth-century English novel like *Tom Jones*, "the young man from the provinces" travels to London and achieves outward successes: wife, fortune, and public recognition. The Bunyanesque pilgrimage has been transposed to a secular plane. In a representative eighteenth-century German novel like *Agathon*, though Wieland granted his debt to Fielding, the pilgrimage is still to a large extent Bunyanesque. In other words, the health of the hero's soul is what counts, while only a slight nod is given to his material connections with other people or to the affairs of society at large.

While we would make a category mistake to praise *Wilhelm Meister* as "realistic" in the *Jane Eyre* or *Vanity Fair* mode—it is much more freighted than such Victorian novels with fairy tale motifs, forced coincidences, sudden deaths, paranormal sexuality, outbursts of poetry, seminar-style philosophical disquisitions, and self-reflexive meditations on *Hamlet* and aesthetics generally—the book does advance well beyond the *Agathon* model of exclusive inwardness. By yoking a Lutheran, at times even pietistic concern for the soul with an intelligent interest in its "material base," broadly conceived, Goethe creates a hybrid realism that Mr. Boyle suggestively compares to the "magic" variety recently offered by Umberto Eco, Gabriel García Márquez, or Günter Grass—or, to put it in eighteenth-century terms, he has blended Voltairean *conte*, Johnsonian fable, and Smollettian travelogue (Boyle, 2.424, 240). He does in any event a better job than he had in the *Theatrical Mission* of presenting the quiddities of mid-century burgherly life and, importantly, of distancing Wilhelm's post-adolescent story from his own by pushing him *beyond* the said mission. In the *Lehrjahre*, more specifically, Goethe integrates Wilhelm's life with that of his son Felix and with the activities of the Tower, and in the *Wanderjahre* (begun in 1807, published in 1821 and, much expanded, in 1829, and, largely ignored by Anglophone writers and readers, not under consideration here) he has his hero qualify as a surgeon, ready to accompany some Germans to America, where they will establish their own sort of Brook Farm.

Goethe is also shrewdly cognizant of money—the theater's struggles for gate receipts, the Tower's income-sharing corporation—which a Wieland or a Humboldt would never have stooped to mention. Goethe knew that any life, internally rich or not, depended on external resources. Characters who, like the Harper, detach themselves from the pursuit of material well-being lose touch not only with their fellows (save as beggars beseeching alms) but also, as in the Beautiful Soul's case, with their very bodies.[12] The "hollow empty Me," as the Physician calls the inner self (2.16), can and will be filled—with ideas, feelings, memories, the products of experience. Only, Goethe unpietistically maintained—and it was a conviction his Italian journey had reinforced—the products of experience ought to be those that ground the inward in the outward: the soul (to employ the common antitheses) in the body, the self in the society, the mind's work in the hands' work, spirit in nature.

The separated theses needed to be brought closer together, as we can see by starting with "nature," which for Goethe is a very complex word, with both a material and a spiritual charge. It is the world's body—the land, sky, and waters—and the unseen providence, or "program" as we might say, within or behind that body. Providentially, Goethe is convinced, "she" will favor any person who takes up almost any job with a view not to making money or treating other people instrumentally, necessary as such means usually are toward whatever end, but to building (a process implicit in *Bildung*) his character. In other words, she encourages the progressive evolution of her creatures' adaptive powers, though not in a higgledy-piggledy way. Creative evolution—many of Goethe's researches into the common principles governing plant and animal *Bildung*, during the very months he is writing *Wilhelm Meister*, anticipate the Lamarckian riposte to Darwin that Samuel Butler and Bernard Shaw would later offer—most often occurs when an organism cunningly deviates from a pattern nature has given it, only to see how soon it will become uncomfortable enough to make a change.[13] A person will have a particular vocation (*Bestimmung*) to which nature has called him, but not forever. (You want to be an electrical engineer? "Fine," says nature, "and what will you become after *that*?") Call it Goethe's post-feudal, Lutheran heritage or simply his psychological restlessness: for Wilhelm, as for himself, there is no standing still. Any desired object, as soon as it is obtained, turns out to be as limiting and unsatisfying as the ones he already has. Small wonder that "contentment" is low on the list of Goethean desiderata. When discomfort or crisis occurs, "becoming" trumps "being" again and again, in a Faustian movement toward greater, or at least different, (dis)satisfactions.[14]

Wilhelm's self-evolution depends upon his readiness to respond to whatever turns up, both nature's material offerings (the warmth of spring or the happenstantial encounter with a woman to enjoy it with) and nature's spiritual promptings (his sexual, aesthetic, or reverential impulses). Readiness to respond doesn't mean "uncritical surrender to." Goethe is no amoralist. Wilhelm is supposed to learn how to moderate and direct his impulses—this is the educative hyper-self-consciousness that Lawrence and others would object to in Goethe—recognizing and accepting what even inspired impulse *cannot* alter, be it Mariana's lack of imagination, the actors' lack of aesthetic ideals, or his own lack of Shakespearean genius, while he recognizes and goes to work on what inspired impulse *can*. Like what? To begin with, his vocation. It is to some degree in his power to fashion it as a painter fashions a picture. Certain materials are given—the number of paint tubes and brushes, possibly the size of canvas and sometimes even the subject—but the artist is free to choose his method of handling and arranging these things. So, by analogy, Wilhelm can choose to join a theatrical troupe instead of the commercial business his father has pointed to.

This act of rebellion brings on the usual paternal disapproval and the usual filial guilt. His father, kindly and fierce enough in the heavy paterfamilias way, dies when his son is yet very young, and so occasions another absence the youth has to deal with—again by seeking paternal surrogates among older men. (Wilhelm's *mother*, one might note, may as well not exist, she gets so little mention, and he therefore has to seek the requisite feminine energies, often among older women, outside his childhood home.) Such

absconded or absconding parents—Wilhelm's are more vividly present in the
Theatrical Mission—are characteristic of many canonical *Bildungsromane*, not just
because of mortality rates within older societies but because novelists have sought the
broader, often richer acculturation that the world beyond the childhood home can offer.
Much is obviously suffered when one loses one's parents, but with luck one can suddenly
contemplate possibilities that were before unimaginable. The storyteller can do more
with an orphan than with a normal child. For Wilhelm, however, the transition is hard.
His father's influence has been potent enough to require that he fight him off even after
he is dead, once on the opening night of *Hamlet*, when he is certain that the king's ghost
is his actual father's, come to rebuke him, the trembling prince, for not doing his
burgherly duty; and again in the bedroom, where the specter of "the harnessed King" is
dissipated by the kisses of Philina, whom he is too drunk to push away. Intercourse with
her confirms the sexual initiation he has had with Mariana. By making him feel more
like a father himself, Philina helps quiet his father's perturbed spirit.

While a *Bildungsheld*, like any son, needs to assimilate his father's positive as well as
to reject his negative energies, from *Wilhelm Meister* to *Sons and Lovers* many
Bildungsromane foreground the rejection. The sons want so desperately to be themselves
that patricide (and often matricide) seem figuratively a kind of test of their manhood.
As we see, Lawrence's exploration of this process, specifically in Paul Morel's passional
search for a more balanced method of assimilating as well as rejecting his parents' qualities, is much more complex and deft than what we behold in Goethe, and suggests that
within this subgenre of the novel, at any rate, something like creative progress from
the late eighteenth to the early twentieth century was made. But to everything a
season. In Goethe's epoch, it was genuinely revolutionary—it seemed quite adequately
complex—to insist that a son might freely choose to do something different from what
his father had done. Wilhelm's father is a merchant, so he tries to become a strolling
player. The father of his boyhood friend and eventual brother-in-law Werner is a bon
vivant, so the son tries to become a frugal capitalist, and succeeds with a vengeance. His
"there but for the grace of God go I" function in the story is to warn Wilhelm and us
against the fetishizing of money and the physical and mental stresses that go with too
many years on an office stool. That is the older Werner, however. When he is younger,
he argues a good case for reinvesting dividends (or in Keynesian phrase, having his cake
and not eating it) and for mercantile activity in general: it not only fosters peace
through trade, but generates the circulation of money and goods by which Wilhelm
himself, like every German burgher, is supported (1.65). Werner's *apologia pro Fortuna*—
he adores the world of Shakespeare's *Merchant of Venice*—reaches epical heights that
moved even the very *spirituelle* Schiller to praise (*Correspondence*, 1.38), and is proof,
should we require it, that filial rebellion needn't always be in a Bohemian direction.

Wilhelm's Supposed Theatrical Vocation

Wilhelm understands economics well enough to follow Werner's *apologia*, but like
Christian Buddenbrook in Mann's novel of multigenerational *Bildung*, he dismisses economics as trivial and shallow, and politics as venal and boring. Of science, unfortunately,

he knows nothing and has been taught less. His lively brain and sympathetic heart can be stirred only by the arts, and given his childish play with puppets, he assumes that the right art for him will be the theater. It does at first seem to be his *métier*, for if, as Aurelia says, in practical affairs he is as innocent as Adam "standing agape" on the morn of Creation, in literary affairs he is as knowing as Shakespeare himself: "one would think you had just descended from a synod of the gods, and had listened there while they were taking counsel how to form men" (1.285). In Wilhelm's case it is all right that he never learns how to *act* Shakespeare at even a journeyman level. Reading him critically is the main thing, since understanding the characters and stories of those plays is tantamount to understanding human nature itself. (Samuel Johnson had made the equivalent claim, but when Goethe and other Weimar classicists made it, English writers such as Coleridge and William Hazlitt really took notice, and the great age of "character appreciation" in Shakespearean criticism began.) So, on the strength of a lead role in a school play and a field trip to Stratford a young man wants to study theater at the university? *Let* him! Experiment with life—*placet experiri*, as Mann's Settembrini classically phrases it— and make the usual mistakes. There will be no *Bildung* without a measure of folly along the way.[15]

This sounds insouciant enough, but in fact Wilhelm considers his theatrical move quite deliberately. Writing to Werner, he declares himself unable to find fulfillment, as his friend can, in "boundless acquisition" and "light mirthful . . . enjoyment." Why not? It is because, among the opulent and the mirthful, he feels aspects of his sensibility are muted. No one responds to his wit, his melancholy, his subtle insights—a typical gifted youth's complaint. This late eighteenth-century gifted youth, living in a country where the ancien régime is the only régime, puts his problem in Beaumarchais-like terms, the abilities of one class versus the disabilities of another:

> I know not how it is in foreign countries; but in Germany, a universal, and if I may say so, personal cultivation is beyond the reach of any one except a nobleman. A burgher may acquire merit; by excessive efforts he may even educate his mind; but his personal qualities are lost, or worse than lost, let him struggle as he will. (1.319)

"Personal cultivation" means, at base level, making himself look good—to have the qualities of voice, dress, carriage, "a polished manner" in "his figure, his person," those Chesterfieldian graces that a nobleman seems to have by birthright and that for those lacking such a birthright could most easily be acquired in the theater. Looking good—today one imagines supermodels and movie stars with some justice thinking this way—has no more to do with "capacities, talents, wealth" than the Apollo Belvedere does. All we care about, with such figures, are line, molding, texture, proportion, color, and so on.

Wilhelm rather innocently believes that his neighbors gaze at a nobleman (*Edelmann*) in a similarly aesthetic way. How democratically presumptuous, how ridiculous it would be for a burgher, regardless of his natural endowment, to pretend to *this* sort of Apollonian beauty (or social decorativeness):

> The burgher may not ask himself: "What art thou?" He can only ask: "What hast thou? What discernment, knowledge, talent, wealth?" If the nobleman, merely by his personal carriage, offers all that can be asked of him, the burgher by his personal carriage offers

nothing, and can offer nothing. The former has a right to *seem*; the latter is compelled to *be*, and when he aims at seeming becomes ludicrous and tasteless. The former does and makes, the latter but effects and procures; he must cultivate some single gift in order to be useful, and it is beforehand settled, that in his manner of existence there is no harmony, and can be none, since he is bound to make himself of use in one department, and so has to relinquish all the others. (1.320)

The burgher must settle into some one mode of production, service, or entrepreneurship, and never venture beyond. The noble need produce nothing in any mode: his "doing" consists of recreation, his "making" consists (one assumes) of directing and administering the labor of other people, and between his recreational and managerial efforts he is able to achieve a "harmony" of talents and interests that is denied the narrowly grooved burgher. (Don't ask about the yet narrower groove of the proletarian, for this is a preindustrial Germany; the peasant isn't under consideration, either, but one needn't be a devotee of George Sturt's *The Wheelwright's Shop* to imagine ways in which the peasant's groove is rather wider than his burgher cousin's.) Wilhelm is—social circumstances compel him to be—Teutonically nonpolitical. He doesn't dream of a constitutional change that would make Germany more like England or America, perhaps because he has a profound intuition that Germany, like any other nation, will change organically not mechanically, and that written constitutions have but slight effects on the process. Goethe's alarm at the social engineering going on in France since 1789 was very like Edmund Burke's.

In any event, Wilhelm addresses his self-cultivation problem as—well, an individual self, intent on "consider[ing] by what means I may save myself." This salvific project sounds like the introduction of a northern burgher into the southern court Baldassare Castiglione had described in *Il cortegiano* or *The Book of the Courtier* (1528), and must indeed reflect Goethe's own transplantation into Duke Karl August's court at Weimar—a place in which to look good, as noted, but also to develop "my mental faculties and tastes, that so, in this enjoyment henceforth indispensable, I may esteem as good the good alone, as beautiful the beautiful alone." Physical and mental aptitudes, in brief, are to be cultivated in tandem, and since Wilhelm has no entrée into aristocratic court circles, he turns to the theater, after all a kind of poor man's court. For in it the poor can pretend to be rich, or indeed to be whatever sort of person the play calls for. Playacting is only pretending. It isn't the serious, Castiglione-like pursuit of many-sided development—the *uomo universale* ideal—that Goethe himself made strikingly his own: part courtier, part mineralogist, part painter, botanist, zoologist, architect, poet, playwright. Doing a little of everything well is reserved for the one-in-a-generation person who has a Goethean endowment. Wilhelm is more like some—by no means all—of us when we were very young, in that he wants to be different from his middling father. And finding himself attracted to those beautiful people, the nobles, he channels his envy, or emulation, into theater work. It seems likely merely to feed his already advanced narcissism, but at the end of the day it leads him *out* of it, which is what education—the Latin *educere*—literally means.

Even if Wilhelm had the talent for acting more than Hamletesque roles, the situation of the eighteenth-century German theater would materially frustrate the ideal "harmony" of physical and mental development he is striving for. Not only are there the fiscal problems that harass most artists, and that force Serlo to turn the company into a light opera troupe pandering to Philistine taste (more along the lines of *The Sound of Music* and *The Fantasticks* than *King Lear* or *The Three Sisters*); but there are also the limitations of the company itself, which is scarcely more ready to perform Shakespeare than the Philistines are to watch him. During the best days of Serlo's deep thinking and vivid acting, his players are too easily given to debauchery—their joyful talk about doing high drama soon dissipating into a drunken supper that ends with glasses and punch bowl broken. Nor are their spirits aided, at other points, by the way the nobles treat them as hired servants, or by the way marauders from some beastly army set upon them in the woods. This is clearly not a country friendly to the theater, and when Philina decamps—she whose wit and quickness have amid scenes of William Hogarthian squalor held them together—the company simply dissolves.[16]

When, as it were, the cardboard theater and wooden puppets are put away, what can Wilhelm be said to have gained from this experiment? Contact with Bohemians, for starters. They are "bad company," as some readers have thought, but among them sex and conversation are, with Goethe's evident approval, freer than in burgherly circles, and they enable Wilhelm, as Goethe told Eckermann, to recognize the contrastingly *better* culture in the Tower.[17] In addition, he has had the opportunity to try on different roles, both on and off the stage, which will help him discover the one, or ones, he is truly good for. Acting is a kind of therapy, as the Second Stranger says: it is "the best mode of drawing men out of themselves, and leading them, by a circuitous path, back into themselves again" (1.146–47).

To act Hamlet is, for Wilhelm, a homeopathic therapy. In his interpretation, the Prince doesn't conceive and execute a "scheme of vengeance"; rather, the original murder "rolls itself along with all its consequences," dragging the good into an abyss with the wicked—all as "Fate alone" decrees. How close this is to Shakespeare's dramatic poem isn't the question. Wilhelm sees in Hamlet what he sees in himself: indecision, intellectualism, and an interest in the theater. More importantly, he wants to believe there is a "fate" that has ordered him to become an actor, and that can therefore be held responsible for his having defied his father. His streamlining of the play—eliminating Fortinbras, the active prince who represents what Hamlet himself in happier times might have been, and the mission to England, wherein Hamlet outfoxes Rosencrantz and Guildenstern—may overemphasize Hamlet's passivity, but it also serves to purge Wilhelm of his own. By overdosing on passivity he can, so to speak, spit it out and thus leave that particular adolescent phase behind him. It is like the undergraduate who drinks too much beer: his unconscious lets him do it—I am offering a benign theory— till his stomach discovers the mistake and teaches him to say no.

The Tower rather heavily declares that "we should guard against a talent which we can't hope to practice in perfection. Improve it as we may, we shall always in the end, when the merit of the master has become apparent to us, painfully lament the loss of time and strength devoted to such botching" (2.125). True enough, and everyone can think of tryouts that should never have been attempted. But Wilhelm's experience in the theater has not been merely widening or purgative. It has revealed a genuine vocational possibility. If his histrionic range is small and the epoch in general unripe for a Shakespearean renaissance, we needn't altogether endorse Mr. Boyle's judgment that the whole experiment has been an "expensive disaster" and waste of time (Boyle, 2.245, 372). We can imagine him, not too foolishly, doing good journeyman work as a provincial theater director. He is at his best when urging the players to attend to often overlooked fundamentals such as moderating their gestures and speaking loudly enough, and to be *critics* of the pieces performed. And when he passionately demands that the ensemble *practice* till their timing and coordination are as sharp as an orchestra's, we can hear echoes of the director of the ducal theater in Weimar, who himself never rose above the level of amateur acting, but who still could believe in the possibility of intelligent performance, shrewdly prompted. In the *Wanderjahre*, Goethe may temporarily have despaired of such possibility, but neither that nor Wilhelm's sighs of regret should eclipse his small but distinct satisfactions in rehearsal and show, or the rightness of his quest for *any* avenue of freely creative self-expression. A piano player may never become a pianist, but no Goethean would call his hours at the keyboard wasted.

Feminine Modalities: Philina and the Beautiful Soul, Theresa and Natalia

The novel's gallery of women—from Mariana, the not too clean actress whom Wilhelm's imagination transmogrifies into a Rubensian goddess of art, and who he at last learns has borne him a son, Felix; to Natalia, the fair virgin of the Tower who is so consummately developed that she helps transmogrify *him* into a responsible citizen and will after their marriage become Felix's stepmother—provides some instructive models for development. And not just female development. Two complementary pairs of women—Philina and the Beautiful Soul, Theresa and Natalia—are like mirrors, well beyond what the types even in *Hamlet* suggest, in which Wilhelm can glimpse analogous male possibilities of his own. Lawrence thought the whole gallery typical of Goethe's "grand orthodox perver[sity]"—his refusal of intimacy, his drive "to intellectualize and so utterly falsify the phallic consciousness"—Laurentian longhand for male sexual desire.[18] It is true that Theresa and Natalia don't stir Wilhelm's "phallic consciousness" very profoundly, and even Mariana has only "shown him a new experience," namely procreative intercourse. But Lawrence must have forgotten Philina.

She who can charm readers as divergently fastidious as George Henry Lewes and Henry James must possess a vitality that appeals to something deeper than sex-in-the-head prurience. One moment she is flirting and dining with some rich city merchants, only to send them packing when they impudently assume that she will take off her clothes to pay for her meal. Next moment, like Mary Crawford in *Mansfield Park*, she is expressing her impatience with a sentimentalist's adoration of the landscape: "to look upon a pair of bright black eyes is the life of a pair of blue ones. But what on earth have we to do with springs, and brooks, and old rotten lindens?" (1.128). No doubt she and her companions are arrested in what Schiller would call the sensual stage of develop-ment. Happy with simple changes, "their highest wish" is merely "To eat daily in a different spot" (1.145). That is believable, but it feels like a calculated caricature, meant to affirm the physical basis for any happiness involving *all* the faculties we call human. Philina may never augment her happiness with the Beautiful Soul's kind of intellectual exploration, but then the Beautiful Soul, afflicted as she is by tuberculosis, never augments her happiness with the other's kind of sensual exploration. Each offers only a partial happiness but, as Lawrence and Santayana would quickly have agreed, Philina's is the more fundamental. Any *healthy*, long-lived spirituality depends upon it. Not that Wilhelm can choose such sensuality; like the Shavian Life Force, it chooses him: "if I have a touch of kindness for thee," Philina tells him, "what hast thou to do with it?" (1.263). He is distressed to find her so beautiful, especially when she dozes in cat-like sleep. He thinks her tawdry next to Natalia, but it won't do to try to stay virtuously aloof from her. Her delightful song in praise of night, with its social and sexual inter-course, may offend Aurelia as too blatant an invitation to go to bed, but its energy succeeds in turning Wilhelm from what Aurelia herself has called a "sparkling bird of Paradise" that frankly never wert, into an ordinary bird of the fallen world—which, with his constitution, is what he *should* be.

Goethe was entirely in earnest in presenting Philina's opposite, the Beautiful Soul, whose "Confessions" make up Book VI. This "religious book," he told Schiller, "is based upon the noblest illusions and upon the most delicate confusion between the *objective* and the *subjective*" (*Correspondence*, 1.60–61). As noted, the model was Susanne von Klettenberg, a pious and by no means prudish woman who had attracted him to the Moravians, though finally that group's doctrine of original sin had offended his sense of man's potential goodness. The Beautiful Soul represents Lutheranism's advance on Catholicism, the latter being represented by Augustin, who superstitiously believes that divinity and salvation are objectified in rituals and relics. Any religious or moral truths, she understands, can have no such objective grounding: they are entirely a matter of emotion, passion, and feeling—in a word, subjective (which, in his counterstatement to G. W. F. Hegel, was to be Kierkegaard's central thesis). She may be "objectively" wrong to call God her "Invisible Friend"—that is, no such assertion can be verified—but she is "subjectively" right to say, with Spinoza, that God doesn't require anyone to love Him, and that He would be no less good if *He* chose not to love anyone. In other words, such an assertion jibes first with her imaginative idea of what a majestic Wholly Other would be like, and second and more importantly with her ethical comportment: when she loves someone or something, it isn't because she thinks God is watching her, but because the person or thing is lovable and she has love to give. Subjectively of a piece, she errs, from Goethe's Kantian point of view, only in fixing her subjectivity upon specifically biblical stories and doctrines. Her niece, Natalia, won't abandon the Bible but will read it along a continuum of other profound texts, thus giving her own ethico-religious subjectivity a properly rational, universalist basis.

The second sentence of the Beautiful Soul's story reads: "About the beginning of my eighth year, I was seized with a hemorrhage; and from that moment my soul became all feeling, all memory" (1.387). As Dostoevsky would see, there is a potential connection between religiosity and illness of any sort, for whoever can't find happiness in the body may seek it in the spirit. It was a common romantic myth that tuberculosis in particular lent a person a spiritual air—the wan complexion, the sunken eyes, the saintly visage, the graceful thinness—but as Mann understood, it had in the *German* romantic tradition also suggested spiritual illness, a something wrong with the "spiritus" as well as with the breath. For contrary to the Platonic idealists' belief, the spirit, when detached from the body, *is* sick—Rudolph Bell's *Holy Anorexia* contains some nasty medieval and Renaissance examples—just as one might perversely say that the vigorous body, detached from its spirit—think of whatever cerebrally challenged athlete you will—is sick too. There seem to be advantages to such sicknesses. By dint of *its* detachment, the "sick" spirit is capable of adventures into the suprahuman—the realm of pure spirit—that the merely healthy spirit, well integrated with its body, is incapable of. By dint of *its* detachment, the "sick" body can, on the other hand, have adventures in the infrahuman realm—represented by Philina's sensuality—that the merely healthy body, well integrated with its spirit, can't have. Full health—the well-bonded body and spirit—remains desirable, but the alternatives have their allure.

The Beautiful Soul's suppression of sensual pleasure hasn't been easy. There is a wonderful moment when she has to have her clothes removed, because they are stained with the blood of Narciss, who has been wounded in a quarrel: "I must confess, while they washed the blood from me, I saw with pleasure, for the first time, in a mirror, that I might be reckoned beautiful without help of dress" (1.397). Having accepted Narciss's proposal, she studies how to become a conventionally submissive bride, but it won't work. He expects certain premarital "dainties" that she can't bring herself to grant; he is a Voltairean skeptic, she is a mystic; and in spite of his advanced opinions, he is a masculinist who wants her to keep her intellectual gifts under a bushel, while she is a protofeminist who wants to employ them openly. She loves him, but she loves and esteems herself and her "invisible Friend" more. This is to choose "the good" over "the delightful," which for her means renouncing the idea of marriage altogether, in order to follow unimpeded her spiritual interests. Going into a Moravian convent as a canoness is an independent move. She certainly won't marry someone who expects his wife to be a worldly hostess, and what she is devoting herself to is a life not of simple-minded prayer and disabling asceticism, but of aesthetic contemplation and scientific study. She has "valued God above her bridegroom," and the richly intellectual activity that follows therefrom is, Goethe might add, what it actively *means* to value God, at least for someone whose illness has made a spiritually and physically integrated *Bildung* impossible. She may have an orthodox conviction of sin, but the Christ she turns to is Arianly heterodox—a visitor from the "shining Heights" of heaven, "whither we too must rise in order to be happy" (1.421). And rise she mystically does: "I could mount aloft above what used to threaten me; as the bird can fly singing and with ease across the fiercest stream, while the little dog stands anxiously baying on the bank" (1.422). For her, the final stage of *Bildung* is the spirit's departure from earth, the "little dog" who "stands anxiously baying" being of course her own body. In the final days of her illness, she looks upon her body's sufferings and responses to medicines with scientific detachment. Her lungs and liver, hurt as they do, are just parts of "the kindred objects of creation" where God has done "his handiwork," and where decay is as natural as gestation (1.442).

Worried that such mysticism might lead his children, Natalia and Lothario, toward hyperspirituality and morbid self-denial, the Beautiful Soul's uncle has raised them along strictly secular lines. Still, as the grown-up Natalia recognizes, it is important to tolerate, even to reverence, the ideal her older cousin has stood for. Such an ideal is extreme, but that is how ideals should be: "such persons are, without us, what the ideal of perfection is within us: models not for being imitated, but for being aimed at"—not copied verbatim but borne in mind as one fashions a self of one's own (2.94–95). The Beautiful Soul's model of perfection is there, like the depiction of

Jesus' suffering and death in the temple of the Pedagogic Utopia, in case Wilhelm or anyone else may need it. It is an exemplum for those who by illness are forced to withdraw from the world, or who by temperament can't fully realize the happiness afforded by the senses. And it is an ethically liberal recognition that, with regard to styles of virtue, one size does not fit all.

Theresa has had no need to withdraw from the world or to deny the senses, but her manner of involvement isn't Philina's. She is a superlative bread-and-butter woman, and Wilhelm is for a short time engaged to her. Trained by her father, she manages her estate, attending to details of forestry, agriculture, and accounting, with an expertise only Lothario can match. She is much too *terre à terre*, in the commendable sense, to be able to find any value in the theater—all those people, "every one of whom I knew full well, trying to pass for something else than what they were" (2.27). This prejudice has naturally something to do with her supposed mother's theatrical career, tainted by a deep insincerity and promiscuity. Women such as Lydia, a pretty creature raised under that actress' influence, may be born mistresses, paid to pretend. But as Lothario says, Theresa herself is a born wife, free to order the affairs of the house while her husband, whatever man he may be, vexes himself in the pursuit of wealth, or in the futile attempt to govern the state: "for the sake of an object which he never reaches, he must every moment sacrifice the first of objects, harmony with himself,—[while] a reasonable housewife is actually governing in the interior of her family; [having] the comfort and activity of every person in it to provide for" (2.31). Theresa is too inner-directed to regard this as a masculinist's separate-spheres trap. As long as she can rule thus over her domestic kingdom, she doesn't mind what her husband does to amuse himself outside. He will always come home when he gets tired. She won't be dictated to by anyone else's rules against casual adultery, nor be depressed by a man's inseminating vagaries. When she learns that, because he has had an affair with her supposed mother, Lothario can't marry her, she simply puts her pants back on and returns Griselda-like to her creamery and sawmill. Not that she is void of sexual passion: she holds quite fast onto Wilhelm until it becomes clear that he really wants to marry Natalia, and she him.

Why, though, should he want to do *that*? It is a hard question to answer concretely. Natalia's image (*Bild*), what she stands for in Wilhelm's mind, is evidently more important than what she actually is. When, attired as a mannish Amazon, she succors him in the forest, it is her angelically "lovely figure" that leaves him stammering: not only does she momentarily eclipse Philina in his mind, she becomes his *anima*, his idea of the fully feminine. And when, wearing a dress, she greets him at the Tower, she takes the place of Stratonike, the hopelessly loved woman in the painting of the sick prince (*kranker Königssohn*) Antiochus in his grandfather's art collection, which has been his favorite as a boy and is now in her possession. It is as if "a fairy tale had turned out to be true," Natalia telescoping in life the mother- and lover-roles that the painting depicts in story. Her pagan upbringing helps connect her also with Clorinda, the pagan heroine of Tasso's *Gerusalemme Liberata* or *Jerusalem Liberated* (1581), whom Wilhelm as a boy had preferred to Tancred, her Christian lover and conqueror. Like Natalia's, Clorinda's dress, figure, and features are decidedly androgynous. And when we recall that Wilhelm is first attracted to Mariana when he sees her in soldier's uniform (she has been playing a male role on stage) and that he is initially unsure whether Mignon is boy or girl, we realize not so much that he is bi- but that his notion of beauty is transsexual. It is a question not of practice but of ideality, hinted at perhaps by Wilhelm Meister's initials matching those of *Weib* (woman) and *Mann* (man).[19] As Mr. Boyle has pointed out (2.238), Goethe concurred with Humboldt, who in essays published in 1795 expressed the theory that the Greeks had often represented beauty in hermaphroditic forms: if beauty was a unitary ideal, then *both* sexes could partake of it partially, and any "full" representation of it had necessarily to borrow qualities from both. Beautiful appearances aside, what in Natalia is superior to Christianity, as Clorinda is superior to Tancred? It isn't her sensuality, certainly, since for all her loveliness she has none to speak of. It is rather her comparative self-forgetfulness—an alertness to others' claims and needs that the Beautiful Soul has been too mystically transported, or too buried in research, to notice. Which comes down to saying that Clorinda or Natalia are, morally, better Christians than Tancred or the Beautiful Soul.

Like the Eternal Feminine at the end of *Faust*, Natalia is a symbol of the Kantian, transcendent good Wilhelm longs for—something he in fact wishes he did *not* long for, so difficult is its attainment. When in the end he does attain it, or when rather it is given to him like a lottery prize he has done nothing to deserve, we have very little to do but cheer his good fortune and hope Natalia will give him the several kinds of love he requires. We have to take on faith what we hear of her acts of charity, her personal beauty, her intelligent connoisseurship. She hasn't the sensually magnetic presence of Philina, or the comfortably domestic presence of Theresa. We feel dissatisfied, and yet we are no doubt making demands that are too high. As a symbolic figure—half Spinozan deity, passionlessly perfect in the manner of the godhead whom the Beautiful Soul expects and demands nothing from, and half Kantian deity, coolly providing other people the things and qualities they lack—Natalia can hardly be expected to radiate the life of (to instance other fictive embodiments of goodness) Dickens's Little Dorrit or even Agnes Wickfield, or Dostoevsky's Alyosha Karamazov or Prince Myshkin. One might complain that even as an embodied bit of goodness she is limited, that like her brother Lothario she is quite unable to do a lot of important things, but we might in all tolerance reply "so what?" Take her as she is meant—as an image of the *Humanitätsideal*—and we will understand "image" in a properly Platonic sense, as an approximation to the good and the beautiful, not those ideals themselves. In any event, it is (to repeat) neither necessary nor possible for her, or Lothario, or Wilhelm, to be harmoniously developed along the lines of the Renaissance *uomo universale*. On the ground—beneath the Platonic empyrean—each person is unique, able to do some things but not all. The desiderated universal harmony will come from the combination of goods, of well-done specializations, effected not by the individual, after all, but by a group—a small secret society, to begin with, that might influence the larger open society beyond.

Masculine Modalities:
The Tower Brotherhood and Politics

The mésalliance of Wilhelm and Natalia, like that of Lothario and Theresa or Friedrich and Philina, is incredible even on the novel's own terms: as Schiller said, there has been "so little [previous] '*sansculottism*,'" and so much lordolatry. Such minglings of aspiring burghers with inspiring nobles are plainly wish fulfillments—or rather, emblems of a late-eighteenth-century *bürgerlich* utopia, in which a person like Wilhelm would have an unearned income and, above the mind-suffocating commercial struggle nearly everyone else is engaged in, could therefore shape his life more freely. His body, spared the etiolation suffered by Werner on his office stool, could be cultivated as an aesthetic object, groomed to please himself and others. So far, so health-clubby selfish. But we mustn't in reverse-snootiness overlook the genuine social benefit in this commoner's visionary project: the nobility would give access to the talents of people born beneath it. This French Revolutionary, Napoleonic program—the outward manifestation of the implicitly liberal presumption of making the question of life's meaning and purpose central to the story of plain Wilhelm's career—is precisely what *must* be instituted, Goethe implies, if Germany at large is to rise to an economic and cultural level worthy of being called civilized. Such after all was the principle Karl August had acted on when he saved Goethe from the drudgery of a legal career in Frankfurt by inviting him to Weimar, getting the Emperor Joseph II to ennoble him in 1782 (hence the "von"), and affording him maximum opportunity to develop all sides of his genius.[20]

The novel's Karl August stand-in is Lothario, the Tower's exemplary noble. Wilhelm's awed O-brave-new-world exclamation—"O what a man is he, Fräulein; and what men are they that live about him!" (2:22)—is met with no demurrers because, apparently, to see the man is to worship him. Lacking that privilege, readers are at liberty to follow Goethe's lead and critically analyze the contradictions he himself has put in play. The force of the novel's utopian vision depends in large part on the viability, not so much for the progressive cause in our time as in *his*, of Lothario's ideas about sexual and political activity.

In his sexual affairs, he relegates wives like Theresa to the escritoire and the lying-in room, and demimondaines like Lydia to the divan and the ballroom. Any *Bildung* beyond what is required for housework and amorous recreation is reserved for aristocratic males like himself. Mistresses are to be used as long as they are pleasurable and untrou-blesome, and discarded as soon as they aren't. He has forsaken Aurelia for Theresa, he explains to Wilhelm, because the former has been too passionate and unpredictable—too likely, perhaps, to demand that he be monogamous. "Alas!" Lothario wails, "she was not lovely when she loved." This is apparently enough to content Wilhelm, who has come to the Tower in the first place to chastise Lothario for abandoning Aurelia, but who now joins the phallocratic (for once the miserable neologism seems apt) position without protest. Lothario's hectic philandering is, if we will, a sign of his "natural" vitality, but as Wilhelm's behavior suggests, it is also "natural" to want to stay with the mother of one's children in order to form a family. One natural urge is obviously at war with another, yet so assertive is the promiscuous one that anything like a fair fight between them, as the Victorian novelists would amply demonstrate, can be ensured only by elevating the familial urge into a categorical imperative. Given Lothario's time and place, which are coincident with Beaumarchais' Count Almaviva's, it isn't surprising that such moral discipline should be foreign to him. It was pretty foreign to Goethe too, but his emphasizing Wilhelm's *desire* to be faithful and to have a family—a desire frustrated by Mariana's death and by his long-time ignorance of who Felix really is—indicates an awareness of the *need* for such discipline, and therefore of relations between the sexes based on concepts that begin to transcend masculinism.

In his political affairs Lothario is a significant improvement on his uncle, who had simply immured himself with his art collection and manuscripts. The nephew is of a more cosmopolitan, progressive generation. Having run into debt helping finance the American colonies' war for independence, he must now renew his fortunes, and in a way that will help Germany. His Horatian formula, echoing the end of *Epistles* I.xi, declares "Here or nowhere is America!" (2.11). The republican outlines of his patriotic policy are clear enough. He thinks nobles should be taxed like other people, and in return the state should relieve them of "feudal hocus-pocus," for example, the laws of primogeniture that keep the landed estates undivided in the hands of a few, while younger children are condemned to perpetual dependency or hit-the-road hazards. If a father could will his land in equal parts to all his children, and if each child could marry regardless of class origins, how many "we might thus introduce to vigorous and free activity . . . . The state would have more, perhaps better citizens, and would not so often be distressed for want of heads and hands" (2.84). That is to say, fewer would emigrate to America, the land of equal opportunity across the sea. They could stay home in an Americanized Germany. The virtuous rentiership Wilhelm agrees to practice on one of Lothario's estates, the job that ironically Werner has had in mind for him, will presumably further these republican aims, and begin to substantiate the life-for-others rhetoric of the Tower's indentures. The particular plan at the end, as Jarno sketches it, is for the members to form a new international secret society, to work nonpolitically behind the scenes on behalf of anti-Jacobin liberalism, the protection of private owner-ship, and therefore the encouragement of scientific and commercial enterprise.

It is all mere proleptic "telling," however, not unlike the usual politicians' campaign promises. Little wonder that readers, German or otherwise, have questioned the necessity of Wilhelm's move into "politically significant" work. They have assumed, on the force of *Wilhelm Meister* itself, that the individual's singular life, or at most his familial life, is suf-ficient ground to cultivate. This asocial emphasis could hardly have been otherwise in Germany—not until the political structure itself was opened up by a slow organic process peculiar to indigenous circumstances, and the burgherly citizen could realistically con-template helping govern the nation. To take *Buddenbrooks* as a representative social his-tory, it is clear that throughout the nineteenth century only the mercantile élite could offer to assist the nobility in running political affairs, and that the range of their contribution was severely limited by the failure of the democratic revolution of 1848. Thanks to events in 1688–1689 and in 1789, revolutionary years that of course summarize (not contain) much wider social and economic developments in England and in France, opportunities for the middle-class or bourgeois individual were more promising than for the burgher. Which, as I have said, gave the English and then the French novelist trans-individual themes largely denied to the German. Largely but, as Goethe's case shows, not entirely.

Dialectic of Freedom, Necessity, and the "higher hand"

The central idea emerging from the lives of Wilhelm and his Tower brethren is that a person is in some measure free to shape his own life. The palmary debate isn't vocational, sexual, or political. It is about freedom, and how that debate is resolved affects our approach to the more topical issues. The issue has been oversimplified by Eric Blackall, who speaks of everything turning on either "fate" or "chance" (136).[21] These are false alternatives. What everything turns on is Wilhelm's "cunning," the intelligence that can create something out of the opportunities given by the lucky or unlucky agencies not of fate—which, as he must repeatedly be told, doesn't exist—but of necessity, chance, or anything he himself might freely have effected. His early fatalistic conviction that "Heaven" has destined him for the theater and will make sure he gets there—it is similar to his belief that Hamlet the Prince has no plan but *Hamlet* the play is full of plan (1.282)—is rebuked by the First Stranger, who doesn't pretend to settle all the problems of free will and determinism, but who does wish to find the "mode of viewing them [that] will profit us the most": "The fabric of our life is formed of necessity and chance; the reason of man takes its station between them, and may rule them both; it treats the necessary as the groundwork of its being; the accidental it can direct and guide and employ for its own purposes." Easier said than done, but to treat the accidental as if it were the necessary—"to bestow on the result of such a vacillating life the name of providential guidance" (1.97)—is to abdicate our humanity. The accidental is something we can "direct and guide and employ" as we wish, limited only by the necessary. That is, one can do the possible and must forego the impossible. Good. The bad news is that it is often very difficult to distinguish the one from the other. Still, platitudinous as such a bare statement makes it sound, this is a commonsensical middle course between a radical doctrine of free will, which would pretend in brash early-Sartrian fashion (and it *was* a fashion) that absolutely everything in life is a matter of choice, and a complete determinism, which would leave us to the capricious winds of natural selection. Wilhelm's being too young to understand the First Stranger's doctrine doesn't in the least undercut it. It is the secret to "the art of living" that he must apprentice himself to, and become in time what his surname suggests he potentially is—a master. There can be no apprenticeship without the freedom to learn—to follow, within however wide or narrow a range, one's own intelligence, and not be needlessly imposed on by any external imperatives. We must remind ourselves how inspiriting, especially for a burgher class on the cusp of vast social upheavals, this anti-Calvinist message was in Goethe's own era.

What in practice does this message imply for Wilhelm? Goethe would have him free, first, to choose his sexual partners, his aesthetic interests, his career and companions, all with a view to giving his life the shape that pleases not other people—his father, Werner, or the Count—but himself. His apprenticeship ends when for a sufficient while he has "pleased himself" alone, and is ready, a little less self-centeredly, to please himself by pleasing others—to become in brief the citizen, the social man, the *master* that the Tower rightly thinks the fully adult person ought to be. (Again we hear more of this than we see.) He is free, second, to "Think of living," and of this we see a great deal. The quoted phrase is the motto of the Tower's Hall of the Past, its sepulcher decorated, like ancient Greek and Roman sarcophagi, with vivid scenes of earthly life. There are no grim reminders of death and decay. When Mignon dies, everyone celebrates the physician's embalming skill, which leaves her corpse with such an admirable "show of life" upon it, making her, for a day or two, but another work of art within the Hall. Death, the Tower insists, is the final moment of life—nothing more, nothing less. This denial of death's horrors, some have felt, betrays an almost unGerman shallowness in Goethe, but in context the entire episode closing out the story of Mignon and her parents, the incestuously coupled Harper (Augustin) and his sister Sperata, signals an essential if painful maturation of the poet–novelist's sensibility.

The French Revolution had marked the end not only of the ancien régime—the civilization of the Abbé, the Marchese, and the long-deceased friend, Natalia's great-uncle—but also of Enlightenment hopes about the redemptive power of poetry, especially the Storm and Stress poetry (a) of infinite desire exemplified by Mignon; and (b) of suffering under some brooding fate exemplified by the Harper. Goethe's putting this sort of art behind him and turning instead to a poetry of renunciation entails explaining away "Know'st thou the land where the lemon-trees do bloom" (*Kennst du das Land*)—quite lovely in itself and lovelier still as one of Schubert's best *Lieder*—as a bit of geographical information about Italy, or some of the Harper's haunting songs as the mind-altering effects of incest. A hopelessly inadequate reduction. As Schiller splendidly said, these Italian figures enter the "beautiful planetary system" formed by the novel's recognizable German social types "like comets," and thereby connect it with a "poetical" system, a stranger beauty that is alien to it and that finally, through death, passes outside it again (*Correspondence*, 1.174). Robert Bly might construe this passing-outside as the poet's betrayal of the "night side" of his intelligence. But I don't think it is that: Goethe is acknowledging the night side's deep longing for sensual beauty, or its more obscure desire for incestuous consummation—an "impossibility," like the several androgynes, that perhaps symbolizes an unattainable ideal of bliss or beauty—and then matching it with the "day side" of his intelligence, its recognition of impossibles, and its ability to sublimate the darker energies. Which, at bottom, is what Mr. Bly comes round to recommending.

In any event, the motif of Mignon's funeral isn't any medieval "memento mori," nor any romantic "half in love with easeful death" swoon, but "Travel, travel, back into life!" (2.151). Night is the time for sleep and dreams, and has its appointed place in the diurnal round, but day is the time for "earnest" living. Keeping night and day thus well-balanced is a matter of free human choice, Goethe implies, just as through the story of the Physician's treatment of the Harper he implies that we may choose sanity, and not allow specters from the grave or from the dark basement of the unconscious to cast on us any morbid spell. We may, with Schiller, wish that Wilhelm would in public pause to grieve more for Mignon, and to consider his own responsibility for her dying, but it is better to be a little brisk about the subject of death than, like some later romantics including Dickens, to turn lachrymose and hysterical. The same unromantic attitude toward death will be found in Mann's Settembrini.

How much freedom should mentors allow young Wilhelm, or any other subject of pedagogical experimentation? Goethe's approach to this question is characteristically multivalent: contrasting rational positions are tried, some absurdities are rejected, and the debate is hung between plausibilities.

The Tower's practice is defined by the Abbé, who maintains that everyone is born with a "capability," one aptitude more promising than others, and that the mentor's task is to get out of the way and let his pupils realize their capabilities through trial-and-error adventure. Once the pupils have discovered their capabilities, they will stick to them. For what they have found by themselves, they will cherish more than what others have assigned them (2.96–97). Still, Wilhelm wonders how the Abbé could tolerate, even encourage, his erroneous pursuit of a theatrical vocation. Why has he offered no "guidance"? The answer is simple. Wilhelm has been right in his own case to reject the stultifyingly conventional life proposed by Werner and the paternal tradition, and to look for a medium through which to shape and express himself. The theater has been the wrong medium, but—the homeopathic argument again—he wouldn't have known it without having tried enough of it to get sick on. But what about someone who doesn't get sick, and therefore persists on a wrong path? The Abbé can't or dogmatically *won't* help such a person. This hands-off method, as Natalia points out, has been successful for her and Lothario because their capabilities have manifested themselves early, but the capabilities of their sister the Countess and their brother Friedrich have been recessed for years: they have *needed* more prompting and haven't gotten it. Natalia is therefore more directive with the orphan girls she teaches. She doesn't leave them "to search and wander, to pursue delusions, happily to reach the goal, or miserably lose themselves in error." Rather, she impresses them with a sense of law, holding it better to live by rule, even if it is a bad rule, than to flounder outside any rule at all (2.103). Goethe concurred in Kant's belief that rational lawgiving is—*imitatio Dei*—the principal sign of our ability to govern ourselves as God governs Himself. In the margin of Kant's "Critique of Teleological Judgment," as Mr. Boyle reminds us, Goethe wrote in a large hand: "Feeling of human dignity objectified—God—." This is what, in the text of *Wilhelm Meister*, he endeavored to show in the character of Natalia, the story's eminent legislator.

Not that human life can be all law, all the time. In Wilhelm's case, the Abbé's laissez-faire and Natalia's interventionist approaches have had to move, in pragmatic compromise, toward each other. The Tower has let him wander, but never completely: the Strangers have entered to give him little lectures, Jarno has put him onto Shakespeare, the Ghost has urged him (all cryptically) to "FLY . . . FLY!" And at the end, everyone conspires to provide him with a wife, a job, and the support of the brotherhood itself. When in turn he comes to the problem of educating his son Felix, he plainly intends to be even more directive. The boy may have the innate Rousseauvian compassion, shown in his anger toward people's cruelty to animals; but he also has a dash of the innate Hobbesian savagery, shown in occasional cruelties of his own— "unmercifully tearing sparrows in pieces, and beating frogs to death" (2.80)—or in his bad table manners. He needs to be civilized. That is why, in the *Wanderjahre*, Wilhelm places him under the care of the Pedagogic Utopians, who don't privately tutor him, as the Abbé would, but put him into a community where the value of rules of behavior is immediately obvious, and where everyone receives "religious instruction" in reverence for the earth, for God, and for humanity—reverence that, since nobody is born with it (it is different from compassion), must be inculcated. Wilhelm realizes that he himself hasn't earlier been conspicuously reverent toward anything but his feminine and masculine ideals, Natalia and Lothario, and he wants to make sure Felix won't suffer from the same lack. More spiritual depth, in short.

Whether permissively or directively pursued, the end of education, as Goethe here conceives it, isn't simply a balance of the individual's physical and spiritual capacities, or of his several intellectual aptitudes. Such a balance may be wished for, but it isn't finally necessary or even possible. The end of education—we needn't repeat it more than Goethe himself does—is rather a harmony between the several specialists that belong to the brotherhood, and to the body politic beyond. Emphasis shifts from "me" to "us": I will attain satisfaction through the successful functioning of the collective to which I belong. And having learned something about the several arts and crafts the other people in my collective have chosen for themselves, I can well imagine *how* they do what they do, and vice versa. I have become a landscape architect, for instance, and you have become an orthopedic surgeon. What we both understand about proportion, unity, and connective sequences enables us to comprehend and appreciate each other's work (see 2.218 and Eckermann, 115–16). Sounds like the formulas of a curriculum review committee, heaven help us, but Goethe rightly felt the importance of bringing the constituent parts of a collective together. Only then could there be a community of minds as well as of material interests.

What the Tower believes it must promote isn't the education of engineers and military strategists, whom material interests will produce anyway, but rather that of artists, teachers, physicians, government administrators, estate managers, connoisseurs. Some like Lothario will have a bent toward theory, others like the Physician toward practice, but all will grow beyond the egoism natural and proper to their earlier years, when they have tried to "attain many eminent distinctions" and "make all things possible," into a dutiful life "for the sake of others." These enlightened grown-ups can then compete, as they cooperate, on civic projects (2.69). The end is no thorough self-transcendence—that is left behind to the Middle Ages—but a responsible, classically eighteenth-century amour propre. My self-worth depends on your approbation of my contributions to the general good, just as your self-worth depends on my approbation. Nor do these eighteenth-century characters need to pretend to poverty. They can add to the general good only if they aren't harassed by economic want; therefore the Tower spreads investments among several countries—their own European Growth and Income Fund—both to maximize profits and to have the wherewithal to ensure a competence to any brother whose property has been confiscated by Jacobins.

Goethe meant us to conclude *Wilhelm Meister* as we would a successful laboratory experiment—not with a myopic view of these procedures and data alone, but with a grasp upon a hypothesis that we can then apply through similar procedures to similar data. The experiment in this case is in social psychology, trying to find out how an individual sensibility might develop in this time and that place, and how it might be integrated with others to increase the common wealth. Thus Lukács could say that what begins as a secret society of the élite might become a model for an open society of burghers and workers.[22] The secret society in question, the Tower, is actually an extended family, including in-laws, friends, and spiritual and medical advisers. This may represent a contracted field of action after the ambitious schemes for social rejuvenation entertained earlier in the eighteenth century, whether in treatises or in legislative or executive chambers—any enthusiasm Goethe felt had been chastened by experience—but at least the focus hasn't narrowed down to the radical, alienated self. That diminution, as Santayana has taught us, would be left to the heirs of Leibnizian idealism in Germany or, in the same line, to some modernist descendants of Emerson in America. As long as one is an integral part of a family, however compassed, there is at least the potential for a wider community, a broader politics.

When Goethe thought back on *Wilhelm Meister*'s "express tendency," however, he didn't mention politics. Instead, he spoke to Eckermann about a "man, despite all his follies and errors, being led by a higher hand, [and] reach[ing] some happy goal at last" (91–92). But Wilhelm is *apparently* led by two higher hands, first the Tower with its several timely interventions, and second his own unconscious, what the narrator calls the "inborn inclination of [his] soul" (2.1) that wants to develop his varied potential and that helps improve his natural and social milieux. As we have seen. The organism wishes to grow in all directions, and to do so in salubrious environments. Like Samuel Butler and Lawrence, Goethe is more interested in freeing up the unconscious' intelligent, life-favoring energies than, like Sigmund Freud, in distrusting, repressing, or at best cautiously sublimating them. Here more romantic than classic, he concurs with Rousseau's belief in the soundness of all human faculties, and in the unconscious' ability to tell the difference between long- not just short-term satisfaction and dissatisfaction. Given the requisite amount of freedom, time, and luck, the unconscious can through trial and error find its own proper path to gratification. Thus in defiance of the super-egoistic, repressive voice of his father, Wilhelm's unconscious, hungering for a return to playing with the puppets of his childhood and vaguely seeking the erotic excitement that might be found outside the home, pricks him into the theater. Such a life satisfies him only up to a point—again, he is no great actor or playwright, and the time is out of joint for a Shakespearean renaissance—and so his unconscious prompts him to follow the clues that lead toward the Tower. The clues are so well-placed, he benefits from such an extraordinary run of almost preternatural fortunate coincidences, that we are likely to protest that the game is rigged. Our philosophic sense says it is rigged by Goethe's Kantian faith in life's transcendental purpose, based on what seems like the incontrovertible observation that human beings are constituted (as in "genetically programmed") to believe that their lives have a goal. (Fear and ignorance alone surely can't account for all those religious people out there, or can they?) Our common sense, though, says the game is rigged by Goethe's willful *desire* to entertain such a faith. He likes his hero and, along the lines of a Shakespearean comedy, simply contrives a happy ending for him.

But of course the novelist isn't as puerile as that. For one thing, the comic ending is remarkably open-ended, with many problems unsolved and with Wilhelm and the rest still afloat on the stream of history. Yet for another, the tidying up is in response to an authentic intuition on Goethe's part. However much he might want to believe in an overarching, transcendental purpose to Wilhelm's or anybody's life, and whatever the Kantian terms in which such a purpose might be couched, he is indicating what I think no one would deny: namely that some people—Wilhelm in this representative instance—have all the luck. Their unconscious makes such felicitous choices because nature has favored them with muscular strength, a sharp eye, a quick brain, good looks, a fluent tongue, and so on, or some combination of these and similar blessings that has given them leverage in the games creatures play.

There is *really* then only one "higher hand"—nature's, manifesting itself in the moves Wilhelm's unconscious makes. The Tower's Masonic-style machinations and rituals are at last a serio-comic parody of the deeper, natural scheme. On the *qui vive* for such a scheme, we would today watch a "Nova" program on PBS and talk about fortunate gene pools, which the scientists kindly try to explain to us. In Goethe's day the talk was of a personified nature, though a century before it had been of God's

Providence and half a generation on, with Hegel, it would be of History, and soon after *that* would come the father of those scientists on "Nova," Darwin and his talk about fortuitous modifications that do or don't help in the struggle for existence. In any case, the individual life must be understood as part of a larger life, which inclines toward some, such as Wilhelm or the Tower partners, and away from others, such as Mariana, Aurelia, Mignon, and the Harper.[23]

Any election or nonelection seems just as capricious in *Wilhelm Meister* as in *The Christian Institutes*: John Calvin did realize that at some level there is no *reasoning* about winners and losers, and Goethe, for all his believing in freedom more than Calvin could, had to admit that luck, grace, natural endowment (call it what we will) is often determinative. The lucky ones will make plenty of mistakes, and will appear to waste time pursuing things they really aren't cut out for, yet (as Goethe writes in a letter of 1819) "it is possible that all their apparently misguided steps may lead to some inestimable good." The "misguided steps" have often led them to the edge of "despair" and all the way "into a strange state of melancholy," but they let the next "wave of circumstance" sweep them on till something better turns up.[24] This exalted Micawberism marks the end of *Wilhelm Meister*. Without his in the least planning, striving for, or deserving it, Wilhelm attains happiness, and can only promise now to behave so responsibly that others will eventually say that after all he has *come* to deserve it. The series of false steps—of taken-up illusions—that comprise his life is objectively all he can point to. Subjectively, however, he can, retrospectively and with a little help from the masters of the Tower, perceive both pattern (the motifs of the art collection, the androgynes, the paired characters, the instances of incest, the botanical metaphors, the connection between the "sick prince" and Natalia, etc.) and purpose (adumbrated by his acceptance of paternal responsibilities toward Felix, his marriage to Natalia, and his commitment to the ideals she embodies). Kierkegaard would say that we live life forward and understand it backward. Forward, Wilhelm's life is a one-thing-after-another business of "just growing," like a plant. It has what Forster would call a mere story. Backward, his life can be seen to have a minimally scrutable shape and direction, a Forsterian plot.[25]

No doubt Wilhelm, like his author, takes himself very seriously. To do so became, as in *The Magic Mountain* Clavdia Chauchat says to Hans Castorp, the German way:

> Passionate—that means to live for the sake of living. But one knows that you [Germans] all live for [the] sake of experience. Passion, that is self-forgetfulness. But what you all want is self-enrichment. *C'est ça.* You don't realize what revolting egoism it is, and that one day it will make you an enemy of the human race?[26]

Goethe himself, though, was one of egoism's greatest critics. *Wilhelm Meister* identifies as *inhuman* the tendency to look at the world as stuff for one's self-enrichment; the *human*—it is one of Clavdia's favorite words—is the commitment of one's affections to others that renders any self-enrichment a mere by-product. Which is what Wilhelm's "happiness" is—a by-product of the work he takes up as father, citizen, and ultimately surgeon. His adolescent narcissism is, one last time, transformed into an adult amour propre.

If his or Goethe's amour propre can still be derogated as egoism, it is from the point of view of latter-day, mostly academic progressivism. For instance, Wilhelm's or

Goethe's dominant principle—that the individual is born not for society's sake but for his own, and that society is essentially an arena in which individuals can collectively realize their own "capabilities"—applied mostly to upper-class or upwardly tending males like himself. Natalia, Aurelia, Theresa, the Beautiful Soul notwithstanding, aspiring women and the working-class had in general no need to apply. The individuals whom nature favored seem to fall into the two or three categories central European societies tended to favor—Goethe making the not uncommon mistake of thinking that the way some things are and have been ("historically") is the way the "hidden [or 'higher'] hand" wants them to be ("naturally"). This prejudice of class and sex was of course shared by his contemporaries, and passed on to his successors elsewhere. But let us do him the justice of thinking historically ourselves. In the era of the French Revolution it was cutting edge to declare the rights of a burgherly man like Wilhelm, for whose talents the nobles of the Tower open a career. It was cutting edge, also, to intimate the career possibilities of gifted women, from the stage (Philina) to the laboratory (the Beautiful Soul) to the manager's office (Natalia). Equality of opportunity, not equality of results, was (and actually still is) the beckoning ideal. Goethe merits praise for having, in art speech, given body to that ideal at the birth of a democratic European civilization. "Here or nowhere is America!" If the English novelists who read Carlyle's translation of *Wilhelm Meister* broadened and enriched the applicability of Goethe's concept of self-cultivation, it was sometimes because, qua novelists, they were better artists than he, but it was also because they wrote about and for a society whose economic and therefore political circumstances already provided a reasonably high baseline of equal opportunity, which they could plausibly imagine going higher still.

Chapter 2

The Idea of *Bildung* and the *Bildungsroman*

Having examined Goethe's treatment of the *Bildungsroman*, I now want to place it in relation to the German tradition and, my main concern, to the Anglo-American. As I mentioned in my Prologue, the idea of *Bildung* was conceived by the late-eighteenth-century Weimar classicists, and in the following century was adopted in England by writers such as Carlyle, Mill, Arnold, and Pater, and in America by Emerson, Thoreau, and other transcendentalists—all romantics or heirs of romanticism—who helped create the climate of concepts and assumptions that novelists in their day and after worked within. Germans, Englishmen, and Americans sustained the idea of *Bildung* in different ways. Very simply, the Germans tended to focus attention on the individual's cultivation, while neglecting responsibility for the national culture. The English tried, with marked success, to be attentive toward both: one's development as an *I* depended not only on the richness of one's inner life, but on the affiliations one had with the people—family, friends, acquaintances, and strangers—who constituted and shared one's social environment. The American note, which I won't sound till my chapters on James and Santayana, was struck somewhere between the German and the English. Nineteenth-century Americans could be very civically responsible, but material conditions—from the greater privacy afforded people within a still largely rural or small town population, to the cushion provided by widely shared wealth—favored a Germanic sort of profundity about the individual self.

This is highlighted in Goethe's *Wilhelm Meister* or its serio-parodic successor, Mann's *The Magic Mountain* (1924), each a magnificent inquiry into how a young man's sensibility spirals through a sequence of impulses, passions, and dialectically opposed philosophies till a well-articulated but still changeable ego is formed. Other people are essential to the hero's growth, and it is a tribute to Goethe's or Mann's skill at characterization that we feel as complexly sympathetic toward them as we do. Still, as I have noted in Clavdia Chauchat's remark, these other people are plainly subordinate: their job is to water, fertilize, and prune the growing "plant," the *Bildungsheld*, whose nursery is the world. Take, on the other hand, the hero of a typical English

Bildungsroman, Thackeray's *Pendennis* or Dickens's *David Copperfield*, who is usually presented quite otherwise. He is decidedly part of his social milieu, and his social milieu is part of him. Intersubjectivity—life with, for, and through other people—is an inextinguishable determinant of his identity, and the question of his responsibility to them isn't sidestepped. The *Bildungsroman* in England has been an intensification of what Q. D. Leavis called the novel of family life, works such as *Clarissa*, *Mansfield Park*, or *Middlemarch*, which ground individuals' destinies in complicated domestic settings, and which she regarded as a peculiarly Anglo-Saxon achievement.[1] Finally, a representative mid-nineteenth-century American novel of family life such as Hawthorne's *The House of the Seven Gables* is known for its almost morbid interiority, while James's *Washington Square*, *The Portrait of a Lady*, *The Princess Casamassima*, and *What Maisie Knew* (to cite his best novels combining themes of family life and an individual's growing up) manage to present a complex interiority without the morbidity, while aspiring to but never achieving the dense exteriority, the thick description of social setting that Thackeray and Dickens were famous for. Santayana's *The Last Puritan*, as we will see, leans still more toward Germanic inwardness, though with an English-inspired chariness about what he called "the egoism of German philosophy."

That phrase comes from the vigorous discussion, undeservedly neglected, conducted by Santayana and the German theologian Ernst Troeltsch (1865–1923) during and after World War I, when intellectuals on both sides went behind the military conflict to analyze the philosophical contradictions between German and Anglo-American (indeed Western European) ways of thinking. The discussion vividly situates the English idea of *Bildung* in relation to the German, and from it one can draw appropriate inferences about any distinctly American idea. Here then is the order of this chapter's topics:

(1) Troeltsch and Santayana; then (taking a step backward)
(2) the development of the specifically German idea of *Bildung*, growing out of the Reformation, in Schiller's *Aesthetic Education*;
(3) Carlyle's introduction of the German idea into English thought;
(4) Mill, Arnold, and Pater's appropriations of the idea, which helped establish the climate of opinion the novelists worked within; and
(5) a definition of the *Bildungsroman* as such, which grew out of Goethe's novel.

Obviously, I have thought it best to begin with Goethe's novel before proceeding to the ideas that fed into and grew out of it. After this chapter, in any case, we will have enough philosophy to appreciate the achievements of the English and American novelists with whom I feel a stronger affinity.

Troeltsch and Santayana

Professor of philosophy and civilization at Berlin from 1915 till his death, Troeltsch wanted to know why the war had happened; to find out, he wrote in 1922 a short history of the idea of natural law, which can also be read as a history of *Bildung*. He argues that the balanced medieval emphases on God-given natural rights and duties—on what the state owed to individuals, and on what individuals owed to the state—gave way, from the Renaissance to the Enlightenment, to an increasingly singular emphasis on natural rights, from then on the school of natural law as such. "Enough about *you*," the new man said to the civil and ecclesiastical authorities, "let's talk about *me*!" Leave people alone, contract-theorists such as John Locke and Adam Smith eventually insisted, and they will simply pursue their self-interest, solving (in Troeltsch's phrase) "every problem rationally by the standard of utility,"[2] whereby the aggregated good of all will both be created by, and will guarantee, the good of each. Of course the hidden hand that would bring about this general happiness was sometimes very hidden indeed, and in late-eighteenth-century Germany there was a philosophical revolt, particularly in the works of Herder, Johann Gottlieb Fichte, and their fellow historicists. Man in the abstract—the *homo economicus* of Locke or Smith's vision—could have no natural rights or duties. Only concrete, flesh-and-blood individuals can have such things, and always in their own way, for flesh-and-blood individuals are fundamentally different from one another, depending on which "organic" group, which nation state, they belong to. God reveals Himself not to a generalized humanity, but piecemeal, each community expressing its mind (*Gemeingeist* or *Volksgeist*) through its inspired leaders, and each struggling against all the others in a war to glorify His infinite diversity, His own psychomachia. The hegemonic torch would be passed, over the years, from reluctant player to eager player, England to France, France to Germany, and so on. Talking about *me* was all right, as long as it was incorporated into talk about *us*, with the *us* defined racially, ethnically, and culturally over against *them*—who naturally from their own perspective regard *us* as *them*.

In Germany, the political circumstances for the evolution of these historicist themes were unfavorable. Given the return to "the old enlightened despotism" after 1815, the failure of democratic revolution in 1848, and then the relentless work of national unification, German thought had no chance for the free, unprejudiced dialectic that might have corrected and purified its principles by experiment. The romantic idealism of Herder finally sank into the political realism of Bismarck, "the conception of a wealth of unique National Minds turn[ing]," in Troeltsch's words, "into a feeling of contempt for the idea of Universal Humanity" (214). Today we recognize this debasement of Herder's relish for cultural diversity into the ethnocentrisms that would subdivide America if they could, and that are subdividing, what in innocent phrase we used to call the comity of nations, into Samuel Huntington's clashing civilizations. But in the eighteenth-century historicists' day, Troeltsch helps us remember, the romantic stress on the individuality of the person was a genuine moral advance beyond the homogenization of people according to religious confession, social position, family or "birth," or (among philosophers) an abstract notion of the human being—just as, in Herder, the stress on the individuality of the community was "surely something richer and more living . . . than any conception of 'contracts' and 'controls' intended to secure a common diffusion of prosperity" (219).

Yet in practice the ethics of German romanticism, in its own variation on a Lutheran theme, subordinated the individual's needs and rights to those of the community (there was no German counterpart to Robinson Crusoe) and confined the blessings of community to Germany alone—partly, as Mann suggested, because of her geographic, cultural "in the middle" status between a rationalist French ethos on one side, and a mystic Polish–Russian ethos on the other. Thus when German writers thought of the individual's self-cultivation, it was usually of its happening in relative isolation: his duty was to realize that portion of godhead that lay within him, with little emphasis on his fellow Germans' claims, and a great deal of emphasis on non-Germans' otherness. But what if others started pushing *their* claims, and political life, on the international stage at least, became unavoidable? Then the state would do the individual's thinking for him, and tell him what to do.[3] Thus, with ample glosses by me, we have Troeltsch's hypothesis—the war had happened because in Germany *I* and *we* were always finally German, and because the *we* hadn't developed democratic institutions.

Santayana's "English Liberty in America," the final chapter of *Character and Opinion in the United States* (1920), extends a thesis already found in his remarkable wartime polemic, *Egotism in German Philosophy* (1916), and anticipates and fills out Troeltsch's history at many points. According to Santayana, because the Weimar humanists had nothing more than a toy state to administer, they were driven inward to the things of the mind. Their successors were more perversely solipsistic: they brooded on their a priori ideas about good organic communities and, given access to large areas of Europe and other continents, they tried to impose those ideas upon them, regardless of what people there might think. "Liberty" after all signified, to these German transcendentalists, being forced to be free—in a mold of the perfect state as fashioned by a heroic leader. That isn't how the English have practiced politics. Their idea of liberty is that everyone should give in a little and, knowing that competing groups in fact have many compatible interests, should go along with the majority vote. "It makes impossible," Santayana contends, "the sort of liberty for which the Spartans died at Thermopylae, or the Christian martyrs in the arena, or the Protestant reformers at the stake"—for these died out of a refusal to cooperate, "to lead the life dear or at least customary to other men."[4] Like these martyrs, German thinkers have been fanatically self-referential, at "liberty" to be themselves forever, and summoning others either to be free in the same way, or to be liquidated.[5] Viable politics, as Santayana and Troeltsch—meaning *democratic* politics—both contend, requires persons and communities to give up lost causes, however dear, and to negotiate the compromises that they and their opponents can accept. If Germany for so long lacked a viable politics, it was because her writers were excessively bound to their own egos, and this, to complete the circle, because the communities they lived in were excessively bound to their governing nobilities and their small territories. It was under such conditions fairly easy to pretend that other people and places did not matter, or even exist.

Thus the development of the theory of *Bildung* in Germany remained incomplete till Mann's *The Magic Mountain*, where Naphta, the death-loving Jesuit–Communist, may always win the arguments, but where Settembrini, the life-loving republican, "means well, means better"—an object lesson for the Weimar Republic in the 1920s that didn't, in that decade, take deep enough root. The practice of *Bildung* went better in West Germany after the destruction of the Nazi Reich, and since the fall of the Berlin Wall and reunification, it has made progress in former East Germany too. No one would accuse Heinrich Böll, Günter Grass, or Siegfried Lenz (Christa Wolf is another matter) of neglecting either sort of cultivation. The point however is that these recent writers are playing—that Goethe himself was already playing—catch-up.

In England and, Santayana believed, in America, the concept of *Bildung*, thanks to a more tolerant political climate, has enjoyed a fuller development, in both theory and practice. Novelists from Dickens to Forster and Lawrence to Santayana himself saw, more responsibly than most of their German counterparts, that the self would grow up only at the moment it came to terms with the demands of other people—with the exigencies of marriage, of vocation, and of socioeconomic realities. If these novelists still to some extent evaded the exigencies of political commitment, it is because the liberalism that made them open to other people made them chary—not always but most of the time—of absolute ideas, which, they feared, might be *imposed* on those other people. Besides, England and America have, not always but most of the time, enjoyed the benefits of a liberally open market economy, on which political freedoms, and the general absence of demands for absolute life-and-death political commitment, really depend. The politically exigent, in short, has with us English and Americans often kept itself in abeyance, freeing us for more personalistic pursuits. That is one reason why we are, politically, often asleep at the switch, but we are nonetheless sufficiently socialized to wake up and recover.

From the Reformers to Schiller

The German Romantics' emphasis, clearly shared by the Anglo-American tradition, on "personalistic pursuits"—on the *duty* to realize our individual uniqueness—can be traced back to the Reformation. Medieval philosophers believed that a person's work, indeed his very identity, was divinely sanctioned, inasmuch as the hierarchy of jobs and stations was a manifestation of God's will. It was considered impious to stir from one's God-given niche. While Martin Luther generally shared this presumption, he introduced a notion that effectually overturned the tables in the medieval temple: he said that an active life in the marketplace pleased God more than a passive one in the monastery, and was accordingly an immediate, positive means of salvation. Hustling in the marketplace created new fortunes, while not-hustling ruined old ones, and the resulting shifts in status and political power made people wonder whether their social niches were God-given after all. Hence the equivocations of the English reformers. Emphasizing the past tense, they translated I Cor. 7:20 as "Let every man abide in the same calling to which he was called," but in the Prayer Book's catechism they emphasized the future: "My duty towards my neighbour is . . . to submit myself to all my governours . . . and masters . . . and do my duty in that state of life, unto which it *shall* please God to call me" (my italics). That "shall" suggests what would become increasingly commonplace by the nineteenth century, and had been implicitly acted on since the seventeenth at least, namely the understanding that the station one was born to was only the beginning; the station God *would* call one to depended on one's own talents and perseverance. One's father might be a cooper, but one might at age 30 find oneself an agent for the sherry importer who always bought father's casks, and at 40 an independent importer, opulent enough to endow a school or hospital, and so on. It was evidently not enough to say, with Luther, that worldly work was a means to salvation. One must *listen*, as Calvin said, for one's call, attending to intellect, sensibility, and physical prowess, to see where one's best, most profitable work lay. And this, not primarily for the sake of material aggrandizement, but to demonstrate that one was of the elect. God after all would not allow his saints to fail in the world, although troublingly He could, to test them, allow some of the nonelect to succeed. Besides, a saint had the duty of cultivating those capacities God had endowed him with, a task impossible if he chose the wrong work—coals for Newcastle instead of sherry for Hull. Just as important could be his choice of mate, with whom he might pray, read the scriptures, rear children according to the Commandments, and of course keep the family business sailing boldly on, an outward sign of inward grace. In short, the Protestant youth had some decisions to make.

All the Weimar humanists did was to widen the problem: one had to select not only a vocation and a mate, but an ideological and ethical point of view. This was something that the premodern man of the Catholic and then the early Protestant consensus had comfortably inherited from his elders and betters, his parents and teachers. It was the modern man's anxious opportunity to find it out—to think it through—for himself. This anxious opportunity was the later, secular upshot of Protestantism: what Luther, and Joan of Arc for that matter, had said about the individual's relation to God, Wilhelm von Humboldt and Schiller said about the individual's relation to everything. It was first and last his or her own business.[6] Between first and last a great many intersubjective factors must be dealt with, of course. But that was something Weimar had to wait for Goethe to insist on.

The supreme Weimar meditation on *Bildung* is Schiller's 1793 work, *Über die Ästhetische Erziehung des Menschen* (*On the Aesthetic Education of Man*). It not only focuses the implications of one's duty to realize an innate individuality; it also projects a history of and a model for such realization that would influence Goethe and the English novelists who came after. The Terror in France had persuaded Schiller that men could not solve the political problem until they had solved the aesthetic—until, in his transcendental idealist terms, they had clarified their sense of the Beautiful, and of the Good and the True that the Beautiful subsumes. This educational project would be less intellective than emotive: it was men's enervated, selfish, and obtuse feelings that, once recharged and ethically sensitized, needed to be integrated again with the rational faculties. Modern Europeans would find their best models for such an integration among the ancient Greeks. Schiller imagines that among *them* "sense and intellect" were cooperatively and equally alive, each person manifesting in large measure the potentialities of the species. The Greek citizen did so many things well—from gymnastics to music, from fighting to reciting Homer, from amateurishly practicing an art or craft to patronizing those who were truly good at it. Among "us Moderns," however, each person seems reduced to one "stunted" specialty— the merchant, the soldier, the singer, who is that and nothing else. Yes, one must pay for scientific, economic, and intellectual advancement: Newton didn't have time to be a poet as well as a mathematician (and when he tried to theologize, played the fool); Kant could not have written his critiques if he hadn't narrowed his mind to abstractions, and left concretions to somebody else.

However, what has been good for the race has been bad for the individual, and something might yet be done to better his or her life. The Good, the True, and the crowningly Beautiful: these reside in individual lives or, for practical purposes, nowhere at all. And while we must be thankful for the benefits of specialization, which have brought us from the Chaldeans and Thales to Newton and Kant, it is now, Schiller says, "open to us to restore by means of a higher Art the totality of our nature which the arts themselves [the specializations of intelligence] have destroyed."[7] This "higher Art," as Arnold would later argue in England, is culture. The Schiller–Arnold thesis is straightforward: brainwork can—if the brain is properly, aesthetically educated—put back together the Humpty-Dumpty wholeness that brainwork has broken. All we have to do is entrust the work not to the king's horses and men, but to the nation's clerisy—its teachers, preachers, writers, and public intellectuals.

But of course not all the young broken Humpty Dumpties are the same. Schiller indicates two roads for the desiderated acculturation—a high one for the few, a low one for everybody else. The high one is for those with potential to become artists and connoisseurs, the people who create and contemplate the beautiful forms that, in their regulated grace and elegance, are above mean considerations of usefulness, money, or duty. As Schiller famously puts it, man "*is only fully a human being when he plays*" (107), though mythically it is the gods alone who, in their "*idleness and indifferency,*" can play without ceasing. This *homo ludens* conceit will do very well for fastidious *Bildungshelden* like Joyce's young artist and Santayana's young mystic, who seem specially elected to "play" at thinking, forming, or writing from a very early age, either rapidly compassing or blithely skipping the "work" less gifted tyros have to per-form. For these less gifted tyros, Schiller marks a low but broad and perfectly respectable road that recapitulates the three stages gone through, ideally, by the race as a whole. First is the sensuous stage, where man is mostly intent on material provision, but where he does have the laws of the Good, the True, and the Beautiful written on his heart—or, as we would say, genetically coded in his unconscious. Second is the rational stage, in which he becomes *aware* of these laws, and his intellectual character awakens—conscious of distinctions between good and evil, true and false, beautiful and ugly. In the sensuous stage, nature has led him automatically from want to satis-faction to new want. In the rational stage, "the hand of *Nature* is withdrawn from him," and he becomes free to choose what he will do (137). At the moment he *knows* he is free, he enters the third, the aesthetic stage. It subsumes the other two, since to educate him for Beauty is also to educate him for physical health and for intellectual and moral understanding. This, because physical health and intellectual and moral understanding are, well, *beautiful* in ways comparable to a song, a poem, or a statue being beautiful. Cultivating "the whole complex of our sensual and spiritual powers in the greatest possible harmony," Schiller insists, the aesthetic individual achieves the comely *Humanitätsideal* that was the ideological center of Weimar humanism (141).

This third stage of the low road takes ordinary people up into the rarefied air where the playful artist and his audience spend much of their time, and by implica-tion makes them capable, in a leisure hour, to join that audience—see a play, look at a picture, read a book—and even, dilettantishly but harmlessly, to dabble at acting, painting, writing. The modern European may not be able to develop himself as fully and harmoniously as the Greeks, but he is still their heir, in his civilized condition free to rise above the search for animal comforts and to delight in appearance, ornament, and play for their own sakes—not to deceive anyone, but for the sheer joy of disjoin-ing and recombining the stuff of nature. And like Wilhelm, he may do this without needing to be a professional painter or a playwright, a scientist or an engineer. The everyday social world, where people have to get along with each other, is itself a sphere for creative engagement, whether on the notable occasions of writing constitutions, as the American founders had recently done, or in the quotidian process of developing manners. Like Molière's Philinte, in *The Misanthrope*, defending polite "*aesthetic semblance*" against the uncouth criticisms of Alceste, Schiller reminds the boor within us that

> Only a stranger to polite society . . . will take the protestations of courtesy, which are common form, for tokens of personal regard, and when deceived complain of dissimulation. But only a bungler in polite society will, for the sake of courtesy, call deceit to his aid, and produce flattery in order to please. (199–201)

The "aesthetic" burgher needs to cultivate the social graces quite as the troglodyte cultivated ornament and dance: he must be happy no longer in what he *owns*, though having "things" is necessary, but in what he *is* (211). What he *is* can be as pleasing as the arts he contemplates. Gentling and invigorating by turns, those arts can still transform the Philistine into the aesthete, just as, through their manifold depictions of chivalry, they once transformed the robbing and pillaging barbarian into a knight—"the sword of the victor spar[ing] the disarmed foe, and a friendly hearth send[ing] forth welcoming smoke to greet the stranger on that dread shore where of old only murder lay in wait for him" (213–15). We are, to a great extent, what we are conditioned to be: the chivalric epic now and then turning berserkers into knights, the sentimental novel turning marriages of convenience into love matches, and so on—just as morally debasing art, which we usually call not art but pornography or propaganda, can turn amorists into onanists, the religious into terrorists.

That Schiller was joined in this project of morally uplifting art education by Wieland, Herder, Humboldt, and Goethe, shows that burgher-bred intellectuals were becoming conscious of their own importance, wishing to pursue aesthetic ends previously reserved for the nobility. On the ground, in other words, they not only aspired to be creative artists: they wanted to be connoisseurs and critics, and to speak, dress, dance, and converse like cultivated men, combining what the English Lord Chesterfield called "the graces" into a beau ideal, the gentleman. This was an advance beyond the ambitions of the eighteenth-century English middle class, at least as reflected in their novels. The readers of Defoe, Richardson, Tobias Smollett, Fielding, and the rest most frequently left the Chesterfieldian program to the lords and lordolators. For themselves, as for Robinson Crusoe, it was enough to produce things and turn a profit, or like Tom Jones, to live adventuresome, energetic, and finally morally upright lives. Milton's earlier injunction to make their lives like a poem, in which all their pursuits would be woven into a harmoniously colored, symmetrically patterned cloth, seemed to them frivolous—a typically impractical poetic fancy. But it was hardly frivolous to Schiller and his implied audience. Their lives, like Milton's, *could* be poems. To Goethe, the *Aesthetic Education* was like a call for a fictional portrait of such a poetic life, a projective experiment to see how far, under modern conditions, a promising youth might go toward putting his several parts all together. Hence, as we have seen, *Wilhelm Meister*, which he began seriously to revise just as Schiller's book came out.

Translation into English: Carlyle and His Contemporaries

Goethe's novel having been introduced to English readers by Carlyle's 1824 translation, it was reissued in America in 1865 and reviewed, as noted, by the young Henry James: "It might almost be called a treatise on moral economy,—a work intended to show how the experience of life may least be wasted, and best be turned to account. This fact gives it a seriousness which is almost sublime."[8] To compress the story of the English appropriation of Goethe's work is to acknowledge the Victorians' sense of their belatedness vis-à-vis both him and his cherished Greeks, and to underscore, for all that, the Victorians' convictions about the importance of such a sublime "treatise on moral economy." One could become *Il Ponderoso* at this point and do a Harold Bloom description of Victorian sons wrestling with—misreading, appropriating, and overcoming—their great precursor, whom Arnold called "Physician of the iron age." But one has no real need of *that*. The Victorians were themselves pretty clear about what they were up against with this Teutonic immortal, and we can follow them in their own terms.

Carlyle translated *Lehrjahre* as "apprenticeship" rather than the more expressive but vulgar "trampship," a Scots term for the journeying wild-oats time of youth before the stay-at-home productive time of adulthood.[9] This hesitation over the title was in fact part of a deeper uneasiness about the book's value. For one thing, it did not correspond to what he and his wife Jane Welsh, along with most of their contemporaries in the 1820s, thought a novel should be: of sentimental love interest it had none, and of pathos little. More damning in Welsh and Carlyle's eyes, however, was the presentation of Bohemian sexual activity—the several hoppings into bed and the unmarried pregnancies that sometimes follow—which we now would call nothing more than frank, but which they, as much as William Wordsworth and Thomas De Quincey, considered profligate and bestial: all these "players and libidinous actresses," Carlyle wailed, rendered in "floods of insipidity, which even I would not have written for the world."[10] On the other hand, "There are touches of the very highest most etherial genius in it," which make him want to "fall down and worship" the novelist: he may be "the greatest ass" in three centuries, but he is also "the greatest genius" in one.

Carlyle's public expressions, to be sure, were straightforwardly reverent: Goethe had after all saved him from the cultivated, indolent despair of the Werther, the Everlasting-Naysayer, inside himself. "For I was once an Unbeliever," he wrote to Goethe, "not in Religion only, but in all the Mercy and Beauty of which it is the symbol." So alienated and despairing had he been, "that Faust's wild *curse* seemed the only fit greeting for human life, and his passionate *Fluch von allen der Gedult!* [*sic*] was spoken from my very inmost heart" (4.248). It was *Wilhelm Meister* that had saved him, in an epiphany he was to recall half a century later:

> I had at length, after some repulsions, got into the heart of *Wilhelm Meister*, and eagerly read it through;—my sally out, after finishing, along the vacant streets of Edinburgh (a windless, Scotch-misty Sunday night) is still vivid to me: "Grand, surely, harmoniously built together, far-seeing, wise and true: when, for many years, or almost in my life before, have I read such a Book?"[11]

Carlyle had had a metaphysical problem. Goethe's novel taught him, in effect, to get over it: what mattered was its idea of *Bildung*, the ethical assertion of the individual's capacity to shape some part of his own life. Taking Goethe at his word, Carlyle turned his back on his metaphysical anxieties and, very much on his own hook in works such as *Sartor Resartus* and *Past and Present*, he told his countrymen to do the same. Then he told them to get to work: believe in Spirit, disbelieve in Mammon, and proceed with the matter-transforming task that it is the essence of Spirit to perform. As he told William Allingham in 1877, Goethe had shown him "that the true things in Christianity survived and were eternally true; [he had] pointed out to me the real nature of life and things."[12] Not that Goethe would have accepted Carlyle's version of essential Christianity and "the real nature of life and things," his dismissal of "happiness" in favor of a spiritual clarity, or his "Worship of Sorrow," once practiced under "the Cross of Christ" but now looking for a different symbol. Goethe's approach to life was rigorous yet at bottom eudaemonistic. True, the *Wanderjahre* does give reverence for Christ-like Sorrow a place in its Pedagogic Utopia's religious instruction, but it is an exclusively small place, and Carlyle's excessive fondness for it, like the Puritanic, self-annihilating emphasis he gives to Goethe's *Entsagung* (renunciation), is an instance of a critic straining from an author what he needs—or what he can.[13]

A Scot of Carlyle's background was almost bound to find a soul-saving message in Goethe, just as an Englishman of Arnold's background was bound to find a prescription for the diseased psyche. But hadn't Heinrich Heine pertly said that "When the spirit was denied existence here in France, it emigrated, as it were, to Germany and there denied the existence of matter"?[14] It was almost enough for Carlyle that, in this sense, Goethe was a proper German. Carlyle was blamelessly unable to follow all the arguments of Kant and the transcendentalists, but he could tell that the German romantics knew, first, that though the medieval "divinities and demons, the witches, spectres, and fairies, are vanished from the world, never again to be recalled . . . the Imagination which created these still lives, and will for ever live in men's soul"; and second, that the burden of imagination is henceforth to create *new* "angels and demons . . . of another and more cunning fashion than those that subdued us" in old time. Earlier idealizations decay, but fresh ones can be invented. Whether he knew it or not, Goethe had effectually begun this remythifying. He had, to switch to Carlyle's best-known trope, woven some of the new philosophical clothes people required, now that their Judeo-Christian fashions (to say nothing of the thin stuff spun by what he called the logic mills of the eighteenth century) no longer fit their sensibilities. And the style of the new clothes? Carlyle recommends that we look directly to Goethe's own well-rounded development, an embodiment of successful *Bildung*. To be sure, he specialized (as we have noted) in writing literary German instead of pursuing painting or botany, but considering how many *kinds* of literary production came from him, it is "an obvious cavil" to suggest that he ought to have concentrated only on lyric poetry or travel literature, in order to gain greater perfection of form, and thus greater fame. Goethe knew "that intellectual *artisanship*, however wondered at, is less desirable than intellectual *manhood*."[15]

Carlyle's mode of praise—"wisdom" is the recurring word—became standard among the Victorians who followed him in admiring Goethe, much to the annoyance of many post-Victorians who have thought "wisdom" boring. But Carlyle's sentences, if we pierce through their rhetorical *sfumato*, make Goethe's wisdom the reverse of boring:

> This is the true Rest of man; no stunted unbelieving callousness, no reckless surrender to blind Force, no opiate delusion; but the harmonious adjustment of Necessity and Accident, of what is changeable and what is unchangeable in our destiny; the calm supremacy of the spirit over its circumstances; the dim aim of every-human soul, the full attainment of only a chosen few. ("Goethe," 1.24–25)

This may be a falsification, but if we slow down to weigh each phrase, we will begin to understand that Carlyle's portrait is less distorted than those sketched by Wordsworth, Francis Jeffrey, or De Quincey, who when his translation of *Wilhelm Meister* came out jeered at that low-minded kraut over in Weimar.[16] What Carlyle grasps is Goethe's conjoining of humanism and pessimism, and he is faithfully paraphrasing nodal passages in the novel, particularly the one in which, as we have seen, the First Stranger rebukes Wilhelm's fatalism (1.97–98). Goethe displayed a serene belief in free will that appealed to Carlyle, who had lost his old religious faith. It was all right, Goethe seemed to say, in a voice that carried its own divinity:

> He knows the good, and loves it; he knows the bad and hateful, and rejects it; but in neither case with violence: his love is calm and active; his rejection is implied, rather than pronounced; meek and gentle, though we see that it is thorough, and never to be revoked. ("Goethe," 1.27)

Like God or Shakespeare, Goethe is "a builder-up"—not, like Mephistopheles or Voltaire, a "destroyer."

Godlike writers aren't to everyone's taste, and for every Carlyle, Arnold, Lewes, or James there was in the Victorian age a denying Wordsworth, De Quincey, Dante Gabriel Rossetti, or Max Beerbohm—all of whose dissatisfaction was summed up by Henry Sidgwick when a German visitor remarked that in English there was no word quite corresponding to "*Gelehrte*": "Oh yes there is. We call it 'prig.'"[17] Decidedly humorous but really just an excuse not to do one's homework. To appreciate Goethe, the English would have to overcome their aversion to thinking. Their true difficulty, as Henry Crabb Robinson saw, lay not with *Wilhelm Meister*'s sensuality—"like the crossing of flies in the air," Wordsworth told Emerson[18]—but with its "directly philosophical purpose," as earnest and witty as *Don Quixote* itself.[19]

Mill, Pater, and Arnold's Appropriations
of the Idea of *Bildung*

The Englishmen notoriously non-averse to thinking—Mill, Arnold, and Pater—were fascinated by Goethe's intellectualism and by all of what Nietzsche called "the dull lustre, the enigmatic Milky-Way shimmer" still glowing round classic Weimar culture.

"Could it be," Nietzsche imagines the English asking, "that the Germans have quietly discovered some corner of the heavens and settled down there? We must try to get closer to the Germans."[20]

Initially it was Humboldt to whom Mill tried to get closer. He cites him in *On Liberty* as the champion of the idea of self-cultivation, but recognizes in the *Autobiography* that he was only part of "a whole school of German authors" headed by Goethe, who pushed "even to exaggeration" "the doctrine of the rights of individuality, and the claim of the moral nature to develop itself in its own way."[21] Mill's immediate inspiration came of course from Coleridge and Carlyle, who had naturalized German ideas about how an intuitive, emotive education, open to the importance of passion, community, natural beauty, and feminine presence, had to be called in to complement and correct the sort of rational, quantifying education Mill had received from his father. The theory behind this humanly necessary balancing act was resplendently told in Mill's essays on Bentham and Coleridge. In practice the act was difficult—as it would be for any of us if we had Mill's IQ and early conditioning. He had an extraordinary dream about the Herculean choice between virtue and pleasure, each embodied in female form. He quite rightly wanted to have both: why could not "a sincere friend & a sincere Magdalen" live chastely side by side, in his ideal woman as in himself? But "the woman [in the dream] said 'no, that would be too vain'—whereupon I broke out 'do you suppose when one speaks of what is good in itself, one must be thinking of one's own paltry self interest? no, I spoke of what is abstractly good & admirable.'" How "queer" dreams are. When he heard the remark about a "sincere Magdalen," Mill thought "it wrong & that the right words were 'an innocent Magdalen' perceiving the contradiction."[22] There is no call to scoff at Mill's sexlessness, as the young Freud did; we need only underscore the special individual Mill was. He wished to transform the sensuous woman who would be "sincere" when she kissed, into an "innocent" who would simply not know about kissing—which would be like fusing Goethe's Philina with the Beautiful Soul. One can appreciate the pathos of such a young man's dream.

As the first draft of the *Autobiography* shows, Mill had abundant and bitter knowledge of the practical and affective debilities imposed on him by a Benthamic education. To know about one's debilities, however, isn't necessarily to be rid of them. Mill could never approach the choice between pleasure and virtue as robustly as, in 1773, Goethe had done: "If I had really met those two ladies, you see, I would have grabbed one under this arm, the other under that arm, and forced both of them to come along!"[23] That is the true Goethean vim, in a style banteringly attractive—"Oh, to be so cool!"—and bullyingly repellent—"Here's another person telling me how I ought to live!"

Mill's father had done enough of that, and the son needed all the backing he could get, German and otherwise, for his desire to be a separate individual. Separate and unique, not according to any paradigm, which is what he mistakenly thought Goethe was forwarding: "his idol was symmetry: anything either in outward objects or in characters which was great & incomplete, or disproportioned (*exorbitant* as Balzac says of a *visage d'artiste*) gave him a cold shudder." As Mill protested to Harriet Taylor, no modern person can achieve symmetry in his life or work. However tightly he laces himself, he has more bits to balance than the Greeks ever dreamt of. No, "it is too soon by a century or two" for symmetry either in art or in character. "We all need to be blacksmiths or ballet dancers with good stout arms or legs, useful to do what we have got to do, & useful to fight with at times—we cannot be Apollos & Venuses just yet."[24] As we have seen, Goethe *too* had understood the need to postpone the Schillerian goal of complete, many-sided, symmetrical development for "a century or two," that is, indefinitely. Wilhelm Meister cannot be an Apollo "just yet"; he has to specialize—to become a sort of blacksmith or ballet dancer—like everyone else.

Mill's ambivalence toward Goethe comes down to this. He very much wanted, on the one hand, to effect a Goethe-like "rounded completeness," synthesizing the rational analytic Benthamic and the emotional intuitive Coleridgean sides of his nature. On the other hand, he rebelled against what he took to be Goethe's Apollonian prescriptive-ness—rebelled in the name of his deepest desire, which was to be his own necessarily jagged and incomplete self. Man isn't a machine or a work of art, to be either meanly Gradground or lovingly sculpted into an ideal form. Man is an organism like "a tree, which requires to grow and develop itself on all sides, according to the tendency of the inward forces which make it a living thing."[25] No bonsai nipping, no pollarding: just let the tree grow as it will. Which, as we have observed, is precisely the creed of the Tower in *Wilhelm Meister* and the tenor of Goethe's remarks throughout the *Conversations* and the letters. There is no template for development, Greek or otherwise, which one is supposed to conform to; there are only the trial-and-error experiments to discover what peculiar shape, in the play between aptitude and circumstance, nature wants one's life to take.

Like Hegel, Ernest Renan, and Jules Michelet, Goethe provided Pater with a lode of ideas first to mine, then to compound and transmute in the white heat of his imagination—a slapdash but not plagiaristic procedure which yielded essays that were works of art. The first such essay he published, "Winckelmann" (1867, reprinted six years later in *The Renaissance*) contains an invaluable assessment of Goethe's *Bildungsidee* derived primarily from *Dichtung und Wahrheit*, a book that, among other things, caused him to burn his poetic juvenilia.[26] Winckelmann was the source of Goethe's love of "balance, unity with one's self, consummate Greek modelling," though Goethe realized, as Pater correctly says, the impossibility nowadays of achieving such a balance, whether like Phryne "by Perfection of bodily form, or any joyful union with the external world," or like Pericles or Phidias by the narrow "exercise of any single talent." One must choose, as William Butler Yeats would later say, perfection of the life or of the work. Only, one must be resigned to getting neither. Moving on is more important than bringing a project to an exquisite close. As Pater writes, "Goethe's Hellenism was of another order, the *Allgemeinheit* and *Heiterkeit*, the completeness and serenity, of a watchful, exigent intellectualism. *Im Ganzen, Guten, Wahren, resolut zu leben*"[27]—meaning by *im Ganzen* an absorbing of the essence of one special pursuit after another, straight through the whole curriculum.

There ought to be no obsession with either body or mind. Goethe's "gift of a sensuous nature" was such that he might easily have "let it overgrow him," just as he might "easily and naturally" have let his "otherworldly" nature expand into the Beautiful Soul's "ideal of gentle pietism." To his "large vision," however, each nature, sensuous and spiritual, was in its extreme form but "a phase of life that a man might feel all round, and leave behind him." Exactly so. Where Pater errs is in attributing to Goethe more belief than he really had in the possibility of a person's becoming an *uomo universale* who would be and do all things human, taking them one by one.

This is a Renaissance aspiration obviously dear to Pater, and it isn't surprising that like Mill he should have projected it onto a writer whose enthusiasm for Periclean Athens seemed to match Schiller's own. But, to repeat, Goethe maintained that a man is called to be Somebody, not Everybody, and like Wilhelm he must renounce certain experiments that don't truly suit his capacities and find a particular work that does.

Nothing is to be gained, at this time of day, by emphasizing how Mill, Pater, or in broader ways the biographer Lewes misprized one of Goethe's central themes. Winckelmann, Schiller, Byron, and the Elgin marbles had taught them a love of Greek wholeness that they would project onto Goethe willy-nilly, and when they thought of *Bildung* it was in terms of the Greek ideal. Not a fatal mistake, since the great novelists were on hand to correct it, quite as Goethe himself had done in *Wilhelm Meister*.

Finally there is Arnold, who in principle applauded Mill's call for individual development, but who in 1867, the year Pater's essay on Winckelmann appeared, worried in *Culture and Anarchy* that in England ungoverned self-cultivation had gone too far. People's doing "as they liked" would not be a trustworthy program till they learnt to "like" the best that had been thought and said. That best was what "culture" offered, and by schooling people to harmonize their Hebraic-moral and their Hellenic-intellectual capacities into a living *whole*—there is that word again—culture could defeat "anarchy." *Pace* his critics then and now, Arnold's brief for culture was not being argued for the sake of the state, instrumental as, through its schools, say, the state could be for culture's purposes. Arnold's brief was for individuals—starting with those class-transcending intellectuals whose task it was, as writers, teachers, and ministers, to educate the classes, whom Arnold dubbed the Barbarians, the Philistines, and the Populace.

The phrases Arnold uses to describe the properly acculturated individual sometimes derive from Humboldt—"the harmonious expansion of the individuality," the "unified and complementary" ordering of "all elements" of one's personality, and so on. But more often they derive from Goethe, whose praise of the ancient unity of sensibility—especially in the "Antikes" section of his essay on Winckelmann—yielded *Culture and Anarchy's* famous definition of perfection as "a harmonious expansion of *all* the powers which make the beauty and worth of human nature."[28] No more than Mill and Pater does Arnold notice Goethe's sense of the obstacles facing the modern paladin of culture in pursuit of such a harmonious expansion. He simply remembers his first reading of Goethe's *Bildungsroman* with fond excitement: "The large, liberal view of human life in *Wilhelm Meister*, how novel it was to the Englishman in those days! and it was salutary, too, and educative . . . [with all its] poetry [and] eloquence."[29] Well, the excitement was justified, if not by any endorsement of Arnold's dream of Greek completeness, then by Goethe's conservative–liberal endorsement of free individual choice, which as I have said was quite revolutionary enough for his time and place. Arnold did get it right in "German and English Universities," where he says that for Germans "*the essential thing*" is that the individual become what he will "*not out of youthful habit, vague disposition, traditional obedience, but . . . upon scientific appreciation, critical verification, independent decision.*"[30] The charge of the major English (and American) *Bildungsromane* was to dramatize, concretely and complexly, the possibilities of independent decision. They were not infinite, needless to say, but they were larger than authors before Goethe had supposed.

Defining the *Bildungsroman*

Now to cut to the chase. Everyone says that *Wilhelm Meister* is the prototypical *Bildungsroman*, but exactly what type of fiction is that? It is best not to say too exactly, as any perusal of precisionist taxonomies will show.[31] A stringent definition will limit the number of bona fide *Bildungsromane* to two or three, a result so frustrating that critics usually drop their arms and let in novels as widely varying ones as Mann's *Joseph und seine Brüder* (*Joseph and His Brothers*) and Thomas Hardy's *Jude the Obscure*.[32] Some traditional markers are nonetheless worth noting. German critics refer to two near relations of the *Bildungsroman*. One is the *Erziehungsroman* or novel of education, such as Rousseau's *Émile* or Johann Heinrich Pestalozzi's *Lienhard und Gertrud*, which is explicitly and pointedly pedagogic. The other is the *Entwicklungsroman* or novel of personal development, which is broadly about the evolution of a hero—Lambert Strether in James's *The Ambassadors*, say—from any one stage of life to another. The *Bildungsroman* is between these, not as narrowly pedagogic as the one—being about general acculturation or, as Martin Swales says, "the clustering of values by which a man lives"[33]—and not so merely transitional as the other—being about the early childhood-to-young-adulthood stages of life.

The term *Bildungsroman* itself was first coined by Karl Morgenstern in lectures in the early 1820s, with specific reference to *Wilhelm Meister*: "it portrays the *Bildung* of the hero in its beginnings and growth to a certain stage of completeness; . . . further[ing] the reader's *Bildung* to a much greater extent than any other kind of novel."[34] The term didn't gain currency, however, till Wilhelm Dilthey used it in *Das Erlebnes und die Dichtung* (*Poetry and Experience*) in 1913: the *Bildungsroman* examines a "legitimate course" of an individual's development, each stage having its own specific value and serving as "the ground for a higher stage," an upward and onward vision of human growth nowhere "more brightly and confidently expressed than in Goethe's *Wilhelm Meister*."[35] That novel projects the normative pattern that, optimistically, parents, teachers, and adolescents themselves like to contemplate: life is a tussle, no question, and Goethe isn't shy about pointing this out, but children become youths and youths become happily initiated grown-ups, ready to invest their talents in *Liebe und Arbeit*, the love and work of the civil society they belong to. Which presumably is why Dilthey designated the novel's plot as "legitimate," and why Morgenstern had been able to recommend it to younger readers, who might themselves be seeking models for, or reassurance about, their own movement toward adulthood.

Susanne Howe's foundational study, *Wilhelm Meister and His English Kinsmen* (1930), in effect takes over Dilthey's idea of the type:

> The adolescent hero of the typical "apprentice" novel sets out on his way through the world, meets with reverses usually due to his own temperament, falls in with various guides and counsellors, makes many false starts in choosing his friends, his wife, and his life work, and finally adjusts himself in some way to the demands of his time and environment by finding a sphere of action in which he may work effectively. . . . Needless to say, the variations of it are endless.[36]

The snag is that she demands a *successful* coming of age—the normative comic ending that Morgenstern and Dilthey had in mind—and therefore appears to think more of

Bulwer Lytton's *Pelham* or Benjamin Disraeli's *Vivian Grey* than of *Richard Feverel, The Mill on the Floss, Sons and Lovers*, or *A Portrait of the Artist as a Young Man*, which end with heroes dead, blocked, or deracinated, to say nothing of *Pendennis* or *Great Expectations*, whose heroes aren't intellectually interesting to her. Well, different professors, different syllabi. Howe is, though, most informative about the non-Goethean prototypes for the *Bildungsroman*, ranging from the Bunyanesque hero looking for salvation through a world peopled with allegorical representations of virtue and vice, to the picaresque hero whose adventures take him instructively through various strata of society, to the quester hero like Parsifal, who learns through painful experience how to reach his goal, and what his goal is worth.[37]

The *Bildungsheld* stands not only for a synthesis of these various earlier heroes, but for modern, post-Enlightenment youth in general. Someone like Wilhelm Meister, as Howe finely says, is

> Every Young Person. Only in this light can we be very much stirred by him. His enthusiasms and his confidence, his indecision and his errors, his spongelike way of absorbing every influence to which he is exposed without profiting visibly thereby, his lack of humor—all these are vaguely touching only as youth is always touching, when it is not maddening.[38]

And of course we find him "touching" as well as "maddening" because the writer of a *Bildungsroman*, exploiting the confessional vein opened up by Rousseau, Byron, and Goethe's own *Werther*, has made us privy to his hero's thoughts and feelings. An intensely Jamesian center of consciousness he need not be, but a focus on the development of his inner life is nevertheless essential. His social relationships matter less for themselves than for the *Weltanschauung*—the "lay religion or general philosophy of life," as W. H. Bruford says—they help him articulate.[39] He is thus more likely to be a dreamer, even an artist, than a man of action. Hence any novel about such a coming-of-age is what, in his postscript to *The Magic Mountain*, Mann called "the sublimation and spiritualization of the novel of adventure,"[40] the picaresque become *Seelengeschichte* or spiritual history, wherein what is inside a character—how he loves his mother, misses his father, prefers the theater to the stadium, and so on—is as important as what is outside—how his father is a merchant or a miner, his school nurturing or dehumanizing, his first girlfriend sexually shy or eager, and the like. Not just the hard facts of growing up, but the youth's soft feelings and thoughts about them.

One study of this kind of novel, referred to briefly in my prologue, is Franco Moretti's *The Way of the World* (1987), which, for all its Marxizing and constitutional distaste for Victorian works like *David Copperfield* that strongly appeal to me, is superior to Mark Redfield's subsequent book, *Phantom Formations* (1996).[41] Mr. Moretti reads these "inward" stories in the "outward" context of modern European political history, "modern" dating from its most decisive event, the French Revolution of "year zero," 1789. The Revolution dissolved the "feudal" system in which young people grew up to fill the social roles they were born to—a dissolution that, as I have said, can be traced back to the Reformation and to the revolutionary political events occurring in England well before France's 1789, but that, after the Reformation, failed to become fully political in eighteenth- or nineteenth-century Germany (which is why between *Wilhelm Meister* at the one end and *Buddenbrooks* or *The Magic Mountain* at the other there are scarcely any German *Bildungsromane* now worth reading). Growing up became a problem when people's roles ceased to be "feudally" prescribed, and could to some extent be written by themselves—just as their forms of government could be written and rewritten. This, says Mr. Moretti, made youth "a specific image of modernity": restless, semi-inchoate, in a state of what Karl Marx called "permanent revolution" (Moretti, 5). A *Bildungsroman* is a fiction that could not be written before the era of democratic revolutions, since the coming-of-age of any such bygone youth was too socially straightforward to be interesting. The modern youth, representative of the coming democracy, is a self-expressive ego confronted with the community's demands for self-repression—demands that don't go out the window just because barons have given way to burgomasters and villeins have become citizens. In the modern state, all are "free," but only within the constraints of citizenship. They can't, and shouldn't, always do as they like.

Mr. Moretti's argument continues thus: *Wilhelm Meister* resolves the conflict between the individual's ego and the community's requirements for compromise in paradigmatic fashion. Wilhelm realizes he has got to fit in, that is, in a mature can't-beat-'em-join-'em accommodation, he internalizes the community's norms by getting married, that classic comedic symbol for the self-limiting social contract. The same is true in *Pride and Prejudice*, *Waverley*, *David Copperfield*, and *Jane Eyre*, which narrate "how the French Revolution could have been avoided" or, since it was too late for that, how it might be "disavowed" or undone. (If everyone would only marry and stay married, and just do their jobs, then we wouldn't see barricades and guillotines in the streets!) In France too there was a reaction, but the spirit of the Revolution had gone too deep (Moretti, 72–73). Stendhal and Balzac renounced the too-cozy Goethean ideal of "happiness" and "maturity," with its attendant marriages and reclassifications. They celebrated "freedom" and "youth," the hero's dynamic metamorphoses that (a) "dismantl[ed] the very notion of personal identity"—why be a son, father, tinker or tailor "somebody" when you can hit the road and become "anybody" you please?—and (b) privileged the adventures of adultery, where so much seems dangerously to happen, over the insipidities of marriage, where so little does (Moretti, 8).

Now (still following Mr. Moretti) Jane Austen, Walter Scott, and their successors in England sought to disavow, avoid, or undo the French Revolution because their own society had *had* its "glorious" middle-class revolution a century before. Which, for a Verso critic, must be a species of joke: "A revolution that appeals to a 'pedigree' of privileges, while disregarding normative and universal principles! . . . [that] aims at the revival of the 'original contract,' and has no interest in future utopias!"—isn't very revolutionary. Mr. Moretti is sufficiently historically minded, however, to acknowledge that this "legal" revolution did give England a culture of justice, in which rights were protected by the courts—a "legacy . . . which the more pulsating and plastic continental Europe (and certainly Italy) can only envy dusty old England" (207), and which has spread its justice from protection of commercial rights to protection of civil rights. Not bad for a polity unguided by universal norms and utopian visions.

We have a fundamental division here between those who dislike and those who like and are grateful for liberal democracy, with its attendant free market and class structure. Santayana and Troeltsch liked it and were grateful, not least because such a society had yielded high aesthetic dividends, its economic mobility and social heterogeneity giving artists a lot of life to look at, and from many perspectives. Mr. Moretti dislikes it and can see only aesthetic losses, liberal democracy having afforded less life and fewer perspectives, and given us artists who are too moralistic. Because English novelists assume that the rule of law reigns everywhere, "Any type of conflict or diversity—whether of interests, ideas, ethical options, or erotic preferences—is removed from the realm of the questionable and translated into the fairy-tale-juridical opposition of 'right' and 'wrong'" (Moretti, 210). Instead of interesting plots of "transformation," we allegedly get inert, convoluted plots of "classification"—Bertha Mason burnt, Micawber exiled, and Jane Eyre and Copperfield married to their respective dears. Charlotte Brontë and Dickens leave Moretti with an "empty stomach. One enjoys oneself, without ever being carried away; one finds plenty of certainties, but no way of addressing problems. . . . Let us therefore say that, due to a unique historical conjunction, the novel was born in England precisely when the ideology of the law reigned supreme. The result was the worst novel of the West [he means *Copperfield*, absurdly], and the boldest culture of justice" (214).

This is the return of Mario Praz, and it is characteristic of the left-radical attack on what G. K. Chesterton long ago called the Victorian Compromise. It has at times invigorated nineteenth-century literary studies, if only by shaking them up, but it has in the long run more often depressed them by producing shelves of utterly predictable celebrations of diversity, uncertainty, and the subversive, hand-in-hand with denigrations of unity, assurance, and consensus. One must not err by over-correcting, however. I have no desire to offer a reactionary defense of the stabilities of a Goethean or Dickensian *Bildungsroman*, precisely because such novels are also rich with their own "transformations," their own sexual and ethical aporias, just as the Stendhalian or Balzacian *Bildungsroman*, *The Red and the Black* or *Lost Illusions*, gives us heroes who are transformed within typifying if constantly shifting social "classifications." It is a matter of degree, each tradition doing what it needs to do, and well-advised to learn what it can from the other.

That is why I recommend the late Jerome Buckley's able study, *Season of Youth* (1974), also mentioned in my prologue. Tolerating and profiting from European and Anglo-American traditions alike, Buckley defines the *Bildungsroman* by reference to an archetypal plot. A sensitive child grows up in the provinces, where his lively imagination is frustrated by his neighbors'—and often by his family's—social prejudices and intellectual obtuseness. School and private reading stimulate his hopes for a different life away from home, and so he goes to the metropolis, where his transformative education begins. He has at least two love affairs, one good and one bad, which help him revalue his values. He makes some accommodation, as citizen and worker, with the industrial urban world, and after a time he perhaps revisits his old home to show folks how much he has grown. No single *Bildungsroman* will have all these elements, Buckley says, but none can ignore more than two or three.[42]

This synopsis is adequate as far as it goes, but I would supplement it with a list of initiatory tests that every inwardly developing *Bildungsheld* must at least try to pass, and that constitute the rite-of-passage peripeties of Buckley's archetypal plot. There are three such tests. First is the sexual test, in which the *Bildungsheld* moves beyond (if he or she doesn't absolutely reject) the affections of one or both parents, and finds someone else—an appropriate partner outside the family—to love. Second is the vocational test, in which the *Bildungsheld* must find a way of relating himself not just to someone but to everyone in the society at large. He must do work that will contribute to the commonwealth, and as I insist along with Mr. Moretti, compared to his forebears he has more freedom—it is both a burden and an opportunity—to choose how he will contribute. Some canonical *Bildungsromane, The Mill on the Floss, The Ordeal of Richard Feverel,* or *Great Expectations,* for example, follow *Wilhelm Meister's* lead by featuring heroes who aren't artists. Their authors wanted to transcend the narrowly autobiographical by portraying characters that ordinary people—those on Schiller's low road of aesthetic education—could see themselves in. No few canonical *Bildungsromane,* however, shade into the *Künstlerroman,* the novel about the growth of the artist (Joyce's *Portrait* preeminently, and *Copperfield, Pendennis,* or James's *Roderick Hudson*), or project the hero as artist manqué, someone not talented enough to be an artist but sensitive enough to be a critical member of the audience, and reflective enough to philosophize about the cultural scene. Instances would include *The Magic Mountain, The Last Puritan,* or Woolf's *Jacob's Room,* though one must admit that even these novels skirt around the problem of what, aside from ruminating about art, ethics, and metaphysics, a person who doesn't live year-round up at Bread Loaf is supposed to do in the everyday loaves-and-fishes market down the hill. The third test, back up the "magic" hill, is that business of ruminating, but specifically about the *connections* between art, ethics, and metaphysics, the practical stress falling on the middle term. Happily, the novelistic presentment isn't as schoolish as my last sentence makes it sound. It is a hero's lived experience of keeping or not keeping promises, of telling or not telling the truth, of being faithful or unfaithful to parents, friends, and spouse, with or without respect to income and class, that gives rise to his conceptual beliefs about (to conjure up Schiller's traditional categories once more) the Good and the True, or fashions his taste for some instance of the Beautiful.

Significant work toward our understanding of ego development was done throughout the twentieth century by psychologists from Freud, Carl Jung, and Jean Piaget to Erik Erikson, D. W. Winnicott, and Robert Kegan (I leave Jacques Lacan to those who find him *lisible*), but their observations and theories are simply part of the deep background of my analyses in this book. For one thing, though I can ask questions or remain silent with the best of them, I have no credentials in psychology. For another, reading Adolph Grünbaum and his disciple Frederick Crews has persuaded me that it would be vain to seek scientific truths—the kind that stand up to experimental trial and have predictive value—in psychoanalytic writing. The founding father himself offers more as a poetic genius than as an empirical researcher. Hence, my manifest sources are literary—and chiefly the novels under consideration here.

They are of course constructs of the human mind—that is a high-school realization, I would think—and like all constructs they are governed by formal conventions that build on and react against one another. To some degree, for example, it is a convention of the *Bildungsroman* to have a young man go through several love affairs, in order to make him aware of what kinds of female presence satisfy what kinds of male needs, just as it is a convention to have him weigh a commercial career against an artistic one, or to have him throw off the intolerable bonds of the village in order to take on more tolerable ones in the city. Nor is it only the novelist who is making his hero conform to conventions. The hero himself has often read young-man-from-the-provinces stories, as

Copperfield has read *Roderick Random* and *Tom Jones*, and will therefore recognize the type of situation he is in and respond appropriately. The coherence of the *Bildungsroman* tradition, then, can to some extent seem artificial—a line of authors who, wittingly or unwittingly, have organized their tales around some arbitrary conventions or semiotic flags.

But for my money the ability to recognize a story of *Bildung* depends not merely on literary training, necessary as that obviously is, but on the story's imitation of patterns of development endemic to the race itself, the psychic round the ego must pass through, analogous to the biological round the body must pass through. Thus what Northrop Frye might have called the archetype behind the archetype of *Bildung*, the tale of a god's growing up and finding his "vocation" as a messiah for a people, or as a slayer of the Evil One, whether dragon, father, or mother, would itself emanate not from an earlier literature—for in theory one could go back to a point where there *was* no earlier literature—but from the psychophysical experience of human beings themselves, leading, in sidereal time and ecospheric space, their creative but bounded lives. Their culture, their stories, which Frye modestly did not want to go behind, must ultimately derive—in ways understandably difficult for academic intellectuals to imagine— from the pre- or scarcely linguistic, largely physical, homo-erectian encounter with the world. The view from the faculty club or the local Starbucks doesn't usually extend that far, but we should, as "common readers," try. Life comes before literature, however true it is that literature (and then more life) then comes after literature. Lawrence, as we will see, says it better, but the "it" amounts to this: in the black dawn of the world there was no Word, just the stuff that words have for millennia endeavored to be about.

Chapter 3

David Copperfield's Self-Cultivation

To move from Mill, Pater, and the rest, and more particularly from Goethe's *Urbildungsroman*, to Dickens's *David Copperfield* is to reverse the ratio between philosophy and character. Dickens (1812–1870) listed Carlyle's translation of *Wilhelm Meister* among his books in 1844. We can't be sure he actually read it,[1] but we can confidently say that he never offers Goethe's sort of critical disquisitions on the national theater, the freedom of the will, or the relation between pedagogy and profession. He has ideas right enough, yet (to play with William Carlos Williams's famous dictum) for him there were no ideas but in character—and, yes, in things. As I have already twice maintained in this study, it is an allowable hyperbole to claim that in England there were more characters, if not more things, for a novelist to discover ideas *in*. The relative fluidity and openness of the social structure, particularly in the dense jostle of London, made it possible for Dickens to know and appreciate many more human types than Goethe could have access to, and he therefore didn't have to philosophically prose about them so much. He could *situate* his hero's growing up—placing it in relation to parents or parent substitutes, to friends and lovers of both sexes, and to the variegated neighbors, nice or not so nice, who help constitute the culture his *self*-culture must fit into—and fairly safely leave us to draw the proper ideational inferences. I will endeavor to draw a few such inferences here, but must first and last insist that *Copperfield* isn't a "novel of ideas" in the way *Wilhelm Meister* or *The Magic Mountain* is. Nor, as a novel primarily of character, is it quite as disturbing a book as *Great Expectations*, especially on the subject of the conflict between social classes. Still, there is no broader, warmer, more humorous field full of folk in fiction, and while everyone complains, with reason, that David himself is less vividly *there* for us after Dora's death, the folk whom he observes and lives with fade not by a single candlepower, even after they have died or gone to Australia. The whole lesson of Dickens, as Chesterton flamboyantly insisted, was "that we should keep the absurd people [those Micawbers and Doras] for our friends."[2] And this, even if at the end we, like Chesterton, fear that David and Dickens might be embarrassed by their eccentricities. No, *Copperfield* is clearly the irreplaceable English example of the *Bildungsroman*, the one we have to read before we proceed to any others.

Everyone who has read the novel remembers the characters, though the plot may be something else. Many early episodes parallel those in Dickens's own experience, as we know from the irreplaceable *Life* (1872–1874) written by his friend John Forster, to which one might add the recent one-volume though still massive lives by Fred Kaplan (1988) and Peter Ackroyd (1990). In any case, *Copperfield*, told in autobiographical form, goes like this. In spite of his father having died before his birth, David's earliest years are idyllic, both because he is cared for by his tender mother and their servant Peggotty and because, on vacation, he is welcomed into Peggotty's brother's quaint seaside home in Yarmouth. The idyll ends when he returns from Yarmouth to find his mother remarried to the handsome but cruel Mr. Murdstone, whose metallic sister soon takes over the management of the house. When Murdstone canes David for failing to know his sums, David bites the man's hand and gets himself packed off to Salem House, a very stupid school but one where he makes two important friends, Traddles the amiable nobody, and Steerforth the dashing cock-of-the-walk. David's mother dies shortly after the death of the child she has borne to Murdstone, who promptly sends David to drudge in a London warehouse. He lodges with the ebullient Mr. Micawber and his family, who are forever falling into debt, even into debtors' prison. Soon, however, the Micawbers are able to seek opportunities elsewhere, and David runs away to his Aunt Betsey Trotwood in Dover. She adopts him, tells off the snooty Murdstones, and sends him to Dr. Strong's school in Canterbury, where he lives with Mr. Wickfield and his daughter Agnes. Clerking in Wickfield's law office is Uriah Heep, an 'umble (read: sneakily ambitious) young man who gives David the creeps.

Having reencountered Steerforth in London, David takes him to meet the Peggottys in Yarmouth—all very charming, but the resistless Steerforth ends up seducing and carrying off Mr. Peggotty's niece Emily, the fiancée of his nephew Ham and David's playmate during his childhood visit. His schooling over, David is articled to Mr. Spenlow, a respectable London lawyer. Soon he is spooning over Spenlow's pretty daughter Dora. The tippling and depressed Wickfield mismanages Betsey's money, which drastically reduces her fortune and David's expectations. He sets to work first as a parliamentary reporter, then as a novelist, and earns the wherewithal to marry Dora, who, upon her father's unexpected death, has inherited nothing. Though fetching in a light romantic way, she can't keep house or bear children, and gradually wastes away. Meanwhile subplots revolve around Dr. Strong and his young wife, who appears to be (but isn't) committing adultery with her handsome cousin, and around Uriah, who appears to be (and is) subverting Wickfield in order to seize the hand of Agnes. Traddles, one of the few good lawyers in Dickens, works with Micawber to expose Uriah's perfidy, liberate Wickfield, and restore Betsey's property. After Dora's death, David goes once more to Yarmouth, where a terrific storm drowns both Steerforth and Ham. Mr. Peggotty has discovered the fallen lost Emily in London, and with her, the Micawbers, and some minor characters, emigrates to Australia. In time, David marries Agnes, who keeps house very well, and bears him children. The fascination, as always in a Dickens novel, lies in the details.

What follows, besides details, is an analysis of the *sense* Dickens thinks David's life makes. He would have agreed with what George Eliot said of "aesthetic teaching," in a directive that Goethe too would have endorsed: it must offer not a "diagram" but a "picture" of "life in its highest complexity." The novelist's charcoal may draw an outline—probably does—but her brushes fill it in thickly, giving us "breathing individual forms, and group[ing] them in the needful relations, so that the presentation will lay hold on the emotions as human experience—will, as you say, 'flash' conviction on the world by means of aroused sympathy."[3] Accordingly, a sympathetic critical analysis ought to focus on the groupings of figures within the picture—how this character connects thematically with that—and the ways in which episodes and images, tropes and tones, mass to suggest the ideas and emotions that give purpose to what the characters, especially the tyro David, say and do. Trying to avoid the diagrammatic but still trying to retrace some of the *Copperfield* picture's architecture (what in the Preface Dickens himself praised as his narrative's "long design"[4]), I shall address, by a logic that will become plain as I go, the following elements:

(1) the myth of an orphaned or semi-orphaned Edenic childhood, David and Emily's primarily, and, that paradise soon lost, the adult project of trying to regain it;

(2) the abused child's fight-or-flight struggle to defend itself, and in particular David's quest for allies in that struggle, most notably Peggotty and his Aunt Betsey Trotwood;

(3) his education in mortality, which conditions his attempts to recreate some version of his childhood paradise in this world and prepares him for its wished-for re-realization in the next;

(4) the vocational question posed to him, Steerforth, Traddles, or any tolerably educated youth, who must decide—and no-decisions and wrong-decisions are here as instructive as right ones—what public work he will do while, more privately, he attends to his double-sided paradisal project;

(5) these young men's relations to women, from their mothers to their girlfriends to their wives, the love of whom is crucial to the paradisal project;

(6) Micawber's Dionysian energies, which emanate from the Life that gives David's life much of its spunk, elasticity, and pleasure; and

(7) the intimations of Providential concern, got mainly through the mythy character of Mr. Peggotty, tending to the belief that the *sense* of David's or anyone's life, with all its pains as well as pleasures, is coscripted by his and by a *higher* hand.

This promises to be a complicated, sinuous analysis, but what at this moment strikes me is how much, regretfully, I have had to omit on every page: *Copperfield* is a huge canvas, and even as one focuses on a single section or zone, one has now to neglect color in favor of line, or then line in favor of texture, tonality, or perspective. All one can do, this side of discouragement, is to remind oneself and others that this well-peopled picture is a unified work of art, more (say) Peter Paul Rubens than William Powell Frith, with whom Dickens is often compared. And then, of course, to reread the book.

A Brief Eden

Reread, at a certain age, for maybe the umpteenth time, though as a teacher my ordinary task is to persuade students to read such a massive book, for the first time, all the way through. Back in the days of fewer media distractions, when Dickens was read aloud in the family circle, Virginia Woolf could write that "There is perhaps no person living who can remember reading *David Copperfield* for the first time."[5] There must be exceptions in a few deliberately backward households, but I think it incontestable that Dickens isn't read like that anymore. What we thus have to do is tweak Woolf's remark to say that once people, even students today, have read *David Copperfield* it is *as though* they had always known it—a book presenting something so *like* childhood and youth that it has *become* childhood and youth. Not "my" childhood and youth, nor "yours" exactly, but "ours"—what Woolf calls one of the "myths of life."

"Ours" has of course become an anathematized word among academic critics who, against any writer's claims to speak universally, insist on the particular distinctions based on gender, class, and race (though with *Copperfield* this latter category hasn't to my knowledge been addressed even by deconstructionists who believe what is textually absent—say, the lives of Australian aborigines whose interests might conflict with those of the immigrant Micawber and company—is often more important than what is textually present).[6] Dickens and any current reader may disagree about what ideas and feelings can be communalized as "ours," but any such disagreement can be instructive only if his concept of what is "ours" is rightly defined. And so with differences between "ours" and "theirs," me and you, his and hers, his and his, etc. The current reader is likely to insist that *all* such differences are acculturated ("constructed"). Dickens thought that *many* indeed were. Steerforth, Traddles, David, and Uriah Heep for instance, because they come from families with unequal incomes and are treated unequally in school, will in roughly similar situations—when confronted with a desirable young woman, for example—think, speak, and act unequally. Steerforth will charm and seduce, Traddles enthuse and pledge himself, David spoon and then half-regret his choice, and Heep plot, hug himself, and wait. Learned behaviors.

What aren't learned are physiognomies, temperaments, special talents. These, Dickens believed, mark innate differences, and (though it is another of those things now practically unutterable at academic conferences) I think he is being commonsensical. Steerforth, for example, can sing, Traddles can draw (after a fashion) and grind through details, David can tell tales and master sign-systems (his native English, or the shorthand that transcribes the English used by parliamentarians), and Uriah can autodidactically master Tidd and Blackstone and jump counters—each as the others can't, and as the others, whatever amount of coaching they might receive, finally couldn't. As we all realize on the playing field or in the music room, some people have a gift that can be developed to the level of stardom; some, not altogether hopeless, can play a subordinate role; and others need to be counseled toward (say) the laboratory, the factory, or the bank. As with Schiller's high and low roads for aesthetic education, it is a question not of prejudice but of discrimination. And Dickens was at one with him and with Goethe in arguing, often explicitly, that the criteria for discrimination should be based not on whether a person is born male or female, rich, poor, or in-between, but on his or her innative, developable qualities. In short, Dickens was a nineteenth-century liberal.

What, then, cutting across these innative differences, is—or *ought* to be—"ours" is the opportunity, for each of us, to develop our special talents, express our temperaments, and make the best of our phizes and physiques. *David Copperfield* like

Wilhelm Meister is an enlivening plea for the "right" to do so without prejudice. Take the way, half descriptive, half prescriptive, in which Dickens presents childhood as Edenically happy. Such a childhood needn't be in a two-loving-parents, economically solid milieu, helpful though that can be. The portraits of young Emily and David show us that orphaned or half-orphaned children can for a while be happy too. For a very brief while, David absorbs all his mother's love and Emily all her surrogate father Mr. Peggotty's, without rival. Her Eden-by-the-sea is at Yarmouth, while his is more traditionally centered in the garden, "a very preserve of butterflies" behind Blunderstone Rookery, "where," as he recalls in the present tense of eternity, "the fruit clusters on the trees, riper and richer than fruit had ever been since, in any other garden, and where my mother gathers some in a basket, while I stand by, bolting furtive goose-berries, and trying to look unmoved" (15–16). Maternal (or in Emily's case paternal) love, oral gratification, and outdoor play: Dickens thought every child deserved some version of this, but unlike George Eliot with the Tulliver children in *The Mill on the Floss*, he doesn't linger oversweetly on the paradisal period of David's or Emily's childhood. *They* may not be aware of the days passing but, like his fully adult character and soon to be spokesperson Betsey Trotwood, *he* the novelist is certainly aware.

What marks their passing is, among other things, changing social relations. David's mother, it is easy to forget, was a nursery maid before his father, David, Sr., married her and raised her up to gentlewoman's status. When her husband dies she is left moderately well-off, but she is instantly prey to fortune hunters like Murdstone, and David himself, with no separate testamentary provision made for him in the event of her remarrying (an instance of folly regrettable but excusable in so young a father, who no doubt thought he would live forever), is prey too. The entrance of Murdstone into the Rookery garden is in any event like that of the serpent into Eden—a turning of the calendar's page. Clara Peggotty can recognize him for what he is (a cousin of Captain Murderer), but Eve-like Clara Copperfield mistakes him for a guardian archangel, giving him—allowing him to take—gate, padlock, garden, the whole rookless Rookery itself. Her cozy life with her boy, provided for by the capable Peggotty and her small independence, has made her too credulous, as of course it has made David, who will later fondly try to regain paradise by marrying Dora—someone with all his mother's affection, prettiness, and musicality, which is okay, but also with all her inability to examine the people who come through the gate, or to keep the key in her own pocket, which isn't okay.

Dora is also prefigured by Emily, except that David's relation to *her*, in an Eden colored *à la* Wordsworth, is as presexual as it gets. The two children cavort or cuddle "as if Time . . . were a child too, and always at play" (37), while the summer Yarmouth vista itself, with its monotonously flat land, broad sea, and big sky, suggests the eternal shore the children in the "Immortality Ode" sport upon. There is no doubt a hint of dullness in all the flatness—it is the first thing little David notices—but the chief emphasis is on its healthy simplicity. Living in direct relation to the calms and storms of nature, the Peggottys and everyone else in Yarmouth aren't distracted by any too-high social pinnacles or too-deep social depths. Like their undertaker Mr. Omer, they can hear together, and without anxiety, the ringing of wedding bells and the tapping of the coffin-maker's hammer. The Steerforth episode that destroys David and Emily's innocence destroys, even before the great tempest, something of Yarmouth's too. His intrusion is like Murdstone's—a calendar-page-turning signal that children can't play along the beach of prepubescence forever. For a while, however, the children's affection for one another rests on a "greater purity and . . . disinterestedness" than any affection between grown-ups can.

Nor is this the nostalgic older David's fantasy. Next to little David and Emily holding hands in the corner or building castles in the sand, the mature sexuality of Rosa Dartle, Steerforth, or even Mr. Peggotty himself presents an obviously more vexed picture, made less "pure" and "disinterested" by people's wanting sexual excitation, progeny, or a renewal of the intimacy they originally had with the parent (or parent-substitute) of the opposite sex. Little Emily seems like "a very angel" because of latency: she doesn't, at the moment, have to contend with a bothersome sexual appetite that, going unsatisfied, could madden her. The older David is so dismayed at the later, unregulated eruption of this appetite in her infatuation with Steerforth that he wishes she had drowned as a child—Dickens pointedly inserted into the galley-sheet this not atypical male wish where, in eighteenth- and nineteenth-century English novels, a female's chastity or fidelity is at stake—and thus, in a short circuit back to the first intimacy, had joined her father under the waves. This, rather than pass through puberty and run away with a man who will never marry her. It is like the dismay David comes to feel even about the *regulated* eruption of his own sexual appetite in his marriage to Dora. The complications of that partnership are so confounding that she believes, with no convincing demurrer from him, it would have been better for them to have remained puppies and not tried anything big.

But to return. Blunderstone's paradisal prelude to life seems extended during the Yarmouth idyll, in which the enchanted David imagines Mr. Peggotty's house to be "a sort of ark" for orphans whose parents have "drownded." By which logic Mr. Peggotty is a sort of Noah, a sufficient hint to us if not yet to little David that this isn't the Eden world after all but at best a haven of righteousness amidst Steerforths and storms. "Time" has taken no holiday; indeed it has stolen a march on David, the whole Yarmouth excursion having been contrived to get him out of the way so his mother could remarry. At her age, and with her ignorance about money management, she naturally feels she needs a man, especially one who flatters her vanity. But to David the "new Pa" simply evokes mephitic ideas of the old pa's "grave in the churchyard, and the raising of the dead" (42), and of a handsome brute horning in between himself and his mother. After this shock, which there is no undoing, her having a second child (also behind David's back) is nothing. Coming home after his first half at Salem House, he discovers her suckling the baby and singing softly to it. Any jealousy is banished at once, for she calls him "her dear Davy, her own boy!" still, and lays his "head down on her bosom near the little creature that was nestling there," assuring him that there is room for two at the sacred founts. The older David wishes he had died on the spot, just as he has wished Emily would have drowned, because he was then most fit for "Heaven"—accepted and accepting (109). As his mother's hair droops over him "like an angel's wing," the demonic Murdstones are forgot: "nothing [was] real in all that I remembered, save my mother, Peggotty, and I" (112)—the "I" being himself and his new sibling mystically melded, and for the moment protected from the big male world, with its ugly competition for women's love and, as he has seen at Salem House, for other men's goods and favors.

Children fit for heaven, mothers with angels' wings: the kitschy romantic tropes can drive us bats, but we need to suspend our distaste and see what Dickens, wiser after all than his persona David, is getting at. While he, the man, rather resented *his* mother, he saw that most of his male contemporaries were excessively attached to *theirs*. Thus David, as their representative not his, should be too.[7] Why the excessive attachment? Why, for all these boys and no few of their sisters, did the mother alone seem to provide some version of paradise? Back in the days before steam, on the farm or in the cottage shops, fathers had used their muscles, made decisions, and served as observable models for their children. Fathers and mothers together had stood as pillars, and beneath the arch that spanned them their children felt secure. When steam came, though, with its new modes of production, there was a great movement of people from country to city, and the men went *away* to work in mills or offices. Their wives had to command the house and educate the children by themselves. (We see the same dynamic in *Sons and Lovers*.) Dickens establishes this situation not by dramatizing a man's transition from (say) village carpenter's shop to city insurance office, which would have been difficult and interesting in a Dreiserian mode, but simply by presenting literally fatherless households in David's, Steerforth's, Traddles's, and Uriah's cases, and otherwise a line up of amiable but weak men—Barkis, Micawber, Mr. Omer, Mr. Wickfield, and Doctors Chillip and Strong. Being attached to the mother alone isn't such a good thing after all: it leaves David at a loss when choosing friends or fiancées, as it leaves Steerforth acting with crudely clever imperiousness in his dealings with everybody, but especially women, who like mama and Rosa have always appeared to exist for his exclusive use. Absent fathers and intensely present mothers—depressed masculine and hyperburdened feminine energies—become a principal theme of English as of German *Bildungsromane*.

The mother's image, in any event, is hypostatized for David when, as he drives away to school, she holds her baby up in farewell: "It was cold still weather; and not a hair of her head, nor a fold of her dress, was stirred, as she looked intently at me, holding up her child" (121). She and the baby—she and David's infant self—freeze into a piece of romantic funerary sculpture. *That*, unaffected by her actual death, is who she henceforth will be for him. To have identified himself with his infant brother has been made easy by the latter's having died before he became a nuisance, but the more edifying point is that love for the other grows out of love for oneself. To imagine the baby's, or anyone else's, needs in situation X is to imagine one's own needs in situation X, and vice versa. This means starting to think of the baby as his mother does—the urchin needs milk and honey—and to think of anyone else as a humanitarian does—we *all* need milk and honey. Note, for instance, the focus fade after David, fleeing London, has arrived at Dover, led there by the image of his mother and by the echo of her saying that Betsey had touched her with a not ungentle hand—after he is safe in bed, with the candle out—when he sits "looking at the moonlight on the water," hoping "to see my mother with her child, coming from Heaven, along that shining path, to look upon me as she had looked when I last saw her sweet face." He feels grateful to be lying in such a soft bed, and thinks

> of all the solitary places under the night sky where I had slept, and . . . . [I] prayed that I never might be houseless any more, and never might forget the houseless. I remember how I seemed to float, then, down the melancholy glory of that track upon the sea, away into the world of dreams. (199)

Again the rhetoric tends to cloy around such sacred subjects, but we can cut through it well enough to see that a mother's hosting a parasite child is natural and necessary during the early years, but disturbing, as in a pietà, as the child gets older. And it is a dependency that David, in an age-appropriate trope, is here beginning to free himself from. He obviously can't get to "Heaven" by walking "that track upon the sea," nor by simply dreaming. The way to "Heaven" lies in reciprocal generosity: he is praying never again to be without a roof over and a pillow under his head, and never to forget those who *are* without them. He must repay Betsey's taking him in by someday taking in someone else. Granted, it is a serious question as the story proceeds whether he ever does much more than *pray* to be so good. But as a child he is quick to see needs in others because he has felt them himself: he can *remember* what it was like to be a tramp upon the road or, later with Dr. Strong as earlier with Creakle, a new boy at school, and he can *remember* the gentleness he then wanted, and sometimes got. If he can be gentle in turn, perhaps he can "get to" where the hypostatized image of gentleness, his mother, has in spirit "gone." It doesn't matter whether this eschatological project is literally possible. It is enough that David understands that he must do more than remember paradise; he must endeavor to *recreate* it, for himself first, and then for others. That, to simplify, is what his mother has been for: without her, no paradise, however imperfect and fatherless; no paradise, no template for trying in future to make himself or others even imperfectly happy.

A Child Abused and Defended

David is fortunate to be able to recall his mother so vividly and to find good, and more practical, substitutes for her in the rough-but-tender Peggotty and the initially scary Betsey.[8] He is most unfortunate, as I have indicated, never to have known his father or to find an adequate substitute for him. The boy's imperfect paradise appears for a while to have been little more than a fool's paradise, quickly lost and with an exile that's not for sissies. First frightened and then neglected by Murdstone, David begins to panic over the possibility that he will grow up to be a derelict, "lounging an idle life away, about the village," a nightmare against which he can pit only the daydream of "going away somewhere, like the hero in a story, to seek my fortune" (134–35). What he clearly wants is paternal guidance in the ways of the world—to be "taught something, anyhow, anywhere!"—even if it is at the wretched Salem House. When he has been rusticated thence, after the death of his mother, the story begins to reverberate with echoes from Dickens's autobiographical sketch, full of wonder "that I can have been so easily thrown away at such an age . . . [and] that nobody should have made any sign in my behalf"; full of "little gent" shame, once he is in London, at being cast among the likes of Mick Walker and Mealy Potatoes and having "my hopes of growing up to be a learned and distinguished man, crushed in my bosom"; full of terror that, were it not "for the mercy of God, I might easily have been, for any care that was taken of me, a little robber or a little vagabond" (149–61). These plaintive cries issue from an appropriate self-solicitude. He will never be able to improve the lot of Mick and Mealy if he dies at age 12, or if, taking the robber-and-vagabond route, he sinks to a sub-Mick and -Mealy level, as Oliver Twist briefly does. There is a real danger of that in David's case as, breakfasting on twopence-worth of bread and milk, supping on "another small loaf, and a modicum of cheese," he slowly starves. And "From Monday morning until Saturday night, I had no advice, no counsel, no encouragement, no consolation, no assistance, no support, of any kind, from anyone, that I can call to mind, as I hope to go to heaven!" (159–60). Sundays he presumably has the comfort of the Micawbers at the King's Bench, but they look on him as a sort of miniature adult, not as the orphaned waif in need of adoptive parents that he in fact is. This London deprivation is only a foretaste of his suffering on the road to Dover, when he truly becomes a poor forked creature with no name. He is, in this neglectedness, an Everychild, our rage being not just that he but that *any* child should be so abused. He is more poignant than Jo in *Bleak House*, because with admirable restraint, even as a child, he can express, as the illiterate Jo can't, the feelings of a person to whom such injustices happen. And as an adult looking back, he can speak not only for himself but for the young abandoned everywhere.

How might a boy respond to those who bring suffering on him? One way is to strike back—a move that, along with other realistic touches about children's experience, Dickens may have depicted in *Copperfield* as he hadn't in *Oliver Twist* or *Dombey and Son* because, as Q. D. Leavis unprovably but plausibly insists, Charlotte Brontë's *Jane Eyre* had very recently given him the artistic courage to do so (109). In any event, the instinct for self-preservation drives David to bite the hand of Murdstone in that terrifying scene of child-beating—to bite "through" the hand in a way that still "sets my teeth on edge to think of it" (58)—and then to feel criminally guilty, as underlings are always made to feel when they defend themselves. The instinct has been reinforced and tutored by what then counted as children's literature. The book about "Crorkindills" that he reads to Peggotty isn't just about "a sort of vegetable" or amphibians laying eggs. It is about killing the tropical dragons that grow up from those eggs, and at the dangerous crises David and Peggotty, like audiences now watching *Jurassic Park*, unreflectingly identify with the killers: "we went into the water after them, as natives, and put sharp pieces of timber down their throats" (18)—an idea that easily translates into a counterthrust against the more immediate dragon, Murdstone. David has learnt another response from boys' romances, which is to strike against himself—an unconscious, roundabout method of self-glorification. For example, when telling Emily he adores her he adds "that unless she confessed she adored me I should be reduced to the necessity of killing myself with a sword" (37). If she doesn't love him, he is no good and deserves to die; if he dies, she will of course feel bad and maybe love him. Just so with Murdstone. If David bites him, he must be wicked enough to be locked up; if he is locked up a long time, someone, admittedly not Murdstone, may take pity on him. Thus, convolutedly, justice will be done against and for him.[9]

Most of the time, though, David hits neither his tormentor nor himself. He just runs away, which for any outgunned organism is the perfectly sensible thing to do. Yarmouth and Dover are literal places to run to, but more convenient are the figurative places revealed in books—*Don Quixote*, the *Arabian Nights*, the *Tales of the Genii*, eighteenth-century English novels—alternative worlds where Murdstone's "five thousand double-Gloucester cheeses at fourpence-halfpenny each, present payment" can be fancied as just another obstacle magnificently overcome. He soon learns to imitate the heroes of books not just in thought but in deed—bringing the figurative into contact with the literal. Not surprisingly, he cries when forced to leave his mother for school; but then he thinks that there isn't much use in that, "especially as neither Roderick Random, nor that Captain in the Royal British Navy, had ever cried, that I could remember, in trying situations" (63). So he won't either. He applies Smollett to someone *else's* problems later, when he calls on the Micawbers at the King's Bench: "at last I did see a turnkey (poor little fellow that I was!), and thought how, when Roderick Random was in a debtors' prison, there was a man there with nothing on him but an old rug, [and] the turnkey swam before my dimmed eyes and my beating heart" (165). Pity for himself is characteristically expressed between parentheses; what makes him weep is pity, prepared in him by a book, for the all but naked man he might find in the prison. David's running away from real life tormentors to the refuge of imagination turns out to be a route back into real life, now better armed to cope with its difficulties. Evidently, literature does instruct as well as please.

Something similar may be said about his most dramatically literal act of running away—the one from Murdstone and Grinby's in London to his Aunt Betsey Trotwood's in Dover. The entire pilgrimage, through all the goroo-men, tramps, drunks, and thieves of merry England, is like King Lear's journey, and not just because both end at Dover. Like Lear, David discovers his essential nakedness, the common pangs of hunger and cold that link him to "the houseless." Only a few touches of culture—soaped hands and face, a buttoned waistcoat, perhaps a set of parents or guardians—stand between him and the respectable churchgoers, they musically congregated and lazing in Sabbath peace, he "quite wicked in my dirt and dust, with my tangled hair," a hobo boy glowered at by the beadle (182). Only a few touches of culture—but the chasm seems infinitely wide. Like the wretches of the road, David can at any moment be reduced to an anonymous "scrap of newspaper intelligence," his body "found dead . . . under some hedge" (180). Against these horrors, even the carceral Salem House, against whose wall David sleeps the first night of his journey, can seem a haven. Unlike Lear, though, David is too young—or rather, too lucky—to be "found dead in a day or two." He will later be given an extended opportunity to capitalize on this experience of kinship with the outcast, and to do something to deserve his good luck. For now, however, what matters is the sheer *fact* of his luck: he is picked up by Aunt Betsey, stripped of his rags, immersed in a sort of baptismal bath, swaddled in some clothes of Mr. Dick (the wise simpleton who is Betsey's ward), and rechristened Trotwood. The name is meant to signalize his best self, the sisterly alter ego who will always, at a crossroads, tell him what she thinks: "Be as like your sister as you can, and speak out!" (203). She is the female conscience, in short, that the male mind and body apparently need if they are to realize their full humanity. In any event, Betsey shortens Trotwood to Trot, implying a brisk mean between a lazy saunter and a mad gallop, and enlivening the stiffness of backbone suggested by the "wood."[10]

So David is reborn, the journey to Dover having been a painful trip down the birth canal, with the umbilical cord tightening around his neck. He arrives looking rather "like Cain before he was grown up," he can in retrospect afford lightly to say, for when the true Cain—"the murderer"—is properly marked and sent packing with his metallic sister, he (David) has a pretty fresh start. Will he now be mindful of his prayer, and remember the houseless whose fate he has for six days and sixty miles had to share? Of course he won't—not altogether. He just feels relieved in having found his aunt, whose treatment of the parts-on-order Mr. Dick "not only inspired my young breast with some selfish hope for myself, but, warmed it unselfishly towards her" (206). The most he can attach himself to is the particular person who is aiding him, a blood relation after all, and no one should at this point expect more from him. We do, however, desire him to remember what he has gone through, and in something other than Bounderbyesque fear, whereby he would tell himself that he will never let anything like *that* happen to him again, and will ruin anybody who even *tries* to unhouse him. Such an attitude is precisely what, in the war of all against all, would sooner or later unhouse everybody, including David. We want him bravely to acknowledge what he has been through, and to devote at least a tithe of the energy he spends helping himself to helping others. We want it, in some measure, because *Dickens* wanted it, as we can tell by his delight in confronting his hero with reminders of the harder time. Micawber is the usual agent for these, as when he blunders in on the tea party David is having at the Heeps'—"what are you doing, Copperfield? Still in the wine trade?" (257)—and sends the boy into a panic over the chance that, in another minute, the appalling differences between him and the nice boys at Doctor Strong's will come out. And this in front of the groveling Heeps! Not surprisingly, though, these reminders of affiliation with the dispossessed soon cease. The more securely middle class David becomes, the more certain he is that a curtain has fallen over his tenure at Murdstone and Grinby's (the time that, as Dickens pathetically said in his number-plans for Number IV, Chapter 9, "I know so well"[11]):

> No one has ever raised that curtain since. I have lifted it for a moment, even in this narra-
> tive, with a reluctant hand, and dropped it gladly. The remembrance of that life is fraught
> with so much pain to me . . . . Whether it lasted for a year, or more, or less, I do not know.
> I only know that it was, and ceased to be; and that I have written, and there I leave it. (215)

The curtain should be lifted more often, many of us believe, but it will take a wind from Australia—the one that in *Great Expectations* brings Magwitch back to Pip—really to lift it. Which, however, is not to say there aren't some morally interesting winds in *David Copperfield* itself.

Education in Mortality

Copperfield is morally interesting because it is mortally interesting. "What draws the reader to the novel," Benjamin says, speaking of fiction in general, "is the hope of warming his shivering life with a death he reads about" (101). Benjamin is referring to our inability to experience our own death—in the sense of going through and remembering it—and thus to our inability to grasp the meaning it finally gives our life. We read about the deaths of others, he argues, in order to guess at what our own full story will be—to understand, proleptically, what dying will be like, and what it will "say" about all that has gone before. *Copperfield* is as edifying in this regard as Tolstoy's "The Death of Ivan Ilych" or the Nicholas sections of *Anna Karenina*—granting of course that Dickens doesn't concern himself with the psychology of patient and caregiver as Tolstoy impressively does—for David's *Bildung* is to a great extent focused on mortality. Throughout his story he encounters the deaths of others, as though he were willy-nilly trying to warm *his* shivering life beside them, till he at last becomes aware that his body, like theirs, is dust, while a little more than faintly trusting the larger hope that his spirit will like theirs endure.

He begins his mortal studies with the contemplation of his father's tombstone in the churchyard, feeling an "indefinable compassion . . . for it lying out alone there in the dark night, when our little parlour was warm and bright with fire and candle, and the doors of our house were—almost cruelly, it seemed to me sometimes—bolted and locked against it" (2). He is doubtless glad to be enjoying his mother's company without having to share her with his father, but he is still sorry that his father has to lie outside in the cold and dark. There, however, he *does* lie, and David isn't in the final analysis eager for him to come in—partly because it would be horrible to greet a decomposing man draped in graveclothes (hence his fright upon hearing the story of Lazarus [62]), and partly because, with natural shortsightedness, he doesn't want a "new Pa" in *any* form, for he is quite happy as he is. Though not as large as some critics have supposed, David's fears of the churchyard are common enough, but in fact it seems to him a predominantly quiet sanctuary: "The sheep are feeding there, when I kneel up, early in the morning, in my little bed in a closet within my mother's room, to look out at it; and I see the red light shining on the sun-dial, and think within myself, 'Is the sun-dial glad, I wonder, that it can tell the time again?' " (14). The sheep familiarly grazing on the lawn enriched by those of the church's "flock" who have died; the sundial reminding those who haven't died that their time will come, yet also, in this pastoral setting, rejoicing that there is after all *a* time for things to be *in*—the passage evokes what Phillippe Ariès has called "the tame death," an attitude of calm acceptance of one's own and others' dying, and a ritualized concern that the dead, once underground, stay put.

When David's mother dies, the tame death becomes, in Ariès' terms, "the death of the other." He has known his mother as he hasn't known his father, and her loss is something he needs to make up for, first by marrying Dora, and last by dying himself and going to the paradise Agnes always points to. In God will occur the omnium-gatherum of dear ones, his mother above all, that is anticipated in the novel's last pages. This, as Ariès has massively shown, was *the* romantic conviction. One's personal identity, especially in its loving communion with others, was simply too precious to cease. The personal had advanced as the anonymous and communal life of the Middle Ages had retreated; and when God appeared to have retreated too, the belief in personal immortality became more insistent because it was less certain. In Dickens, we can sense this in the exaggerated pathos of the deaths of Little Nell, Paul Dombey, and Jo, which, according to Humphry House, were so popular because a post-supernaturalist, humanistic religion "is very poorly equipped to face death, and must dwell on it for that very reason."[12] Compared with the morbid scenes House bemoans, however, those devoted to the deaths of David's mother, Dora, and even Barkis are pretty restrained. The focus isn't on David's needing assurance about what will happen after death; it is on his needing to realize that *he* is the one who someday will have to do the dying.

He takes a step in that direction when, imaging himself as the infant in his mother's coffin (a point Dickens underscored in his notes [*Plans*, 821]), he defines and accepts the death of his childhood. Having done so, he gives few morose thoughts to joining his family in the churchyard. He may invoke his mother all he wants, but he understands that she can come only in spectral form:

> Can I say of her innocent and girlish beauty, that it faded, and was no more, when its breath falls on my cheek now, as it fell that night? Can I say she ever changed, when my remembrance brings her back to life, thus only; and, truer to its loving youth than I have been, or man ever is, still holds fast what it cherished then? (24)

Her spirit, that is, "still holds fast" to him, as it did when he was a boy, and so proves (to him, at least) that women are "truer" to their first affections than men are. But, inconstant "man" though he is, he can remember her and, when he is older, write his memory down, and then get on with the job of living, which in his case entails attempts to replicate, only in better terms, the scene of his earlier version of family happiness. In due course *he* will die and his children, visited "thus only" by the "breath" of his spirit—the imagery of Tennyson's almost contemporaneous *In Memoriam* (1850) is similar—might remember him.

Why, compared with someone like Lawrence's Paul Morel, David has so little trouble "getting on" after his mother's death is explained by his having in effect another mother. Peggotty's Christian name, Clara, is as we have noticed the same as David's actual mother's: they divide the maternal functions between them, the one being pretty and playful, the other toughened and practical, and both of them caressive and warm. After his mother's death, Peggotty again takes David to Yarmouth, where, in bed at night, he hears the moaning wind and thinks how the sea might rise to sweep them all away, just as it has risen "and drowned my happy home." Next, though, "as the wind and water began to sound fainter in my ears," he thinks of something else, "putting a short clause into my prayers, petitioning that I might grow up to marry little Em'ly, and so dropping lovingly asleep" (143). Emily is the new life to which Peggotty has led him. She happens to be the wrong girl for him, as in a similar way Dora will be. Yet both answer to his chief desire, the reincarnation of the pretty playful careless femininity he has lost. It seems cruel and is yet profoundly comforting: a child can recover from the death of its opposite-sex parent by marrying an age-appropriate replacement. Only, as David discovers, the replacement shouldn't in his case be identical in temperament with the original.

To return to my mortal subject, the ocean is David's image for the great "deep of Time" that receives all the dead and at the last will in judgment give them up again—an event adumbrated by the washing up of Steerforth's and Ham's bodies after the storm. But grief for their loss and hope for their final reconciliation aren't all that concern David in the admired "Tempest" chapter. Robert Lougy may go too far in saying that the *real* focus is David's anxiety about his own death,[13] but such an anxiety is certainly there, and has been since the onset of Dora's illness. The long adolescent holiday has begun to end—the holiday of success at Dr. Strong's school, renewed companionship with Steerforth, and busy penetration of the "forest of difficulty" necessitated by Betsey's loss of money, during which his mother's funeral, the "high rock in the ocean" of memory (131), with all it has insinuated about his own mortality, has been obscured by the crisply blown spray of activity. One doesn't look squarely at death when the weather is gay, quickening, and fresh. But with the loss of Dora's baby, and then with what we take to be her consumption, comes a change, solemnized for David by intimations of her fate as a "Little Blossom" when he sees "the trodden leaves ... lying under-foot, and [feels] the autumn wind ... blowing" (664), or when he carries her upstairs, still lighter than before, and feels "as if I were approaching to some frozen region yet unseen" (700). Winter isn't far behind, yet how is her fate, or his, different from anyone else's when seen *sub specie eternitatis*?

> The rooks were sailing about the cathedral towers; and the towers themselves, over-looking many a long unaltered mile of the rich country and its pleasant streams, were cutting the bright morning air, as if there were no such thing as change on earth. Yet the bells, when they sounded, told me sorrowfully of change in everything; told me of their own age, and my pretty Dora's youth; and of the many, never old, who had lived and loved and died, while the reverberations of the bells had hummed through the rusty armour of the Black Prince hanging up within, and, motes upon the deep of Time, had lost themselves in air, as circles do in water. (742–43)

To be lost like an echo in air is the fate of everyone, whether delicate like Dora or puissant like the Black Prince, whose "rusty armour" hangs in those towers as grimly as a corpse in a gibbet. To die young, like "the many, never old," is undoubtedly sad, but from a sufficiently "towering" point of view the differences between young "motes" and old are inappreciable.

With broodings like these, David paces away the night as the storm rages over Yarmouth. He stops "several times" to gaze out the window, "but could see nothing, except the reflection in the window-panes of the faint candle I had left burning, and of my own haggard face looking in at me from the black void" (790). The passage is haunting—so much so that Mr. Lougy, pretending that Dickens had read Heidegger, centers the entire novel on it.[14] Pretending that Dickens had read Kierkegaard, with whom he would have had a stronger affinity, I think one can find something in the passage that Mr. Lougy misses. Directly after it, David goes downstairs where "A pretty girl . . . screamed when I appeared, supposing me to be a spirit," and where the men are discussing whether "the souls of the collier-crews who had gone down, were out in the storm?" It is as if David *had* for the moment become "a spirit": he has looked past his own grave into "the black void," the abyss of Time, whence his soul, his "face," stares haggardly back. But stares back at what? It stares, first, back at itself: that is, David stares back at David, reviewing himself, replaying his life, which is a traditional occupation for spirits "on the other side." It stares, second, back at the "faint candle," which, reflected in the windowpanes, recalls the candle Mr. Peggotty leaves burning in the window of the ark-home for Emily to see if she returns at night and needs a light to guide her. David, in other words, is appropriately full of existential dread at the knowledge that he will die, but he also possesses the existential hope, however "faint[ly]" burning at this moment, that some Mr. Peggotty-like presence will, in "no time," leave a light to guide him.

After the "Tempest" chapter, and after the departure of the Micawbers, Emily, and Mr. Peggotty for Australia, David knows as much about his own death as, through "reading" those of others, he can. Marriage to Agnes isn't death itself, as James Kincaid with his usual reverence proposes,[15] but it *is* a preparation for death. David has had too much taken from him: he therefore curtails his worldly hopes and adopts a classical Epicureanism leavened by supernaturalism—a position that devotes no intemperate affection to people and things that tomorrow will vanish, regrets yet accepts the loss of youthful naïvety and passion, and settles down to a dutiful routine. He has kept warm by the artistic task of memorializing the early days, when the world seemed worth the hustle; and he has kept cool by the bourgeois task of rationalizing the late days, and of knowing something about seeming.

What I mean is this: David's dilemma in the final chapters is that, on the one hand, everything valuable in his character reaches back to his childhood, when he has first learnt what tenderness, fidelity, laughter, and perseverance are; and that, on the other, his childhood has bristled with degradation at Murdstone and Grinby's, and with shabby gentility among the Micawbers. He is embarrassed by any reminder of these bad times, and he no doubt feels guilty about being thus embarrassed. He must therefore *seem* not to be troubled by guilt—to be glad that the curtain is down over Murdstone and Grinby's, and that half the globe divides him from the Micawbers and, for that matter, from the horny-handed Mr. Peggotty and the deflowered Emily. In his autobiography, however, the book we have been reading, David can be bolder. The curtain can be raised on the scene at the warehouse, Micawber can be relished, Mr. Peggotty and Emily can be honored and wept over, and so on. Memorializing the past will then be more important than rationalizing the present: memorializing the past could indeed help David to *stop* rationalizing the present, at least to the extent of caring less about whether the jolly Traddleses have Britannia Metal or Georgian silver beside their plates at table.[16] If he can look again, in all justice, at those who have been taken, he may be able to look properly to those who remain. Otherwise, "It's in vain, Trot, to recall the past" (347).

The Vocational Quandary:
David, Steerforth, and Traddles

Between birth and death, as everyone knows, there are taxes, and the question for all the *Bildungshelden* I am looking at in this book, with the exception of the independently wealthy protagonists of *The Portrait of a Lady* and of *The Last Puritan*, is what sort of work will they do in order to pay the tax-collector—and, if possible, achieve a measure of personal satisfaction in the process. The work of someone who is just punching the clock might be called mere labor; that of someone who is personally satisfied with the work he is doing might be called vocation. It is what, at length, we have seen Wilhelm Meister in quest of. In *Copperfield* the issue jumps into focus when Micawber complains that his son "has contracted a habit of singing in public-houses, rather than in sacred edifices." The boy naturally feels bullied. There have been no openings in the cathedral choir, and in any case, what else is he to do?

He demands to know

> Whether he had been born a carpenter, or a coach-painter, any more than he had been
> born a bird? Whether he could go into the next street, and open a chemist's shop?
> Whether he could rush to the next assizes, and proclaim himself a lawyer? Whether he
> could come out by force at the opera, and succeed by violence? Whether he could do
> anything, without being brought up to something? (762)

Quite right: a child must be *trained* to do this or that. What, one may ask, has been
David's training? He has been given the usual ill-focused schooling of middle-class boys
aping aristocratic boys—that is, an indifferent grounding in classics, mathematics,
ancient history, and sports, first under Murdstone and Creakle, who, because they are
sadists, teach him very little; then under Doctor Strong, who, because he is gentle and
respectful, helps him, all vaguely, to get on. Hectoring and beating versus trustfulness
and kindness—"evil" versus "good"—that is about as far as Dickens's pedagogic criticism goes in this novel, or in any of the others. David's real education occurs outside of
school, learning *how* to read from his mother, and *what* to read from his father's library
of eighteenth-century novelists and travel writers. He derives from these a certain moral
sensitivity (recall what Smollett does for him) and certain skills as a storyteller, which he
exercises on Steerforth at Salem House. But—he may as well be an English major—
there is no one to suggest the specific vocational turn he might give these capacities.

Here is where a father would be welcome, and (once more) the absence of fathers
in the novel may be an indication of a general crisis of succession—a crisis of vocation—
which Dickens sensed throughout his country's middle class. The hereditary system
whereby a Mr. Peggotty brings up a Ham, or a Mr. Omer a son-in-law, to do the work
he himself has done is inoperative in the middle class because, on that level, little real
work is *being* done. David's and Steerforth's fathers apparently lived off modestly
independent incomes, as does Betsey. And the worst thing about a liberal, classical
education, as Butler came to remark, is that it cuts the youth off from any artisan-like
pursuits, which are thereafter as "beneath" him as manual day labor. Among the liberally
educated in *Copperfield*, we do have the physician Mr. Chillip and the headmaster
Doctor Strong, but their jobs aren't sufficiently interesting, it seems, for David to
describe them. But there are no civil servants, clergymen, military officers, or (excepting
Murdstone) businessmen. The only professional world Dickens investigates is the
law, along with one of its offshoots, parliamentary reporting. What we hear from parliament, or from the papers of Wickfield and Spenlow, seems however too close to the
Circumlocution Office to give an imaginative person much to cheer about. Micawber
may enjoy parodying the orotundities of officialese, but he pertinently objects to the
dryness, under Wickfield and Heep, of his usual office pen-pushing. It is precisely
this lawyerly world that the fatherless David, "a young man at his own disposal,"
drifts into. Betsey has asked him what he would like to be,

> But I had no particular liking, that I could discover, for anything. If I could have been
> inspired with a knowledge of the science of navigation, taken the command of a fast-
> sailing expedition, and gone round the world on a triumphant voyage of discovery,
> I think I might have considered myself [*à la* Micawber] completely suited. But, in
> the absence of any such miraculous provision, my desire was to apply myself to some

pursuit that would not lie too heavily upon her purse; and to do my duty in it, whatever it might be. (273)

This is youthfully, romantically, honorably said: if given a chance to be Captain Cook, fine; but if not, he will do whatever task comes his way and be the "morally . . . firm fellow" his aunt exhorts him to be (275). Following Steerforth's hint that Doctors' Commons is "a very pleasant, profitable little affair of private theatricals, presented to an uncommonly select audience"—a place where "They plume themselves on their gentility" (343–44)—David obediently sits down, faute de mieux, in the articled chair Betsey's neat £1,000 has bought him. What he likes is the "tolerably expensive" appearance of Spenlow's office and the repeated emphasis on the genteel (350), which suggest a London version of the boathouse in Yarmouth or the book-filled attic at Blunderstone: "Altogether, I have never, on any occasion, made one at such a cosey, dosey, old-fashioned, time-forgotten, sleepy-headed little family-party in all my life" (352).

David's reactions to this "soothing opiate" are perfectly understandable if we recall the subterranean London he has last been acquainted with: "when the coach was gone, I turned my face to the Adelphi ['such a noble residence'], pondering on the old days when I used to roam about its subterranean arches, and on the happy changes which had brought me to the surface" (355). The joy of having come up keeps him from thinking overlong about the signs of *Bleak House*–like corruption around Spenlow's practice. Having had no strong vocational expectations to begin with, he lacks any criteria by which to explain and clean up the dirt, and the chance of living easy makes him go along with Spenlow's not wisely passive but merely indolent belief that "the principle of a gentleman [is] to take things as he found them"—a "system" of "good and evil" mixed (480). The faculty of social criticism *does* develop in David: it is manifest in his older self's presentation of his younger self's lazy credulity. But development would never occur if he stayed on his stool at Spenlow's: he needs the threat of poverty—Betsey's loss of money—to push him off.

Compared to Traddles, David is at this crisis hardly impoverished. His articles have been paid for, and he could simply bide his time before taking his "cosey, dosey" seat in Doctors' Commons. Still, remembering how a quick succession of accidents has desolated him once, he looks upon this present pass in life-and-death terms. Besides, this is a chance to justify Betsey's good opinion of him. He therefore switches fairy tales: before, he has been the grateful inheritor of godmotherly riches, whose only arduous chore has been to wear a waistcoat too florid and boots too tight; now, he becomes the heroic woodsman, whose labors will clear a path through the "forest of difficulty" till he gets to Dora. He here finds a positive use for the experience got in the Murdstone and Grinby's time: a "little gent," he has felt, should be able to work as hard as Mick Walker and Mealy Potatoes. He *can* work hard, but he must do it alone. Dora merely screams at the idea of such activity, as though he were a perspiring navvy who "went balancing . . . up and down a plank all day with a wheelbarrow" (542).

David's first great project, mastering the "Egyptian Temple" of the stenographic alphabet, is something we can believe in because we *see* something of his struggles to learn. He deserves the frank praise he gives himself. His second great project, becoming a novelist, is harder to believe in because we see nothing but his scribbling away in the evenings and mercifully turning to Dora as often as he can to ask for a new pen.[17] The fact is that he is caught in a rhetorical dilemma. On the one hand, he doesn't want to destroy his own credit by "flourish[ing] himself before the faces of other people in order that they may believe in him" (690). It would be too much like watching Barry Bonds pumping iron and taking steroids, for the sake of learning how he got strong enough to hit so many home runs. On the other hand, David wants to insist that success in writing, as in anything else, comes only through "punctuality, order, and diligence"—his (or Dickens's) main target being the Gowans and Steerforths who think that dashes of talent, cheek, and wishful thinking are enough to produce a successful anything. To be sure, he sketches his "education" as a novelist—his retention of the child's ability to attend to incongruous details (the "I Observe" chapter: note his "I saw everything" when visiting Traddles's lodgings [402]); his list of stories read and then retold to Steerforth; his fondness for inventing vignettes about people in houses glimpsed from the road; his habit, when in mourning for his mother or in rags on the road to Dover, of looking objectively at himself as though he were someone else; and indeed his very colorlessness, a consequence of his having self-negatingly drained so much color into the portraits of characters who surround him, even those he dislikes. Yet a mere list of aptitudes explains neither David's choice of vocation nor (leaving choices of that sort to augurists of the imponderable) how, once he has made his choice, he seizes on a theme, gets it onto paper, revises his copy, peddles his book, and so on.

But so what if we don't have any of David's Jamesian notebooks, or even Dickensian number-plans? Dickens himself seems to have thought the writer's vocation a sort of divine given, and any further inquiry impertinent. What counts in David's case is that, like any other respectable Victorian, he desires to *do* something with what has been given him—a desire that implies a large measure of legitimate ambition, prior to any specific vocational summons. "My reflections at these times"—he is speaking of when he walked round Blunderstone during his and Steerforth's visit to Yarmouth— "were always associated with the figure I was to make in life, and the distinguished things I was to do. My echoing footsteps went to no other tune" (320). He remembers how, in the days before the Murdstones, his mother and Peggotty used to puff him; and more recently Betsey has encouraged him to establish himself as an independent creature—as someone who is and shall be worthy of respect. Of course, at this point he simply equates the respectable and "the distinguished" with the genteel. Hence the drift into Doctors' Commons, and into some of the still more shadowy ganglia of what Carlyle called the Dandiacal Body. There, for a while, he is guided by Steerforth, who is unwittingly following the mode of the archdandy Byron, and who, as his failure to find his own vocation shows, is himself in need of a guide.

There are too many things to say about Steerforth, his interwoven attractive and unattractive qualities, but we can achieve some concentration by noting how the latter derive in large measure from his lack of a father, a condition shared inter alia by David and Uriah, and how fatherlessness in turn has led to his feeling flummoxed around the question of what he ought to "do" when he grows up—a feeling exacerbated by his having an ample unearned income, which is one problem the other two lads don't have. Steerforth's wonderful name, suggesting all his power of "steering forth" toward whatever object he desires, is finally ironical, for the fact is that neither he nor anyone else is providing the steering—the purposeful, charted direction—he needs. He says it himself: "David, I wish to God I had had a judicious father these last twenty years!" (322).

Mrs. Steerforth has persuaded her son that the world is a three-layer birthday cake, baked and frosted for him alone. The birthday boy may realize that he is being greedy and, with reference to his stomach, even stupid to eat it all by himself, but as his mother hasn't invited anyone else to the party, he may as well go ahead. Being fatherless really does mitigate some of his offenses. Not only has his mother selfishly put him in the place of her dead husband; she has done so just at the time when he couldn't possibly know how to resist. She has sent him to Salem House instead of to a reputable school because she has wanted him first to find "himself the monarch of the place," and then "haughtily to be worthy of his station" (296)—which isn't quite as insane as it might sound, for there are advantages in a talented child's attending a small school, where the chances to shine athletically, musically, academically and so on are statistically better than at a large one. This queen mother, however, is more insane than not, for she actually plumes herself on having "gratified . . . every wish" of her son, from whom she has "had no separate existence since his birth." Well, if this Hampstead Oedipus got into this incestuous mess unconsciously, he can try to get out of it unconsciously by running away with Emily. He isn't planning a wedding, but an extended affair will at least begin to loosen his mother's choke hold on him. The incestuous union—unlike Sophocles, Dickens is thinking psychology only, so I use the adjective figuratively—hurts the Hampstead Jocasta too. Once her son has cut himself loose, nothing is left for her but a life of paralysis and bitterness behind closed blinds.

It is ludicrous for Mrs. Steerforth to complain that marriage to Emily "would irretrievably blight my son's career" (469), for he has none—not yet, and not in prospect either. Brought up to the pursuit of fashionable idleness, he says he has "never learnt the art of binding myself to any of the wheels on which the Ixions of these days are turning round and round. I missed it somehow in a bad apprenticeship, and now don't care about it." And then the masterly segue: "—You know I have bought a boat down here?" (324). The boat, which he has named "The Little Em'ly," will help him carry off the no-longer-little Emily, and unlike Ixion, who bungled his approach to Hera, he isn't going to get caught—primarily because he isn't poaching on anyone as formidable as Hera's husband. Steerforth has a Faustian energy, but it never progresses beyond the pursuit of a Margaret: "[Looking] after him going so gallantly and airily homeward," David recalls, "I thought of his saying, 'Ride on over all obstacles, and win the race!' and wished, for the first time, that he had some worthy race to run" (427). It is good that Steerforth frankly *knows* he has no worthy race to run, and is ashamed. It is also good that he has charm—what Angus Wilson has called "that secular semblance of grace,"[18] and what Butler would call, simply, the only grace there is. David's determination to remember Steerforth at his best, even after he has learnt the worst, is based on the latter's charismatic qualities, which in themselves are not only admirable but, for a nascent storyteller, enviable: "There was an ease in his manner— a gay and light manner it was, but not swaggering—which I still believe to have borne a kind of enchantment with it" (104). There is abundant evidence of Steerforth's "enchantment"—"some inborn power of attraction"[19]—in the visit to the Peggottys on the evening of Ham's and Emily's engagement, the happy "little picture" of which "was so instantaneously dissolved by our going in" (311–12). That dissolving is portentous enough, as are the sailor's song and the "Story of a dismal shipwreck" with which Steerforth regales the company. But "so pathetically and beautifully" does he sing "that the real wind creeping sorrowfully round the house, and murmuring low through our unbroken silence . . . [seems] there [only] to listen"; and so grippingly does he tell the "dismal" tale, and so gaily a merry one, that everyone—not just Emily—is bound in "irresistible sympathy" to the moods he generates. We ourselves forget the portentousness, we want the entertainment to go on all night, and are for the moment like an audience mesmerized by a novelist reading his work—obviously a situation of intense interest to Dickens or David.

Only with an effort, then, do we notice, and take offense at, Steerforth's calling Ham "my boy" to his face (and "a chuckle-headed fellow" behind his back), or his describing his pleasure with the Peggottys as "quite a new sensation" (317). Such remarks shock David, till he sees laughter in Steerforth's eyes and concludes that he is joking. Yet he isn't joking. He is exercising the same will to power that has driven Mr. Mell from his camp stool at Salem House, less out of hatred for poor people than out of pique at anyone's trying to exert authority over him. When Traddles has bravely cried shame, Steerforth has "disdainfully" replied:

> His [Mr. Mell's] feelings will soon get the better of it, I'll be bound. His feelings are not like yours, Miss Traddles. As to his situation—which was a precious one, wasn't it?—do you suppose I am not going to write home, and take care that he gets some money? Polly? (100–01)

This belittling of people's feelings, disparagement of girls ("Miss Traddles," "Polly"), and conviction that the injured poor can be bought off, will characterize Steerforth's behavior toward Emily too. He never has to pay in a manner that affects him. When Steerforth laughs in church and Traddles is punished, Traddles doesn't tell. Steerforth gives him "his reward," saying "there was nothing of the sneak in Traddles" (91), but he takes no punishment on himself. What after all are fat boys with no money *for* if not to do unpleasant things for sixth-form Apollos?[20] What indeed is a storytelling boy like David for, but to stay awake till the small hours diverting the same?

> The drawback was, that I was often sleepy at night, or out of spirits and indisposed to resume the story; and then it was rather hard work, and it must be done; for to disappoint or to displease Steerforth was of course out of the question. In the morning, too, when I felt weary, and should have enjoyed another hour's repose very much, it was a tiresome thing to be roused, like the Sultana Scheherazade, and forced into a long story before the getting-up bell rang; but Steerforth was resolute. (93)

The offer of some pointers in Latin and arithmetic, and a few Sultanic smiles, may be adequate return for little David, but a grown-up should protest that the exchange is most unequal. Steerforth, in short, treats Traddles and David as he will later treat Emily and the Peggottys: they are tools or toys to be picked up and discarded at whim. What the older David can't at first see in *his own* class-proud attitude toward the Peggottys, his condescension toward Traddles, or his treatment of Dora, he can *learn* to see by studying Steerforth's behavior. As genteel charmer, as misdirected man of parts, he finally rouses David to mix some criticism in with the praise.

Steerforth is a standing warning, Traddles a standing invitation. The key to *his* character lies in the skeletons he draws to console himself after being caned by

Creakle, or to console David after the news of his mother's death. The skeletons don't have any psycho-morbid significance, nor are they memento mori hints that the days of caning shall soon be over. They are just easy to draw "and didn't want any features" (91). That is to say, Traddles is beautifully simple: nothing keeps him from responding appropriately to Steerforth's cruel snobbery or to David's untimely bereavement, or later from expressing himself professionally in straightforward, hearty language—a talent, as Mr. Waterbrook concedes, which will impede his rise up the legal ladder, where circumlocution keeps the "cosey" "dosey." His originality consists in what David calls his freshness—his devotion to Sophy, "a curate's daughter, one of ten, down in Devonshire," a county he *walks to* whenever he goes a-courting; his preparations for house-furnishing (the round table, "two feet ten in circumference," to put a book or a teacup on, etc.); or his thundering of parliamentary orations and invectives at Betsey and a somewhat frightened Mr. Dick while David practices his shorthand (546). Traddles's married life with Sophy is a delightfully unreasonable affair of puss-in-the-corner, "tea and toast, and children's songs," all insinuated into Gray's Inn's gray "grim atmosphere of ponce and parchment" (830). Anyone can hiss "grow up!" at this happy pair, but how utterly beside the point—which is that some people "grow up!" without losing the ingenuousness of their "wonder years." As Traddles says of their on-the-town pleasures, taken in the spirit of Charles Lamb's "Old China": "Now, you know, Copperfield, if I was Lord Chancellor, we couldn't do this!" (847).

Fortunately, he doesn't become Lord Chancellor (though like Micawber he *is* "eligible"), but we are told that he does become a judge, and purchases one of the houses he and Sophy used to ogle on their walks. This, of course, passes all understanding, in spite of "the clear head, and the plain, patient, practical good sense," which, credibly enough, Traddles has shown during the exposure of Heep. The England of *Copperfield*, to say nothing of the England of Dickens's other novels, is incapable of rewarding the Traddlesian virtues. In fact, any country this side of Never-Never Land would be incapable. But even supposing in high circles an outbreak of enthusiasm for clarity and practicality, Traddles still lacks the sort of magnetism, the complex public appeal, that would bring him wide notice. In this regard he is *too* simple, and is therefore an inadequate foil to Steerforth, David's manly angel. The only adequate foil turns out to be a womanly angel—one very much, and very honorably, "of the house."

Relations Between Male and Female

David's approach to "the womanly" will strike most of today's readers as naïve. The double-edged innocence of his childhood—now producing amusingly candid observations, now being exploited by waiters, carters, and older boys generally—extends well into his adolescence. The older David refers at one point to "the simple confidence of a child, and the natural reliance of a child upon superior years (qualities I am very sorry any children should prematurely change for worldly wisdom)" (69–70). Yet what is "premature"? When should David start to possess a bit of "worldly wisdom," particularly of a sexual variety, and how? The "child's Tom Jones" David reads about can remain "a harmless creature" (56) till he (David) reaches puberty, an event that then came later in life than it does now (at seventeen he may have danced with the eldest Miss Larkins, but to his mortification he still has no use for the shaving water the hotel maid brings him in the morning). That the shaving water is even thinkable means, to take a wild guess, that sexual maturation is thinkable too, and that David could profit from the advice a Fielding, a father, or a liberally (that is to say a conservatively) reconstructed Steerforth might offer. Even they, however, could only *prepare* him for the essential things—the physical and spiritual accommodations a relationship between grown-ups asks for—which (like it or not) he must learn on his own.

The *Bildungsheld* has to experiment if he is to learn—Dickens shares this semi-risky conviction with Goethe—but no vital experiment occurs in a vacuum. David's experiments with the opposite sex are conditioned by his memories of his mother. When he thinks of her in sublunary terms, he sees the dancing and singing young woman who likes men to call her bewitching and believes that to marry one of them might justify getting herself a new parasol. In short, she is the "very Baby" Aunt Betsey descries at the beginning of the novel. She conforms to the Kate Greenaway ideal of feminine beauty, the pre- or barely-pubescent, long-dressed and therefore seemingly legless girl—"legless" was George Orwell's oft-echoed jeer at Agnes—who shouldn't be troubled by marriage and childbearing. David's mother, to be sure, has borne him, but since her husband was in the churchyard, the success of the birth has almost appeared to depend on its being virginal. There is no suggestion of virginity about her next birthing—she has been horribly tupped by Murdstone—but by then the question of her fitness as a mother has been settled in the negative, and she and her second child flicker out. Dora too finds marriage and motherhood beyond her: her oysters are never opened, and her child is either stillborn or miscarried (it "took wing" [698], as David euphemistically says).

Where Kate Greenaway girls are concerned, we don't expect any more sexually straightforward language. All the palpable sexuality in the novel is funneled either into the dirty river that the prostitute Martha (she would be one of some 8,000 sex workers in the London of 1850[21]) walks along in London, and that Emily knows something about; or into the brackish pool that Rosa Dartle, Mrs. Steerforth, Mr. Wickfield, Mr. Peggotty—the whole cast of repressed, obsessed, or imperfectly sublimated characters—stare at. Any attempt to let sexuality flow cleanly and naturally seems to frighten David: he won't even mention to Agnes the possibility of Annie Strong's sexual interest in her cousin Jack for fear that it would sully her mind, and perhaps confuse his own. This does them both the injustice of implying that they aren't adults. In brief, David's whole attitude toward "good" girls' and boys' sexuality is uneasy. The material cause is the impression he has got from his undeveloped mother; the essential cause is the very English tribal notion—painted by Greenaway and upheld by her correspondent John Ruskin, both of them participating in an abreaction against what Carlyle in *Latter-Day Pamphlets* called the "phallus worship" of the age,[22] the stews of the city and the irregulated couplings of people of all social classes—that his (David's) mother is just the sort of turtledove men like.

Dora is an admirable imitation of a turtledove, but the capacities of such birds are severely limited. With the education she has had—taught to play the guitar, to paint flowers (most inaccurately, but never mind), to look ornamental at her father's dull weekend gatherings, all this a suburban imitation of a dreamt-of aristocratic life of leisure—she has never been expected to be responsible, and therefore isn't. She is treated like a prerational doll by everyone, even Betsey, who in nicknaming her Little Blossom not ungently insinuates that she isn't fit for anything past the springtime of life. David calls her "my pet," lets her call him "Doady" ("doting" yes, "toady" no), and generally comes down to her funny but exasperating level of frivolity, where cookbooks become platforms for Jip's pagoda. She hasn't had the benefit of a mother who could show her the duties and pleasures of housekeeping and rational conversation. She has had the protection of her "confidential friend," Miss Murdstone, but, she pouts, "Who wants a protector?" Not *she*. She is like a fairy tale doll that wishes to be ensouled and animated as a person. But both nurture and nature—her Little Blossom daintiness—have conspired against that. As Dickens's notes for Number XV, Chapter 44, say, "Carry through incapacity of Dora—But affectionate" (*Plans*, 845).

Dora's being a damsel imprisoned by the she-dragon Miss Murdstone offers David a replay of the time of troubles back at Blunderstone Rookery, only now he is older and can imagine himself capable of rescuing his sweetheart. His exertions are comically, self-tolerantly remembered: "I was almost as innocently undesigning then, as when I loved little Em'ly" (393). He thinks not of money, marriage, or sexual consummation, but only of dotage, both as excessive fondness (the doting/Doadying) and as a second, or rather an uninterrupted first, childhood. What matters is that Dora be always thinking of him, and he of her, or that he be free to circle about her house, blowing kisses at her window, "and romantically calling on the night, at intervals, to shield my Dora—I don't exactly know what from, I suppose from fire. Perhaps from mice, to which she had a great objection" (474). The spoony insubstantiality of it all, like one of Miss Mills's romantic plots, makes David look back not just with amusement but with pity:

> When I measured Dora's finger for a ring that was to be made of Forget-me-nots, and when the jeweller, to whom I took the measure, found me out, and laughed over his order-book, and charged me anything he liked for the pretty little toy, with its blue stones—so associated in my remembrance with Dora's hand, that yesterday, when I saw such another, by chance, on the finger of my own daughter, there was a momentary stirring in my heart, like pain! (489)

The Proustian poignance of this, if we are at all susceptible, is just right: the ring of perishable little blossoms made imperishable in stones, and now worn on the finger of another perishable child.

Dora soon knows herself to be unworthy compared to Agnes, and the honeymoon is scarcely over before David knows it also: to think, he says, "how queer it was that there we were, alone together as a matter of course . . . all the romance of our engagement put away upon a shelf, to rust—no one to please but one another—one another to please, *for life*" (634, my italics). It sounds like what it nearly is—a prison sentence. His cell mate believes that to be "reasoned with" is worse than to be scolded, and that if he had planned to act this way, he shouldn't have married her. Now that he has married her, however, Betsey's counsel is pertinent: he must

> "estimate her (as you chose her) by the qualities she has, and not by the qualities she may not have. The latter you must develop in her, if you can. And if you cannot, child," here my aunt rubbed her nose, "you must just accustom yourself to do without 'em." (639)

Of course Dora can no more bring forth the qualities she doesn't have—rationality, level-headedness, and housewifery, which are virtues instrumental in everyday domestic management, not (*pace* Mary Poovey) in "class exploitation"[23] —than petunias can bring forth eggplant. She can only point to her petals and shrug. "Child-wife" she asks to be called after the hilarious but disastrous dinner party, following which her duties are reduced to holding David's pens. Her joy in this occupation is as touchingly naïve as Mr. Dick's joy at being able to do copy work for Doctor Strong. It isn't quite the counsel, conversation, and partnership he needs, yet by keeping silent about it, he discovers that, lying down in the bed he has made, he can pretty much rely on himself. His novels get written regardless of wifely support or opposition, as did Dickens's own. Which means that when he finally turns to Agnes—worrying less about the upper-middle-class refinements his mother and Dora have evoked in his fancy, and more about the any-class good sense the friend of his Canterbury school days has evoked in his imagination—he can bring almost as much to the table as she can.

Not that David's marriage to Agnes was part of Dickens's original plan. She was clearly positioned to play for David and Dora the sisterly role Georgina Hogarth had played for Dickens and Kate. Dickens's notes for Number V do indeed indicate that Agnes will be the real heroine (*Plans*, 824), and therefore presumably David's eventual wife, but the decision to "kill Dora" (Dickens's tears-checking order to himself) seems not to have been made till the due date for the seventeenth number was nearly upon him.[24] What thematic motive did he have in removing this poor girl? Her death gives David an unwanted but necessary portent of his own, a phase of what I have called his mortal education. It also gives him a second opportunity to marry, which will help us contrast the ways of foolish and wise male virgins, romantic and "disciplined" hearts. Would it have been better, as Dora thinks, for her and David to have known each other as children and then been sundered? Not at all: they need to be inoculated against romantic infatuation, even if it means that one of them won't survive.

There is nothing romantic, in Dora's a*dor*able way, about the sanctified Agnes, who in Michael Slater's phrase "trail[s] clouds of Mary Hogarth,"[25] Dickens's beloved sister-in-law (Georgina and Kate's sister) whose early death so moved him. We see her first as a girl, but already she is a "staid and . . . discreet . . . housekeeper," with "a little basket-trifle hanging at her side, with keys in it" (223). Her home economy surpasses even Peggotty's (515), thanks, we infer, to her higher mental organization, evident also in her conversation and her affective literary judgment. David's chief praise, though, is saved for her moral intelligence. She is a figure of holiness, an Anglican saint who never talks about dogma or about going to Africa to be martyred, but who nevertheless reminds David of the "tranquil brightness" of "a stained glass window" he has once seen in a church (223).[26] This is vague, but deliberately so. "I love little Em'ly," he has as a boy insisted, "and I don't love Agnes—no, not at all in that way— but I feel that there are goodness, peace, and truth, wherever Agnes is" (232). Emily means profane love, which he reserves for the child-figures who remind him of his mother in her earthly guise. Agnes means sacred love, which reminds him of his mother in her spiritual guise, as we have seen her receding moonward or resting in the sunlight of a street in Agnes's own Canterbury.

He calls Agnes his "sister" throughout most of the story, and thus acknowledges her as the fleshly counterpart to Betsey's make-believe niece, "your sister Betsey Trotwood," the ego ideal he is supposed to emulate. It is as if she were the other half of himself, with which, as in Aristophanes' myth in Plato's *Symposium*, he must spend his life trying to reconnect. This must be the meaning of the several hints that Agnes and he are liter-ally predestined for one another, complementary double-yokes of the same egg: he brings the naïvety, child-likeness, and romantic imagination, she the earnestness, maturity, and rational intellect—antithetical qualities they are supposed not merely to meld together but to encourage in each other.

As it turns out, Agnes is more successful at educing her peculiar qualities from David, than he his from her. The reason is that he doesn't want her to change: he leads together the brilliantly stained pieces of her windowed self, and expects her to remain enshrined above the casement. He also assumes the not uncommon possessive attitude of brothers toward sisters: "there is no one that I know of, who deserves to love *you*, Agnes" (276). Which is to say, he denies her the right to marry anyone. She is expected to be the sisterly–auntish guardian of the hearth, who will help him and Dora keep the dog out of the mashed potatoes, and the baby, if there is one, out of the fire. Practicing for this career, she warns him against his "bad angel" Steerforth, adding that "I feel as if it were someone else speaking to you, and not I" (367). Such moments are only inter-mittent with Agnes, though; she isn't a full-time prophetess speaking for God, but a woman needing, and wanting to give, physical tenderness.[27]

She says that "if any fraud or treachery is practising against him [her father], I hope that simple love and truth will be strong in the end. I hope that real love and truth are stronger in the end than any evil or misfortune in the world" (511). This is optimistic, but it isn't shallow. The qualifying words are "simple" and "real," the one meaning pure and unconditional, the other vigorous and discerning. The good that Betsey does for little David, Mr. Dick for the Strongs, Traddles and Micawber for Mr. Wickfield, or Agnes for Dora, David, or Emily depends in each instance on the capacity to discern what needs to be done and why, and then vigorously to do it. Agnes' special activity is with the outcast (Emily), the desolate (David), or the dying (Dora)—activity that, leaving behind the followers of the nastier side of Nietzsche, deserves respect, and that, because Dickens doesn't dramatize *too* much of it, is believable. She does a par-ticularly good job with David when he is mourning the death of Dora:

> She commended me to God, who had taken my innocent darling to His rest; and in her sisterly affection cherished me always, and was . . . proud of what I had done, but infinitely prouder yet of what I was reserved to do.

Rhetorically, we must understand, she is trying not to be clever but to be good. So she says that sorrow has come, and will in the course of nature come again, but David's duty is to accept it as God's inscrutable will, and as the door opening to "His rest." So much for theology (hers if not altogether yours or mine). But as for ethics, she also speaks of the work David is "reserved to do," which requires a renewed interest in the things and people of this world, not a premature translation into the next.

> I resorted humbly whither Agnes had commended me; I sought out Nature, never sought in vain; and I admitted to my breast the human interest I had lately shrunk from. It was not long, before I had almost as many friends in the [alpine] valley as in Yarmouth.

It is hard to believe the bit about "Nature, never sought in vain," because nature's presence in the novel has been oceanic not alpine, and David wouldn't know how to respond to the mountains without the aid of the Wordsworth he alludes to. But we do believe that he makes friends, just as Emily has done during her fearful Italian days, and that these contacts, plus the confidence placed in him by Agnes, get him writing again—"a story, with a purpose growing, not remotely, out of my experience" (816)—which in turn draws him back to England.

The Agnes he finds there is in deeper trouble than she knows, and for once *he* can do something for *her*. She has restored the Canterbury house to the way it has been in their childhood, with "the basket-trifle, full of keys, still hanging at her side" (840). She is living with the past if not exactly with the dead, and David calls her from it, after a maddeningly obtuse period of imagining she loves someone else. It is a nice touch, nevertheless, that the purblind David should for a while be prepared to give Agnes up if she loves someone else: renunciation isn't the moral necessity Goethe or James usually thought it to be, but the *willingness* to renounce is. So, to Betsey's joy and to ours, David and Agnes return to life. He in particular eschews what Carlyle would have called unhealthy introspection—whether it is amorphously about how he misses Steerforth or Dora, or scrupulously about how he may be to blame for their deaths[28]—and decides simply to get on with life. He and Agnes embrace with as much physicality as a Dickensian love scene can allow, and fruitfully enough to have a family. Readers should not therefore be displeased with Agnes because she is sexless, for that side of her nature simply wanted calling out by someone whom she has known as a gentle boy and who has become a virile man. David's gentleness is what makes this breaking-up of an "incestuous" intimacy between Mr. Wickfield and his daughter so welcome, in contrast to what we feel when the virile Murdstone breaks up a similar intimacy early in the story. In fact Agnes, who, as Peter Gay argues, has properly played sister to David till he has worked through his Oedipal problems, will if anything teach *him* about the open expression of amorous affection. Our displeasure with her, if it must come, should center instead on the fact that she is without humor—that the largest life of the novel resides in someone with whom she has practically nothing to do. I mean Mr. Micawber.

Micawber Dionysus

Micawber's elasticity contrasts, quite obviously, with the "firmness" of the Murdstones. But he is only a little less distant from another kind of "firmness" found in Betsey, Agnes, and Mr. Peggotty, who, while not so repressively puritanical as the Murdstones, do keep their appetites on a tight rein. And for good reason. The moral projects they are "firm" about—personal independence and the defense of weak and exploited people like Mr. Dick, Mr. Wickfield, and Emily—require all the energy they have got. There is none to spare on Micawberian good times.

To define himself ethically and temperamentally, David tries to steer his boat between Micawber and the honorifically firm trio. It isn't surprising that, with such a wide channel, he does discover a route, but like most captains who sail a middle way, he has a hundred passengers who want to get closer to one point or another (usually Micawber Rock rather than the Moral Archipelago) for every dozen who simply feel glad that the weather is brilliant enough to allow a glimpse of everything. No need to dwell on the power of the morally firm characters' example: David learns self-reliance, charity, and a degree of tolerance from them. The only problem is that the degree of tolerance isn't large enough. Betsey and Agnes deal very sympathetically with Dora's weaknesses, and thus encourage sympathy in David, but they are less sympathetic than they should be with what Micawber stands for.

The crucial episode is David's "first time of getting tipsy," as Dickens prompted himself for Number VIII, adding "Description of it exactly" (*Plans*, 830). Well, David "exactly" has a jolly time getting drunk with Steerforth and his companions, and very few readers have much minded his making a fool of himself by speaking too loudly in the theater, falling downstairs, or conflating seven words into one. Ishsurlynorworse' anaswiv'leror'cawber. And having joyed in a Dick Swiveller, a Micawber, or a Pickwick, who can wholly condone David's excessive morning-after reaction to his adventure, and all because his behavior has embarrassed Agnes?

> But the agony of mind, the remorse, and shame I felt when I became conscious next day! . . . my recollection of that indelible look which Agnes had given me—the torturing impossibility of communicating with her, not knowing, Beast that I was, how she came to be in London. (363)

"Beast that I was"? The pertinent Chestertonian rejoinder is that the beasts are the ones who drink only water. Dickens knew that there are human, Dionysian mysteries deeper than Littimerian respectability—mysteries that pleased the subversive in him. But he also knew that the contemporary reality of drink had almost nothing to do with Dionysus, and it is therefore not surprising that he makes David, under Agnes's influence, confuse a tippling dinner party with a scene from William Hogarth's hammered gin-lane. David's problem is analogous to that of the prototypical English *Bildungsheld*, Prince Hal, who must find a golden mean between the liberating looseness of Falstaff and the straitening discipline of his sovereign father. David's Falstaff is Micawber, his sovereign Agnes, scion of Betsey. And the rejection of Falstaff—is Micawber's emigration.

To describe Micawber is as difficult as to describe Falstaff, but one telling approach is to see him mythically, as though he were a Dionysian figure like Mynheer Peeperkorn from the novel I have referred to several times when discussing Goethe, Mann's *The Magic Mountain*. Peeperkorn is Dionysian not merely in his love of alcohol, the gift of Ceres, but in his manic-depressive swings, which mime the rising and falling of the Life Force. His speech pattern is dithyrambic, usually consisting of a tumble of words, baroquely ornamented, which stammer down to a breathless "in short" —the whole performance tending toward the throbbing up and down monotony that, in Mann's Schopenhauerian, Nietzschean imagery, is *there* in the world's pulse, and that the story of the now broken, now whole Dionysus continually repeats. His speech is also a Dionysian parody of all the Apollonian attempts to order the world rationally and economically. Just so, the Latinate, obfuscating diction of parliamentary debate or judicial pronouncement loses its frightfulness when it issues from Micawber. (As Dickens's notes for Number X, Chapter 28, say, Micawber is "relieving himself by legal phraseology" [*Plans*, 835].) Delighting in what David calls his "portly" grandiloquence for its own sake, as the tauroscatological rhetoricians Pecksniff and Chadband never do, Micawber bends highfalutin euphemism and triplets to strictly personal uses—to describe the state of his own exchequer, to expose the perfidy of Mrs. Micawber's family, to analyze a core sample of the Heep-Heap of Infamy—and thus satirically translates the public world of parliament and courts to the latitude of Lilliput.

This satire, however, is something Dickens asks us to discern for ourselves. David himself seems to miss the force of parody: he can't distinguish the circumlocutions of officialdom, which muffle reality so that protest can't break out or reform break in, from the circumlocutions of Micawber, who consciously plays with words in a fugue of mock heroics. Or most of the time it seems conscious: I admit that *occasionally* his orotundities seem mechanical, as if he were an actor who can't get *out* of a role. But that is only on a bad night. For the most part he is an actor who is alert for his cue—the knocking of a creditor, the setting out of a tray of rum and oranges, or the proposing of a jaunt across the sea and into the Australian bush—and who on the instant knows how to arrange his costume and improvise his lines. Like many actors, Micawber often isn't sure *who* he is. Speaking to little David, he cryptically remarks that "If, in the progress of revolving years, I could persuade myself that my blighted destiny had been a warning to you, I should feel that I had not occupied another man's place in existence altogether in vain" (175). "Another man's place" refers to his belief that he was meant for something better in life, but it also suggests an estrangement from himself, as though he had no "place" of his own in this world, and were condemned to acting out a hectic series of parts, from that of a man of "blighted destiny" to that of one for whom something has at last turned up.

Still, he does much better in the first part than in the second. The elasticity we admire in him depends on an "Annual income [of] twenty pounds, annual expenditure [of] twenty pounds ought and six" (175), with the god of day going down upon the weary scene, and his own person "floored." He and his wife are so used to insolvency that, on the rare occasions when they are flush (i.e., sixpence in the black), they simply don't know how to act (172). It is as though a dinner on-order were better than one actually served up. The time of dreams and insolvency is often the time of youth, and the Micawberian elasticity depends on that as well. He frequently refers to David as "the friend of my youth, the companion of earlier days" (407), though he was already then a bald-pated father of four. No matter, for youth in this context means the readiness to take on a new "career," a new costume, and new habits, all at a moment's notice. The old are the people who can't or don't want to change—the pathetic Mr. Wickfield, the honored but doddering Doctor Strong, the Murdstones, Mrs. Steerforth, Littimer, and so on. One remembers, with Mr. Kincaid,[29] Falstaff's wonderful "They hate us youth," with the "they" being the respectable people for whom speech is always supposed to be straightforward, behavior sensible, roles apportioned out one per person, dreams separated from reality, and each person's hands in his or her own pockets. The youthful Micawber doesn't think much of these rules. He offers Traddles an I.O.U. precisely as if it were solid sterling, just as he relishes his bag of walnuts or glass of punch precisely as if his granaries were stored for the seven lean years ahead. Note that Micawber isn't the picture of *helpless* youth. His handiness with the chops over the fire is a sign of how he has got through life without a large establishment; like Huck Finn, he is a "boy" who knows how to camp.

Note also, however, that when Traddles innocently lends Micawber his name and accepts his I.O.U., he in fact suffers the loss of the little stock of furniture he has been saving against the day of his marriage to "the dearest girl"—a loss he doesn't recover without much hard work. W. H. Auden thought it a fair exchange: other people give Micawber money, while he gives them florid rhetoric and well-spiked punch. Orwell however was perhaps not unjust in frowning at Micawber's cadging: he is charging Traddles and the others more than the rhetoric and punch are really worth. And there are sufficient other hints of the underside of the life insolvent to give us pause: *chez*-Jellyby images of Mrs. Micawber unconscious, with her head sticking through the railings; the screaming and hungry twins; the unschooled Master Micawber; their father's not always histrionic threats of suicide; and the lugubrious period of depression caused by his having to work for Heep. (He can see that Agnes and her father are being robbed, but for a long while, in debt to Heep as he is, he doesn't see how he can prevent it.) Let Micawber, like many another nineteenth-century n'er-do-well, go off to a New World and become as much of a success as he likes.[30] The fact remains that in the Old World he has been better as a mythy Dionysus than as a provider for a family, and it is to David's credit that he says so. He understands that much of life is inescapably material, and that, by whatever economic system we will, goods have to be produced and distributed. To parody the given system, to live forever drinking the cup that another has made and filled for you, isn't, David realizes, an adequate basis for living. He appreciates Micawber—as his masterly recreation of him evinces. But he knows that he and most of us can't *be* like Micawber. Not all the time, anyway. Sending Micawber to Australia is a way of placing his irresponsible example seventy-times-seven leagues off. David's responsibilities aren't perhaps very exciting— providing bread and butter for Agnes and their children, and writing his books without the harassments of duns—but anyone who doubts the value of his fulfilling them has (I will wager) always been provided for by somebody else.

Those anti-Malthusian children who keep dropping from Mrs. Micawber may be the family's jocund way of bidding the philosophical radicals to go to, but nonetheless they are most of the time unfed, all the time uneducated, and definitely, as Thomas Hardy's Little Jude would have darkly said, "too menny." Micawber finally understands this himself, and proceeds in Australia to secure his tribe against further crimson imbalances of income and expenditure. It is admittedly hard to put this Micawber together with the Dionysian figure a world of readers has lost its heart to, though those letters and newspaper articles from down under suggest that the spirit is very much alive. Dionysian figures aren't indeed easily sustainable in novels that are at one level meant to be realistic, having to do with how people make their day-to-day living. Mann solved this problem by importing a Peeperkorn who is an immensely wealthy Dutch planter, and who nobly kills himself when he becomes too old or ill priapically to serve Clavdia Chauchat with quite the desired frequency. Dickens could not, for once, be quite so fantastic.

A Higher Hand

What Aristotelians would call the final cause of David's *Bildung* is religious understanding. He wants to know what ultimate reality could legitimate the ethical principles he masters under the teaching-by-example offered by Betsey, Agnes, Mr. Peggotty, and others. Agnes is good at gesturing up toward such an ultimate reality, but Mr. Peggotty's speech and action, and the imagery surrounding them, are more theologically definite. If we want a grip on Dickens's version of the Christian myth, we have to attend to the man who is going for to seek his niece.

As we have seen, he is a Noah-figure, the benignant man in a malignant generation, whose ark is loaded with the orphans no one else would take in. He is also a shepherd who, leaving the others to their collective security, goes in search of the one lost sheep— a symbol whose poignancy depends not a little on the lost sheep's reminding us of ourselves. Like Joe Gargery, he is a Christian hero. His charity has always been given "unto one of the least of these," as Mrs. Gummidge says (516). He has forgiven Emily already, and to find her he goes out into a "glow of light," a "solitary figure toiling on, poor pilgrim" (473). Like Bunyan's pilgrim, he has his own sins to expiate, particularly his harsh judgment of the prostitute Martha, who, he at last sees, is no different from Emily—a woman taken in adultery.[31] The link is nicely made. In the Phiz illustration showing Martha earlier being succored by Emily, the picture on the wall is of Jesus with the accused woman; and when Mr. Peggotty recovers Emily, he obliquely recalls that story by saying that he has seen her "humbled, as it might be in the dust our Saviour wrote in with his blessed hand" (725)—Jesus having written in the sand while, unable to cast a stone at a woman whose heart is like their own, the accusing men cleared out. This in turn faintly suggests that Mr. Peggotty is acknowledging a venereal speck in his own heart, inasmuch as he may have loved Emily with a more than paternal or avuncular sort of old-man interest.[32] But whatever the extent of his waywardness, he has absorbed the lesson of the "woman taken" story: he goes forth determined to sin and judge no more.

Charity aside, Mr. Peggotty is unwavering in the other cardinal virtues, faith and hope. He allows no evidence to count against his conviction that Emily is alive, and one supposes that if she were proved to be dead, he would expect to have her restored to him in heaven, or to have God send him another Emily in the form of another little girl. Outside the Christian myth, this looks like obstinate self-delusion; inside the myth—I am recalling Kierkegaard's handling of the Abraham and Isaac story—it looks like faith, and of a very active sort:

> His conviction remained unchanged. . . . And, although I trembled for the agony it might one day be to him to have his strong assurance shivered at a blow, there was something so religious in it, so affectingly expressive of its anchor being in the purest depths of his fine nature, that the respect and honour in which I held him were exalted every day.
>
> His was not a lazy trustfulness that hoped, and did no more. He had been a man of sturdy action all his life, and he knew that in all things wherein he wanted help he must do his own part faithfully, and help himself. (714)

He "does" all sorts of prodigies: walking to Yarmouth in the middle of the night to see if the candle is still alight; going elsewhere, sixty or eighty miles, to see if a report of a lost girl applies to Emily; or traveling over the Alps down to Naples and back. This round of journeys is deliberately larger than life, meant to conjure up affinities with Noah or Abraham, Jesus or Peter. Mr. Peggotty is a fisherman partly in remembrance of Peter, whose rough virtuousness was as superior to the smooth Pharisees' self-righteousness as his own is to Mrs. Steerforth's. It is Emily's status as a "Fisherman's daughter," not as a "Pretty lady," that appeals to the decent common Italians who take her in after she has run away from Casa Littimer. Their kindness, Mr. Peggotty says, "is laid up wheer neither moth or rust doth corrupt, and wheer thieves do not break through nor steal. Mas'r Davy, it'll outlast all the treasure in the wureld" (728). The common people have produced their Heeps and highway ruffians, too, but it is in general clear that Dickens subscribed to the Gospels' sentimental belief in their superior decency. When seeking incarnate holiness, he felt, one generally does better looking down than up. As Emily writes to Ham: "When I find what you are, and what uncle is, I think what God must be, and can cry to him" (785).[33] Sophisticates may smile at the rhetoric—Dickens (I keep apologizing for him) is at his worst when fallen into his iambic pious pentameters—but if one is looking for clues to decent behavior, this revelation-through-personal-example is more to the point than the often baffling displays of nonnatural supernaturalism we get in the Bible.

   Not that we can ignore Dickens's trafficking in the supernatural. Ham and Mr. Peggotty are slow as cold molasses, intellectually, but they are credited with strong powers of divination. Mr. Peggotty's, again, are concentrated on Emily's whereabouts. Ham can more broadly sense the current of Providence—"the end of it like"—in the stirring of the sea "lying beneath a dark sky, waveless—yet with a heavy roll upon it, as if it breathed in its rest" (456). David worries that, should Ham again meet Steerforth, "the end" will be murder, but of course it isn't that. He has just "supernaturally" foreseen his own death by drowning—a family tradition after all. What *is* "deep" in Ham is the understanding—not supernatural at all but simply psychologically adroit—that he is partly responsible for Emily's flight: "'Tis more as I beg of her to forgive me, for having pressed my affections upon her" (737), than as he should forgive her. Hence he won't hurt Steerforth, who has exploited a situation he (Ham) has helped create. Not that the two are reconciled. Ham probably never recognizes the figure on the wreck as Steerforth, and when their bodies are brought into town the people agree to lay them out in different rooms. But surely the *effect* of their deaths is reconciliatory: what are their enmities now, when they have been drowned in the ocean that, as we have seen, figuratively claims everyone in the end?

   The Providence whose end Ham dimly understands is imputed as a shaping force throughout the story, manifest now in the suggestion that David's "caul" is an equivoque for an *opus Dei* "call," now in the portents of Emily's seduction or Steerforth's death, now in the hints that David and Agnes have been predestined for each other. The role of Providence doesn't leave David's imagination, the *apparent* shaping force in the story, in quite the embarrassed position one might suppose. Providence may ordain a particular order for David's life, but his imagination must cooperate, both by discerning that order when it impinges on him as portent or déjà vu, and by retracing it when he comes, in the Kierkegaardian terms I have used for Wilhelm Meister, to understand backward what he has lived forward. His life's *telos*, like everyone else's, is never certain as he goes forward. If all things have worked together for him, it isn't just because he has quietly loved God but because God has, through so many of the characters we read about but also in propria persona, even more quietly and obscurely loved him—the obscurity diminishing slightly only upon retrospection, fully articulate in this three-volume autobiography. It is a conviction, as among others Garrett Stewart has rightly remarked, that Dickens himself had about his own great good luck: only God's mercy could overcome probabilities and keep him from becoming a little thief back in the bad days of Warren's blacking warehouse (845). Providence won't "work," orthodoxly here as in Goethe's heterodox Kantian picture, unless there are human agents willing to go along and *choose* their fate. It isn't enough for David to "sense" that Agnes has been meant for him: he actually has to marry her. Nor is it enough for him to "believe" that his sufferings at Murdstone and Grinby's or on the road to Dover served the higher end of making him compassionate the oppressed: he actually has to go out of his way, like the Samaritan, *to* compassionate them. In doing so he makes himself according to the specifications by which an infinite Other has made him already.

This philosophically having one's cake and eating it troubled Dickens less than it has his modern critics.[34] As J. S. Mill would say, the question about Dickens's version of the Christian myth need not be a Benthamic "Is it true?"—true that Providence has elected Agnes for David, or decreed "the end of it like" for Ham and Steerforth? To which, after all, one can honestly give no more than an agnostic reply. The question can and ought to be a Coleridgean "What does it *mean?*" Why should David believe in foreordination on one hand, and in a heaven-opening eschatology on the other? There are common-sense psychological answers, some of which I have offered. They have to do with David's desire to return to the comfortable paradise he has known in the garden of his childhood, on the warm bosom of his mother, with his ghostly father a well-disposed but invisible presence. This desire can, through a series of domestic arrangements, be only partially satisfied on earth. Thus Agnes' pointing to the omnium-gatherum God will arrange—the fête for which David is rehearsing on the final pages of his story as he reviews the faces that have been dear to him: now they fade, but hereafter they will shine. His enthusiasm for this psychic solace derives less from the need to comfort himself, though that is strong, than from the wish to comfort others. He is like the Bachelor in *The Old Curiosity Shop* who pursues antiquarian research in a country church. Whenever he comes upon two versions of a legend, one cynical and one sentimental, he always chooses the latter. He wants to make people believe that virtue not vice is rewarded in the end, on the hopeful supposition that people will then act more virtuously, and without despair. There is, however, a deeper psychological reason why David should believe in Providence. He needs to feel that the act of writing is justified. If Providence isn't something he is just imagining, then his imaginings are really something. They are discoveries—insights into the way things are. The connections in his life that he half-creates, he also half-perceives. They were authentically there, they were meant to be there, and his efforts to realize them then, and record them now, are cooperative in the large design of history itself.

And what designs do David's particular purposes have on us? As James said of *Wilhelm Meister* and as I at least implicitly argue throughout this book, reading about another's self-cultivation should in some manner influence our own—whether we are living it forward or understanding it backward. It goes without saying that David wishes us to emulate the good and to shun the bad characters in his story, but beyond that is the tacit invitation to emulate his own authorial work. The novel isn't offered as a narcotic, an inducement to daydream. It is offered as a spur to agency. To watch the characters act can enable us to act—as Roderick Random's bravery helps David stop crying when he leaves home, or as the bold action of *Julius Caesar* disposes him to boldness, and enables him (for better and worse) to hail Steerforth in the London inn when he might otherwise have shrunk back. But to emulate David's specifically authorial work? To be like the hero we have to do more than hold the pen. Dora can do that. We have to retrace our own lifeline, to present it in such a way that its pattern is clear, its sense manifest. To read the autobiographical novel should lead, ideally, to writing one. If we were able to do *that*, we might better know what to do with the life left us.

Chapter 4

From Pink to Yellow: Growing Up Female in *What Maisie Knew* and *The Portrait of a Lady*

The account of childhood, orphaned in all but fact, that James offers in *What Maisie Knew* (1897) plainly derives not only from *Copperfield, Oliver Twist, The Old Curiosity Shop, Little Dorrit,* and *Great Expectations,* just to name the obvious instances in Dickens, but also from classic sketches of "the young idea" he had studied from *Wilhelm Meister* to *Jane Eyre* and *The Mill on the Floss.* Nor is *Maisie* a sport within the Jamesian canon itself, as the early chapters of *Washington Square* (1881), a tale such as "The Pupil" (1891), or a novella such as *The Turn of the Screw* (1898) amply attest. He was fascinated by examples of superior human consciousness—great intelligent seekers and finders from Isabel Archer in *The Portrait of a Lady* (1881) and Hyacinth Robinson in *The Princess Casamassima* (1886) to Lambert Strether in *The Ambassadors* (1903) and Maggie Verver in *The Golden Bowl* (1904)—and he could naturally be keen on discovering just where such sensibilities came from, and how they were cultivated.

In a word, the problem of *Bildung* was as interesting to him as it was to his English and European counterparts in the nineteenth century, and along with Mark Twain in *The Adventures of Huckleberry Finn*, he offers the best American explorations both of the child's unfolding self and of its growth into adulthood. *Roderick Hudson* (1876), his first substantial novel, puts the whole childhood-to-adulthood story together. It is a portrait of the American artist as a young man, but finally it is more revealing about America and art than about young manhood. *The Princess Casamassima* is in effect a portrait of the artisan as a child, boy, and youth, but instead of becoming the American *Copperfield* it becomes the American *Under Western Eyes*—that is, a novel about revolutionary European politics on par with Conrad's later one.

The fact is, James was more interested, more often, in the growth of fine female sensibilities, the fullest treatment of which comes in *Portrait*. After a brief but revelatory glimpse of ego-shaping girlhood experiences, he brings Isabel to the period of courtship, where the sexual and marital questions that preoccupy Wilhelm Meister or David

Copperfield are tellingly explored. I will come to *Portrait* in the last section of this chapter, but for the most part I will examine the lesser known but powerful *Maisie*. Putting them together will give the proper stereooptic depth to James's understanding of psychological and moral development. That, more than any other discipline in his tonic "live all you can" embrace of experience, is what mattered to him most.

Reading *Maisie* is like reading an eighteenth century comedy,[1] in that much of the amusement, and no small part of the pathos, derives from symmetries of situations and echoes of speeches that progressively exhibit characters and ideas. Here is the story. Six-year-old Maisie is the only child of Beale and Ida Farange, a tall handsome English couple who have gone through an acrimonious divorce. The court in its Solomonic wisdom has divided Maisie between them, six months with one, six with the other, which predictably leaves the girl bereft of love or even of attention, except when her parents use her as a deliverer of hurtful messages. She does get attention and love from her governesses, though. At her mother's there is the young, lovely Miss Overmore, who follows Maisie to her father's. He makes her his mistress and finally his wife, after which she is known as Mrs. Beale. Back at her mother's, Maisie's second governess is the old, dowdy Mrs. Wix, who, no big trick, is more motherly than her mother.

Meanwhile, as Beale has taken up Miss Overmore, Ida picks up Sir Claude and marries him. He is almost certainly a baronet, but James isn't like Thackeray or, in this matter at least, like Jane Austen, and so we know hardly anything material about this character's estate. What counts is that he is a "family-man" by instinct. Therefore he devotes himself to his stepdaughter Maisie, who is the occasion for his getting together with the similarly devoted Mrs. Beale. Not really in love with their respective spouses, these young stepparents are drawn to one another while, in a sleep-with-whomever-you-like fashion, Beale and Ida pursue new paramours of their own. While not needing to work, neither of them is rich, and so they trawl the fashionable waters for mates who *are*. Compared to the marriage of Maisie's parents, the coupling of Sir Claude and Mrs. Beale is a love match, for while he has a small competence, his affairs are always "involved" and her fortune lies entirely in her face and figure. At any rate, like the mirrored bits of colored glass inside a kaleidoscope, Maisie's stepparents come together just as her actual parents split off—and off again. The stepparents and Maisie first discover the pair's perfidy in matching recognition scenes, and then Maisie alone rediscovers it in matching repudiation scenes. Finally relinquishing all claims, her parents dump her onto her stepparents, whom they plan to divorce, though in the last phase of the story the custody fight is resumed between Sir Claude, Mrs. Beale, and Mrs. Wix. Maisie would prefer to stay with Sir Claude the handsome prince, but, jealous of Mrs. Beale, whom he can't give up, she chooses to stay with Mrs. Wix.

What is interesting, aside from our aesthetic pleasure in reverse-images, is how Maisie perceives them: how she knows what she knows, and what, through the *mazy* twists of her thoughts and feelings, she *makes* of what she knows.[2] She isn't the cipher my synopsis may imply, though like young David Copperfield she often is so helpless as to *need* to be passive. Like him, she is an eminently imaginative observer, and if in her shorter tale there are fewer episodes and characters, she has almost as much to ponder about personal relations as he does, and rather more to ponder about adult concupiscence—and about the threshold between childish ignorance of sexuality, on the one hand, and adult theory and practice, on the other. Her famous "moral sense" is centered on sex and sensibility, no less "knowingly" than what we find in the older, coyer Copperfield or in the franker heroes of Forster, Lawrence, and Santayana.

My discussion dwells on the following:

(1) James's concern for the dissolution of traditional family life, and the notable lack of help Maisie can expect from the adults around her;

(2) his record of how she finds out things for herself by using her eyes and ears, and by interpreting the information those organs take in;

(3) the novel's patterns of images and figures of speech, from the morally neutral to the morally charged, particularly the symbols of Edenic gardens spoiled by concupiscence and Maisie's intellective journey from darkness into light;

(4) how Boulogne, a place of light, challenges and enriches her moral sense, which turns out to be more than merely English;

(5) her models for goodness among the adults around her, and the "operative irony" of her embodying goodness in her own person;

(6) the portrayal of her nascent sexuality, as she moves from "pink" prepubescent innocence into "yellow" pubescent experience; and

(7) Isabel Archer as a representative instance of what, in James's vision, happens to the psyche and moral sensibility of the young woman, "a lady," Maisie might plausibly become.

Unhappy Families

I forfeit, at the start, any ambition to explain James's 1890s fascination with prepubescent adolescents such as Maisie, Morgan in "The Pupil," Flora and Miles in *The Turn of the Screw*, or, in a throwback to *Portrait*'s precious pathetic Pansy Osmond, Nanda Brookenham in *The Awkward Age* (1899), who is at the age of coming out and entering the marriage market. James's biographers—Leon Edel remains the most authoritative—have speculated that his failures as a playwright in this decade made him feel particularly vulnerable, as if the wounds of his childhood had been reopened. Identification with sensitive, assailable but imaginative, boys and girls may have seemed a double resource, providing now a withdrawal from the brutalities of adults, not least their sexually motivated ones, and now an opportunity to study those brutalities through the eyes of gentler organisms. Vis-à-vis the grown-up world, children are outsiders, and their point of view had an obvious if not precise attraction for a writer who, as an American among the English, a celibate among the promiscuous, a repressed homosexual among expressive heteros, and a great artist among Philistines, was an outsider too. James's unconscious was no less swampy than the next person's, and with all those letters, notebooks, essays, and fictions he afforded it plenty of opportunities to give itself away. Which is why the biographers have been legion and their claims so often non-verifiable. With so much evidence, more than one thesis can seem arguable.

The action and cast of *What Maisie Knew* have no less and no more to do with the data of the author's life than the other *Bildungsromane* I am addressing have to do with the lives of their authors. Beyond the author's life are the social conditions of his time and place, and his novel will disclose something about them. It can also, transhistorically, disclose something about our own social conditions—the manifestly crucial ones, then and now, being those of disintegrating families. What in this book I am calling the crisis of paternity is generalized in *Maisie* as a crisis of parenthood *tout à fait*. Maisie knows, to begin with, what Maisie sees, and what she sees is that parents—who, according to the adult conversation she overhears or the romantic tales Mrs. Wix tells her, usually come in pairs, a bonded mother and father—in her case come singly. Now she is with one, now with the other, and at each transition she bears a greeting, as at six years old her "innocent lips" convey to mamma papa's declaration "that you're a nasty horrid pig!"[3] The people around the Faranges may tsk-tsk or feel amused by this running battle, but they don't appear to have been much more successful in their own marriages.

Sir Claude says that at bottom he is a "family-man" who truly enjoys caring for and playing with children, but he will be "hanged" if he can find any "family-women." Witness his wife Ida, who despises a man willing "to accept a menial position about" another man's daughter, "potter[ing] about town of a Sunday" when he might, like her, be putting out "feelers" for new sexual partners at pleasant country houses (110–11). Witness Mrs. Beale herself, who, though approving of his nurse-like qualities, doesn't want a family as much as a good place in society. Perhaps she had too much family back home. Like many governesses in nineteenth-century fiction, she comes from people who are "nice" but have more children than they can afford. Therefore she must go into the one respectable profession open to women—namely teaching—and, employing tactics from a profession that is older but not respectable, seek her fortune. Her governess-precursor isn't Jane Eyre but Becky Sharp.

In any event, it is evident that James was troubled by the breakdown of the normative family—the breakdown that by now has become so pervasive that many commentators simply eschew the word "normative" and are often uncomfortable with "normal."[4] Why, however, should he put Maisie's consciousness at the center this novel? For two reasons. First, he could register the effects of a fissured family on its offspring. If something is wrong, can the child's point of view help us define and measure it? Second, he could exhibit her piecing bits of information together, listening to adults' interpretations, and ultimately drawing her own inferences. What brings men and women together, and what should they do when children begin to appear? To have a child investigate these questions, as it were from the ground up, was to concede that certain ethico-social fundamentals were no longer regarded as, well, fundamentals by many of his advanced contemporaries—the sort of people who would be reading a highbrow novel like *What Maisie Knew*. Among our own contemporaries, for whom divorce, custody arrangements, and blended families are commonplace, either James's novel is as datedly quaint as *Anna Karenina*—What's the *big deal* about having an extramarital affair and bearing a child by someone other than one's husband?—or, like Tolstoy's novel, it is urgently relevant. Even if all happy families were boringly alike—and of course they aren't—a fair number of readers would have to be curious about the norms on which the happiness is based. Compared to Tolstoy, James handicaps himself by omitting any picture of a happy family to play off against the unhappy ones. Possibly it is because he doesn't believe his society affords him a model. But he works with what he has got, "courting [Maisie's] noiseless mental footsteps" as she studies the unhappiness around her, weighs her seniors' dicta, and—like a Rousseauvian savage drawing up, in concert with other nobles, the original social contract—imagines a set of norms that happen to chime with those of her country's traditional, now endangered, culture.

That country and that culture are always endangered as far as its writers are concerned, and we have seen how even in the relatively sunny *Copperfield*, especially when regarding the neglected, abused, or miseducated young, Dickens fingered his worry-beads. His *Bildungsheld* is surrounded by people, however, many of them beneficent as well as benevolent, and he comes through—is brought through—tolerably well. How unaccompanied and immured, by contrast, little Maisie is. She rarely sees her parents. Sir Claude is for a long time only a sympathetic photograph and then a merely occasional visitor ("And this is what you call coming *often?*" she challenges him like a duchess). She does see a great deal of her governesses, but Miss Overmore is short on accomplishments and distracted by her hunt for men, while Mrs. Wix is even shorter on accomplishments—indeed she is a pedagogical joke—and distracted by her delusions about men in general and Sir Claude in particular.

Delusions, yes, but—like those silly sentimental novels she reads and relates to Maisie, which have "the blue river of truth" winding through them—Mrs. Wix's delusions are irrigated by insight, albeit in the shallowest of ditches. She knows that all men are sexually susceptible, and that none of them can, without aid from a good woman, be trusted with a bad one. She was married once, but either her husband abandoned her or, like their daughter, he died. (As Ralph Touchett in *Portrait* might say, the husband of Mrs. Wix "would be likely to pass away.") She doesn't know Beale, but assumes that, with respect to promiscuity, he is like Ida, only, being male, worse. Sir Claude, she insists, has the congenital male problem with "passions"—he is "a slave" to them—but because he is "the perfect gentleman and strikingly handsome," he is worth trying to save from all the "bad women" who would use sex to get into his wallet. When Mrs. Wix is for a long time out of Maisie's life, Sir Claude himself begins to direct her education, treating her to some volumes of essays that to all appearances never get read, a series of free public lectures so hideous (as Mrs. Beale says) they "*must* do us good," and excursions to cricket matches and window-shopping around London. In short, Maisie's three monitors are feckless, their knowledge superficial, their wisdom middling at best, their behavior and tone (the amiable Sir Claude almost always excepted) frequently objectionable.

Finding Out for Herself

In a poignant bit of play therapy, Maisie has told her doll Lisette, who has wondered where she has been all day, to "Find out for yourself!" That, sharply, is what mamma once told *her* to do, and it is what, in real life, she *does*, not just with respect to information about what people have been up to, but with respect to what it means. Her finding out, just like little David's, is perceptual in the beginning. First she sees, then she hears. First there are things, then there are words for them. The words help her turn "sight" into "insight," adding (it is a central Jamesian procedure) moral sense onto aesthetic sense.

Let us consider the visual data and her way of interpreting them. Initially, she sees that mamma is grand and glamorous, Mrs. Beale delicate and lovely, father handsome and fond of looking at himself, Sir Claude's face sympathetic and his manner kindly, Mrs. Wix gray and greasy but, while protecting, in need herself of protection, and so on. With admirable registering of surface detail, James makes as much of the child's ocular stage as Freud does of its oral:

> it would have been difficult to say of him [Mr. Perriam, one of Ida's lovers] whether his head were more bald or his black moustache more bushy. He seemed also to have moustaches over his eyes, which, however, by no means prevented these polished little globes from rolling round the room as if they had been billiard-balls impelled by Ida's celebrated stroke. (91)

Of course the words are James's, but—it is like Mr. Potato-Head, animated by Maisie's impressions of her long-armed mother's power with a cue-stick—the eyes are the little girl's.[5] Her initial interpretations are naturally hit-and-miss. She scores a bull's-eye with the Countess, the mulatto who might have been "a dreadful human monkey in a spangled petticoat," with "a moustache that was, well, not so happy a feature as Sir Claude's" (193).[6] True, the woman suffers from racial prejudice, an outgrowth of Maisie's childish reaction against a phiz so palpably *other* than she is used to, and it is to combat that prejudice that she showers some of her superfluity, got from who knows what South American enterprise, onto Maisie—that cab fare plus the handful of sovereigns she ends up surrendering to Mrs. Beale. But dropping sovereigns onto Beale in payment for sex and companionship *is* morally as "dreadful" as Maisie finds the woman's appearance. The child's instinct is fortuitously right. She scores a bull's-eye with Sir Claude, too. He really *is* sympathetic, now teasing Maisie about how many buns she has eaten, now self-denigratingly admitting that "He can't, he can't, he can't!" give up Mrs. Beale, and on the whole showing her, the daughter of a woman he soon comes to loathe, the greatest affection. But Maisie's interpretations are wide of the mark with the Captain, who, because he has a face as "informally put together" as Mrs. Wix's, she thinks must be as kind. And she misses, more seriously, with Miss Overmore, the later Mrs. Beale. Her lovely features, fine manners, and—James registers this with exquisite Austenian irony—staggering accomplishments seem to give her a leg up on Mrs. Wix:

> Miss Overmore . . . could say lots of dates straight off (letting you hold the book yourself) state the position of Malabar, play six pieces without notes and, in a sketch, put in beautifully the trees and houses and difficult parts. Maisie herself could play more pieces than Mrs. Wix, who was moreover visibly ashamed of her houses and trees and could only, with the help of a smutty forefinger, of doubtful legitimacy in the field of art, do the smoke coming out of the chimneys. (27)

Maisie will learn that there is something merely facile about Miss Overmore's sketches, and indeed about the love and attention she directs toward her. Learning this depends on developing a good ear.

What she listens to, and then repeats, are the words people use. She discovers that their meanings can be multiple and that, when in France she starts to learn another tongue, cultural differences can make translation, indeed moral understanding, puzzling. The key words are "sympathetic," "square," "brute," and "angel" (applied respectively by Sir Claude and the Captain to mamma), "*plage*," "amour," and "*free*," and later I turn most of them over. For the moment it is essential that we appreciate how words in general, and the tones of voice that convey them, enable Maisie to elaborate her interpretations of the visual. Again, her experiences with her two governesses show the process. For openers, Mrs. Wix looks drab, cross, and frightening, and Maisie stands off. After an hour, though, the old woman's voice wins her over, with its maternal tale about a crushed-in-the-road "little dead sister," whose place Maisie will now fill. Having heard and understood what Mrs. Wix says, Maisie perfectly knows what to think about the funny goggles, the greasy hair, the scalloped dress—and, it goes without saying, how to reciprocate her gentle taps and hugs. The process with Miss Overmore runs in reverse. After a favorable opening visual impression and the pleasant enough patter of her conversation, Maisie gradually shies away from the woman whom, as Mrs. Beale, she unconsciously regards as a rival—not for her father's affections, of course, but for Sir Claude's. Mrs. Beale's *voice* doesn't throw out clear signals till the end, when that rivalry is in the open: Give Sir Claude up "To *you*, you abominable little horror?" There is no missing the feeling in *that*.

So much for Maisie's eyes and ears. With regard to Mrs. Beale's harsh tone, we may, in our mature wisdom, have seen it coming. The one-time governess, with no resources beyond those given by nature ("I'm good and I'm clever. What more do you want?"), *does* have to make her own fortune—for which purpose Sir Claude is essential, Maisie merely instrumental. Of course Mrs. Beale has *wanted* to love Maisie, and has hoped to hold on to her. Hence the idea of marrying Sir Claude, and the two of them adopting the cast-off waif. Maisie has liked that idea, and for a long while insists, against the tug of her unconscious, that her first ideas about Mrs. Beale were correct: "She's beautiful and I love her! I love her and she's beautiful!" (276). Once she becomes conscious of their rivalry, however, she permits Sir Claude to speak to Mrs. Beale on her behalf: "She hates you—she hates you" (359). Which is in line with Maisie's own "I'd *kill* her!" when telling Mrs. Wix what she would do if Mrs. Beale were unkind to him. It is the child's offer of a "guarantee [of] her moral sense," matching the squinting Mrs. Wix's own "wild grunt" (288). In the primitive competition to defend those one loves—and this governess and pupil "adore" Sir Claude—the operative command, at the salient, is hatred of and death to the enemy.

Knowing as Maisie Knows: Patterns, Symbols, and Moral Meanings

In real life there is no certainty that a child will piece together her sensations and arrive at a unifying interpretation, but James evidently feels that a *bright* child's chances are pretty good. Maisie herself may have few conscious moral designs beyond wanting both to avoid being a "low sneak" and to have everyone "squared," but (to play on Wilhelm's mot about *Hamlet*) her life is full of design—psychological and moral. James's patterns of images, metaphors, and symmetrical couplings and sunderings are intended as artful mirrorings of the probabilities of life. That the divorced Beale and Ida should quarrel over who is to take care of Maisie is more than just probable, it is practically inevitable, and the same holds true for their new spouses' entering into negotiations over their stepdaughter. Granted, we descend into the merely possible when Mrs. Beale and Sir Claude fall in love, Maisie serving both as a cover and as an irresistible charmer in her own right. But such a daytime-television looping isn't unthinkable, given the narcissism of *their* new spouses, Maisie's parents, and given the chance, occasioned by Maisie's passively bringing them together, of their finding a better deal in one another. The leisured set in London, which the original Faranges and Sir Claude belong to by birth and Mrs. Beale by adoption, is small enough to make the subsequent recognition and repudiation scenes involving Maisie, her parents, and their new paramours seem simply in the cards. The geometric logic of these and similar game-like movements burrow into Maisie's consciousness, giving her "a sense of something that in a maturer mind would be called the way history repeats itself" (172).

As, mutatis mutandis, it surely does. Geometry is morally neutral, however, and the good and evil of any particular movement will emerge—half discerned, half attributed—as Maisie draws on logical resources deeper than the geometric. I don't mean her moral sense, for James says there is something deeper than that. It is when she starts to break down in front of the adults who want her, as in a school exam, to *out with* her moral sense:

> her arms made a short jerk. What this jerk represented was the spasm within her of some-thing still deeper than a moral sense. She looked at her examiner; she looked at the visi-tors; she felt the rising of the tears she had kept down at the station. They had nothing—no, distinctly nothing—to do with her moral sense. (354)

The tears emanate from her desire to be nurtured, recognized, loved—and from her fear that, with all these adults busy promoting or, in the sole case of Mrs. Wix, preventing sexual promiscuity, nobody will take the trouble to fulfill it. Her tears have "distinctly nothing" to do with her moral sense? Perhaps they don't, inasmuch as they are preverbal and as James is no quantitative Benthamite, for whom good consists of what is plea-surable and evil of what is painful. But the tears—of desire for pleasure and fear of its opposite—must at some residuum be *part* of the foundation of her moral sense, if only as motivators.[7]

Definition, in any case, isn't James's purpose. He does go out of his way at the start to reassure us that Maisie's soul is and will continue to be "unspotted" (6), but he doesn't explain whether that indicates she is to remain ignorant of sex, or kindhearted, or what. And so with his express condemnation of Beale's moral stupidity. Does it entail meanness, abusiveness, obtuseness, or all three? It isn't a case, as in T. S. Eliot's shrewd comment, of James having a mind too fine for any idea to violate it. Rather, the novelist wants *us* to conceive the ideas—by working through the same experiential data Maisie works through. Of course she is short on vocabulary, but that is actually lucky for us. To know as Maisie knows is to come to grips with the concrete, palpable sensibilia of her world—to attend to the novel's imagery, in short—and especially to the figures of speech that reflect her way of mentally connecting dissimilar things. The imagery and figures involving beasts, battles, games, and mirrors are everywhere, and have a nonce vividness.

In the novel's architecture, though, are two series of images and figures pervasive enough to become symbols—namely those evoking gardens and those evoking a movement from darkness into light.

The gardens are the kind we expect in a Judeo-Christian culture: initially they look Edenic but then turn out to be either threatened or already subverted. At the very beginning, tiny Maisie gets orientated to life in Kensington Gardens. It is the paradisal green where she can do what she will, but it is also a place of possible abandonment— she wonders what would happen to her if Moddle, her not very watchful nurse, should be gone when she "came back to see if she had been playing too far"—and a place of invidious comparison between her toothpick legs and the robuster limbs of other children. Moddle's diagnosis is that she is so thin because she "feel[s] the strain" of a broken home. "Thus from the first Maisie not only felt it, but *knew* she felt it" (11, my italics). Which is to say that she comes to consciousness with the taste of the fruit of the tree of knowledge of good and evil already in her mouth. The temptation scene happened long before, when at the very latest her parents sued for divorce. She knows she bears the burden of her parents' infidelities, a species of original sin, and never more than on the day when, as she is walking with Sir Claude, the pleasance of Kensington Gardens is changed into a battlefield. Sir Claude has been chatting about how the rural-seeming park is like "the Forest of Arden":

> "and I'm the banished duke, and you're—what was the young woman called?—the artless country wench. And there," he went on, "is the other girl—what's her name, Rosalind?—and (don't you know?) the fellow who was making up to her. Upon my word he *is* making up to her!" (139)

At which point Maisie recognizes that Rosalind is in fact mamma, Sir Claude's wife. He is the banished duke indeed, and together he and Maisie try to guess who the usurping fellow might be: Mr. Perriam, Lord Eric, the Count? It turns out to be the Captain, who has "his season-ticket" to that "illuminated garden, turnstile and all," suggested by Ida's face, with eyes painted "like Japanese lanterns swung under festal arches" (144–45). The paradisal gardens are eclipsed by an amusement park, a kind of outdoor bordello where brawls might break out between the madame and her "frequenters."

The counterpart to this episode occurs in the indoor garden at the Earl's Court exhibition, where Maisie pauses with Mrs. Beale in front of the "Flowers of the Forest" sideshow, a "tropical luxuriance" of "bright brown ladies" (171), whence issues, on the arm of papa, the brown Countess with a scarlet feather. Compounding such an appalling emanation from this faux paradise—"She's almost black," Maisie reports to Mrs. Beale, who, referring to Beale's pickups in general, replies that "They're always hideous"—is the Countess's *plus* faux paradise of an apartment, which Beale whisks Maisie off to. The atmosphere is as in an "Arabian Nights" storybook, brilliant with "more pictures and mirrors, more palm-trees drooping over brocaded and gilded nooks, more little silver boxes scattered over little crooked tables and little oval miniatures hooked upon velvet screens than Mrs. Beale and her ladyship together could, in an unnatural alliance, have dreamed of mustering" (176). What is faux about this scene is its mishmash, the loot of empire—what a nice equal-opportunity touch that James puts it into the arms of a mulatto—bespeaking not love of beauty but the vulgarity of sheer acquisition. The palm trees and silver boxes are on a level with the "jolly" candies Beale offers Maisie:

> He spied a pink satin box with a looking-glass let into the cover, which he raised, with a quick facetious flourish, to offer her the privilege of six rows of chocolate bonbons, cutting out thereby Sir Claude, who had never gone beyond four rows. "I can do what I like with these," he said, "for I don't mind telling you I gave 'em to her myself." The Countess had evidently appreciated the gift; there were numerous gaps, a ravage now quite unchecked, in the array. (179–80)

That, literally, is delicious—especially the bits about the looking-glass, enabling one to watch oneself eat, and about the topping of Sir Claude's meager rows.

The final garden is in Folkestone. Sir Claude and Maisie are sitting before dinner on a bench in the hotel garden when her mother appears—a silken apparition rising from the ground like a goblin gaudily damned. She doesn't expel Maisie from England—she and Sir Claude are leaving on their own—but she does expel her forever from the primal maternal presence. Maternal is the right word, despite the absence of that presence for most of Maisie's young life. For as she passionately insists that the Captain, whom Ida now calls "the biggest cad in London!," was sincere when he said such "beautiful" things about her, Maisie senses within herself

> a fear, a pain, a vision ominous, precocious, of what it might mean for her mother's fate to have forfeited such a loyalty as that. There was literally an instant in which Maisie fully saw—saw madness and desolation, saw ruin and darkness and death. "I've thought of him often since, and I hoped it was with him—with him—!" Here, in her emotion, it failed her, the breath of her filial hope.

And so her desolated, possibly tubercular mother abandons her entirely, withdrawing the ten-pound note she was about to tip her with ("Dear thrifty soul!" Sir Claude exclaims) and, her wrath melting to pity, murmuring "You're a dreadful dismal deplorable little thing" (225). Alliteration intensifies the sentiment, no doubt, and for a moment the after-image of departing mamma merges in Maisie's eyes with that of departing papa. But questions about both receive "a sudden gay answer in the great roar of a gong" announcing supper, just as Sir Claude approaches.

> "She's gone?"
> "She's gone."
> Nothing more, for the instant, passed between them but to move together to the house, where, in the hall, he indulged in one of those sudden pleasantries with which, to the delight of his stepdaughter, his native animation overflowed. "Will Miss Farange do me the honour to accept my arm?" (226)

"Native animation" indeed! Sir Claude is full of secular grace, as he wittily imagines Ida's ten-pound note "Rolled up in a tight little ball, you know—her way of treating banknotes as if they were curl-papers!"—which sparks Maisie just as wittily to imagine it having "at any rate rolled away from her for ever—quite like one of the other balls that Ida's cue used to send flying."

And so what? when "Everything about her . . . —the crowded room, the bedizened banquet, the savour of dishes, the drama of figures—ministered to the joy of life," and when afterwards "she smoked with her friend—for that was exactly what she felt she did—on a porch, a kind of terrace, where the red tips of cigars and the light dresses of ladies made, under the happy stars, a poetry that was almost intoxicating" (228). Bedizened, maybe bedazzled, but James isn't just notating Maisie's heady experience among grown-ups who for once are noncombatants, and with a man whom she adores more than in the end she should. He is also inducting her into the visual, aural, tactile, olfactory sensations of "the joy of life," more of which can be found by her and Sir Claude's turning "back into the garden," a sort of Eden restored now that mamma has been purged, whence "they could see the black masts and the red lights of boats and hear the calls and cries that evidently had to do with happy foreign travel" (229).

Travel to France, that is, and on the morrow with the sun. This finally brings us to the second major symbolic pattern in the novel, for that "crossing of more spaces than the Channel" (202) completes Maisie's journey out of the darkness of her London childhood by bringing her into the light of Boulogne. From the start, her childhood has been buried in "the tomb" (5), an allusion to her bare, badly lit schoolroom where she follows her thoughts as though they were "images bounding across the wall in the slide of a magic-lantern. . . . strange shadows dancing on a sheet" (9). This sounds very like the cave in Plato's allegory, flickering with shadows cast by an artificial light—the cave of illusion and ignorance out of which she must mount, in the climax to her story, "as if France were at the top" (230). There are moreover, in that schoolroom, darknesses within the darkness—the high dusky shelves and the deep closets where Moddle stashes the shadows too monstrous for Maisie to play with. Under Mrs. Wix's tutelage some of these are brought out for examination, a procedure that is necessary if Maisie is to understand how terribly cast away she is, and that is safe if in fact she can depend on being rescued by Sir Claude, who shines "in her yearning eye like the single, the sovereign window-square of a great dim disproportioned room" (159). When not in her schoolroom Maisie is in some other enclosed place that is either dim or lit by gas: in a hansom or a lecture room, in the National Gallery or a tea shop, in the Earl's Court "thingumbob," in the Countess's jungly apartments, or in her parents' smoke-filled drawing rooms. There is nothing ruthlessly consistent about Maisie's immurement: she does go on walks in the streets and parks. Still, if only because a child in London must live mostly in rooms and put up with London weather—when it isn't dark, it is rainy and the streets are "all splash"—one has the impression that Maisie's childhood is dank and suffocating, and that her voyage to France will be to her what it has been to many others, a voyage into sunlight, where she can see things as they really are and where "You're free— you're free" can mean something for her that it hasn't meant for her stepparents.

What's the French for "moral sense"?

The "larger impression of life" made upon Maisie in Boulogne inspires some of the most luxuriant writing in the book, intended to fulfill those happy anticipations that have seized Maisie at Folkestone. James goes for the verbal reflection of a Eugène

Louis Boudin painting, declaring, now Maisie is "abroad," that "she gave herself up to it, responded to it, in the bright air, before the pink houses, among the bare-legged fishwives and the red-legged soldiers, with the instant certitude of a vocation" (231). Her luminous curiosity gives her the lead over Susan Ash, her questionable companion still attached to the Edgware Road, and propels her beyond those benighted English ways of eating boiled eggs for breakfast and jam for supper. Breakfast in Boulogne is in a place "along the quay" where bran is sprinkled on the floor such that for Maisie it possesses "something of the added charm of a circus," and where the waiter, serving café au lait out of two steaming "spouts of plenty," performs "as nimbly with plates and saucers as a certain conjurer her friend had in London taken her to a music-hall to see." Circuses, music halls, *la vie de bohème* led by "the irregular, like herself—who went to bed or who rose too late" (324): what an immensely beguiling change after so many dingy repasts with dear frumpy Mrs. Wix. Even the weather round Boulogne turns sparkling as if by Sir Claude's particular arrangement during his absence, till "the joy of the world so waylaid the steps of his friends, that little by little the spirit of hope filled the air and finally took possession of [a] scene . . . in which, to English eyes, everything that was the same was a mystery and everything that was different a joke" (266–67). Of course there is an immensity of Gallic infatuation in these passages. Maisie is wowed by Boulogne just as Hyacinth Robinson, in *The Princess Casamassima*, is wowed by the Place de la Concorde in Paris, though unlike him she is fortunate never to learn anything about the nation's politics. James is usually only half-a-step away from ambivalence about the seductions of France, and at certain moments with Maisie his irony is unmistakable:

> Best of all was to continue the creep up the long Grand' Rue to the gate of the *haute ville* and, passing beneath it, mount to the quaint and crooked rampart, with its rows of trees, its quiet corners and friendly benches where brown old women in such white-frilled caps and such long gold earrings sat and knitted or snoozed, its little yellow-faced houses that looked like the homes of misers or of priests and its dark château where small soldiers lounged on the bridge that stretched across an empty moat and military washing hung from the windows of towers. This was a part of the place that could lead Maisie to enquire if it didn't just meet one's idea of the middle ages; and since it was rather a satisfaction than a shock to perceive, and not for the first time, the limits in Mrs. Wix's mind of the historic imagination, that only added one more to the variety of kinds of insight that she felt it her own present mission to show.

Maisie's "middle ages" are mostly secular, her historic imagination dyed in whatever Walter Scott colors have stained the popular romances Mrs. Wix has recounted to her. That woman's own vision of the Middle Ages is centered on "the great dome and the high gilt Virgin of the church" that they on several occasions focus their meditations on, she sighing, like many a Jamesian Protestant, that "she had probably made a fatal mistake early in life in not being a Catholic"—causing Maisie to wonder if she herself still has time to convert (267). At the end even of a sunny day on the Continental side of the Channel, it isn't too difficult to distinguish James's earnest from his ironic encomia to French culture. On the one hand, Maisie's head is turned by separately trivial details of diet, dress, architecture, and social customs—from devotion to that "great golden Madonna" above the church to the way an "ear-ringed old" woman says

"'Adieu mesdames!' . . . in a little cracked civil voice" (270). Really, Maisie might as well be a Jamesian American tourist, so superficial is her experience of Continental life. On the other hand, "the institutions and the manners of France," the accumulation of these trivial details, suggest to her "a multitude of affinities and messages" (231) that do beneficently broaden her insular outlook on a transculturally deep subject—profane love.

Profane because Mrs. Wix harps so exclusively on her special subject, sacred love, that Maisie can't quite understand how the two are connected. It is like asking, as they sit on "their battered bench" on the rampart, flanked by "their gilded Virgin" up there and by "the semi-nude bathers" on the *plage* below them (286), what the one can possibly have to do with the other. James favors this grouping for the strong advantage it gives him in putting the natural and the ethical (if not the out-and-out supernatural) in play with one another.

> Maisie had seen the *plage* the day before with Sir Claude, but that was a reason the more for showing on the spot to Mrs. Wix that it was, as she said, another of the places on her list and of the things of which she knew the French name. The bathers, so late, were absent and the tide was low; the sea-pools twinkled in the sunset and there were dry places as well, where they could sit again and admire and expatiate: a circumstance that, while they listened to the lap of the waves, gave Mrs. Wix a fresh support for her challenge. "Have you absolutely none [no moral sense] at all?" (280)

Now, Maisie is an apt pupil, but she must wonder, amidst the monotony of sand, sea-pools, and lapping waves, about the pertinence of Mrs. Wix's probings for a moral sense. It is a moment that looks forward to the morning when Mrs. Wix darkly declares that "God knows!" what Sir Claude might be up to in Mrs. Beale's room, and "Maisie wondered a little why, or how, God should know" (312).

Well of course human beings aren't anemones living in "sea-pools"; they must develop a morality to guide them through the conflicts they inevitably have with one another. And if the God they have built temples to doesn't visibly concern himself with the goings-on in Mrs. Beale's bedroom, or isn't altogether encapsulated in the Bible where Mrs. Wix finds her morality "branded" once for all, we would be rash to suggest that James is discounting religious tradition and biblical literature entirely. Fair enough. The question is, where between a naturalistic amorality and a supernaturalistic bibliolatry does he want Maisie to come out? Mrs. Wix wants her to condemn her stepparents simply because they desire to live together out of wedlock. Maisie, with "a vague sigh of oppression," escapes her governess's queries by going out onto the balcony. There, hanging over the railing,

> she felt the summer night; she dropped down into the manners of France. There was a café below the hotel, before which, with little chairs and tables, people sat on a space enclosed by plants in tubs; and the impression was enriched by the flash of the white aprons of waiters and the music of a man and a woman who, from beyond the precinct, sent up the strum of a guitar and the drawl of a song about "amour." Maisie knew what "amour" meant too, and wondered if Mrs. Wix did. (284–85)

Thinking that perhaps Mrs. Wix doesn't know, Maisie asks, "*Is* it a crime?" Being given the bibliolator's definitive answer, she finds that she "didn't even yet adequately understand." Mrs. Wix is at this reduced to that adult appeal, mandatory more often than people with no experience with children may think, of "Just *trust* me, dear; that's all!" (285). The girl would be glad just to trust, but knowing the French word for love complicates her ideas rather more than knowing the French words on the menu at the table d'hôte. The immediate complication is that amour involves physical passions that aren't merely "enslaving," as Mrs. Wix would have it, but are so sweet that people can, while escaping slavery (sex addiction), find them positive incitements to, and reinforcers of, more spiritual affinities. Mrs. Wix's either/or of sex/no-sex verges on the literally senseless.

That is the easy part, and it makes James and his little heroine seem more like Forster and Lawrence than they actually are. Where they *are*, spiritually and physically, is closer to Dickens, which is why what Maisie knows about amour, beyond the birds-and-bees business, is that it is bristling with categorical imperatives. Love mamma—"Do it always!"—she tells the Captain. "Tell the truth always," she all but tells Sir Claude. To be sure, these are counsels of perfection quite impossible to realize, and any attempt to do so would bring society to a halt. But, as we see Santayana maintain, they are morally requisite nonetheless. They are the ideals that situationists—casuists—navigate by. Less impossible is Maisie's conviction, as we must infer it, that amour makes one free—free, as her stepparents more and more hollowly cry, from the legalisms and taboos of society, but free more substantively to love without being master or slave. That anyway is the suggestion at the end, when Maisie bids Sir Claude to liberate himself from the almost sadomasochistic relationship he has with Mrs. Beale and live all chastely in never-never land with herself.

But about those counsels of perfection. In spite of the "relish" with which he beholds Maisie's goodness, Sir Claude isn't likely to "do it always" with Mrs. Beale: he is far too fond of gazing after young fishwives on the beach or perfumed young women in the hall. Nor does he, or can he, tell the truth always. He lies to Maisie about not having been overnight with Mrs. Beale (his "stick" is in her room, not in London), and for the very good and very human reason that, as an adult, he doesn't deem the girl mature enough to be told, even indirectly, about sexual intercourse. At least not told by a man. There is also, one must admit, the *temptation* to lie about the kind of love that he entertains for her, and that she more than filially entertains for him. The pedophiliac impulse is strong in him, but he recognizes it, checks it, and effectually sends Maisie back to the motherly Mrs. Wix while he pursues his chosen, age-appropriate partner, Mrs. Beale. Instead of Vladimir Nabokov's *Lolita*, a novel several critics have superimposed on this one, we get an overlap with *Copperfield*, where the almost pedophiliac relation between Mr. Peggotty and Little Emily is checked—just in time, most readers will say—by the need to pack up for the voyage to Australia.

The ability to be absolutely truthful about sex in all circumstances, not least to and about oneself, is notoriously rare. But if it is understandably rare in adult conversation with children, it could helpfully be more common in adults' conversations among themselves. In Sir Claude's case, what needs to be faced is his dependency on women, which Mrs. Wix has in mind when referring to his being "a slave to his passions." Slave to the orgasmic experience women provide, obviously, and to the spoiling—the way they fool him into thinking that he is a conqueror and adored. But also, what he keeps returning to, slave to his "fear." On the one hand, it is fear of what he would do without them: Be a homosexual? Hang out with girls like Maisie, whom he calls "old man," "dear boy," and so on? Suffer in abstinence? On the other, it is fear of what, in return for sexual favors, women can *make* him do: marry them, buy them expensive gimcrackery, accompany them to salons and museums (no aesthete, he is bored in the National Gallery)—and all, in his case, without the compensatory satisfactions of family life. His books don't balance when it comes to women. He is damned and afraid *with* them, and afraid he would be damned *without*. Maisie's promise that she will give up Mrs. Wix if he will give up Mrs. Beale is "beautiful" not just because it has a sacrifice-tat-sacrifice-tit symmetry. Maisie in effect challenges him to overcome his fear of doing without women—or more precisely, without women of the age and attractiveness that he desires sexually—in order to withdraw into the aforesaid never-never land of stepfather, stepdaughter bliss.[8] Is *this* what James in his "Preface" means when declaring that his "interesting small mortal" "really in short, mak[es] confusion worse confounded by drawing some stray fragrance of an ideal across the scent of selfishness, by sowing on barren strands, through the mere fact of presence, the seed of the moral life" (viii)? Not Nabokov's Lolita but Lewis Carroll's Alice, only in purpler prose? Yes, as we will see, and no.

Moral Models and "operative irony"

If Maisie can sow "the seed of the moral life," did someone give it to her or was she born with it? James seems to believe, unprovably, that, like everyone else only more so, she was born with the seed—or, as one now might say, she was hardwired with the capacity for moral reflection—and the pertinent question is how that capacity has been developed. How has she learned "what 'amour' meant"? There is little doubt about the importance of two decent people, Sir Claude and Mrs. Wix, who have set some salutary examples for her. Granted, Sir Claude uses Maisie to facilitate his connection with Mrs. Beale, but he is almost always affectionate and kind to her—the exception being the afternoon when, acting on her "pacific art of stupidity," she doesn't tell him what the Captain has said about mamma. This exasperates him. The dominant point about Sir Claude, though, is that he is "sympathetic" (48), not just in appearance, nor just when in the supreme moment he promises Maisie, with a breast as agitated as hers and with "tears . . . as silently flowing" (108), never to forsake her, but also when, in the face of her questions about Mrs. Beale, he gravely says, "Let her be. I don't care about her. I want to see *you*" (320). The moral import of Sir Claude's being sympathetic tells in his manners—that amiable princely style complementing the princely phiz, and that way of "making love to her." The phrase is tricky because to our ears it implies sex, but in their day, and to Maisie's ears, it implies making up to—as at Boulogne she notices Mrs. Beale "make love" to Mrs. Wix, whose help she needs. Sir Claude makes love to Maisie insofar as he is nice to her, and this (my only point now) serves her as a model for how *she* might be nice to others.

Mrs. Wix's kindness to Maisie isn't romantic in Sir Claude's way, of course. It is a maternal kindness, rather, giving her a "soothingly safe," "tucked-in and kissed-for-good-night feeling" (26). Mrs. Wix is "safe" because she is like this "always": what she has done on behalf of her own little girl, long ago "crushed by the cruellest of hansoms," she pledges to do on behalf of Maisie. True, Mrs. Wix needs to feel wanted, and one might argue that any fetching slip of a girl would do as a substitute for the daughter lost, but the fact remains that the woman *is* faithful. It is a felicitous example for this particular discarded daughter to imitate, and at her age no harm can come from the "swarms" of illustrative tales Mrs. Wix passes on from Bovaryesque "novels . . . all about love and beauty and countesses and wickedness . . . and gushing fountains of homeliness" (27). The morality derived from that sort of fiction—the bits about love, wickedness, beauty, homeliness—is bolstered if not broadened by the only other book Mrs. Wix appears to know, the Bible, and James grants her a formidable say in the deliberations in Boulogne. We have heard her negative opinion on the question whether Sir Claude and Mrs. Beale should be living together outside of marriage, and whether Maisie ought to be mixed up in anything so forbidden. She speaks, out of "her deep, narrow passion," as though "she had been a prophetess with an open scroll or some ardent abbess speaking with the lips of the Church" (203). Her thunderings remind Sir Claude of his mother—he even admits it might have been better if she *had* been his mother—but, he explains in the kindly tones one uses when addressing demi-idiots, "My dear friend, it's simply a matter in which I must judge for myself. You've judged *for* me, I know, a good deal, of late, in a way that I appreciate, I assure you, down to the ground. But you can't do it always; no one can do that for another, don't you see, in every case" (260). Which, looking no further ahead than to *Sons and Lovers*, is exactly what *every* son must sooner or later tell his mother—or her stand-in. Not for nothing, in any case, did James propose in his notebook that one of Maisie's governesses should be "frumpy," and after Sir Claude's "Mother, do you *mind*?" speech, we behold her in a posture that leaves us unsure whether to hoot or weep:

> "Here I am, here I am!"—she spread herself into an exhibition that, combined with her intensity and her decorations, appeared to suggest her for strange offices and devotions, for ridiculous replacements and substitutions. She manipulated her gown as she talked, she insisted on the items of her debt. "I have nothing of my own, I know—no money, no clothes, no appearance, no anything, nothing but my hold of this little one truth, which is all in the world I can bribe you with: that the pair of you are more to me than all besides, and that if you'll let me help you and save you, make what you both want possible in the one way it *can* be, why, I'll work myself to the bone in your service!" (263)

Sir Claude is naturally uninterested in erotic substitutions, and Mrs. Wix's plangent promises, which sound like Dickens at his most sentimental, are of increasingly limited interest to Maisie.

Given the fallibilities of these two monitors, it should be apparent that Maisie can't be "saved" by either of them. Accepting their cultivating hints about amiability, making love, and being faithful (not to mention telling the truth)—all of which, to repeat, nourish the "seed" of morality mysteriously innate within her—Maisie must proceed to save herself. To conceive an ideal that no one is quite able to teach her, she has to heed what, in his "Preface" to "The Lesson of the Master," James calls the "operative irony" of her situation. Such irony "implies and projects the possible other case, the case rich and edifying where the actuality is pretentious and vain. So it plays its lamp; so, essentially, it carries that smokeless flame, which makes clear, with all the rest, the good cause that guides it."[9] Irony inverts the actual to produce the ideal. Maisie comes up with the desideratum of "doing it always"—loving someone always—in reaction to the behavior of the adults around her, who merely do it sometimes, or never. They are miserable, as she can tell from their grimaces, their violence, their slanders. "Her little instinct of keeping the peace" (182) is simply her inspired hunch that she might attain happiness by pursuing "the possible other case," refusing to be used as a messenger of insult, imploring the Captain to be better than—the opposite of—"all the others," and clinging loyally (she would be a "low sneak" if she didn't) to Sir Claude, Mrs. Wix, and even Mrs. Beale for as long as she can. She posits this ideal as a philosopher might posit the idea of the Good: it is "the possible" she needs if she is to climb out of the fetid air of betrayal and recrimination she has breathed from the start.

James presents Maisie's ironic inferences as extraordinary but nonetheless believable human acts. "To this end," he explains in his "Preface," "I should have of course to suppose for my heroine dispositions originally promising, but above all I should have to invest her with perceptions easily and almost infinitely quickened. So handsomely fitted out, yet not in a manner too grossly to affront probability, she might well see me through the whole course of my design" (viii). The question of "probability" is ticklish. Maisie's "dispositions," her genetic endowment, are plump without being incredible, and she has a terrific sensory apparatus without seeming preternatural. Is she herself an example of "operative irony"—the romantic "possible," a nobly willed instance of the "civic . . . imagination," which James pits against "all the stupidity and vulgarity and hypocrisy"? Well, yes, for if a society doesn't offer the artist any happy probabilities, he is duty-bound to *invent* an instance: "What one would accordingly fain do is to baffle . . . calamity, to *create* the record [of a fine sensibility], in default of any other enjoyment of it; to imagine, in a word, the honourable, the producible case."[10] Not that it hugely matters if James is inventing a figure whom the society at large doesn't typically afford, and about whom we have to suspend a measure of disbelief. It is the essence of Maisie's character that she is atypical. In her exceptionalism she is less like Wilhelm Meister or David Copperfield, both, as I have said, mediocre in the honorable sense, and more like Santayana's Oliver Alden, who has a spark or two of his author's own genius. If Maisie were more typical of children in her desolated situation, the bottom line would be something like "Good kid, tremendous potential, but no chance for development." Given the "miracle" of her innate "dispositions" and sensibility, the judgment is "*Very* good kid, who by force of her will and imagination, and with help from a few grown-ups, comes through beautifully." She doesn't just dream of "the possible other case," she embodies it. What after all would be the point, amid "all the stupidity and vulgarity and hypocrisy"—the calamity of disintegrating families—of depicting a hapless mediocrity, a mere victim? A small specimen of genius has at least a chance of finding a way out. Maisie's genius consists of what James calls the "freshness" of her mind, to wit, her ability to ask ingenuous questions, test the proffered answers, and reach her own deductions. Of course James is inventing all this, but he describes his invention with such clarity that we entertain the precious "illusion of reality," the feeling that we are reading not a fantasy but a report.

Maisie's Sexuality

What especially fosters this sense of reportage are, for starters, the frequent indications of Maisie's fallibility—the things she at first misunderstands about the adults and their world—but more, the quite ordinary unfolding of her own sexuality, the com-mingling of her affective and her physical impulses. To be sure, readers in 1897 were unlikely to clap their hands together in recognition of *this* "quite ordinary" unfolding. These after all were the years in which Freud was having to work so hard to persuade people that children had sexual feelings, compulsions, hopeful and fearful fantasies *at all*, and James was offering his own contribution to enlightenment on the subject. His inquiries are obviously less anatomical than Freud's, but readers who have attended to the imagery and general erotic tensions of, say, *The Turn of the Screw* will readily acknowledge that he could produce a luridness of his own. *What Maisie Knew* is by comparison almost clean-cut, giving us, as I have intimated, a sort of Alice who, if she were totally luckless, could become a sort of Lolita.

The point is that she isn't luckless and, morally speaking, she isn't senseless. I have said that her final proposal to Sir Claude—Mrs. Wix and Mrs. Beale should be given up in order that they, stepfather and stepdaughter, might live alone together—compels him to realize that it's not possible. As he exclaims with a constrained tap-dance gaiety, "He can't, he can't, he can't!" do it (362). Can't, that is, forgo sexual intercourse with an attractive age-appropriate woman—and age-appropriate deserves some stress. James has empha-sized how the predatory Ida is older than Sir Claude, who has himself emphasized how Mrs. Wix (the "ridiculous replacement") is impossibly ancient and Maisie rather too young. But only just. "I *should* be in fear if you were older—there! See—you already make me talk nonsense," he tells Maisie early on, after admitting he is afraid of her mamma (115), and later in France he clearly thinks a life with her alone would have its attractions. There would be no more hectoring from Mrs. Wix, his self-appointed mother, no more demands from Mrs. Beale, his dominatrix, and, since Maisie *isn't* older, no longer any reason to "be in fear." His jocular desexing of Maisie, calling her "Maisie boy" and so on, is a way of defining a platonic heterosocial relationship analogous to the platonic homosocial one we see between Pemberton and Morgan in "The Pupil."[11]

But platonic for how long? Maisie will soon *be* older. Her liminal state is delicately underscored at the station where she and Sir Claude discuss the possibility of taking the train to Paris and leaving Mrs. Beale and Mrs. Wix behind. He has bought her "three books, one yellow and two pink. He had told her the pink were for herself and the yellow one for Mrs. Beale, implying in an interesting way that these were the natural divisions in France of literature for the young and for the old." This is the color code I allude to in my chapter title. While currently in the "pink" of life, Maisie will soon at puberty move into the "yellow," and during the light-orange transition the romantic notion of getting on that train and heading into a life of Parisian irregularity has its allure. "*Veux-tu bien qu'il en prenne?*" Sir Claude asks, referring to whether the porter should buy two tickets.

> It was the most extraordinary thing in the world: in the intensity of her excitement she not only by illumination understood all their French, but fell into it with an active per-fection. She addressed herself straight to the porter. "*Prenny, prenny. Oh prenny!*" (345)

Maisie is childishly fond of rhetorical triplets, but this particular one in baby-French—in the crescendo of noise and indecision James builds up "amid cries of '*En voiture, en voiture!*' "—has the impact of an orgasmic "Yes, yes, oh yes!" It issues from her with a spontaneity recalling her "Lots of times!" response to Mrs. Wix's question whether she has ever felt "jealous" of Mrs. Beale (287). Such jealousy, born of actual or fancied sexual rivalry, is the weft of Maisie's moral cogitations at the close—the cogitations of an extraordinary imagination in, I am insisting, a quite ordinary dilemma, a blended-family variant of the classic family romance.

Fortunately, Maisie and Sir Claude miss that train to Paris, and the warp in her cogitations—and in his—can be get a tightening tug on the loom. The warp is simply their common-sense grasp, hers initially firmer than his, of moral realities such as: (a) how "unconventional" and "rum" would be the ménage he envisages "somewhere in the South—where she [Mrs. Beale] and you would be together and as good as any one else. And I should be as good too, don't you see? for I shouldn't live with you, but I should be close to you—just round the corner" (334); (b) how much more-than-"rum" would be the proto-pedophiliac fantasy of the two of them living together in Paris or wherever; and (c) how lucky for both that there is a conventional, entirely natural way out, namely their separating instanter. Sir Claude will stay with Mrs. Beale. Now that both have been promised a divorce by their respective "fiend[s]"—no difficulty proving the wives' adultery and the husbands' also, plus desertion—we can see no legal impediment, Mrs. Wix's unlettered denials notwithstanding, to Sir Claude and Mrs. Beale's marrying one another. Even if they were formally to adopt Maisie, the already noted rivalry over Sir Claude would turn "her ladyship" into the wicked stepmother of storybooks. Therefore, Maisie's best option is the one she freely chooses—and at last "I'm free!—I'm free!" takes on a certain profundity—when she puts her hand out to Mrs. Wix. Mrs. Beale herself has formulated the normative psychological reasoning behind such a choice: "The essence of the question was that a girl wasn't a boy: if Maisie had been a mere rough trousered thing, destined at the best probably to grow up a scamp, Sir Claude would have been welcome" (302). But as Maisie is a girl, she needs a female guardian, Mrs. Beale of course offering herself in the cited instance, but Mrs. Wix being the preferred candidate in the end. *She* won't pose any rivalrous opposition to Maisie's love for any man (they have always been united, like fans in a club, in adoration of Sir Claude), and while she can be expected to put a brake on the growing girl's desire to go out, among other things, she will know how, eventually, to *let* her go, and meanwhile will have provided the nearest semblance to a home—a place where sexual feelings are muted to a frequency simply out of range—that Maisie has ever known.

That dimension of "wonder at what Maisie knew"—knew beyond what James in the "Preface" calls "the death of her childhood" (xi)—never got written, not at least under her name. I do though propose to consider how, in the line of female *Bildung*, James elsewhere figured the psychological and moral development that a Maisie-sort, first a girl, then a young woman of imagination, might pass through. The possible illustrations are overwhelmingly numerous, from Gertrude Wentworth in *The Europeans* and Daisy Miller early in his career, to Milly Theale in *Wings of the Dove* and Maggie Verver late in his career. It is the middle period *The Portrait of a Lady*, however, that will enable me to forward the necessary points—points that, in line with the title's indefinite article (*a* lady), highlight Isabel Archer's representativeness and make the novel as much "of 1907" (xiv), meaning contemporary, as *Maisie* is.

Isabel Archer

My treatment of *The Portrait of a Lady* is brief and two short paragraphs will do to recall its story. Having grown up motherless, with a spendthrift father who took her and her sisters along on his frequent travels to Europe, Isabel Archer comes of age in Albany, New York, where that father has recently died. She has very little money of her own. Her mother's eccentric sister, Mrs. Touchett, takes her to England to visit her husband, a wealthy American banker from whom she is amicably separated, and her son Ralph, a consumptive too ill to succeed his father at the bank. Back in America, Isabel has declined the marriage proposal of Caspar Goodwood, a textile magnate, and directly she is in England she declines a proposal from Lord Warburton, a duke whose "big bribe" fortune is the stuff of fables. Struck by his cousin's independence—a girl who doesn't marry Lord Warburton must want to do extraordinary things—Ralph persuades his dying father to bequeath her half the money intended for himself, which would give her the wherewithal to *do* the extraordinary. What ensues, of course, is most unextraordinary: Mrs. Touchett's friend Madame Merle puts Isabel in the way of Gilbert Osmond, an American dilettante and widower living in Florence with his teenage daughter Pansy. Though at first hesitating, Isabel finally succumbs to his importunities. They marry, settle in Rome, and, during the three years James lets silently pass, find out how unhappy they truly are with one another.

During the second half of the novel the obtuse Isabel discovers that Osmond married her for her money, and that he did so under the prompting of Madame Merle, whose lover he once had been, and who has schemed not just for his benefit but (it turns out) for their illegitimate daughter Pansy's. That *jeune fille* is touchingly innocent, and has lately been the object of Lord Warburton's attentions. He withdraws, however, partly because he understands that marrying little Pansy would be a dishonorable way of drawing closer to her stepmother (who if she is unhappy in marriage is still not interested in adultery), and partly because he recognizes that the girl is in love with Ned Rosier, an American connoisseur who in adversity also loves her. Downcast because his daughter won't after all become a duchess, Osmond accuses Isabel of untrustworthiness, and of having driven Lord Warburton away. At this, she goes England to sit by the deathbed of Ralph. Osmond opposes such a journey, but she has the more reason to defy him after learning from his sister, the Countess Gemini, the full extent of his and Madame Merle's relations and machinations. Ralph's funeral over, Caspar urges Isabel to bolt with him—why should she return to a husband who has used and now hates her?—but she insists on returning to Rome.

Why a portrait of *this* lady? It is as if she couldn't help announcing to others that she *deserves* a sitting or two. "I don't believe you allow things to be settled for you," Ralph tells her upon their first meeting at Gardencourt, his father's English country house. She replies like a pert American Jane Austen-style heroine: "Oh yes; if they're settled as I like them."[12] That James does rather more than Austen in tracing the origins of this sort of pertness is largely due to his writing eighty-some years after her—years of novelistic preoccupation with questions of psychological development. None of Austen's successors had excelled her at registering the psychology of the *moment*: for instance, Emma Woodhouse's sad realization that she has done Miss Bates a moral injury, or her happy realization, "dart[ing] through her, with the speed of an arrow, that Mr. Knightley must marry no one but herself." These moments are delicately prepared, but the psychology of *development* from childhood to girlhood to young womanhood, which since Goethe we have associated with the *Bildungsroman*, is something Austen attempts only in Fanny Price of *Mansfield Park*, and even there she is offering a mere pencil sketch of early development. Her real interest is in the nubile young woman. That is comparatively true of James's regard for Isabel also, but he had learned too much from *Wilhelm Meister*—I have cited his review of Carlyle's translation, and of course there were countless other inspirations—to be content with a mere pencil.

Painterly analogies are for obvious reasons irresistible when discussing *Portrait*, and so I say that if James worked Isabel's womanly figure in oils—and in the New York Edition of 1908 with plenty of scumbling and varnish—he worked her childish and girlish figures in pastels, with a palette broad in color, rich in texture. What color and texture most obviously bring out is that having early lost her mother she is as bereft of models for growing up female as the representative Copperfield, say, is bereft of models for growing up male. Her charming dissolute impecunious father has freely spoiled her, especially during the family's peregrinations among the watering places of Europe. Indeed, the Archers strongly resemble the Moreens in "The Pupil," with Isabel as preciously "imaginative" as young Morgan is precociously "intellectual." Her girlish sense of right and wrong is quite as worldly as the elder Moreens': when her bonne runs off with a Russian nobleman, abandoning her sisters and herself at Neufchâtel, she coolly considers it "a romantic episode in a liberal education." Which is wonderfully open-minded, but a worrisome instance of "seeing without judging" (1.42–43).

We have noticed this Jamesian (and common-sense) sequence in *Maisie*: first we see, then we judge—and by judging start to know the world morally. Thus Isabel's palpitating excitement during the American Civil War, which began when she was 12 years old, "in which she felt herself at times (to her extreme confusion) stirred almost indiscriminately by the valour of either army" (1.46)—her moral judgment approving "valour" generally, whatever combatant might display it, and avoiding the harder question of war aims (the sustaining of slavery against the ending of it). Thus too her yearning in her later teenage years to move on from innocence to experience. With almost culpable innocence, as she herself might severely say, she has enjoyed the usual benefits of her class—people with moderate and mysteriously derived unearned incomes—which James miscellaneously tabulates:

> kindness, admiration, bonbons, bouquets, the sense of exclusion from none of the privileges of the world she lived in, abundant opportunity for dancing, plenty of new dresses, the London *Spectator*, the latest publications, the music of Gounod, the poetry of Browning, the prose of George Eliot. (1.46)

Although she has never gone to school and reads in secret to keep people from labeling her as bookish, she clearly has intellectual ambitions. When James's retrospective pastel changes focus from panorama to scene, the young woman is trying, on a rainy day in Albany, to give her "vagabond" mind some military discipline. "Just now she had given it marching orders and it had been trudging over the sandy plains of a history of German Thought" (1.31)—exactly what the transcendentalist culture of New England *would* prescribe for her,[13] and exactly the cue for the entrance of "our crazy Aunt Lydia." This stolid empiricist—"One either did the thing or one didn't, and what one 'would' have done belonged to the sphere of the irrelevant, like the idea of a future life or of the origin of things" (2.37)—offers her new-found niece a trip to England and Italy, where the plains are fertile and often garden-like, and where, more than in her "blessed Albany," her "ridiculously active" imagination (1.42) will have something historically richer to work with.

"Ridiculously active"? What James means, if we subtract some of the facetiousness he lends the word, is Isabel's uncritical excitement about anything romantic or uplifting—the valor of both North and South, again, or of all parties during the French Revolution, now the oppressed sansculottes, now the royalists, who in tumbrels look so picturesque (1.100). Her enthusiasms are as higgledy-piggledy as her self-imposed reading list: the London *Spectator*, Browning, a history of German thought. Whatever stimulates. Well, being young, healthy, and tolerably well-off—and not being a player either in civil war or in revolution—she has survived this lack of system. Her life has been mostly pleasant. She did, however, lose her mother early on, and has recently lost her father. She is sensible to the psychological and moral significance of those losses. They qualify as the "unpleasant," something that, she has gathered from literature, can be "a source of interest and even of instruction." Of course there is irony in such phrasing, but of an altogether tender variety. Tender because, as James explains, she will shortly encounter further, sharper forms of unpleasantness: "She was a person of great good faith, and if there was a great deal of folly in her wisdom those who judge her severely may have the satisfaction of finding that, later, she became consistently wise only at the cost of an amount of folly which will constitute almost a direct appeal to charity" (1.144–45).[14] His periphrastic way of saying she has got a thing or two coming.

Anyway, having a "good faith" literary idea that "interest" and "instruction" can be gained from unpleasantness is better than having no idea on the subject at all, or blindly thinking oneself, or wanting prissily to keep oneself, immune. When Ralph tells Isabel that she can't see the ghost at Gardencourt because she hasn't gained the requisite "miserable knowledge," and indeed that she is "not made" for such knowledge, she complains that "if you don't suffer they call you hard"—or possibly shallow. To which Ralph replies: "Never mind what they call you. When you do suffer they call you an idiot. The great point's to be as happy as possible" (1.65). Ralph is right to declare that it is idiotic to suffer needlessly, but Isabel is right to believe that suffering is not only inescapable, it is also morally needful. That is why she tells Lord Warburton she wants to expose herself to "the usual chances and dangers" (1.187), both to suffer when her time comes and to find out about and empathize with others who suffer in their time. Such, in short, is the ethical theme of her story: she undergoes her own tragedy—the sort of thing she has hitherto known about only through literature—when she marries Osmond, and *that* enables her to identify with and defend Pansy, who, as her father tries to make loveless marital arrangements for her, faces similar perils.

But to return to Isabel's teenage palpitations. What makes her more interesting than an American naïf like Daisy Miller is the *use* she wants to make of her spiritual independence: not merely to have "fun" as she tours Europe, but to be "planning out her development, desiring her perfection, observing her progress"—and so indeed to open herself to the dreaded charge of being "a rank egoist" that, as we have seen, Goethe and his fictive children have so often had to face, and that can feel harsher because after all she isn't a Teutonic youth but an "American girl." In other words, she is doubly uppity as a "barbarian" ex-colonial and as a female taking herself as seriously as European gentlemen have traditionally taken themselves. There is promotional intention in the title-word "lady" in place of "woman," to say nothing of the Daisy Millerish "girl." Like a classic *Bildungsheld*, this lady likens her self to a garden that she must cultivate, and in terms only an extended quotation can do justice to:

> Her nature had, in her conceit . . . a suggestion of perfume and murmuring boughs, of shady bowers and lengthening vistas, which made her feel that introspection was, after all, an exercise in the open air, and that a visit to the recesses of one's spirit was harmless when one returned from it with a lapful of roses. But she was often reminded that there were other gardens in the world than those of her remarkable soul, and that there were moreover a great many places which were not gardens at all—only dusky pestiferous tracts, planted thick with ugliness and misery. In the current of that repaid curiosity on which she had lately been floating, which had conveyed her to this beautiful old England and might carry her much further still, she often checked herself with the thought of the thousands of people who were less happy than herself—a thought which for the moment made her fine, full consciousness appear a kind of immodesty. What should one do with the misery of the world in a scheme of the agreeable for one's self? It must be confessed that this question never held her long. She was too young, too impatient to live, too unacquainted with pain. She always returned to her theory that a young woman whom after all every one thought clever should begin by getting a general impression of life. This impression was necessary to prevent mistakes, and after it should be secured she might make the unfortunate condition of others a subject of special attention. (1.72–73)[15]

"Conceit" means both metaphor and haughtiness, but there is very little haughtiness to contemn. She is conscientiously aware of her civilization's "dusky pestiferous tracts," which in London she shows a foolhardy curiosity to explore on her own, though not extensively enough to outgrow the sentimentality about the poor that James registers through the quoted phrase. And—far from narrowly self-serving—she is right to believe that before she can ameliorate "the unfortunate condition of others" she must put herself in training: "getting a general impression of life" in order to learn the facts on the ground (it is "necessary to prevent mistakes"), and doubtless honing whatever skills she has for removing "ugliness and misery." We would have to be tone-deaf to miss the mandarin-comic irony, proof against sentimentality, in the voice referring to "a scheme for the agreeable for one's self" and the prevention of "mistakes," as though life really did resemble school. But James knows as well as Goethe ever did that the young, clever, good-looking person should, while avoiding the "sin of self-esteem," possess a healthy degree of amour propre—should have that "unquenchable desire to think well of herself" that alone makes "life . . . worth living" (1.68).

Thinking well of herself is one thing, actually living well is something else. Like the other *Bildungshelden* here under consideration, after going through the required struggles with parents or their surrogates and firming up her sense of moral if not religious convictions, the adult Isabel needs to do more than emulate Madame Merle. That polyglot expatriate—pianist, watercolorist, embroiderer, and connoisseur—seems to embody European culture's shallow notion of Goethean *Bildung*: "She was in a word a woman of strong impulses kept in admirable order. This commended itself to Isabel as an ideal combination" (1.250). Beyond polish, taste, and self-control, Isabel needs love and work. This last, as we find, is the more problematic for our novelists and their characters, especially when, like James with Isabel, the novelists resist the temptation to offer yet another veiled autobiographical "portrait of the artist." The lone professional "artist" in this novel is Henrietta Stackpole, who in her assiduity, ambition, and probity is more than the anti-American, anti-scribbling-women figure of fun she may initially seem.[16] Isabel rightly admires her friend's man-like careerism, "proof that a woman might suffice to herself and be happy," and proof that journalism was but one of the vocational paths a serious woman might follow. Just what other paths there might be is of course left vague, since Isabel never has to contemplate them. Notwithstanding the rumors among some American men, so frightened of her reputation for cleverness, that she is writing a book, Isabel has no desire for authorship—and is frankly appalled by the disregard for privacy necessitated by Henrietta's labors for *The Interviewer*. (Note how both the prying curiosity about English "specimens" and the all-American righteousness that mark Isabel when she arrives at Gardencourt are soon taken over by Henrietta, at which point Isabel herself assumes Ralph's role of the sophisticated Anglophile.) Neither does that staple occupation of the gentlewoman down on her luck, governessing, ever arise. Isabel may not be a *parti*, as Madame Merle kindly points out, but she is so decidedly pretty and lively that, like the later Miss Overmore who does have to put in her pedagogic time, she attracts proposals from men sufficiently affluent to disregard the absence of dowry. Like most women of all classes in her day—and like little Maisie the day after—Isabel believes her principal vocation will ultimately center on being a wife and mother: "Deep in her soul—it was the deepest thing there—lay a belief that if a certain light should dawn she could give herself completely" to the right man (1.71–72).

If that is a natural belief (and surely in her case it is), it is also natural for her to bide her time. She shies away from, and if necessary defies, those not-right men who want to mate with her, whether it is the phallicly insistent Caspar—"There was a disagreeably strong push, a kind of hardness of presence, in his way of rising before her" (1.162)—or the mannerly insistent Lord Warburton, who courts her

> in the kindest, tenderest, pleasantest voice Isabel had ever heard, and look[s] at her with eyes charged with the light of a passion that had sifted itself clear of the baser parts of emotion—the heat, the violence, the unreason—and that burned as steadily as a lamp in a windless place. (1.147–48)

Isabel justifies her resistance to these suitors on the, to them, maddeningly "theoretic" grounds of wanting to retain her freedom to explore life, avoid routine, take the usual chances with danger and possible suffering, and so forth—all those amorphous youthful *Bildungsheldisch* longings for varied experience that Ralph on the contrary finds beautiful and determines to finance. There is also her understandable fastidiousness. Leaving aside the inevitable, tedious speculations about her Puritanic discomfort with sexuality or her latent lesbianism, we ought to honor her reproductive desire to choose as well as to be chosen, which complements her moral desire to engage a man on terms of affective and intellectual equality.[17]

Henrietta's independence in this matter is inspirational, the two friends agreeing "that a woman ought to be able to live to herself, in the absence of exceptional flimsiness"—that is, as long as she is emotionally and economically stable—"and that it was perfectly possible to be happy without the society of a more or less coarse-minded person of another sex." As for "the subject of marriage," they are unanimous on "the vulgarity of thinking too much of it": they are young enough to wait, and they have other fish to fry. Particularly, they want to travel through Europe. This calculating, rational deferral of marriage suggests in Isabel's case, but also in Henrietta's, "something pure and proud . . . something cold and dry an unappreciated suitor with a taste for analysis might have called it." The something has anyway kept "possible husbands," save at this point the intrepid Caspar, at bay. "Few of the men she saw seemed worth a ruinous expenditure, and it made her smile to think that one of them should present himself as an incentive to hope and a reward of patience" (1.71). She will eventually "give herself completely"—she *wants* to—and one meaning of all those pounds sterling is that she may choose the time and place of giving, and the man who is to receive the gift. Another meaning, which it seems everyone in life and literature must learn afresh, is that money cannot purchase wisdom, affection, vocation, or any of the other spiritual desiderata that make for happiness. Still, it is Isabel's purse and she holds the strings. I will come back to what, at the close, she might beneficently *do* with it.

From the middle of the story on, however, we wonder why, in view of her fastidiousness, the financially independent Isabel should choose Gilbert Osmond. Consciously, to be sure, she marries him because she really likes him: "sweet delusion," as James writes in his notebook, and "oh, the art required for making this delusion natural!"[18] Hence the pages devoted to establishing the grounds for Osmond's claim to being "the first gentleman in Europe" (2.197)—grounds consisting mainly of refined appearances (the beard, the clothes, the bibelots) and of civilized, often artful conversation.[19] So also the indications that Osmond really likes *her*, and for most of the reasons other people do, namely her beauty, her taste, and her vivacity, happily contrasting with the listless tenor of life at Palazzo Crescentini. He likes everything, in short, except her "ideas," which, as he tells Madame Merle, are very bad and must be sacrificed (1.412). The sacrifice, as it turns out, is massive, since Isabel's ideas mean her mind, and her mind means her character or, according to the notebook again, "her own larger qualities."[20] So much for conscious liking on her part, and liking and disliking on his.

It isn't till the admired forty-second chapter, Isabel's wee-hours meditations before the dying fire, that she penetrates to motives either hidden or unconscious. Hidden, that is, from her. What Ralph and his mother suspect has all along been obvious to us, if only because James has made us privy to Madame Merle and Osmond's devilish planning sessions: they—he—married Isabel for her money. He has been glad to spend it on First Empire furniture and variegated objets d'art, while Madame Merle has hoped the establishment at Palazzo Roccanera would attract an opulent husband for her dowerless daughter. Madame Merle may have made Osmond's marriage, just as her aunt says, but she didn't make Isabel Archer's. Isabel Archer has made her own (2.158). With what un- or at best semi-conscious motives? First, she now realizes, was her hope of satisfying, obliquely, a maternal need. After some customary familial charities, she hasn't had any worthy idea how to spend her £3,500-a-year, whereas Osmond, who seems to her to have "the best taste in the world," would have plenty of worthy ideas. To marry him, a "more prepared receptacle," would be all providentially to "launch his boat," to satisfy "a kind of maternal strain," to produce "the happiness of a woman who felt that she was a contributor" (2.192). Since the son they conceive at the beginning of their marriage dies in infancy, it is almost the only maternal opportunity she has left, though as a "filial" beneficiary, it is by now clear, Osmond has no desire to repay her or show gratitude.[21] Second was her unwitting imitation of Osmond's aestheticism, his connoisseur's compulsion to add exquisite "things" to his collection. He doesn't own what he would like—say, a third of the contents of the Vatican Museum—but having once got "an old silver crucifix at a bargain" and discovered "a sketch by Correggio on a panel daubed over by some inspired idiot" (1.382), suddenly he can add to "his collection of choice objects" a figure who has certified her rarity "by declining so noble a hand" as Lord Warburton's (2.9). Treating her as a "thing," making "use" of her, as she will realize Madame Merle too has done, is a sin Isabel herself has been passingly guilty of. Early on we note her American-abroad interest in "specimens": what Henrietta writes up for *The Interviewer*, Isabel prefers to observe as though touring a museum. And once she got used to drawing the income from Mr. Touchett's bequest out of the bank, she must have understood, at some preconscious level, that she was now in a position to *collect* a precious specimen—rather as the Touchetts had collected those Lancrets and Constables.[22] This connoisseur's impulse, after more than three years of living with the "piece" she was introduced to in Florence, is something she becomes fully conscious of. Playing providence to an impoverished aesthete has given her not just the sense of maternal sponsorship, but also the sense of ownership. That princely fellow with "a genius for upholstery" (2.131) is *her* husband!

By acknowledging her sin, obviously very venial compared to Osmond and Madame Merle's mortal vileness, Isabel touches her own ethical tradition.[23] Osmond and Madame Merle's tradition is Old World, sexually exploitative, narrowly self-interested (other people are to be manipulated as means towards one's own profit). Her tradition, while hardly Bostonian, does in a New World way derive from an earnest primitive Christianity, which subordinates sexuality to the procreative purpose of marriage, and which endeavors to treat other people as ends in themselves—not to be exploited or used, but loved or at least respected.[24]

> She was not a daughter of the Puritans, but for all that she believed in such a thing as chastity and even as decency. It would appear that Osmond was far from doing anything of the sort; some of his traditions made her push back her skirts. Did all women have lovers? Did they all lie and even the best have their price? Were there only three or four that didn't deceive their husbands? When Isabel heard such things she felt a greater scorn for them than for the gossip of a village parlour—a scorn that kept its freshness in a very tainted air. There was the taint of her sister-in-law: did her husband judge only by the Countess Gemini? (2.200–01)

She can imagine how Osmond regards her New World way of thinking about ethics: "It was very simple; he despised her; she had no traditions and the moral horizon of a Unitarian minister. Poor Isabel, who had never been able to understand Unitarianism!" (2.201–02).

That wry imposition of mock-pitying authorial dismay upon indirect notation of her inner thoughts is evidently meant to bracket all ethico-theological doctrines in favor of immediate feeling. Isabel's "moral sense" is an adult version of Maisie's. Like hers, it is in part innative, in part acculturated, and the acculturation is distinctly American as against European or, more precisely, communitarian as against cosmopolitan. Madame Merle herself, prior to "clever" Isabel's inheritance and the conception of a scheme for entrapping her, has forwarded some shrewd criticisms of the ways of her fellow American expatriates: "You should live in your own land; whatever it may be you have your natural place there. If we're not good Americans we're certainly poor Europeans; we've no natural place here. We're mere parasites, crawling over the surface; we haven't our feet in the soil." And she has in mind both Ralph— "His consumption's his *carrière*"—and Osmond— "a man made to be distinguished" but who has "No career, no name, no position, no fortune, no past, no future, no anything" (1.280–81). Mr. Touchett opened a London branch of his American bank and, since capital is always welcome in economically free societies, he did very well. But the other Americans living abroad in this novel do no productive work, offer no creative ideas, provide no services to the Europeans around them.[25] Small wonder therefore that an Osmond or a Madame Merle's affective development stops at amour propre, and in her case, finally, can degenerate into self-hatred. Even their child Pansy is someone they regard as a curio to be immured and opened only to qualified buyers. Another reason, especially if Pansy should become "a perfect little pearl of a peeress" (2.175) by marrying Lord Warburton, for them to think of themselves as all the more exclusive. Not that self-worship, greed, adultery, and the rest of the deadly sins are impossible in, say, the Rutland, Vermont, that was Mr. Touchett's home. But if, as an American, one lives in such a town, one can be checked by the disapprobation of one's neighbor compatriots, and possibly even be moved by their approbation. It is the same social dynamic affecting a French person living in a French town. The expatriate Osmond, Isabel comes to understand, thinks of other people not as neighbors or fellow citizens, but merely as "the world"—there to gawk at the show of his wife's Thursday evenings, and there, finally, to be kept out.

The upshot of Isabel's reaction to having been "made a convenience of" (2.410), beyond quiet outrage and the "revenge" of letting Madame Merle, before she retreats in disgrace to America, know that she knows, is a resolution to prevent Osmond's continuing to make a convenience of Pansy. Having left the Rutlands and Albanys of her native soil behind, Isabel has begun to discover the limits to the *Bildungsheldisch* desire for freedom that we are so taken with in the opening chapters, and that Ralph has persuaded his father to underwrite. It is fine to echo the Declaration of Independence about one's individual right to pursue happiness or make judgments: Isabel, as her uncle notes, is strikingly "fond of your own way" (1.35), and she silently admires her aunt's insistence that her own point of view is neither European nor American but, "thank God . . . personal!" (1.81). But it isn't so fine to make up a life of mere personal preferences, in selfish imitation of "our crazy Aunt Lydia," who (per Millicent Bell) in her "sterile eccentricity," restless wandering, and "emotional distance" from husband and son, offers a dry, dispiriting model of independence for its own sake.[26] Just as Goethe brings Wilhelm, or Dickens Copperfield, out of youth into an adult commitment to vocation and (starting with the family) community, so James brings Isabel into something similar. Under the disabilities of nineteenth-century women, as I have said, it is altogether expected that she should find her vocation in marriage. Going back to the one she has made in Rome already seems quaint to an *émancipée* like Henrietta, but as the political theorists say, she is devoted to the office (if not the office holder). As for community—that connection with the wider world of suffering humanity Isabel has begun to sense among the Roman ruins, where "the ruin of her happiness seemed a less unnatural catastrophe" (2.327)[27]—well, there is a "special interest group" within the very Osmond family she so sadly belongs to. In brief, there is her affective bond with Pansy.

We must infer most of this for ourselves. Isabel does not in the final chapter fully explain to Henrietta, Ralph, or Caspar why she intends to go back to Rome. But, on the basis of what I have said earlier about her natural self-protectiveness (see note 17), I think we can affirm that dread of sexuality (Caspar's "white lightning" kiss and his urging her to become his paramour in defiance of the world's "ghastly form[s]") is only a very small part of it. She in any event has a better understanding than, for instance, Mrs. Beale will have in *Maisie*, of the small-print long-term costs exacted by that world from people—the women more than the men—who live with one another outside of marriage. No, Isabel's larger motive is Pansy: "not to neglect Pansy— not under any provocation to neglect her—this she had made an article of religion" (2.162). The repetition makes the article sacredly binding. Isabel has had to learn to regard Pansy morally rather than aesthetically. She isn't the "*ingénue* in a French play" (1.401) or "the small, winged fairy [that] in the pantomime soars by the aid of the dissimulated wire" (2.26) she at first has seemed. She is fully human and—the way she plights her troth to Rosier while gazing into the teapot is the only real love scene in the novel, prior to Isabel's sororal tending of Ralph's deathbed—becoming more so by the week. Her attachment to Rosier being genuine, and the tyrannical opposition of her father seeming immovable, she appears doomed either to a loveless marriage, with whatever alternate suitor, which would be as desiccated as his own, or to a celibate life, the emotional costs of which she clearly can't fathom, though she is beginning to guess. Therefore, it might be well if Isabel were to play the cards in her hand: she could set aside a portion of her £3,500-a-year for Pansy and designate her as first heir to the principal. If the terms of that sort of *dot* weren't enough to squeeze Osmond into consenting to his daughter's marrying Rosier, then the women could just wait out the two years till Pansy reaches her majority, at which point she might marry without his consent.[28] When in any case the young creature, from her penal convent, implores Isabel to return from England, the latter pledges "I won't desert you . . . my child." "My child," of course—her "maternal strain" still has this morsel for devotion—but even more suggestive is James's figuring Pansy and Isabel as "two sisters" (2.386), the younger being the older's fellow lady no longer "in waiting" but fully "out" in Roman society and very much needing the womanly guidance Isabel alone can give. "I think I should like your advice better than papa's," Pansy has remarked. "It isn't because you love me—it's because you're a lady" (2.255).[29]

A girl needs a mother, or a mother-substitute, quite as a boy needs a father or father-substitute. James would make the point again in *What Maisie Knew*, as we have seen, and it is made repeatedly in the *Bildungsromane* under analysis throughout this book. Absent a parent or parent-figure, an older sibling or sibling-figure can serve instead. The crisis of paternity must here be called a crisis of parenthood generally, and James makes it clear that at the back of Pansy's cry of "Ah, Mrs. Osmond, you won't leave me!" is *any* child's cry for protection and guidance through the rites of growing up—like the Everychild's cry one hears in distressed moments of *David Copperfield*. The family, nuclear and extended, is the natural party to heed such a cry. As we see next, however, for Forster the family is in such a shambles that his *Bildungsheld* is forced to start over with a artificial set of "brothers" under an institutional mater. As for Lawrence, who will come after, his hero is too poor to cozy up with acquired siblings in a collegiate den. The family shambles—meaning almost literally "slaughterhouse"— must simply be dealt with: life fought for, and death resisted, in company with an almost too-actual mother and father.

Chapter 5

Forster's *The Longest Journey* and "the code of modern morals"

"Sin was not necessarily something that you did: it might be something that hap-pened to you."[1] Orwell's "'Such, Such Were the Joys,'" here recalling the lunatic dilemmas he was thrown into by his bed-wetting at school, typifies what, in spite of many readings of novels such as *David Copperfield, Great Expectations, The Mill on the Floss, Pendennis, Richard Feverel,* or *The Way of All Flesh,* we may forget: that English authors since the romantic period have been preoccupied with the Blakean "experience" as much as with the Blakean "innocence" of childhood. Written in 1947, "'Such, Such'" harkens back to the Edwardian England that is the setting for the novel I want to examine in this chapter, Forster's *The Longest Journey* (1907), which is heavy with Blakean experience from beginning to end. It may never have as many readers as Forster's more coherent and ambitious *Passage to India* or *Howards End,* on which his reputation will always rest, or his more complaisantly comic *Room with a View,* but it ought to have more readers than it does. Forster (1879–1970) liked it best of all his books, and if we place it in the tradition of the *Bildungsroman,* we can understand why.

The story it tells can be quickly summarized. Congenitally lame, orphaned in adolescence, bored and bullied at school, Rickie Elliot finds his life improving at Cambridge, where his friends, notably the philosophy student Ansell, are bookish without being stuffy. He himself wants to write books of fiction, not to say fantasy, and he is fond of the men at college who encourage him. He is also drawn to Agnes Pembroke, the pretty sister of Herbert, a schoolmaster. When her handsome athletic fiancé Gerald suddenly dies in a soccer game—actuarial probability isn't Forster's strength—she sets her sights on Rickie. They become engaged (a move Ansell warns against) and visit Rickie's wealthy widowed aunt, Emily Failing, at her house, Cadover, in Wiltshire. Her husband Eustace Failing used to be a socialist writer, whom the narrator occasionally quotes. Mrs. Failing informs Rickie that Stephen Wonham, an amiable toughie who hangs about Cadover, is his illegitimate half brother—a kinship Stephen himself knows nothing of. Agnes's conventionally horror-struck reaction gives Rickie his cue, his imagination begins to dry up, and his stories don't find publishers. Thinking himself no good as a writer after all, he decides to marry Agnes, teach at Herbert's school, Sawston, and submit to nature's common plan. It doesn't work for him. Agnes bears a lame child, who shortly dies, and Rickie sinks into depression. Stephen, who has learned he has a brother, appears at Sawston. Agnes thinks he wants to blackmail them. Disdaining the suggestion, he departs— gets himself disowned by Mrs. Failing, who has heard wicked things about him from Agnes—and returns to Sawston, where he meets Ansell. "Hit[ting] out like any ploughboy," this philosopher damns the Pembrokes and rescues Rickie. But not before flooring him with the revelation that Stephen is the son not of his supercilious father, as he has supposed, but of his sainted mother. Rickie learns to love Stephen, but he seems to lose all will to live, letting himself be killed by a railroad train after he has pushed the inebriated Stephen off the tracks. At the happy close, Herbert has found a publisher for Rickie's stories, and Stephen, now married and a father, makes it clear he won't be cheated out of his share of the royalties.

Plainly, this is a *Bildungsroman* in tune with the Buckley criteria I have outlined in chapter 2. We have the sensitive boy suffocating in the provincial suburbs, who becomes the artistic youth breathing free at Cambridge and the young man fronting the "great world." He has his good (Ansell) and bad (Agnes) love affairs, and comes to terms with his family (Stephen) and his country (at least the rural core of it, Wiltshire). He also works through the usual critical quests. In his quest for sexual identity, he cuts his father, looks for a substitute for his mother, and ultimately discovers a set of biological and spiritual brothers. In his quest for a vocation, he variously tries to teach school, publish stories, and somehow earn part of his income—to "hear" his money as Ansell's family can hear theirs. And throughout he tries to clarify an ideology, now with reference to both politics and the world-historical spirit (the British Empire, the depopulation of the countryside, and what he mystically imagines to be the future of the Anglo-Saxon race), and now with reference to everyday moral issues (keeping promises, telling the truth, and staying faithful—all serious matters to a scion of the Cambridge of G. E. Moore).

Here, in assessing Forster's achievement in realizing Rickie's semi-successful *Bildung*, are the topics I address:

(1) What he owes to his alma mater Cambridge, scene of the novel's first half;
(2) his and his fellows' search for satisfying vocations;
(3) Forster's peculiar mythic conception of Wiltshire, Greece, and nature;
(4) his ideal of brotherhood (the novel is dedicated *Fratribus*);
(5) his situating of Rickie's story *sub specie* two notions of eternity; and
(6) the utilitarian regard he gives his otherwise aestheticist view of narrative art.

Alma Mater

We have seen in a previous chapter how David and Little Emily enjoy an early, Wordsworthian-inflected Edenic period—David's especially subsisting within what

Erikson calls "unity with a maternal matrix."[2] Rickie's Edenic period is brief indeed, largely because his mother is distracted by a hateful husband and a soon-lost lover (Robert, Stephen's father), but also because the suburban box his family lives in is stuffed with objects no one likes, and because outside there is nothing but smog and asphalt. This depressing environment constitutes a serious "material" disadvantage for Rickie. Stephen in contrast gets to grow up as a young Huron outdoors in Wiltshire. More subtly, there is the material problem that Rickie's father's disdain for his wife is based not so much on differences of taste about carpets and flower frames, as on his inability to care properly for the carpets and flower frames he himself would choose. He regards them merely as advertisements for his own aesthetic exclusivity.

Cambridge rescues Rickie from this gray suburban snobbery. A mother substitute—alma mater—she teaches him that liking *things* is a function of liking the *people* who share space with them, the people and things together forming a matrix that can substitute for the primal maternal presence one sooner or later loses anyway. In his dell, in his room, friends and things are both "really there" for him—"really there" being a key phrase in the Berkeleyan epistemological bull session the undergraduates are having as the novel opens. The friends and the things are thrown into chummy, eccentric contiguity:

> now his room was full of . . . people whom he liked, and when they left he would go and have supper with Ansell, whom he liked as well as any one. . . . On the table were dirty teacups, a flat chocolate cake, and Omar Khayyam, with an Oswego biscuit between his pages.[3]

Cambridge is a home, the "unity with a maternal matrix" recovered and recreated on a higher plane, with a greater diversity of affections and a more mature sensibility to engage them. Rickie's friends make the things in his room dear, as the Oswego biscuit adds something to Omar Khayyam. This detailed setting, like the ones we get of Sawston and Wiltshire, is crucial: few novelists have appreciated as much as Forster the degree to which *Bildung* is an achievement in space, a reaction against and creative response to physical environments.

"Oxford is—Oxford: not a mere receptacle for youth, like Cambridge," he would write in *Howards End*. "Perhaps it wants its inmates to love it rather than to love one another."[4] An apparently indifferent "receptacle," Cambridge is in fact nicer than many real mothers, for she essentially leaves her sons alone, that they might find affection for one another if they can. And since by the time Rickie "goes up" he is an orphan, he is accordingly eager to nestle with his "brothers" in his own room, in his special dell, in all the enclosures that suggest the womb. College of course can't go on forever, and Alma Mater can't long pass herself off as *Magna Mater*. That is why Agnes offers *her*self as the logically ultimate mother-substitute, calling Rickie from the dell and, when he comes, resting his head on her lap. But her call doesn't sound till his final term. Which means that for three rich years he has felt that, in the "divine interval between the bareness of boyhood and the stuffiness of age," the university has actually been *his*, as it was the fellow's whose name, like a ghost, is still visible on the door through the paint beneath his own. The dons have existed neither to research their lives away nor to administer away the lives of others but, as Forster's favorite don Goldsworthy Lowes Dickinson believed they ought, to induct youth into its own kingdom. "They taught the perky boy that he was not everything, and the limp boy that he might be something" (63). The youth thus favored learn through conversation and reading. "Talk away. If you bore us, we have books," Ansell tells Rickie, not at bottom coldly but in the rough–tender way "the saved" speak to one another. It is the dialect of the benevolent brotherhood.

To be sure, some Cambridge brothers are more benevolent than others: it all depends on one's point of view. Forster's is particularly precious, Rickie, Ansell, and the rest of "the saved" standing in for the Apostles, the Cambridge Conversazione Society to which he was invited in his last undergraduate year at King's. It is a picture held out exclusively to his "aristocracy of the sensitive, the considerate and the plucky"—in short to readers who, if they weren't part of the original group, feel modestly but pluckily that they *might* have been. Glen Cavaliero may be right to say that "the Cambridge episodes have altogether too clubby a ring,"[5] but a "club" is precisely what Forster wants to appeal to: only a small world can, for him, *tell* among the larger, Sawston-like organizations that make up the "great world." When Ansell says that the dictates of the "great world" are meaningless, he means they have no empirical reference to the immediate lives of himself and his friends. The dictates of tiny Cambridge are meaningful because they *do* have empirical reference: they are abstract principles that enable "the heart's imagination" to perceive and evaluate the local facts of those lives (68, 226).

The formula about the heart's imagination is adapted from Keats, but the controlling framework of ideas behind Apostolic thinking is that of Moore's *Principia Ethica* (1903), especially its final chapter, "The Ideal."[6] A few words about Moorean Cambridge—the spiritual environment flourishing in the material environment—are essential to understanding Rickie's crisis of philosophical identity. In a 1960 piece, "Looking Back," remembering "a particular little Cambridge of a particular moment (1900)," Forster says:

> What they were after was not the Truth of the mystic or the ter-uth of the preacher but truth with the small 't'. They tried to find out more [as in more Moore]. They believed in the intellect rather than in intuition, and they proceeded by argument and discussion. I hovered on the edge of the group myself. I seldom understood what they were saying, and was mainly [like a good novelist] interested in the way they said it. I did, however, grasp that truth isn't capturable or even eternal, but something that could and should be pursued.[7]

Trying "to find out more"—even when one allows that "the Truth of the mystic" is unattainable, or that the "truth" of the historian, scientist, or novelist is elusive, transient, and in some measure negotiable—is an enterprise in discrimination. As the Bishop Butlerian epigraph to the *Principia* says, it is to recognize that, at a given moment, "Everything is what it is, and not another thing." This is the sort of knowledge Forster thinks Cambridge *begins* to bestow upon its sons: they can tell by its standards both whether something has material reality (the cow in the college meadow is *there*), and whether it has spiritual reality (Agnes ultimately *isn't*). Which, with respect to *Bildung*, is the good of a sense of the Good.

Bertrand Russell believed that Moore's disciples "degraded his ethics into advocacy of a stuffy girls'-school sentimentalizing"[8]—a criticism Forster had in effect already offered.

For starters, it is hard to imagine Ansell, "the undergraduate high priest," having anything to do with "stuffy girls'-school sentimentalizing." He is much too masculinist. He is also, however, too donnish, and Forster was evidently convinced that the whole brotherhood needed to come down out of their college rooms and have some extramural experiences. Rickie has had a few—Agnes and Gerald's heterosexual embrace, the sudden deaths of his mother and Gerald, and other such incidents—and he sees that they are beyond the ken of "narrow" mollycoddles like Ansell, who talk about abstractions such as "love and death [so] admirably" (61) but who haven't had many red-blood encounters with life. Mollycoddle and red-blood were Dickinson's terms, an improvement on the similarly bifurcating Apostolic categories dividing the world into "reality" (members of the society) and "phenomena" (nonmembers who only "appear" to exist). This is just smarty-pants egoism, and the Kantian lingo is unable to gull intelligent undergraduates for very long. Ansell and Rickie must—and do—learn that some people who have never even visited Cambridge, or heard of Hegel or Moore, are also "real." Stephen is the obvious case, but Agnes too has in the beginning a kind of substantiality that Ansell's homosexual jealousy fails to obscure. There are some things the limpid Moorean states of mind can't take in, and the tale, prompted by what Forster called the "lower personality" of the teller, knows it.

Vocation

It is therefore just as well that, having no hope of a fellowship, Rickie must at last leave Cambridge. But for what? Will he and his friends still be able to help each other? And more urgently, can he find work that will interest him as much as his light collegiate regimen of desultory reading and writing? The regimen has shown him that he likes writing, but he can't abide Herbert's vision of Grub Street drudgery: "the artist is not a brick-layer at all," Rickie protests, "but a horseman, whose business it is to catch Pegasus at once, not to practise for him by mounting tamer colts" (16). The fact is, though, that Rickie isn't yet experienced enough to catch Pegasus, and, like most artists in their nonage, he looks foolish trying: "How could Rickie, or any one," Agnes demands, "make a living by pretending that Greek gods were alive, or that young ladies could vanish into trees?" (165). Public school has truncated his options as severely as, in *Copperfield*, it had truncated Steerforth and David's, or as, in *The Way of All Flesh*, it truncates Ernest Pontifex's.[9] A dozen years of classical languages haven't fitted Rickie to become a manual laborer or tradesman, nor yet a diplomat or administrator. True, he has an unearned income left him by his father, but—hatred for that father aside—he still wants to get money he can call his own. Herbert makes the obvious suggestion: while he waits for the magazines to accept his scribbled fantasies, what is more plausible than that he should stimulate in other people his own love of imagination? In other words, why not teach literature?

Rickie's decision to become a school instructor is queered by his having been thrown off balance by his engagement to Agnes and his disavowal of Stephen (*this* lout his half brother?!). Worried in his myth-mongering way that he has offended some Olympian god, he makes the earnest, plausible Victorian mistake of supposing he can do penance through public service. "Perhaps he had not worked hard enough, or had enjoyed his work too much" (166). Hasn't his best, brightest college friend Ansell's second failure with his dissertation shown that "They were none of them so clever after all" (213)? (I don't think there is a reader who, post-Boise State or post-Yale, can deny having occasionally felt the shock of *that* recognition. After making Phi Beta Kappa, the clever people have to prepare themselves for—sometime, someplace—getting dinged, just like everyone else.) Away with the higher, Paterian hedonism that has deluded "the saved," and get into harness. If Rickie can help pull levers on the "beneficent machine," why then he might "do good! . . . Let us give up our refined sensations, and our comforts, and our art, if thereby we can make other people happier and better" (166). It isn't about *us*, it is about *them*. He becomes an assistant master at Sawston School, where there is some ivy but mostly creeping-charlie, just as Ernest Pontifex becomes a curate in a London slum. It is a Victorian, social-gospel gesture of renunciation.

Not everyone at Sawston School is devoted to renunciation. Mr. Jackson exercises the humanistic spirit of Cambridge (more ivy, less creeping-charlie) and rejects Herbert's "beneficent machine" and all it implies. Boys should be at home with their families when they aren't in class. When they *are* in class—well, "He told his form that if it chose to listen to him it would learn; if it didn't, it wouldn't" (161). When Rickie takes over his own class, his impulses are similarly confident in what he knows, and liberal in how he wants to share it with others. Wishing to rouse his boys with the music of *Pan, ovium custos*, he asks whether they think it beautiful, and is in high spirits with someone's candid "No, sir; I don't think I do." But too young to stand up to Herbert, too wimpish and fey to stand up to Agnes, he soon caves. As teacher and as administrator, he finds it simpler to demand rote learning and frightened obedience. He faces what Forster elsewhere calls "the old problem of the letter that kills but seduces, because being a letter it can be easily memorized."[10] Further, it is the letter that governs the Empire. Hence Herbert's convocation speech about the school as the world in miniature[11]: "it seemed that only a short ladder lay between the preparation room and the Anglo-Saxon hegemony of the globe. Then he paused, and in the silence came 'sob, sob, sob,' from a little boy, who was regretting a villa in Guildford and his mother's half acre of garden" (171). A present-day Herbert might plausibly pooh-pooh those boo-hoos. Schools like Sawston *can* in fact produce the stuff competent functionaries are made of, as now through Rickie and later through Margaret Schlegel the novelist tries to concede. The aesthetic life and the economic life—the inner and the outer—are interdependent, and even if we ignorantly "letter" the first good and the second evil, the task of perceiving and indeed of augmenting their connectedness remains. Thus the famous dictum: "Rickie suffered from the Primal Curse, which is not—as the Authorized Version suggests—the knowledge of good and evil, but the knowledge of good-and-evil" (186).

The inner life has, however, been so long abused or neglected in Dunwood House that the dictum scarcely applies. Forster's account of Sawston's problem erases the hyphens, unfortunately, with the Pembrokes becoming unmitigatedly evil and Mr. Jackson rather inertly good, as though to suggest that *any* attempt to administer the lives of schoolboys is bound to go wrong. Surely more would be learnt about education, and Rickie's capacity to further it, if he were working with, so to speak, a more Jacksonized Herbert. An essential lesson, and one that Orwell would have underscored, is nonetheless learnt: if there must be schools, let them be *day* schools. As Rickie finally rouses himself to say, a boy shouldn't be ordered together with other boys before life within the family has made him ready to enter into good-fellowship. *Bildung* begins, and should for a long time develop, at home. The terrible Varden episode—the little prig is scapegoated by the Pan-angered herd, his already aching ears "wrenched" till he screams in agony and is sent home for an operation that just manages to save his life (200–01)—shows what happens when boys are stuffed into boarding schools. No Pembrokean orations can keep them from worshipping the Lord of the Flies,[12] and only parental care and adult supervision generally can channel their violence away from each other and onto, say, the soccer field.

Wiltshire, Greece, and the Myth of Nature

As Cambridge has adumbrated a myth of brotherhood, and Sawston a myth of anomie, so Wiltshire adumbrates a myth of nature—"the beginning of life pastoral, behind which imagination cannot travel" (92). In other words, a myth about the pre-urban, preindustrial organic communities English people once lived in. A Wordsworthian myth of this sort is easier to entertain in Wiltshire than in India, where Forster, like Aldous Huxley in the tropics, would later notice the sinister indifference of the lower animals, obviously waiting to take over again when man gives up his show of governing the earth. The Wordsworthian temperament is safe in Wiltshire, where if men try to love one another, the earth, through "some rallying-point, spire, mound," will "Perhaps . . . confirm" them (294). That is from Mr. Failing's essay, "The True Patriot," expressing a somewhat confused hope that one might almost believe in, given the setting Forster has described—not after all the Lake District or the Brontëan heath, but a place, if one can for a moment forget England's considerably older cottages, manor houses, and cathedrals, rather like a stretch of mid-American farmland. Wiltshire's animals and rain seemed to Forster a bit more *for* the shepherd than against him. The county had an ordinary rural beauty, which only a few decades of human folly could (and nearly *would*) destroy. As Forster poignantly writes in his 1960 introduction:

> There was a freshness and an out-of-door wildness in those days which the present generation cannot imagine. I am glad to have known our countryside before its roads were too dangerous to walk on and its rivers too dirty to bathe in, before its butterflies and wild flowers were decimated by arsenical spray, before Shakespeare's Avon frothed with detergents and the fish floated belly-up in the Cam.[13]

Rural England's "wildness," made more poignantly beautiful by the author's associating it with the hopeful years before the Great War, is what underpins, though they needn't be aware of it, his characters' indoor lives among teacups, books, and clever conversation.

The makers of "arsenical spray" probably come from cities, those "grey fluxions" of brick "where men, hurrying to find one another, have lost themselves" (290), and where Stephen, if he were to linger long enough, would soon be as etiolated as, in

Howards End, Leonard Bast is. Stephen fortunately isn't clever enough to build "a Heaven in Hell's despair": he has to live his life right where he stands—there, in the world he in the end twists Herbert round to look at: the valley quiet, "but in it a rivulet that would in time bring its waters to the sea" (307). There is no miniature of, no health away from *that*. The worth of that valley and rivulet, and of wildness generally, depends in this novel on the worth of Stephen, the one character truly at home in it.[14] Part Tony Lumpkin, part noble savage, Stephen has the oddly mixed qualities Forster likes, and he expresses them with gesture and accent sufficiently enfleshed to compel my not-much-shared belief that he is "really there."[15] He is the natural son, an animal "with just enough soul to contemplate its own bliss" (229), whose feral life of sensation—riding for joy over the downs, drinking when thirsty, bathing naked when hot, drinking again for the rowdy pleasure of it, and sleeping on the grass with Orion tilted overhead—is frankly a dream. The Stephen who at the end of the story is said to be a farmer can't have time for that much fun. But then it is exactly a dream—a holiday—vision of Stephen's life that most interests Forster, who doesn't know much about farming anyway. Only by projecting a dream-vision can he show the reader what he believes is *behind* Stephen.

He dwells in a state of nature just Hobbesian enough to be credible. "One nips or is nipped . . . and never knows beforehand" (127) is the motto of a creature awake to the fortuitousness of his existence, eager to fight for his share of bread, tobacco, and sunlight, and self-protectingly ready to cry quits when a stronger creature like Flea Thompson throws him on his back. He takes his chances moment by moment, with no thoughts about securing himself against the future, and with no thoughts about the past except, simply and superbly, to ask why he and not someone else, why something and not nothing, should be. Such ontological wonder never detains him for long, however. Those Robert Ingersoll pamphlets he reads dimly tell his brain what his blood knows already, namely that, *materially*, it is he not God who exists, and that, as Forster says elsewhere, to "forget its Creator is one of the functions of a Creation. To remember him is to forget the days of one's youth" (*Two Cheers* 82). To forget the spirit Creator may help one remember—recognize—other creatures. True, Stephen doesn't adore them so much that, if they nip one cheek, he will offer them the other. Nevertheless, he promises that if they don't nip *him*, he won't nip *them*. "Is that the only thing that keeps you straight?" asks Rickie. Stephen answers, " 'What else should?' And he looked not into Rickie, but past him, with the wondering eyes of a child" (285). Those final phrases—certainly a good example of Forster's trying rhetorically to put one over on us—detract only a little from our granting the idea behind Stephen, which is that there is a primal mode of existence, governed by an implicit ethic that Mill could only elaborate on, and that more sophisticated people (like Mill) lose touch with at their peril.

Stephen knows that he exists, and feels little need to know more. Not until Rickie insults him does he vigorously defend his selfhood (the earlier fight with Flea Thompson is like puppies tussling over a bone). Forster diminishes Stephen's "personality" in order to focus our attention on the several myths that he evokes, myths meant to tell us who Western man is and where he has come from. Like Harold in Forster's finest fantasy, "Albergo Empedocle," Stephen has been "back to some table of the gods[;] . . . he belonged for ever to the guests with whom he had eaten" (231). Eaten and drunk. The particulates of Wagnerian or Paterian myths that critics like Tony Brown, Robert K. Martin, and Judith Herz have more or less convincingly filtered out of *The Longest Journey* require experts to identify them.[16] Almost everyone, on the other hand, can see the broadly Dionysian associations in Stephen, as we have seen them in Micawber. Rickie might take pleasure in Micawber, who is a figure in a book. In everyday life, the pleasure is nil: "Drink, today, is an unlovely thing," Rickie believes, and therefore regards Stephen's pub-crawling as simply bad behavior. He can't hear "the cries [that] still call from the mountain," to which Stephen "respond[s] with the candour of the Greek" (286), and which Forster, asserting the semi-silly privileges of the artist, evidently wants us to respond to also. Stephen's drinking, singing, and (as he says) plopping, mime the natural cycles of spring, summer, and fall, or dawn, noon, and evening. Rickie believes "the analogy was false, but argument confused him" (284). Verbal proofs *are* impossible, and probably irrelevant. One does better, Forster thinks, by protracting one's sojourn in the aesthetic stage—looking at a work of art, or a character like Stephen, and not trying to *say* much about it.

A photograph of the Cnidian Demeter ("long picture—stone lady") hangs like a piece of meat in Stephen's attic room at Cadover, moving with every stir of air, glinting with sunrise and moonrise. The naïvety of the symbolism disarms criticism. The statue's nose is gone, her knees are shattered, she is art eroding back into nature, half-lady, half-boulder in her niche in the British Museum. In his 1904 essay, "Cnidus," Forster had chartered his own private cult of her, asserting that she alone on Olympus has "true immortality," since all people, even the anemic English, worship her:

> And Poets too, generation after generation, have sung in passionate incompetence of the hundred-flowered Narcissus and the rape of Persephone, and the wanderings of the Goddess, and her gift to us of corn and tears; so that generations of critics, obeying also their need, have censured the poets for reviving the effete mythology of Greece, and urged them to themes of living interest which shall touch the heart of today.[17]

Lionel Trilling was one such critic, censuring Forster for employing "the most literary and conventionalized of all mythologies."[18] Maybe, but such a complaint dodges Forster's claim, which through Stephen is that *we*, the "generations of critics," are the ones who are "effete." We may be like Aunt Emily, who looks for the natural man to resemble the shepherd in "Lycidas" and therefore misses the significance of Stephen, who "lived too near the things he loved to seem poetical" (260). Or we may be like Ansell, disinherited and embarrassed "among those marble goddesses and gods" in the British Museum, where in Keatsian mood "he could only think of the vanished incense and deserted temples beside an unfurrowed sea" (197). Ansell is the critic we should try to resemble, for he is at least humble. When he hears that Agnes is pregnant, he passes by the Ephesian Artemis and the Cnidian Demeter, and is struck by his own ignorance of generation and decay. Such statues don't abash Stephen because he is at home with the realities their blank eyes are gazing on.

"Those elms were Dryads—so Rickie believed or pretended, and the line between the two is subtler than we admit" (3). Forster's attitude toward the Greek myths wavers likewise between belief and pretense or, to use his terms in *Aspects of the Novel*, between prophecy and fantasy. He grants that from the vantage point of the galaxies, or even of the East, the stories about Greek deities are preposterous and pitiable. (Seeing the film of Peter Brooks's production of Jean-Claude Carrière's *The Mahabharata* [1987–1988] makes a non-Orientalist like myself feel that the Indian epic trumps Hesiod most of the time, and even Homer some of the time.) But as a Western man with a late-Victorian classical education, Forster maintains that, for the practical purposes of his own *Bildung*, the Greek view of life is as normative as it was for Goethe. What hovers between belief and pretense is a fragile wish, a wish—he never gives up on it—for what in "Gemistus Pletho" (1905) he youthfully calls the Greek gods' "radiant visible beauty, their wonderful adventures; their capacity for happiness and laughter" (*Abinger Harvest*, 190). This Paterian fixation is "wrong" in India, where muddle and mystery confound every regulative idea. But it is "right" for any-one born north and west of Suez, where, as Cyril Fielding reflects in *Passage to India*, "The Mediterranean is the human norm."[19] That is a wish on behalf of a proposition Forster himself, most of the time, *believed* in.

Rickie tries to express that prophetic norm through his classically charged fantasies, but these pretendings fail because they are such obvious compensations for his own lack of experience. The failure is amusingly registered by the fate of one story, obviously Forster's own "Other Kingdom," about a girl who turns into a tree. Stephen tries to read it while lying naked on the roof in the late-day sun, drying after a bath. Who is this girl, he asks, why all this to-do about trees? "I take it he wrote it when feeling bad." Agnes's marginalia pointing up the allegorical equations can't help—not under this sun, with the starlings chattering, and Cadbury Rings humped above the village. "In touch with Nature! What can't would the books think of next? His eyes closed. He was sleepy. Good, oh good! Sighing into his pipe, he fell asleep" (131). The "good" that Stephen embodies may go back to an imagined pastoral genesis, but it isn't, in the end, all that Forster is striving for. If Wiltshire is the old, deep, animal center of England, Cambridge is the growing tip, high and spiritual. Swinburne's "Beloved Republic" is realized, fitfully but repeatedly, each time the center and the tip are connected. That, diagrammatically put, is the form the indi-vidual's complete *Bildung* must take, and, as we have seen Goethe asserting more than a century before, that is also the form any national *Bildung* must take. The socioeconomic difficulties such national connections have to overcome are immense. A modest beginning might nonetheless be made by enabling young people from the "center" of the country to be educated at "tip" institutions such as Cambridge or Oxford, or (thinking of Lawrence) at their red-brick counterparts. Forster in any event isn't the writer to consult for policy solutions. His job was to offer eloquent slogans—"Only connect" and the like—and, *qua* novelist, to offer at least a *composite* sketch of what a grown-up individual would be.[20]

The Brotherhood

By offering such a composite sketch, *The Longest Journey* is unusual among Anglo-American *Bildungsromane*. Someone like Wilhelm Meister or David Copperfield clearly has much to learn from other people, but neither they nor Paul Morel enters into the sort of meaningful male friendships that Rickie enjoys, though the American Oliver Alden would come close. Rickie, Stephen, and Ansell are "brothers" forming, as some critics now say, a homosocial *Bund*—obliquely descending from the Tower in *Wilhelm Meister*—each with something to give the others. Ansell, to begin with, encourages Rickie to think more clearly. The latter does well enough among "the saved," following, at a distance, their argument about Berkeleyan epistemology. He gets into trouble, however, when out on his own with Agnes, parroting Ansell's "I have no ideals," then turning red because "he could not remember what came next" (16). Ansell can remember what comes next, but, as his examiners claim, he has read too much Hegel and therefore has become isolated from flesh and blood people. In Mr. Failing's terms, he is "vulgar" (closed off from his neighbors) while Stephen is happily "coarse" (quick to give himself away). By knocking Ansell down—a boorish salutation Forster rather overvalues—Stephen is supposed to be doing him a large favor. He is showing him the "Spirit of Life" as it thrives outside of books. It is related to the lesson Stephen's father Robert had given Mr. Failing, namely that love, like less tender emotions, can't be divorced from muscles and nerves: "there are, perhaps, not two Aphrodites, but one Aphrodite with a Janus-face" (250). In short, the knowledge of love, too, is a knowledge of good-and-evil, spirit-and-flesh.

What few critics have recognized is that Rickie, prompted by Ansell, also teaches Stephen something—namely the importance of remembering their mother: "the Beloved should rise from the dead" (267). True, he is wrong at first to remember her by forgetting Stephen, but he is nonetheless right finally to think that both of them should love her, and that she from her spiritual world can "speak" to them. Like Mrs. Wilcox, Mrs. Moore, and the Greek deities, Mrs. Elliot is "risen" as long as she in memory is "raised," an ancestor authorizing one son to people England and, with equal kindness, telling the other to flicker out. It is as supernaturalistic as Forster ever gets, and it is too much for some readers. In any event, when the survivor, the illegitimate, gropes at the end for words to say what "salvation" the legitimate has bequeathed him, he bends down and reverently kisses his daughter, "to whom he had given the name of their mother" (311). (The name is "Lucy" in early drafts, but, as though Forster were reverently observing a taboo, it goes unmentioned in the final version.) Stephen has been taught that his life is more than a matter of "Here am I, and there you are" (287), in truce or combat. It is also a matter of loyal attachment to important forebears.

What Rickie and his "brothers" would in theory *like* to do is cultivate a wholeness not just as a set, with Ansell's intellect and Stephen's body adding to Rickie's imagination, but—with a push now from one, now from another—to cultivate it as individuals. Yet none of them can. It is the fault of (a) panoptical institutions like Sawston School, (b) the conventions about sexual preference and expression that in different ways plague "the saved" and Agnes, and (c) congenital limitations such as Rickie's lameness and, with a book in his hands, Stephen's fidgetiness; but it is also the fault of (d) the sheer complexities of the modern era, where, as Goethe saw, specialization in modes of knowledge and production is necessary in ways it wasn't to the fifth-century Greeks he and Schiller admired. The nineteenth-century English, notably Keats, Arnold, and Pater, had, as we have seen in chapter 2, admired them also and had helped form the university cult to which "the saved" belong. If the Greek *uomo universale* couldn't be realized now, perhaps he might be in the future. Forster, coincidentally echoing Bernard Shaw's recent cry for a Lamarckian-willed Nietzschean Superman, prophesies just that: the coming of the major *Bildungsheld*, a descendant of Stephen and his kind, slouching from Wiltshire to Cambridge to be born.

What, seriously, will he be like? Forster's requirements are all ethical and thus supplement the myth of nature that his vision rests on. The whole man must love the dead and—we come here to the theme of Shelley's "Epipsychidian" from which the novel's title derives—he must love the living. Correct, but simplistic. Of course, the novelist's task isn't to tell merely, but to show, and thus turn the simplistic back into the elementary "simples" moralists take their aphorisms from. Thus Forster gives Stephen the opportunity to observe how the Ansell family refrains from nipping even when nipped—not because they are cowering Jews, but because they are trying to transcend the more brutal elements in nature. Like Shelley, "a man less foolish than you supposed," the Ansells mean well, mean better than Hobbes. The whole man would also be open to many loves and so, again like Shelley, would in another way transcend what Ansell most detests in nature, its erotic possessiveness. He labels Agnes "the emissary of Nature," the woman who, in Shavian as well as Byronic phrase, "wants to love one man" and who wants that man to be a dutiful husband and nothing else.[21] "But [the whole] man," Ansell says, "does not care a damn for Nature—or at least only a very little damn" (88): he wants to love *more* than one person, as Stephen, whose instinct to take a wife to bear his children doesn't diminish his fondness for Rickie and Ansell, seems to know. More than one person, more than one sex.

This issue of bisexuality, if not entirely of promiscuity, is the most troubling for Rickie. At Cambridge he has appreciated the "Epipsychidian"'s pluralism, but after his engagement to Agnes, who predictably is jealous of Ansell (just as he is of her), he finds it "a little inhuman." Two country lovers walking together, caring for no one else, may "be nearer the truth than Shelley" was (138). As Rickie charmingly if callowly meditates:

> There are men and women—we know it from history—who have been born into the world for each other, and for no one else, who have accomplished the longest journey locked in each other's arms. But romantic love is also the code of modern morals, and, for this reason, popular. Eternal union, eternal ownership—these are tempting baits for the average man. (292)

Abandoning his undergraduate rebellion against "the code of modern morals"—who after all do college kids think they *are*, challenging the way of the "great world"?—Rickie mistakes himself for the "average man" and tries to join the "great sect" of arm-in-arm romantic couples. Of course, part of the blame belongs to Agnes, who can think of only one sort of couple. She wants to *possess* a man, with help from her horsewhip; and she wants in turn to *be* possessed, to be kissed so hard that it hurts—at least as much as when she had had her ears pierced. Gerald has hurt her like that, but Rickie is too soft even to begin. By marrying her he hopes to protect himself against all danger, but as his unconscious shows him in a dream, to escape danger means to escape from life itself—the green earth, the singing birds, the centaur Stephen.

Into the box in Sawston, with a teak monkey to guard the door: his dream calls it "the old plan" (121). We shall miss the point if we rejoin that the new plan, along Edward Carpenter's Uranian line, is for Rickie to marry Ansell;[22] or, along one of Lawrence's lines, for him to marry some country girl like his mother, or not to marry at all.[23] Whatever he does, he should let his affections flow unplanned, outside the box of small people, small moralities. Otherwise, as Shelley has tried to tell him, his life's journey will be not only the longest but the dreariest.

Imagining Two Eternities

What about the philosophical aspects of Rickie's *Bildung*? There is always in Forster a varying blend of hope and despair, the one dominant in *A Room With a View* or *Maurice*, the other in *Passage to India* or certain war-time essays, but neither ever quite cancels the other. Even when his hope is plainly a business of fanciful pretending, as in his 1935 address to the *Congrès International des Écrivains*, he pretends well enough to gainsay the logic of prophetic despair. He is a stubborn player:

> I am worried by thoughts of a war oftener than by thoughts of my own death, yet the line to be adopted over both these nuisances is the same. One must behave as if one is immortal and as if civilization is eternal. Both statements are false—I shall not survive, no more will the great globe itself—both of them must be assumed to be true if we are to go on eating and working and travelling, and keep open a few breathing holes for the human spirit. (*Abinger Harvest* 70)

As he focuses both on the annihilation of all things and on the departure times at Victoria Station, so he simultaneously entertains two concepts of eternity, one genuine, the other make-believe. Take the question of personal immortality. Where, Aunt Emily wonders, is the soul of the child run over by the train? The real answer, one would think, echoes in the Marabar Caves—nowhere. Still, for the same everyday moral purposes that lead him to claim that Demeter is alive, Forster affirms that souls go on living, that they on rare occasions communicate with people still in the flesh, and that their eternal life is like a nice day on earth, where everyone is young and imagination honored. The optative mood of immature fantasies like "The Point of It" and "The Celestial Omnibus" doesn't altogether disappear in the mature novels. True, he admits everywhere, in, for example, the contra-Rousseauvianism of "The Menace to Freedom" (1935), that man is imprisoned today because a million years ago he was born in chains, afraid of the universe, of his tribe, of himself (*Two Cheers* 9); that his brain is too small, his polity too frail. Yet there was Periclean Greece, Dante, Shakespeare—civilization sufficient, he thinks, to justify the millennialism he learned from Lowes Dickinson, which, as he quaintly says in "Pessimism in Literature" (1907), hopes that comedy will again express "joy on a large scale—the joy of the gods,"[24] and that the major *Bildungsheld* will be born, too. The wish of fantasy wants to be the Word of prophecy, which, in *Howards End*, for instance, less quaintly declares that the life of the soul shall "pay" after all.

The Longest Journey is also governed by this double vision. The first is that of the genuine eternity. Robert tells Mrs. Elliot that one day "the fire at the centre [of the earth] will cool, and nothing can go on then" (249). This gives us a Dantescan comedy with no ladder from *inferno* to *paradiso*, no final moral standard by which to place human behavior. From the intense inane, Ansell's speech before the assembled schoolboys looks the same as Herbert's.[25] But the second point of view, that of the make-believe eternity, is more immediately pertinent. While the earth *does* go on, it is reasonable to live as if death were selective, taking the bad and leaving the good;[26] to live as if Periclean Greece could be revivified; to live as if the rose of love, floating down the stream beneath the bridge, would, like Dante's, "burn forever" (293).[27] And while the earth goes on, it is reasonable also *to write* as if these things were true. Thus Forster anoints Stephen, who, kneeling in the water, can see the burning paper when Rickie no longer can, as the brother who will guarantee the race. For though the novelist is ultimately concerned, in Mr. Emerson's words, with the everlasting "Why," he must for the most part be concerned with whatever "transitory Yes" he can create.[28] In brief, though his skepticism seems to make him an incipient modernist, Forster is in this transitional text a still-Edwardian (i.e. belated Victorian) "as if" believer in make-believe eternal verities—a lower-cased trinity of the good, the true, and the beautiful—which is what Dickens might have been if he could have theorized like Arnold, or what Arnold might have been if he had been able to plot and characterize like Dickens.

Love and metaphysics aside, how, with better luck than he actually has, might Rickie say yes to his artistic vocation, and thus pass from apprenticeship to something like mastery? Certainly he would be ill-advised to give up his fancies and rest content, like Ansell and Stephen in their own ways, with nothing but dry facts. If, as Mr. Jackson has affirmed, "poetry, not prose, lies at the core" (189), then Rickie should *continue to imagine, but do it better*. He must learn to invent good metaphors, comparing "real" people with the apposite "unreality," and thus discovering what Ansell, with his mandala, might call the real reality—the invisible inmost circle within a square.[29] How, for example, should he imaginatively apprehend Agnes and Gerald? He *has* to pretend, to imagine they are more interesting than they appear, if he is to know what they potentially *are*. But he pretends wrongly, he compares them to inappropriate objects. The much-misunderstood passage occasioned by the lovers' kiss is an indirect account of Rickie's imagination doing business badly, at the end of which we shift back to Forster's point of view: "It was the merest accident that Rickie had not been disgusted. But this he could not know" (43). If his imagination were in better order, he might have spread less Swinburne and more Hardy on that purple pond and thus have got closer to "the core" of Agnes and Gerald—Medusa in Arcady and the brainless athlete from Aristophanes' *The Clouds*, perhaps.

To imagine is to value. "The soul has her own currency," and "reckon[ing] clearly" is knowing to what we should compare the image on the coin. Rickie's soul has traded in coin bearing his mother's image and has gone bankrupt with the news of her "immorality"—that is, her ability, independent of a marriage license, to love and bring forth life.

Fair as the coin may have been, it was not accurate; and though she [his soul] knew it not, there were treasures that it could not buy. The face, however beloved, was mortal, and as liable as the soul herself to err. We do but shift responsibility by making a standard of the dead.

There is, indeed, another coinage that bears on it not man's image but God's. It is incorruptible, and the soul may trust it safely; it will serve her beyond the stars. But it cannot give us friends, or the embrace of a lover, or the touch of children, for with our fellow-mortals it has no concern. It cannot even give the joys we call trivial—fine weather, the pleasures of meat and drink, bathing and the hot sand afterwards, running, dreamless sleep. Have we learnt the true discipline of a bankruptcy if we turn to such coinage as this? Will it really profit us so much if we save our souls and lose the whole world? (246)

This passage, whose metaphor and phrasing could come straight from Butler's *Erewhon*, needs to be read in the context of the whole novel.[30] We can buy worldly joys neither with God's currency nor with Sawston's. "We do but shift responsibility by making a standard of the dead": by associating his mother with chaste, more-than-human respectability, with both God's Blessed Virgin and Sawston's Victoria, Rickie has made her a "dead" standard in more than the literal sense. If he were reckoning clearly, he would associate her, first, with earthy fecundity, whereby she might be a living standard, her image doubling with Demeter's; and second, with her other son, alive in the literal sense, of course, and alive in his mute respect for Demeter too. But shifty metaphoric argument soon breaks down. What holds up, once again, is a more static objet d'art—the final chapter's tableau of Stephen, the "stone lady," and Mrs. Elliot's namesake, his daughter.

The Uses of Fiction

Forster said that he was not a great novelist, inasmuch as he had managed to represent only three types of character: the person he thought he was, the people who irritated him, and the people he would have liked to be.[31] In *The Longest Journey* the first two types overlap. Rickie is both a gentle self-portrait—someone who "dislike[s] cruelty"—and an irritating stick: "Yes, Rickie—I could kick him for his lame leg, you know."[32] And he *does* kick him—kick him, by Erewhonian logic, to death. Directly Rickie has heard his mother's beyond-the-grave advice to let the Elliot blood die out, Forster says, "he deteriorates" (209)—which is a bit premature, given his rejuvenation after he joins Stephen. He writes a novel, reads books, and rebuilds friendships. Then suddenly, in a confused evening, everything collapses. He is discouraged because Stephen has got drunk after he promised not to, and then he finds him lying unconscious across the tracks. "Wearily he did a man's duty. There was time to raise him up and push him into safety. It is also a man's duty to save his own life, and therefore he tried" (303). Too late, too little, as the locomotive, symbol we suppose of anti-natural industrialism, bears down on the limping artist, who hasn't paid proper dues to nature. Rickie's death borders on suicide, since it is surely easier to pull not "push" a man off the tracks, and since he obviously doesn't "try" very hard to get off himself. Forster's knowledge of Rickie was imperfect, for someone who gives up on life should beforehand *act* like someone who would give up on life. And despite his tendency to make foolish decisions, Rickie hasn't been that sort of person. He has walked out of

Dunwood House with as much energy as Agnes displayed when she dragged him in. A plain case of authorial homicide.

Wilfred Stone gave the earliest persuasive account of Forster's confused feelings toward this most faithful self-portrait among his novels, arguing that Rickie's death is the "ritual sacrifice of a childish self that releases the libido for active life."[33] Elizabeth Heine has described Forster's ambivalence about his homosexuality, a condition that, following Carpenter and Havelock Ellis, he believed to be hereditary, and that he emblematized in Rickie's inherited lameness, something that more broadly marks the self-hating Failing family's failings.[34] What may have begun as an exercise in self-loathing then becomes an admonition to himself to do better than Rickie. On the one hand, he must remain celibate (the "defect" of homosexuality shouldn't be passed on); on the other, he must accept his condition and "make copy" out of the subversive outsider's point of view that the gene pool has given him. In any case, the fact that we are made biographically curious indicates an artistic flaw—one that *Bildungsromane*, which are often veiled autobiographies, not infrequently suffer from. Forster ought to have been contained in the book, but in a weak moment he contained the book in himself, forcing it to be useful for his own narrow psychological purposes.

Yet as James McConkey would have it, *The Longest Journey*, like a Chekhovian tale, *wants* to be autonomous and anonymous—to say "I, not my author, exist really." And to the extent that it succeeds in saying that, it can, if we bring to it those questions about *Bildung* that preoccupy me through this study, be broadly useful to us. The idea of usefulness would seem out of place to the defender of art for art's sake, the Forster who praises lyric poetry, the truly anonymous art, precisely because it has no use. I am thinking, however, of the general usefulness of the "subsidiary dream" that a work of art draws us into, the state of attention near to "the condition of the man who wrote," that brings "to birth in us also the creative impulse" (*Two Cheers* 82, 84). The power of *The Longest Journey* as a whole stirs us to forget the incoherence of Rickie's death, to leave off our ultimately impertinent questions about Forster's motives, and to ask what good there may be in *our* vocations, friendships, houses— or, if you will, our postures in front of the Cnidian Demeter. The novel isn't a hitching post but a signpost, pointing at last to the problem of our own apprenticeship, remembered or ongoing. If we turn away from it, as in *Where Angels Fear* Philip Herriton turns from a painting by an Italian master that is suddenly inadequate to its subject, we do so because the subject is once again ourselves. And our task? Naturally it is to live our own lives, but possibly also, as I suggested at the close of my *Copperfield* chapter, it is to remember, and ideally even to compose, our own version of what Tolstoy, in his fictive autobiography, simply titled *Childhood, Boyhood, and Youth*. That would bring "the creative impulse" full circle.

Chapter 6

Lawrence's *Sons and Lovers*:
"We children were the in-betweens"

And so it was written: "The Word was made Flesh," then, as corollary, "And of the Flesh was made Flesh-of-the-Flesh, woman." This is . . . backward . . . the whole chronology is upside-down: the Word created Man, and Man lay down and gave birth to Woman. Whereas we know the Woman lay in travail, and gave birth to Man, who in his hour uttered his word.[1]

Thus Lawrence (1885–1930) wrote in January 1913, trying to invert the Gospel of John. His third novel, *Sons and Lovers*, one of the supreme *Bildungsromane* in English, was at the printer's. Through luminous descriptions and emotively powerful scenes, he had more than found his novelistic voice, and now seemed compelled to rehearse a prophetic one—as though needing to sum up the message inside the black bottle of what he would later call his "colliery novel." A prophet often begins by putting his right vision in opposition to a precursor's wrong one: if, writing as a Neoplatonist or as a Hellenized Essene, John had privileged the Word over the Flesh and taken nearly two millennia of Christian civilization with him, then Lawrence, working toward a post-Christian civilization, would aggressively privilege the Flesh over the Word.

I expect many readers are as familiar with *Sons and Lovers* as with *David Copperfield*, but a short reminder of Lawrence's plot may prove handy. He begins with the social setting—the lives of coal miners (colliers) in Bestwood, near Nottingham, and particularly of Walter Morel, who marries the better-educated, primly attractive Gertrude. It is a real love of opposites that brings them together, but his drinking and coarseness soon disenchant her. She gives up on her husband and devotes herself to her four children, especially her firstborn William. Rather than go down into the pit like his father, William goes to London to work as a clerk and to engage himself to a Dora-like girl called Lily ("Gyp"). Neither the work nor the engagement lead to anything, and William suddenly dies. Mrs. Morel despairs, but soon commits herself to her second son Paul, who also has the wherewithal to climb out of the working class. He is a promising painter, but meanwhile for money he works in Jordan's prosthetics factory in Nottingham. He has a "Lad-and-Girl" romance with Miriam Leivers, and finds a pastoral world on her family's farm. Theirs is a mostly spiritual relationship—her resemblance to his intellectually inclined mother blocks his desire to connect with her sexually—and so he turns to Clara Dawes, an older woman, separated from her husband, who works at Jordan's. Sexual connection with her is easier, but he misses Miriam's cerebral vitality. When his mother falls ill with cancer, he and his sister Annie nurse her to the end, when they euthanize her with an overdose of morphine. With his first love now dead and marriage to either Clara or Miriam impossible or unlikely, Paul is truly "derelict"—though in the last pages he turns away from death, wherein he might join his mother, toward the hum of life in Nottingham.

That behind all this Lawrence should be targeting something as old as John's Gospel and claiming still more ancient sources for his own isn't surprising to those who know even a little of his work. Much more than the modest Forster, he felt himself possessed of a prophetic vocation. Dark utterances, richly supported by the sensuous imagery and the cadences of the Bible, make his the unmistakably vatic voice of his period in English literary history. And history is the word to stress. He would readily have acknowledged that the collision between John's Gospel and his own was of recent birth, which occasions my opening topics:

(1) the nineteenth-century intellectual and socio-historical background to Lawrence's philosophy; and
(2) his own family history.

This will clear space for the aesthetically interesting questions *Sons and Lovers* raises that I proceed to take up:

(3) What, as a novelist, did Lawrence propose to do with these historical *données*?
(4) What could a tale, as against a mere metaphysic, disclose about sons whose position "in-between" radically different parents makes development exceptionally difficult?
(5) What specifically are the hero Paul Morel's chances to love, to work, or, when the dominant parent dies, even to live?
(6) And what might these questions have to do with readers now?

Background: Intellectual, Socio-historical, Familial

Like Mill and most of the prominent English writers of the Victorian Age, Lawrence's fidelity to fact required him to acknowledge two truths. First is the truth of Bentham: the universe consists of particles, and as the natural sciences study the behavior of atoms and the like, so the human sciences study the behavior of bodies. Second is the truth of Coleridge: the behavior of bodies depends on mental responses far more complicated than Bentham's utilitarian pleasure–pain calculus could account for. Let us for the moment omit the Coleridgean concern for the transcendent power that creates and sustains all the particles, a concern Lawrence, after his education in Darwin,

Herbert Spencer, and Hardy, still felt. The immediately relevant point is that, after reading those writers, he was intellectually a child of Victorian Benthamism as well as Victorian Coleridgeanism. He joined materialism with vitalism. However the cosmos began, it was a "fleshly"—atomic not a "wordly"—spiritual event. At the same time, what animates the flesh in particular is qualitatively different from what moves electrons around a nucleus. A writer who had grown up in the Congregational tradition was unlikely to abandon his sense of the sacredness of life, which is why Lawrence's quarrel with John's Gospel is essentially intramural—a question of prioritizing terms in the manner of a latter-day Carlyle whose authentic gifts, and therefore whose true vocation, were those of a latter-day George Eliot.

What is *not* Victorian is Lawrence's insistence that the Flesh isn't masculine but feminine—that the biblical Father really "should be called Mother." Even nineteenth-century women writers—Harriet Beecher Stowe being an exception—didn't worry much about theological "gendering," but here in the early twentieth century Lawrence suddenly does.[2] His feminizing of the Creator is more than fidelity to biology, which reminds us that "the Woman lay in travail, and gave birth" not only to boys but also to girls. Unable to let well enough alone, Lawrence mythologizes biology. Extrapolating from the labor of mothers, he postulates a Great Mother archetype, sexualizing the originary asexual division of cells in the *Urschleim*, and in terms that can't be satisfactorily explained by reference to his conventional adoption of pagan metaphors ("Mother Nature" and so on). Why this emphasis on the feminine? The answer lies not in natural but in social science, and what it can reveal about the modern crisis our *Bildungsromane* variously expose—that of paternal authority. The imbalance between male and female energies that Lawrence had experienced in his own family was, he understood, a particular instance of a general crisis England had been undergoing since the early days of the Industrial Revolution.

A Laurentian history of that crisis, informed by his own experience, would read along these lines. Before the Industrial Revolution, men and women had worked, close together, on farms, in cottage industries, or in shops. The decades-long series of enclosures of common lands and the ineluctable progress of technological sophistication and concentration had drawn men off the land and into the factories or the mines. This development left women home alone, in sole charge for most of the day of their children's upbringing. In a typical working-class household, then, the father earned the money out in the rough-and-tumble world of men, where long and exhausting hours necessitated the refreshment of drink and mateyness in the pub. When he finally came home, it was often as a tired, grimy, tipsy intruder. The mother's tasks were also difficult—cooking, cleaning, mending, nursing and teaching the children—and her allies tended to be other wives and mothers like herself or, among the few males who weren't part of the industrial enterprise, the local schoolmaster or clergyman. Their help in training and disciplining the children was indispensable, but when disciplinary problems became too acute for her or for them, she would characteristically appeal to the hard hand of her husband. "Wait till your father comes home!" Where did this leave the father? From the children's point of view he was the heavy—the parent who spoke harshly and spanked—as he was the one who performed mysterious and often dangerous work in the still mostly masculine world of the factory or the all-masculine world of the mine. His intellectual and spiritual authority was practically nil: all such concerns were monopolized by the mother and the effeminized-by-association schoolmaster and clergyman.

The girls in such families might have had a strong mother to identify with. She was close at hand every day, and they could model themselves after her. However, they would have missed having what Robert Bly calls that important "love affair" with their father when they were one-and-a-half to three years old—the affair that might have prepared them for loving a male who wasn't their father when they entered late adolescence. And if their father was brutal as well as distant, they would have ended up regarding men generally with distrust and fear. The boys would have suffered even more. When the father was distant, they too would have missed their early, pre-three-year-old love affair with him—the one that, preceding the first Oedipal struggle, would have brought the excitement of the father's rough dandling and wrestling, which the mother typically didn't offer, and would have given the sons a chance to identify with masculinity.[3] Nor, as the boys grew older and memories of the initial relations (or non-relations) with mother and father faded, could they find in a distant father a model for manly behavior, either as workers (his work was far away), as husbands (he was too worn out to show his wife any tenderness, or to cooperate with her in domestic chores), or as "souls" (the stultifying routine in factory, mine, or shop and the dominance of the mother in the verbal nurturance of the children had between them left the fathers with little to offer in conversation or storytelling). Hence the sons, quite as much as the daughters, would have depended on their mothers for soul-tending. In the absence of any initiation experience—say a trade apprenticeship, shepherded perhaps by an uncle or some other father substitute—the sons would enter the adult working world with a shock. In the absence of reliable "coaching"—whether by father, uncle, or neighbor—they wouldn't know how they should treat females who weren't their mother or sisters. To fall back on the cliché, were those females Madonnas or whores? Overspiritualized objects of worship and sources of intellectual stimulation, or brutalized objects of arousal and channels for release?

This frankly simple survey of psychosocial circumstances in the industrial world begins to explain why, in the "Foreword"'s new-gospel sketch of the Creator, Lawrence runs the genders together: he is acknowledging the ahistorical fact of uterine gestation and the pointedly historical circumstances of maternal domination in Victorian and Edwardian households, while also betraying a nostalgia for paternal power—not just the sperm the ovum can't do without, but the socializing male energies that presumably underlay the old-gospel language about the Creator Father. More concretely, the survey should help situate the story Lawrence tells in *Sons and Lovers*. The dynamics of the Morel family, and the conundrums Paul in particular faces, are representative. His questions are shared, in the modern era, by many European and American *Bildungshelden*, from Wilhelm Meister to David Copperfield to Oliver Alden: Who and where is the father? Which is to say, what is an adult male? How does a boy become man? And how, outside the family, does an adult male relate himself not only to other males but to females? We have seen in James the analogous questions female protagonists must front. The Lawrence novel for such questions is *The Rainbow* (1915), where they open onto his central theme, the "relations between men and women" and the sanctity of marriage, which he pursued in *Women in Love* (1920) and returned to in *Lady Chatterley's Lover* (1928). But initially he had to address in *Sons and Lovers* these questions of male adolescent development.

Why did he *have* to? First, there was the self-confessed therapeutic reason: the need to "shed his sickness," to work through his own obvious mother-obsession and apparent fatherlessness by refracting them in the characters of a *Bildungsroman*, after which he could disclose what he had discovered—what "we have come through" *to*—in his marriage with Frieda Weekley, née von Richthofen, in July 1914. Second, there was the educational reason: the desire to help his contemporaries shed *their* sickness. If adults' capacities for a "living life" (as opposed to a dying one) depend on what they have experienced in childhood and adolescence, then they will do well to *understand* their childhood and adolescence—something, Lawrence believed, the novel could enable them to do. Hence he presents his characters as specimens of their generation's moment in history, Paul, for instance, noticing that

> A good many of the nicest men he knew were like himself, bound in by their own virginity, which they could not break out of . . . Being the sons of mothers whose husbands had blundered rather brutally through their feminine sanctities, they were themselves too diffident and shy. They could easier deny themselves than incur any reproach from a woman. For a woman was like their mother, and they were full of the sense of their mother.[4]

And Miriam, the woman with whom in this case Paul is too shy, resembles "a good many of the nicest" women her age who, listening to their mothers' cautionary tales and observing their fathers' elephantine gallantries, have learned to be diffident about sex. It is as though Lawrence were saying to his readers: "Look, what happens to Paul or Miriam, or, if you insist, what happened to me and Jessie Chambers, has happened to a lot of people. This novel is going to show how and why it happened, and try to figure out where they—we, you—might go from here."

Father and Mother

If in *Sons and Lovers* we have a typical son in Paul and a typical daughter in Miriam, who is the typical father? We are given only one, and in sketching the industrial factory hand or miner I have anticipated the portrait of Walter Morel that Lawrence based on his own father. Since it is obscured by the more prominently placed, more carefully worked portrait of Mrs. Morel—an arrangement Lawrence came to regard as a mistake — we need to give the paternal portrait its full due. What are we told and shown about Morel? What are we almost but not quite told or shown? What is hinted at? Morel is the unlettered butty who went down pit when he was eight years old, rarely sees daylight, labors under conditions physically draining and dangerous, drinks with his mates, and feels generally unwanted by his wife and children. He is also the "natural man" who, in wonderfully evoked scenes, has been famous for his lithe dancing and choir-boy singing; who, to his wife's great and pathetic indignation, cuts the one-year-old William's hair so as not to "make a wench on 'im"; who comfortably cooks his own breakfast each morning; who walks to work through the fields and along the hedgerows, off which he may pick a stalk to chew on for the day; and who, having recruited his children to help him make fuses, tells them cunning tales about the mice and the horses in the mine.

To a great extent a man like Morel *is* where he works. To his wife the mine is nothing but an industrial hole in the ground: when the men go into it daily, there is little enough money; when there is a slow down, everyone faces destitution. For Paul, however, that hole and its environs are alluring, as numinous as the tabernacle or the atmospheric conditions in the Sinai: "When I was a boy, I always thought a pillar of cloud by day and a pillar of fire by night was a pit, with its steam, and its lights, and the burning bank,—and I thought the Lord was always at the pit-top" (364). The whole show—the slag, the steam, the trucks—seems to Paul "like something alive almost—a big creature that you don't know." The mine is "alive" because "the feel of *men*," of "men's hands," is all over it (152). But, in a gender conflation similar to the "Foreword" 's, this Yahweh-brooded-over, masculine place is also distinctly feminine: we see for ourselves that it is the orifice of the earth that the colliers each day "die" into and are "born" out of. This crinkled "womb"—swarming with men, horses, and mice—has enabled Morel to incorporate the feminine side of his self, and has made him quite as friendly to life as is the woman whose womb has carried his children. It is a friendliness, a tenderness we perceive in the unbearably poignant scenes showing him first greeting William on his Christmas homecoming, and then grieving for him when Paul brings word of his death in London:

> The two walked off the pit-bank, where men were watching curiously. As they came out and went along the railway, with the sunny autumn field on one side and a wall of trucks on the other, Morel said in a frightened voice:
> "'E's niver gone, child?"
> "Yes."
> "When wor't?"
> "Last night. We had a telegram from my mother."
> Morel walked on a few strides, then leaned up against a truckside, his hand over his eyes. He was not crying. Paul stood looking round, waiting. On the weighing machine a truck trundled slowly. Paul saw everything, except his father leaning against the truck as if he were tired. (167)

This passage, made if anything more moving by Paul's adolescent obtuseness to the fact that his father, if "not crying," is nevertheless stunned and mourning, is finely capped when his father rejoices over his first successes as a painter: he wipes his eyes and says "that other lad," William, would have "done as much, if they hadna ha killed 'im" (297). "They" are somehow the bosses who drive the pencil-pushers in the clerk-stool world Mrs. Morel has sent her "knight" William into. His resistance weakened by the pressures of his job, he dies of pneumonia and "a peculiar erysipelas," a then often-fatal inflammation of the skin that, significantly, begins with the chafing of his clerk's collar at his throat. Say what she will about the miners' unspectacular and iffy paychecks, or about the frequent accidents and the remoteness of the hospital, the sweaty pit seems— the novelist has of course *made* it seem—less hazardous, psychologically as well as physically, than the allegedly unsweaty white-collar world of the city.

While not the full presence in the home that his wife is, Morel hasn't altogether absconded either. He is what Jack Miles has called an "absent presence," a phrase to describe the status of the Yahweh who, having been a "presence" in the Book of Exodus (the aforementioned pillars of cloud and fire), becomes more distant in the Book of Isaiah—and will be a "present absence" in the Book of Psalms and just an "absence" in Proverbs.[5] The father's absent presence in *Sons and Lovers* is something that, especially in its life-friendly mode, Lawrence established in spite of his conscious dislike of his own father. Better, he established the father's absent presence by dint of artistic honesty. What as a young man he was only semiconscious of—the father's vitality and his own filial need of him—he in middle age, which sadly meant near the end of his life, consciously affirmed. There are many statements in the essays and letters that in effect trump the salient judgment of the early novel, as in "I would write a different *Sons and Lovers* now; my mother was wrong, and I thought she was absolutely right."[6] The most extended evidence of retrospective reversal lies in "Nottingham and the Mining Countryside" (1930), where Lawrence recalls his boyhood fascination with the collieries and the colliers. Eastwood was bordered by "the old England of the forest and agricultural past," and like Morel his father would on the way to work "hunt for mushrooms in the long grass, or perhaps pick up a skulking rabbit" to bring home in the evening. The "Nottingham" essay fills a lacuna in *Sons and Lovers*, namely an explicit account of the colliers' conditions underground. Before mechanization, which we hear about in *Women in Love*,

> the miners . . . knew each other practically naked, and with curious close intimacy, and the darkness and the underground remoteness of the pit "stall," and the continual presence of danger, made the physical, instinctive, and intuitional contact between men very highly developed, a contact almost as close as touch.

A miner's wife, Lawrence's mother, for instance, cared most about wages and acquisition (so she had been "taught" and "encouraged" by her culture), and she pushed her sons to office jobs and better pay. The miner himself cared only about comradeship down pit or in the pub, and about "beauty."

Beauty? Lawrence means that, since the real source of beauty is "underground," having to do with intuitive receptivity, the colliers in their dark tunnels understood more about it than their wives up in their sunlit kitchens. He offers the example of a flower. Partly because it is so unlike anything the collier has ever seen down pit, and partly because, working down pit, he has developed an affinity for the earth in which it is rooted, a flower is to him an object of "contemplation which shows a *real* awareness of the presence of beauty," the awareness of "the incipient artist." His wife on the other hand would regard it as a class-enhancing possession—something to pick in order to decorate her dress, her hair, or her window sill. Lawrence rounds off his essay with a John Ruskin-like lament for the betrayal of beauty by nineteenth-century town-planners, and a William Morris-like call for town-renewal. The Arts and Crafts Movement picture we are left with is of Derbyshire hilltops crowned with Tuscan villages, lived in by jocund peasants who make comely furniture and clothes, and, singing and dancing, have never heard of their being underpaid or undereducated.[7] (For what after all would higher wages mean, thinks Lawrence, but the temptation to buy motorcars or cinema tickets? Just as more board-school education would only mean a susceptibility to novels by Ouida and pamphlets by Sidney and Beatrice Webb.)

Stephen Spender was surely right to have pointed out that this collier-cum-agriculturalist community—valorized by the *Scrutiny* group and others as a "chapel-going, Bunyanesque, proletarian" alternative to the Oxbridge and Bloomsbury that Lawrence had in the persons of Russell, John Maynard Keynes, and Lady Ottoline Morrell found so null—was precisely what he spent his many years of exile fleeing. Rather than embracing his father and the proletariat generally, he gave them up as, by the time of the Great War, thoroughly dehumanized by the implacable machine and the meddling state. He therefore sought the vital society he desired among Italian peasants, Aztec or Navajo Indians, and long-gone Etruscans, the very groups that had least to do with the country of Fielding or George Eliot that *Scrutiny* wanted the England of the generation just after Lawrence to connect with.[8] The "Nottingham" essay, or late pieces such as "Hymns in a Man's Life,"[9] do however reveal a Lawrence whose memory of Derbyshire and his childhood had been imperfectly suppressed, and the outright commendations of his father and his unmechanized mates can—his father having died in 1924—be understood as a revision of his own early feelings, especially as they were reflected on the surface of *Sons and Lovers*. That revision should not dictate how we read the novel, any more than Tolstoy's *What Is Art?* should dictate how we read the *War and Peace* or *Anna Karenina*, which he repudiated on ethical grounds. But that revision, building on what is already in the depths of the novel, can alert us to the problem of the father's "absent presence" that we might otherwise be unable to articulate. "I would write a different *Sons and Lovers* now": the "pit" of the tale, if we "mine" it alertly, reveals that in a sense he *already had* written a different novel. That he had done so is evident with the father. Which means we can't look complacently at the mother as either balm or bane for the males in her family. Balm-and-bane, as Forster might say, is more like it.

We may see Mrs. Morel more complexly if she steps forth, backlit, from the withheld "Foreword." Written as a letter to Edward Garnett, Lawrence's editor for the novel, it allows us to register, as I have said, both a transvaluation of the Word and the Flesh, and a diagnosis of an imbalance of power in the realm of domestic politics. As Christ the Son proceeded from the Father and uttered his Word—that is, created as a carpenter tables and chairs and as a prophet miracles and sayings—so every son proceeds from his mother. To illustrate, Lawrence spins his own fable of the bees: The filial "bee . . . comes home to his Queen [his mother] as to the Father, in service and humility, for suggestion and renewal, and identification which is the height of his glory, for begetting." "Comes home . . . as to the Father" means not only as Christ comes home to God the Father but—the context makes it clear—as a son turns to his mother *in place of* his father, a "demanded" process by which the bee, in the language of servitude, "carries and fetches, carries and fetches" (471). The relation of son to mother becomes, implicitly, that of husband to wife: the Queen Bee (Lawrence called Frieda by that name, "q.b." for short) is, like the conventional Muse, the divine inspirer who sends her son or her husband to do the world's work, the "I am I" declarations of achievement, whether by "Galileo and Shakespeare and Darwin," or by a butty at Brinsley Colliery. Trouble begins when the husband-bee, already an absent presence for the son, fails to come home. The Queen in that case expels him, "as a drone," from her hive. Does she then, in the hunger of Flesh, take another man? Hardly ever, because the thou-shalt-not "Law," a "Word" we remember that is inferior to the Flesh, forbids it. He too may feel inhibited from finding another woman. In which case "shall they both" destroy themselves, he with alcohol "or other kindling," she

> in sickness, or in lighting up and illuminating old dead Words, or she shall spend ["her surplus" vitality] in fighting with her man to make him take her [not a bad idea], or [not a good one] she shall turn to her son, and say, "Be you my Go-between." But the man who is the go-between from Woman to Production is the lover of that woman. And if that Woman be his mother, then is he her lover in part only; he carries for her, but is never received into her for his confirmation and renewal, and so wastes himself away in the flesh. The old son-lover was Oedipus. The name of the new one is legion. (472–73)[10]

To be sure, the new Oedipuses marry women who aren't their mothers, but it is their mothers who have their passional love. A wife despairs of such a momma's boy husband, and perforce "hope[s] for sons, that she may have her lover in her hour." While Lawrence may here be trying out some of the Freudian categories he was then picking up from Frieda, he is well on his way to articulating his own peculiar myth, what in *Psychoanalysis and the Unconscious* (1921) and *Fantasia of the Unconscious* (1922), his "polyanalytics," became his puissant misreading of Freud.

It is as if Lawrence were revising not only Freud but *Hamlet*. Paul's mother's name is Gertrude; she is the Queen Bee in this Bestwood Elsinor. There is no King Hamlet-like first husband, though in her youth she was attracted to a boy who wanted to become a clergyman. Her Claudius, Mr. Morel, could keep up with the Danes in drinking, and his dialect places him socially on the level of the Gravedigger. The essential analogue is that Paul often feels as fatherless as Hamlet, and that he feels a deep ambivalence toward the man his mother is married to—his father and yet somehow not his father. She might have married someone who, from her point of view, was Hyperion. How then did she end up with a satyr? It has been an attraction of opposites—the pale civilized lady startled yet warmed by the ruddy native collier—marked in the too-brief but unforgettably vivid scene at the Christmas dance. Though passionately happy with him during the first months of their marriage, she soon decides that, since he has been less than honest about his financial situation and has proved fonder of the pub than of her company at home, he is no good and her marriage has been a mistake. His earnings are often predictably low because his superiors at the mine punish his snideness by assigning him inferior stalls. Too much of the money he does manage to earn goes to drink. Sober and conscientious husbands are so rare in Bestwood that, when Mrs. Morel meets the worthy Mr. Leivers at Willey Farm, she pours into Paul's ears a resentful and enthusiastic if-only: "Now *wouldn't* I help that man! . . . *Wouldn't* I see after the fowls and the young stock! And *I'd* learn to milk, and *I'd* talk with him, and *I'd* plan with him. My word, if I were his wife, the farm would be run, I know!" (158). Mrs. Leivers fails her spouse because she isn't tough enough; Morel fails his because he is too tough. Thus the unsquared accounts of the mismatched.

What Mrs. Morel wants isn't so much erotic satisfaction, though the occasional rekindling of the flame she initially shared with her husband shows that she wouldn't be ungrateful for it, as the socioeconomic satisfaction of earning the money that could boost their children into the middle class. Like Shakespeare's Gertrude, she finally cares most about her offspring. For her, the parental team's goal is acquisition and merger—*acquiring* the wherewithal that guarantees the respectability of a smart house, the chance at a grammar-school education (the ancient universities were still largely out of the question for all but sons of the very well-to-do), and the clothes and manners that could introduce them into circles where they may meet the daughters of families still higher on the social ladder, with whom they might *merge* through marriage. I don't think we are meant to scoff at this goal, which even in "static" feudal times—a late moment of which we have seen in *Wilhelm Meister*—had been pursued by noble and burgher. Lawrence puts us *inside* those scenes showing Mrs. Morel's careful shopping for a new vase for her precious flowers (those decorative "possessions") or a new blouse for herself; or showing the painful pleasure of their going out to dinner in a Nottingham restaurant, which is awkward for Paul, who realizes that his mother is no more competent than himself at dealing with the snooty waiter, and which perhaps is eye-opening to us, who must realize that this woman is so impoverished she has never before eaten in a restaurant. Her desire to push her sons into the middle classes isn't exclusively focused on shops and restaurants. She is convinced that, because the middle classes have the education and the leisure, they read and discuss ideas in ways that can fulfill the intellectual side of her sons' characters. Lawrence the essayist, or indeed some of the voices he has introduced into this very novel, will declare some of her ambitions to be brummagen: her own cooking is better than anything a six-shilling Nottingham restaurant can offer, and the middle classes, whatever their power to buy books and go to concerts, can often be the very Philistines Arnold had both bemoaned and quixotically hoped to educate. Paul and Miriam are, we may confidently say, intellectually leagues in advance of the Miss Jordans and their friends in Nottingham. Still, Mrs. Morel is right to want her children to be given bread instead of a stone when they are hungry, and to develop and deploy their imaginative and ratiocinative powers.

Whatever direction their character formations take, it will go best if they draw on the energies of both mother and father. Lawrence's view, articulated throughout his *oeuvre*, is that any character, for good or ill, will be formed through the play of contraries. Mr. and Mrs. Morel aren't simple embodiments of Blakean "Reason and Energy," but their marriage does seem a yoking of heaven and hell, and it leaves their offspring in a fix as to what "party," angel or devil, they belong to. The higher doggerel that Lawrence wrote in "Red-Herring" (1929), though obviously referring to his own family, neatly encapsulates the war of "Attraction and Repulsion" the Morel children are drawn into:

> My father was a working man
> > and a collier was he,
> at six in the morning they turned him down
> > and they turned him up for tea.

> My mother was a superior soul
> > a superior soul was she,
> cut out to play a superior rôle
> > in the god-damn bourgeoisie.

> We children were the in-betweens
> > little non-descripts were we,
> indoors we called each other *you*,
> > outside, it was *tha* and *thee*.

The poem ends by declaring that, while the Lawrence children have risen ("a servant-maid brings me my tea"), they remain in-betweens longing to curse "the god-damn bourgeoisie" and "kick their ___ses."[11] The simplicities of the poem, or sometimes of Lawrence's late essays, displace what in *Sons and Lovers* is a tensely complicated debate. Our task as readers is to pay due attention to both sides—the defenders of "*you*" (Blake's Heaven) and those of "*tha* and *thee*" (his Hell)—as Paul, stuck *between*, endeavors to negotiate a way *through* them.

His mother won't let her sons go down pit, to become moles with pickaxes. The eldest, William, thanks her for the ineffable privileges that go with the white collar, and innocently complains about the absence of his mother's sensible conversation among his girlfriends, even the more socially ambitious. But, to repeat, professional and psychosexual pressures soon conspire to kill him. His suffering contributes to Paul's doubts about the advantages of upward mobility. He thinks genteel poshness is nothing compared to the intrinsic something—"life itself, warmth"—he feels in "the common people." Of course he can't explain how they have more "life" than the middle classes, and his mother points out that, "among the common people," he spends all his time with "Those that exchange ideas, like the middle classes. . . . She frankly *wanted* him to climb into the middle classes, a thing not very difficult, she knew. And she wanted him in the end to marry a lady" (298–99). It is a collision between the mother's wisdom, not invalidated for being conventional, which hopes for a life for her son that will in every way be richer than his parents', and his youthfully inconsistent argument, pursued with saurian evasiveness, which expresses his desire to choose his own friends.

His *you*-talking (U-talking) mother has pointed to the candidates she considers eligible—"educated" girls like Miss Moreton—and Paul squirms. What friends would his *tha*-talking father recommend? Paul may not be comfortable with his father or his "father's pals," but by yearning for "the common people" he clearly, his denial notwithstanding, *misses* him. He senses that his father has a potency necessary to a boy who wants to become a man—a potency his mother can't give. She can scrub her pans in the morning as she scrubs her husband's back in the evening, she can stand the pangs of childbirth and the pain of cancer, but she recoils from the colliers' singing, dancing, and drinking. She can't see how it is cold homes that make warm taverns. Cold homes? Lawrence understood, in his own terms, what we would describe as the hormonal differences between the sexes—differences exaggerated by the above-glimpsed cultural changes brought on by an Industrial Revolution that, separating men from women for most of the day, brutalized the former and provoked the latter to a seraphic reaction. That is, if the men *will* imbibe the ethos along with the beer offered by the tavern, then their wives, insisting that they aren't barmaids, *will* turn their eyes up to heaven—or just to the ceiling. Like Mrs. Leivers, who in spite of all her children dreads the actuality of sex, Mrs. Morel wishes life were delicate and more spiritual. When it proves not to be, she clenches herself against it—or, rather, she channels her reserved warmth toward her son, with whom she may sleep ("in spite of hygienists," that is, the psychiatrists of the day) safe from the crudities of intercourse. What then transpires, in the terms of the "Foreword," is that Morel the father is more maternal—more "Fleshly," more rooted in "life itself"—than his wife is.

It is confusing enough, even without the linguistic gender conflation, and one can understand Paul's quandary about what kind of life he belongs to. He is caught between a mother for whom life is spirit, ideas, acquisition, and status; and a father for whom it is the naked contact of flesh. Each partakes of a truth that is distinct, but only partial. Paul has to negotiate his own combination of powers inherited from each of his parents, trying to use the prepotencies of the one to overcome the inadequacies of the other. It will be an extremely difficult task, not least because his mother has stolen a march on his father, thereby placing herself in formidable position to resist, often unconsciously, not only him but all other influences Paul may encounter.[12]

Odi et amo

Lagging in the march though he is, Morel isn't the melodramatically "bad father" who beats his wife and children and gambles away whatever money he doesn't drink. There *are* flashes of violence: his locking his wife, pregnant with Paul, out into the night; his angry flinging of the table drawer that strikes her above the eye; his actually hitting her in the face (an episode merely reported); or his near fisticuffs with William and later with Paul. But he is also capable of warm tenderness towards these same kin, and it is sad if not surprising when his wife's disillusioned stand-offishness proves a model so irresistible that even the last-born Arthur, the collier's favorite, comes to hate him. That said, the wife and children's hate, or our own, mustn't entirely eclipse the love that for her was there in the beginning, and for them has been fostered by those admired scenes of fuse-making or of telling stories about the life down pit. The summary comment near the end of the evocation, quite beyond praise, of William's first Christmas visit—"Everybody was mad with happiness in the family. Home was home, and they loved it with a passion of love, whatever the suffering had been"—has the ring of authenticity. *Odi et amo* was Lascelles Abercrombie's suggested subtitle for this novel.[13] Whatever the ratio between these Catullan verbs, both must be kept in play.

Hatred and love toward Morel, on the page and in our minds, clash intensely on the day of Paul's birth. He comes home from work, too tired to think. Served his beer by the neighbor Mrs. Bower, he "drank, gasped . . . drank, gasped"—for all the world like a gorilla—without a care "that his wife was ill, that he had another boy." True, since he must sweat several pints every shift in the mine, he had better drink something, and no real miner is going to ask for lemonade rather than beer. But must a real miner grunt how thirsty he is, or point self-pityingly to his black face "smeared with sweat"? He will behave the same way before the Rev. Mr. Heaton, Paul's godfather, who drops in to talk theology with Mrs. Morel. This miner may be the blue-collar salt of the earth, which is admirable, but he habitually reminds women, children, and clerics of his sacrifices, which is deplorable. In any case, after he has drunk his pint, Morel reluctantly mounts the stairs to see his wife. No wallowing in suffering for her:

"I s'll be all right."
"A lad, tha says," he stammered.
She turned down the sheet and showed the child.
    "Bless him!" he murmured. Which made her laugh, because he blessed by rote—
pretending paternal emotion, which he did not feel just then.

"Go now," she said.

"I will my lass," he answered, turning away.

Dismissed, he wanted to kiss her, but he dared not. She half wanted him to kiss her, but could not bring herself to give any signs. She only breathed freely when he was gone out of the room again, leaving behind him a faint smell of pit-dirt. (44)

How nicely poised are the emotions here. Morel's affections for wife and child are real enough; only—stammering, murmuring, exhausted, shy (how many nights ago did he throw this woman out of the house?), and not exactly encouraged by her to offer a kiss—he has difficulty expressing them. At the same time, her laugh at his "pretending" a fatherly piety he is too tired *really* to feel at the moment is, if not polite, at least perceptive. Her memory of his recent chucking her out must still be vivid, and surely, given her own social antecedents, it isn't being overdelicate to wish he would eliminate the "faint smell of pit-dirt" before offering a kiss.

In sum, Morel is neither the gorilla we may momentarily mistake him for, nor a kind sensitive controlled Mr. Heaton who can open a seam of coal, but an imperfect husband whose virtues we have to consider seriously, and often in spite of what the not-always-fair teller says about him. And so with Mrs. Morel. Of course she is the heroic little Victorian mother, among whose qualities has been the passional shrewdness to feel, at the Christmas dance where she meets him, that the "sensuous flame of life" in this dancing man, his ringing laugh "soft, non-intellectual, warm, a kind of gambolling," might just be the force to moderate the uncomfortably baffling incandescence of her own intellectuality. But she is also the stern "Puritan" who, once that fateful dance and the nine months of post-wedding happiness are over, simply decides that her husband is fiscally dishonest, intemperate, incorrigible—someone to be "dismissed." Her marriage has been a mistake, and hereafter her own power of "thought and spirit," turning away from his phallic candle flame, will endure apart from him. Which means she will do everything she can for her sons, who she hopes will become men after the middle-class pattern her husband can neither conceive nor respect.

The Sons and Their Lovers

What do these sons have to reflect on when looking for their own women? Initially of course they don't reflect at all: they act and react as the local culture and their unconscious desires dictate. A prize-winning athlete and quite the laddie in a Highlander kilt, William pursues the bold sort of girls who pursue him—that is, the sort who go to dances and incur his mother's disfavor. He assures her, while he burns their letters, that they are only (to use the dialect) fribbles to spoon with; that his real love is still for her. And when in London he becomes engaged to Lily, he feels he has to follow through and marry her, since he has "gone too far" to back out. Meaning, quite obviously, that he has slept with her and, whether she is pregnant or not, that her social position would be cruelly compromised if he jilted her now. It is Hardy's Jude Fawley and Arabella all over again: the woman may be no better than she should be, but the honorable young man, half-falling and half-pulled into bed, will do his duty by her. Mrs. Morel is a realist, properly insisting that her boy not sacrifice himself needlessly. Assuming that Lily isn't pregnant after all, she urges William not to feel bound by any promise implied in having slept with her. If he feels Lily's character (all sex, no ideas) is incompatible with his own, then he should take a lesson from his mother's misallying herself with an all sex, no ideas sort of person two decades ago, and back out. Observe her implied principle: premarital intercourse is hazardous and should be resisted, but if one has escaped the hazard—if there has been no conception—then one remains free to look about. Poor William however isn't looking about; he just stares across the room. "Only his mother could help him now. And yet, he would not let *her* decide for him. He stuck to what he had done" (162, my emphasis). He wants to separate from his mother—by at least making his own decision—but the woman he insists on choosing is what Freud would call a degraded object, so unlike his mother that he can feel no affection. Thus, by the logic of this family romance, he soon dies. As Paul, with popular Darwinism on his mind, will later tell Miriam without really understanding its application to himself, the cause of William's death lay in his having gone "wrong somewhere"—having strayed from the "proper way" nature had mapped out for him, as she has mapped it in different fashions for everyone.

We have to infer for ourselves what, according to nature's map (and not just Mrs. Morel's prescriptions), William's or Paul's "proper way" is, but with regard to choosing a woman other than their mother to love, the tale reveals that someone too *other*—someone in William's case like Lily—isn't the ticket. Paul's Miriam is from one point of view too *similar* to his mother. We can't imagine her dancing or putting up with "the faint smell of pit-dirt," and if anything she goes Mrs. Morel one better in the pursuit of bookish ideas and Congregational religiosity. Paul's Clara, on the other hand, does for him what Lily has done for William—shows him the depths of impersonal, unreflecting sexual intercourse and its connections, peewits and stars in choral accompaniment, with the throbbing cosmos. Neither Miriam nor Clara quite answers his needs, in part because he is still affectively tied to his mother, in part because each is in some way imbalanced or incomplete. Seriocomically put, it is a problem of Miriam being top-heavy (mind and spirit outweighing loins) and Clara being bottom-heavy (loins outweighing mind and spirit).

This is familiar though still-contested territory in the criticism, and the teller tells us much about it. What is never mentioned by him and is scarcely mentioned by the critics is something else the tale directs Paul and us to reflect on. He says he wants unreflective impersonal love, and is angry when Miriam, with her eye contact during coition, compels him *to* reflect, to *be* personal. Reflect about what? Primarily it is about what Arabella in her scheming way gets Jude to consider: the consequences of their coition, not least the possibility of pregnancy.

> "We belong to each other," he said.
> "Yes."
> "Then why shouldn't we belong to each other all together?"
> "But—" she faltered.
> "I know it's a lot to ask," he said. "But there's not much risk for you really—not in the Gretchen way. You can trust me there?"
> "Oh I can trust you!" The answer came quick and strong. "It's not that—it's not that at all—but—" (327)

She is also afraid of what her own mother has for years said to her about the farmyard dreadfulness of intercourse. But Paul's interrogative "trust me"—supposing it to mean that if she gets pregnant he won't play Faust to her Gretchen but will marry her, as his younger brother Arthur has married the three-months pregnant Beatrice—is rather glib. Economically and certainly psychologically, he is even less prepared for marriage than Arthur. He is putting the finally succumbing Miriam at some risk. The youth of Edwardian Derbyshire seem, on the evidence of this novel, to have no access to contraceptives, and abortion is expensively out of reach for farm and factory girls. Thus when Susan, one of the girls at Jordan's, finds herself pregnant and has to quit (company rules? disgrace? needing to join the far-away father?), Paul, in whom she has confided, tells her he is sorry. " 'But you'll see it'll turn out all right. You'll make the best of it,' he continued, rather wistfully" (305). Take that for a dose not just of society's but of nature's double standard.

His wistfulness may stem from more than sympathy for Susan; he may also be thinking about how Miriam or his new lover, Clara, might through his cavalier demands that they "belong to each other all together" be Susanized. Note that his mother bids him think precisely about that possibility with Clara—not exclusively that she might become pregnant but also that she is married to Baxter Dawes, and that Nottingham is sufficiently remote from Bohemia to make her a talked-about woman. It is bad enough for her reputation that she has separated from Baxter; it will be worse if she is seen going around with a young man seven years her junior. This concern isn't maternal jealousy, as Paul Oedipally suggests; it is one woman's consciousness that another woman can be made miserable as well as poor by her neighbor's disapprobation. Paul's reply—Clara "hasn't much to lose"—comes from ignorant bravado: "No—her life's nothing to her, so what's the worth of nothing? She goes with me—it becomes something. Then she must pay, we both must pay. Folks are so frightened of paying—they'd rather starve than pay" (359). Exactly the attitude of the man who bolted with Frieda Weekley, but Clara will soon be furious when, at the court proceedings against Baxter for having thrown Mr. Jordan down the stairs, her name comes up as the *casus belli*. " '*Cherchez la femme!*' smiled the magistrate," but *la femme* isn't smiling. Baxter's violence could as well be directed at her as at Jordan or Paul, and the other women at the factory have already given her the silent treatment. That Paul resists his mother's warnings about the social dangers to which he is exposing Clara is healthy in a way. After all he needs to break free from his mother. Yet in this case we can appreciate how inane that "break free" slogan is, for his mother is offering him a feminine insight into Clara's position that, in his masculine self-centeredness, he could use. "Mum and dad," to quote Philip Larkin, may "fuck you up,"[14] but they can also set you right.

Too Little Dad, Too Much Mum

Of course Paul has other people besides "Mum and dad" to set him right. He has, most pertinently, his antithetical girlfriends, Miriam and Clara. As I have sufficiently remarked, they beckon Paul to a life outside his family, but his capacity for responding to their beck depends greatly on what happens inside it. Therefore here I want to remain focused on his parents, less to damn or praise than to understand. Not that the novelist himself was past damning and praising. As we have seen, the older Lawrence recognized how much he owed to his father's vitality; indeed he wished he had drawn on it more deeply than he had, and through celebrations of primitives and proletarians of various sorts he tried to repay his father for earlier shortchanging. These are belated signals from the "teller," going beyond the "tale," that in this instance we should be alert to, and since Dorothy Van Ghent's brilliant formalist critique in the early 1950s (to go no further back) readers *have* been duly alert.[15] What Morel gives matters, as does what he fails to give, and if we see Paul's *Bildung* as a kind of steeplechase, pitting him against his peers or against amorphous social conditions, then we may hurrah when the father gives him help, and barrack when he doesn't. And it is the same with the mother. But that sort of audience participation not only neglects Paul's own initiatives—his chromosome-transcending, or at least generation-skipping, "genius"—it also violates one of the *tale's* most sympathetic insights, namely that the enabling and disabling powers of both parents are so intertwined as to render moot our specta-torial damning and praising. After we have put the book down we should indeed strive to achieve a better balance between contrary energies, gender them as we will, in our own lives and families—and not just because Lawrence told us to, but because of the sobering crisis for males in the industrial or now postindustrial society that I sketched at the beginning of this chapter.

But enough exhortation. *While* we are reading, moral resolutions, like moral judgments, should be suspended in favor of old-fashioned, Coleridgean understanding. We need to ask not "Is it true? Is it right? Should it be?" but "How is it, and why?" Or rather, we need to begin with the *how* and *why* questions, in order to situate —to complicate without making mush of—our attempts at normative evaluation. To recall the old philosophical distinction, our language about *ought* needs to be grounded in a fully developed language about *is*. I will explain what I mean by taking one last look at Mrs. Morel, paying attention, as earlier promised, to a few cues offered by the teller Lawrence's demi-informed, "polyanalytic" dissent with Freud. A brief summary is worthwhile, both for the light it sheds on *Sons and Lovers* and for the nontheological translation it gives to the novel's "Foreword."

Lawrence regards Freud as an amoralist who has invented an unconscious stewing with fecal waste and incest fantasies. "The true unconscious," Lawrence declares, isn't a catch-basin but "the well-head, the fountain of real motivity."[16] Incest cravings and sexual phobias certainly exist, but as consequences of aberrant experience in a particu-lar social matrix. I say "aberrant" because Lawrence posits a norm whereby a child's parents instinctively coordinate their influences, the mother appealing to his "upper centers," his mind and heart, while the father arouses the "lower centers," the rough life behind and beneath the solar plexus. Such a normative interaction, with parents actually getting it right, sounds like a pop psychologist's golden age, and Lawrence is of course no better than the next prophet at describing or even locating that time. We can at least entertain his assumption that the predominantly agrarian, village-centered England—the civilization Flora Thompson would soon depict in her deservedly classic *Lark Rise* trilogy (1939–1943)—corresponded with his norm rea-sonably well; and that by Edwardian times, thanks largely to the socioeconomic developments that we might title "from Lark Rise to Bestwood," the parental balance has been upset, the norm has been forgotten, ignored, or dismissed, and the aberrant has become the normal.

Thus from Lawrence's perspective the typical husband has ceased to command his wife, to show her a high mission requiring her aid, and she has in consequence carried her love to her son, her surrogate lover. She offers "a final and fatal devotion . . . which would have been the richness and strength of her husband [but] is poison to her boy." Since social taboos keep her from stimulating his "lower centers" directly, she the more excites his "upper" ones, closing a bond of sympathy too like the platonic attachments of the characters Lawrence portrays in Hermione's country house or Halliday's London-Boho crowd in *Women in Love*, with their wavering, polymorphous, and in any case ideational sexualities; or too like the bloodless loyalties promoted by "child-schools, Sunday-schools, books, home-influence."

Since the son's and mother's lower centers were once linked by the umbilical cord, her effort to excite his soul willy-nilly excites his genitals. Unable in conscience to respond to his mother like *that*, he directs his sexuality back onto himself, in reverie and masturbation. And thus he grows older, enthralled spiritually to his mother, erotically responsive to her mentally if not physically, impotent in sum to make what an anthropologist might call a sincerely exogamic commitment. Of course he needn't think exogamically till he is into puberty. Before that—and here the language unmistakably evokes Paul's and his creator's own prepubescence—

> Everything comes to him in glamour, he feels he sees wondrous much, understands a whole heaven, mother-stimulated. Think of the power which a mature woman thus infuses into her boy. He flares up like a flame in oxygen. No wonder they say geniuses mostly have great mothers. They mostly have sad fates.

Sad, since the son of such a mother will have a next-to-impossible time finding another woman who can "infuse" that much "power" into him, and not least because the maternal infusion is, in the family context, so quick and easy, "without the shocks and ruptures inevitable between strangers." A normative romance is thus forestalled, "The cream [being] licked off from life before the boy or the girl is twenty. Afterwards —repetition, disillusion, and barrenness."[17]

What follows "Afterwards" in *Sons and Lovers* itself sounds wretchedly like a "drift towards death," the phrase Lawrence used, somewhat misdirectingly, in his plot summary to Garnett, describing Paul's "derelict" condition at the end. The prepubescent "glamour" sounds—well, "wondrous" and "heaven"-like, as though for the richly endowed male "genius" the brightness of the mother-kindled flame could somehow compensate for his troubles with other women or for the brevity of life. So happy is Paul's relation to his mother, as they innocently keep house together and as they merrily holiday to Nottingham or to Willey Farm, that on first reading we can't easily mark the threshold of his debility. Subsequent readings will suggest that these innocent or merry intimacies are the beginnings of trouble, which might have been avoided had the father been able to draw Paul to himself, both at age 2 and at age 14. As it is, the lad regards her both as his mother, a woman to worry about and be embarrassed by, and as his "sweetheart," a girl to take out on a date. The ambiguity of this relationship becomes painful by the time they go to Lincoln. He is put off by her crow's feet and frustrated by her slowness in walking up hill. "Why can't a man have a *young* mother? What is she old for? . . . *Why* can't you walk? *Why* can't you come with me to places?" (282). This is the thoughtless cry of youth against the extinction of its first friend, what has been its surest joy. When she is dying of cancer, it is clearly intimated that she has taken sick, or at least hasn't consulted a doctor, because she unconsciously understands that she *has* to die before Paul can move on to another woman, in a distinct life of his own. Round her sickbed he may unconsciously understand it too, as he at one moment whispers to her as to a bride, and at the next prepares, with a strange titter, her milk and morphine. It is as though he were saying, "Yes, I love you, filially and more, but I must also, in mercy, kill you—because the 'and more' is killing *me*."

When the drink has done its work and she lies dead, he approaches her almost like the Prince who wakes Sleeping Beauty.[18] She looks "like a maiden asleep," as young now as he is, and since his father is staying away, afraid, *he* can be the lover who rouses her back to life. But the facts—the coldness of the corpse he "passionately" kisses isn't a Gothic touch, it is just the case—say no (443). The contact may be ghoulish enough to suggest to him that in future he should look not for sleeping beauties—who knows what they will be like when they wake?—but for beauties whose eyes are already open. That, surely, is the "hygienic" message. Still, just as surely, Lawrence refrains from condemning all erotic connection between son and mother. The narrator, as we have seen, defies the "hygienists" who would disapprove of the young adolescent Paul sleeping with his mother when he is down with bronchitis, as I believe he would defy those who would expunge every "sweetheart" or "lover" signifier in Paul's account of his late adolescent feelings toward her. In his particular case, the filial and the amatory can't be compartmentalized.

The misfortune of the case has been evident since his and Miriam's frustrations with each other first surfaced. The pity of it is evident in another tremendous chapter ending, that of "Strife in Love," just after he has once more failed to kiss the toothsome Miriam—he *can't*, till he drives "something out of himself" (247)—and then had his bitter discussion with his mother, who has complained that Miriam would absorb so much of him that she herself would be nowhere.

> [Paul] had taken off his collar and tie, and rose, bare-throated, to go to bed. As he stopped to kiss his mother, she threw her arms round his neck, hid her face on his shoulder, and cried, in a whimpering voice, so unlike her own that he writhed in agony:
> "I can't bear it. I could let another woman—but not her. She'd leave me no room, not a bit of room—"
> And immediately he hated Miriam bitterly.
> "And I've never—you know, Paul—I've never had a husband—not really—"
> He stroked his mother's hair, and his mouth was on her throat.

Not that we need a "Don't try this at home" warning label, but such bare-throat kissing is always in Lawrence an indicator of serious foreplay. Mrs. Morel has throughout her life been a heroine of self-restraint, but this "I've never had a husband—not really" is a step in the direction of Goblin Market, and puts a wretchedly unfair burden on Paul, who is promptly driven to deny all amatory feelings for Miriam and to display them, floridly, to his mother instead:

> "And she exults so in taking you from me—she's not like ordinary girls."
> "Well, I don't love her, mother," he murmured, bowing his head and hiding his eyes on her shoulder in misery. His mother kissed him a long, fervent kiss.
> "My boy!" she said, in a voice trembling with passionate love.
> Without knowing, he gently stroked her face.
> "There," said his mother, "now go to bed. You'll be *so* tired in the morning." As she was speaking she heard her husband coming. "There's your father—now go." Suddenly she looked at him almost as if in fear. "Perhaps I'm selfish. If you want her, take her, my boy."

Morel's footsteps remind her that she does in fact have a husband, however un-"really" she has felt the connection, and that the normative next move for Paul should be to cut the apron-strings.

> His mother looked so strange, Paul kissed her, trembling.
> "Ha—mother!" he said softly.
> Morel came in, walking unevenly. His hat was over one corner of his eye. He balanced in the doorway.
> "At your mischief again?" he said venomously. (252)

Mischief indeed. And as Paul and his father square off to fight—the pork-pie meant for the younger and seized by the older is a metonym for the woman who baked it—she moans in pain. To Paul it is the first palpable hint of the cancer that will kill her, as though, again, her body comprehends that in this crisis the only solution is for her to exit, stage right. That is in Act 5, of course. Here in Act 3, stage right is the parents' bedroom, and Paul—it is another palpable reworking of *Hamlet*—begs her not to go there:

> "Sleep with Annie, mother, not with him."
> "No, I'll sleep in my own bed."
> "Don't sleep with him, mother."
> "I'll sleep in my own bed." (254)

Her firmness marks a commendable moral recovery. Better than Paul, she has understood that in the action prior to Morel's tipsy entrance she has, in a collapse of will, been abetting her son's unconscious, fumbling attempt to cuckold his own father. As the last line of the chapter says, "Everybody tried to forget the scene," and if they can't, they can nevertheless endeavor, in future rehearsals, to revise it.

"Tragedy ought to be a great kick at misery"

For Paul, after his mother's death, such a revision should mean trying to emulate his father, insofar as he, for all his mistakes, had at least managed to step out of *his* mother's sphere of influence and find a mate. With his mother gone, however, Paul feels at first as though everything else might as well go too. The general emptiness, in himself and in the mechanical bustle of Nottingham, seems irremediable. He hasn't yet got the requisite belief in himself to ask Miriam to marry, so he wishes that she would ask *him*. When, to her credit, she refuses to "relieve him of the responsibility of himself," he blames her for offering merely another Christian self-sacrifice, or, in a confusion that doubly binds her, he blames her for demanding such a sacrifice of him: "was it a mate she wanted, or did she want a Christ in him?" "Christ" as in sexless spiritual partner or crucified corpse in Madonna's lap. But those are his projections not hers. "Suddenly she saw again his lack of religion, his restless instability. He would destroy himself like a perverse child. Well then, he would!" Miriam's own "religion" has by now become Unitarianism, that halfway house frequented by the lapsed church- or chapel-goer, but in any event we know it isn't entirely sexless and life-denying. And, while it relishes "the moment's attraction," such a religion also cares, as she feels Paul now doesn't, for something "deeper"—for instance the connection between one moment's attraction and another's, or between any particular attraction and the something-not-ourselves source of all attractiveness. So, confident that when he returns to caring for "deeper" things, he will "come to her," Miriam says good-bye.

Though there is no suggestion that in some sequel Paul *will* return to Miriam, the final page does eloquently imply that he will again concern himself with more than "the moment's attraction"—or, as here, the moment's repulsion and despair. After he has stepped off the tram, as he leans against a stile with the countryside black before him, the theme is spatial connection, the phrasing at once of the Bible and of astrophysics, or, as I maintained at the start of this chapter, of Coleridge and Bentham:

> In the country all was dead and still. Little stars shone high up, little stars spread far away in the floodwaters, a firmament below. Everywhere the vastness and terror of the immense night which is roused and stirred for a brief while by the day, but which returns, and will remain at last eternal, holding everything in its silence and its living gloom. There was no Time, only Space. Who could say his mother had lived and did not live? She had been in one place, and was in another, that was all. And his soul could not leave her, wherever she was. Now she was gone abroad into the night, and he was with her still. They were together.

The matter of the cosmos, including the atoms of his mother's body and of his own, while sometimes intensely concentrated, is now immensely scattered. The spiritual stuff of the cosmos—quite undefined, of course, but here we may simply call it memory—can overcome the scattering's distances. And it is less a question of will than of psychological necessity: "his soul could not"—*must* not, if for the immediate future it is to survive—"leave her." We come back to his body, however, which is *not* "wherever she was." Rather it is here:

> his chest that leaned against the stile, his hands on the wooden bar. They seemed something. Where was he?—one tiny upright speck of flesh, less than an ear of wheat lost in the field. He could not bear it. On every side the immense dark silence seemed pressing him, so tiny a speck, into extinction, and yet, almost nothing, he could not be extinct. Night, in which everything was lost, went reaching out, beyond stars and sun. Stars and sun, a few bright grains, went spinning round for terror and holding each other in embrace, there in a darkness that outpassed them all and left them tiny and daunted. So much, and himself, infinitesimal, at the core a nothingness, and yet not nothing.

It is a Pascalian emotion, made uncommonplace by the pleading, biblical naïvety of "speck of flesh" and "ear of wheat lost in the field,"[19] and the stammering "not nothing" affirmation of somethingness.

> "Mother!" he whimpered, "mother!"
> She was the only thing that held him up, himself, amid all this. And she was gone, intermingled herself! He wanted her to touch him, have him alongside with her.

This pathetic "whimper" has been prepared for. It is the verb describing Mrs. Morel's weeping when William's coffin is brought into the home, or when in the scene quoted above she has cried that Miriam is taking Paul from her too, and it carries the full charge of the symbiosis—sometimes mutualistic, sometimes parasitic, never neutrally commensal—between this mother and her sons. The mutualism between her and Paul has paid dividends; the parasitism has hurt them both. It is time, then, for Paul to invest the dividends but to disengage himself from a destructive parasite:

> But no, he would not give in. Turning sharply, he walked towards the city's gold phosphorescence. His fists were shut, his mouth set fast. He would not take that direction, to the darkness, to follow her. He walked towards the faintly humming, glowing town, quickly. (464)

The "gold phosphorescence," like the "glowing," is associated with Paul's father, as "city" or "town" has for Paul and William been the site of the world's work, especially of *men's* contributions to that work. The words are a final reminder of Paul's masculine inheritance — of what he has got and not got from his father—just as, to keep our balance, the shut fists and the tight mouth remind us of his mother's gritty, determined will.

Lawrence called his book, anchoring *ought*-judgment in *is*-analysis, "a great tragedy,"[20] and in conventional terms it is. Two natural laws divide Paul between them, the one telling him to cherish his mother and the other telling him to leave her and take a wife—as his father once left his mother to take the very different lady who became Paul's mother. Further, his struggle, like Hamlet's, hurts more people than himself. In a letter written while finishing *Sons and Lovers*, however, Lawrence gives the idea of tragedy a less conventional note: "I hate England and its hopelessness. I hate [Arnold] Bennett's resignation. Tragedy ought to be a great kick at misery" (*Letters*, 1.459). The "quick" in Paul, evoked in the book's final adverb, comes as much from father as from mother, and it produces such a kick—not directive or programmatic, needless to say, but at least defiant. That was often the response to misery that came from Lawrence himself. The suffering of the war years had shut him in a tomb, he would later write to Cynthia Asquith (March 9, 1916), but not forever:

> The spring is really coming, the profound spring, when the world is young. I don't want it to be good, only young and jolly. When I see the lambs skip up from the grass, into the sharp air, and flick their hind legs friskily at the sky, then really, I see how absurd it is to grieve and persist in melancholy. We can't control the coming and going of life and death. When it is our time to go, we'll go. But when it *isn't* our time to go, why should we fret about those whose time it is? It is our business to receive life, not to relinquish it. (*Letters*, 2.574)

Paul's stride towards town is a diminished form of this defiance, but the grammar of nature still applies, just as it has done when, going for a walk the day before his mother's death, he has met the donkey in the field and embraced it: life recalls itself to itself precisely when the snow and the night say it is over. One can precipitate many messages out of the black bottle of *Sons and Lovers*, and a principal one, as I have here maintained, is that for Paul the call to life comes from paternal as well as maternal energies. Readers will "get" the message, however, only if they steep themselves in all the bottle's juices. Call it the immersion school of literary criticism, the one, if any, I would myself belong to.

For Lawrence, this *Bildungsroman* was therapy as much as art: "[One] sheds one's sicknesses in books—repeats and presents again one's emotions, to be master of them" (*Letters*, 2.90). He offers no T. S. Eliot hyperbole about escaping emotions. The novelist must rather see them clearly, without letting falsehood or pain distort them, in order that we may see them too. Such purposive vitalism is what prompted my earlier comparison of Lawrence with George Eliot, combining Coleridgean comprehensiveness of understanding with a Carlylean demand for active, reverent response to the "nature" that is outside, inside, and between human beings. Art was never for Lawrence an end in itself; it was a means toward more abundant life. If we can see and feel emotions on the page, we can see and feel them in our rooms, streets, fields— spontaneous life welling up from the blood, urged on but not controlled by the brain. As he says in his justly famous credo, "Why the Novel Matters":

> At its best, the novel, and the novel supremely, can help you. It can help you not to be a dead man in life. So much of a man walks about dead and a carcass in the street and house, today: so much of woman is merely dead. Like a pianoforte with half the notes mute. But in the novel you can see, plainly, when the man goes dead, when the woman goes inert. You can develop an instinct for life, if you will, instead of a theory of right and wrong, good and bad. In life, there is right and wrong, good and bad, all the time. But what is right in one case is wrong in another. . . . And only in the novel are *all* things given full play, or at least, they may be given full play, when we realize that life itself, and not inert safety, is the reason for living. (*Phoenix*, 537–38)

The therapeutic aspect of the novel, then, isn't just for the author, shedding his "sicknesses" —"art for *my* sake," as Lawrence informs the aesthetes. It is for us—art for *our* sake—insofar as it places us in the godly position of judging the quick and the dead, and as it helps us find strategies for aligning ourselves with the former, and learning, finally, to join the latter with a little less anxiety. It is his version of Wallace Stevens's frank insistence that poetry is there to help us live our lives, and to do so fully, before, like Lawrence's own great poem, "The Ship of Death," it readies us for "the longest journey."

"The Ship of Death," written in the final months of Lawrence's life, folds that Shelleyan phrase into a graver context than Forster had done, and for medically obvious reasons. I want to return, in the next chapter, to something like the epicene, Austenian atmosphere of Forster's *The Longest Journey*. Santayana's *The Last Puritan*, that genuinely philosophical *Bildungsroman*, offers a psychology less intensely presented than Lawrence's but just as systematically worked-out. And its bazaar of *Weltanschauungen*, through which the Puritan pilgrim passes, displays goods sometimes more durable than the Cantabrigian bric-a-brac of Forster. In short, Santayana provides an instance of Bunyan's Vanity Fair meeting—well, Thackeray's—save that the stalls are set up mostly in New England, and the comedy of manners and sex yields place to the comedy of morals and metaphysics.

Chapter 7

The Philosophical Apprenticeship of Oliver Alden

A faintly amused smile, too ripe for malice, plays over [Santayana's] lips; and as he walks about slowly, picking up a broken lance or turning over a helmet with the point of his toe, he soliloquies on the old Humanism, the three R's of the modern world, the Renaissance, the Reformation, and the Revolution, and the more ancient R of Romance; takes note of the importance of the supernatural as a logical foundation for the moral absolutism or provinciality of the New Humanists, and ends with an exposition of the moral adequacy of Naturalism. This is the reverie of a harmonious and disinterested mind, picking its own path amid the debris of a controversy: in its very allusiveness, its lack of direction, its refusal to follow the line of battle or even to perform any tender offices for the dead and wounded that are lying about the field, it achieves that sense of intellectual liberation which is the better part of philosophy.[1]

Oliver Alden, the *Bildungsheld* of Santayana's only novel isn't called "the last Puritan" simply because he is at the end of a line. It is also because he expresses a kind of spiritual extremity. Indeed Santayana (1863–1952), whose sensibility Lewis Mumford praised in the passage quoted above, originally thought of calling the book *The Ultimate* (rather than the more suggestive *Last*) *Puritan*. Born in 1890, Oliver is a latecomer. He brings together the moral and social traits of the single Old World tradition that had truly taken hold in the New, and that by his time had largely broken free from the theological myths that had alternately comforted and terrified his forebears. Comfort and terror: the Puritan tradition had in fact been double-sided. There is a fine Augustus Saint-Gaudens bronze entitled "The Puritan," about 30 inches high, a muscular striding figure with the characteristic broad pointed hat and long flowing cape. When one of my sons, then maybe four years old, saw the piece in a museum and I asked him who it was, he didn't hesitate: "Dracula!" That is the terrifying, hard, tough-minded side of the tradition, present in Oliver's given name, which derives from the inspired, not to say fanatic politician and general, Oliver Cromwell. Then there is the comforting, soft, tender-minded side, present in his surname, which derives from his ancestor John Alden, the delicately conscienced and decidedly unaggressive amorist portrayed in Longfellow's poem.[2]

Oliver's mother, who likes symmetry as much as the next unwitting Hegelian, hopes that he will harmonize these two mind-sets, growing up to impose comforting values upon the terrifying facts of the world—thus making it a nicer place for a greater number of people. Of course he does—can do—nothing of the sort. After 600 pages of strenuous dialectics, he simply "peters out," a victim of an absurd auto accident shortly after the 1918 armistice that ended a wasteful war.[3] Very unlucky. His consolation, and ours, is that he has begun to intuit what, for his kind of sensibility, growing up all the way might look like. If only he had better luck, we probably exclaim—though that may miss the symbolic meaning of his early death. And if only he had been born into a more propitious time and place—though that might be wailed about any imperfect life. Still, our "if only's" have their point. Knowing what, for a modern philosophical youth, growing up all the way might look like can prepare us for two very important developments: the advent of a new philosophical poet, and the evolution of the new culture that he or she would speak for and help sustain. Which is what, as I implied at the end of my previous chapter, both Lawrence and Stevens understood we need—a supreme fiction to help us live our lives.

But let me briefly say what happens in Santayana's story, which begins with Oliver's ancestry—his uncle Nathaniel, who embodies the genteel tradition at its Beacon Hill highest and driest, and his father Peter, whose rebellion against all that is spirited but feckless. Middle-aged and independently wealthy, Peter marries Harriet, the pretty but bovine daughter of a Hartford psychiatrist. Oliver, their only child, is raised by his intellectually timid mother and by Irma Schlote, his Goethean-romantic German governess. His father absents himself by taking long voyages on his yacht, ably captained by the handsome Jim Darnley ("Lord Jim"), the going-on-thirty Englishman who befriends the seventeen-year-old Oliver. Hitherto he has been educated by women and schoolmasters; now begins his tutelage under Jim, who, rather more than his own father, seems a real man. Oliver's pursuit of real manhood in college—first at Williams, then at Harvard—is both academic (studying philosophy) and athletic (playing football). He excels at both. He also tries sex, first with his cousin Edith in New York, and second with Jim's sister Rose outside Oxford. But in neither case can he be as natural as Jim or as insouciant as his other cousin, Mario Van de Weyer. These two men, like Jim's father the Anglican rector, Caleb Wetherbee the Catholic historian, the meditative but drug-addicted Peter, and even "Santayana" the Harvard professor himself, play master and journeyman roles in Oliver's philosophical apprenticeship. Before his death, he has himself qualified as a journeyman, and if his master's papers haven't yet been signed, their articles have been drawn up—and dramatized—in the most engaging terms.

The distinction of *The Last Puritan* (1935) is undeniably there, yet it is harder to pin down than one would like. For starters, it has the rare merit of having been a Book-of-the-Month-Club bestseller back in a period, which extended through the mid-century heyday of book clubs such as the Readers' Subscription, when high-middle- and even echt high-brow novels, as well as histories, memoirs, and so on were bought and read by self-improving Americans. Into the early 1960s, indeed, *The Last Puritan* was a favorite college text, as evidenced by the numerous copies of the Scribner's paperback available today in used-book stores. Students cottoned to a coming-of-age novel that featured a hero as surrounded by philosophical spokesmen as Hans Castorp is in *The Magic Mountain*, and that like that German work could be read as a capstone-course summa of the Western tradition. But then the left-radical student politics of the late 1960s drove seemingly nonpolitical and therefore irrelevant literature "off syllabus." Which is one reason why I am turning to *The Last Puritan* here. It possesses an enduring relevance for readers who value superb writing—call it Arnoldian high seriousness conveyed with a wit and elegance reminiscent not only of Arnold himself at his most acerbic but of Oscar Wilde at his cleverest—and who still believe that, speaking of high seriousness, a "criticism of life" is what great books offer. In any event, a novel that has been irreplaceable for readers as diverse as Conrad Aiken, Q. D. Leavis, Trilling, Edmund Wilson, Gore Vidal, Robert Lowell, and Stevens ought to be studied and made current again.[4]

Of the Anglo-American novels I discuss here, it conforms most closely to the template fashioned by *Wilhelm Meister*, especially in its direct engagement with concepts of (in modern jargon) early childhood development, psychosexual identity formation, education, and competitive *Weltanschauungen*. The only way to demonstrate *The Last Puritan*'s quality is the old-fashioned Satanic one of walking up and down upon it: getting to know its hero and the people he meets, and retracing the philosophical patterns Santayana has drawn in their midst. With a novel less known than *David Copperfield* or *Sons and Lovers*, such a procedure will also be the most informative. Reader, in any case, beware: *The Last Puritan* is a genuinely *philosophical* novel, and its filiations with Santayana's wider thought are as compelling as those between, say, the ideas in *Sons and Lovers* and Lawrence's "polyanalytics." Therefore some of what follows will find its way into Santayana's autobiographical, literary critical, and more strictly ethico-metaphysical writings, but in doing so I will only be following the promptings of *The Last Puritan* itself, which on every page is nothing if not suggestive.

The order of interrelated topics is:

(1) the boy Oliver's situation as heir to all the Puritan ages, on the one hand, and as scion of particular—make that *peculiar*—parents, on the other;

(2) his several relations with people who, in thought and action, represent philosophical positions for him to test and ponder;

(3) his persuasion, after much testing and pondering, that a metaphorized Christian Platonism—regarding that "ism" as a poetic myth—is the only ethically right posture; and

(4) his realization that, since he is neither saint nor genius, his spiritual service will consist of standing and waiting for a new philosophical synthesis, and a poet to give it dramatic expression.

Such service is sufficiently "no picnic" to please even Oliver, who, as Santayana says, detests picnics. In any event it doesn't last long: the hero, as noted, dies just as the Great War ends. It is a gesture signaling not only an access of the author's mercy, but also the close, discouraged though hardly hopeless, of the major phase of the *Bildungsroman* tradition as such.

Scion of Puritans: Oliver's Childhood

Let us begin by asking where Puritanism, as a religious worldview, came from. If Oliver is the last Puritan, who—plurally—were the first? Santayana often, in- and outside this novel, reaches back before Plymouth Rock to the sixteenth-century Reformation, the climactic episode in the family romance of Christendom in general and of European racial temperaments in particular. The Nordic child, as Santayana would have it, had properly rebelled against the Latin parent, the Protestant individual declaring that he, not the church, was to be responsible for biblical interpretation. Religious individualism facilitated economic individualism and the consequent growth of the burgher class, and in time made plausible the transcendentalist episte-mology of the German philosophers. As we saw in chapter 2, Santayana traces a line from Luther to Kant, Hegel and company in Germany, and thence to Emerson in America, whereby the Reformers' hermeneutical principles were extended until the priesthood of all believers became the isolation of everyone—believer, unbeliever, and agnostic. Each person was like a Leibnizian monad whose knowledge of the world consisted of nothing more than what it alone perceived, and marked by scribblings on its own interior walls. This is called solipsism. Neither facts nor values could exist, these Reformers-to-transcendentalists argued, unless the individual ego created them. As Santayana said to Edmund Wilson, the mistake of the German transcendentalists, as of the British empiricists like Berkeley, was to claim "that the order of discovery of objects comes before the order of their genesis—as if (he laughed) the idea of our grandfather came before the fact of our grandfather!"[5]

Transcendental idealism's mischief wasn't confined to the library or classroom. "*I* define reality" could become "*we* define reality," and "you" or "they" don't count. Thus, in Germany the poison of "egotism" led to the Great War, and in America the intoxicant of exceptionalism led to imperial wars against Mexico and Spain. By 1917, Santayana believed, the intoxicant had worn off: America was entering a war on behalf of the down-to-earth pluralism of English democracy against the still-poisoned Germans.[6] Oliver's story discloses this political conflict within the turn-of-the-century American mind, and situates it in the process of personal psychological development. From the beginning he is more egotistically isolated—more socially disconnected—than any tyro we have considered, certainly more than David Copperfield, Rickie Elliot, or even little Maisie.[7] Like Wilhelm Meister, he has to *become* socially connected, a self living in con-scious *relation* to other selves. He is an American, in short, who for all his New England Puritanism seems more German than English, and Santayana's treatment of his *Bildung* is accordingly focused more on epistemological, metaphysical, or ethical crises than on the sexual or vocational ones characteristic of English, and most other American, novels of this type. Which makes the image of him at Harvard, sculling in a single shell on the Charles like the figure in Thomas Eakins's painting, so poignantly emblematic.[8]

Not that he, anymore than other children, can get through his early years in singu-larity. He is a member of a family, however oddly thrown together. Here and in his autobiography, *Persons and Places*, Santayana shows abundant knowledge of the drawbacks of family life, but he nonetheless thinks the usual domestic arrangement justified. Beyond their animal needs, children need some tips about how to think and act. "The father talks," says Santayana, and at least for a while the children listen; they learn to talk as he does; they imbibe his principles, his judgments . . . A code of morals, a view of events, is transmitted to them ready-made so that they become his children in the spirit as well as in the flesh. And this even if they rebel against all his maxims; for in doing so they frame maxims of their own, and move on his moral level, or above it.[9]

This is admittedly a rather gold-plated account of the patriarchal household to which Santayana himself belonged in Avila, Spain, for the first eight years of his life. When he was sent to his mother in Boston, he lost his father's immediate guidance and consequently idealized the man's wisdom.[10] Yet he had enjoyed his father's direct influence at least over his early boyhood, while Oliver's boyhood and even adolescence are still another instance of a *Bildungsheld*'s suffering from his father's "absent presence." Peter Alden prefers to live on his yacht, leaving Harriet as the "present presence" in young Oliver's life. The boy is part of a family, but like Santayana's in a different way, it is a family that is fractured.

Harriet is pitifully small game—the "unselfish" sort who tries to control your life "for your own good"—but Santayana hunts her down with matricidal glee. He must be reflecting resentment of his own mother's overdominance during his Boston years, and accordingly he is only mildly curious about the social disabilities that *created* "gentlewomen" like her.[11] True, he does insist on Harriet's natural endowment—her superb physique, "elemental and rooted in nature like the hills" (*Letters*, 271)—but since she doesn't go in for sports and has been taught to dislike sexual intercourse, childbirth, and the business of nursing, fondling, and dandling her boy, her Dianaesque body soon softens into the Junoesque. Little Oliver notices that Mrs. Murphy down by the river is different: she holds her child on her lap even when she is trying to sew. Why? Perhaps, Harriet says, it is because the child is sleepy, or because they are too poor to afford an extra chair. "They get almost to *like* huddling together. It's repulsive, and so bad for the little one's health, and so uncomfortable. But," she concludes "a little sadly," "ignorant people are like that."[12]

She is as uneasy about the spirit, specifically the imagination, as about the flesh. Why trouble Oliver with "Poetry and mythology and religion and remote history, [which] had nothing to do with *life*"? The only reason she can see is to help him "understand better why, in the Middle Ages, they burnt people at the stake" (1.84–85). This *is* one thing he could learn, but of course she leaves out all the spiritual positives from the past—the understanding, as Santayana would phrase it, that religion is morally valid "poetry" intervening on, or infusing itself into, "common life." Harriet knows as well as any Unitarian gentlewoman that the poetry of religion has no scientific and little historical validity. That is, it doesn't accurately explain how the world was made, or, entirely, how people have actually behaved in it. Stupider than most gentlewomen, though, she chucks the whole poetic volume and loses the moral truths it figures. The result is a double Gradgrinding: Oliver has no mother-love to guide him in his quest for the affection of eligible women like Edith and Rose, and no religiously imaginative tradition to guide him toward a spiritual language—terms for understanding not only all those medieval autos-da-fé but also the love songs, heroic ballads, and narratives in stone or glass. These latter phenomena are part of the imaginary world that, first and last, is the only world Santayana finds interesting—where, as against the real, natural world, what is "good" for the human spirit comes about not by accident but by express intention.

Fortunately, for these affective and imaginative concerns Oliver has Irma Schlote, the German governess who does what she can to give him what his mother hasn't. She comes to America as (to repeat) a pronounced romantic, with Goethe's own genial amativeness, professing "how beautiful a healthy sensuality was to round out the character" (1.92). She teaches Oliver *Lieder* and prayers, lets him sit on her lap as she beats time on his knee, rumples his hair "so that he might look more like a genius," or sometimes, when he comes to a hard passage, "stroked his legs." The upshot has its predictable pathos: "One day, without any reason, he climbed up from her knee and put both arms round her neck, holding on very softly and very tight for what seemed to her a long time." He needs to put his arms around *somebody*, and while Irma is glad to serve, she also knows that she is finally not the proper somebody. She therefore stops stroking his legs and waits either for his mother to offer him her lap or, more probably, for him to grow up and find an eligible woman.

Irma has given him just enough affective and imaginative education to let him know all dimly what he lacks, but from a Goethean point of view it is already too late. The growth of his "healthy sensuality" has been baffled by early frosts. He would do better as a pastor, he understands upon Irma's hint, always feeling "locked into a pulpit with a big book open in front of him . . . because the persons he ought to love best, like his mother and God, would always be impossible to hug and it would always be wrong to hug the others [like Irma]" (1.102–03). That he possesses something like a saintly if not a priestly vocation occurs to several people in the story, but Santayana isn't recommending early vows of ascetic renunciation. Any saint or priest must *earn* his vocation through a hard struggle with his own sensuality. He ought to discover what hugging "the others," to say nothing of hugging his mother, is like, before renouncing them out of love for someone or something higher. He ought to—he *has* to—wake up to the body before waking up to the spirit.

Oliver begins by waking up to his body, just like everyone else, and Santayana details the phases with an acuity that has little to learn from (for example) Jean Piaget. Oliver's first world is gastrocentric, good or evil being defined by what gives his tummy and bowels pleasure or pain. His nurse soon helps him identify the existence of things just beyond the alimentary, and outdoor exercise soon brings him into intimacy with organic goings-on in the world at large. What is operative out there is the "universal reptilian intelligence which was not thought, but adaptation, unison, and momentum" (1.123). Later, for Oliver, come horseback riding, sculling, motoring, quarterbacking: his adeptness in these activities is notable, and he appreciates the *measurability* of physical contests. You really know who has won the 440-yard run, as you can't really know whether a particular history or philosophy essay is truly superior or just flashy. Being a good athlete isn't enough for Oliver, however, partly because there is no affective contact—his football teammates aren't his intimate friends, at least not off the field—and partly because, qua athlete, his potential for less quantifiable games such as history or philosophy is kept "dumb." As the title of the sports column in my college newspaper used to put it, jocks *can* talk. Only, Oliver's coaches never ask him to.

Back in early childhood, Oliver has felt the desire for something more than the physical the moment he discovered he has a brain as well as a stomach, and found the one more authentically "himself" than the other. In some ways this is no happy discovery, for just as his hands and feet sometimes refuse to do what he wants, his thoughts, among which "he ought to have been able to play as he chose," can also refuse: "The interest would die out, the pictures would fade or become ugly and frightening, and you couldn't stop the silly old words repeating and repeating themselves" (1.82). Inner and outer worlds are alike imperfect and unruly, and the joys they do deliver are transitory and often accidental. To perceive all this—the vanity of life—is for Santayana the beginning of seriousness, and little Oliver, like the Greek philosophers, rapidly moves beyond "the instinctive egotism and optimism of the young animal" by placing his faith not in will but in imagination. It is a Puritan (i.e., ethically "purist") move, for his is a more than commonly *judging* imagination, an "inner oracle that condemned and rejected" what is wrong in the world, and that remains undismayedly "sure of being itself right" (1.83). Call it a *considered* egotism. Anyway, with such a burning light within—one recognizes the morally cocksure type among adults, but here are the childhood beginnings—it is no wonder that he looks almost reproachfully at grown-ups when they tender their moral commonplaces. What do *they* know about real good and evil?

Santayana offers a genetic hypothesis to account for the purity of soul that can't find lasting satisfaction either on the playing-field or in the classroom. The temperamental differences between male and female, he wittily imagines, may reflect their different chromosomal structures.

> It would have been so simple for the last pair of [Oliver's] chromosomes to have doubled up like the rest, and turned out every cell in the future body complete, well-balanced, serene, and feminine. Instead, one intrepid particle decided to live alone, unmated, unsatisfied, restless, and masculine.

As a male, the embryonic Oliver has "chosen"—let us allow Santayana his fantasy—"the more arduous, though perhaps less painful adventure, more remote from home, less deeply rooted in one soil and one morality." He is crossed, however, with a longing for that final doubled chromosome, "a nostalgia for femininity, for that placid, motherly, comfortable fullness of life proper to the generous female." He is therefore uncomfortably androgynous, with too much feminine "sensitiveness," the pitying "capacity for utter misery," to ride roughshod over all obstacles like your male American red-blood, and yet with too much masculine curiosity, too much muscular enterprise, to stay at home like your female American mollycoddle. At which point it should be clear that a tongue-twisting deconstructionist charge of phallogocentrism would be hasty: for Santayana, as for Lawrence or more recently even for Julia Kristeva, masculine and feminine aren't necessarily sex-specific labels. Leaving genetic fantasies to the side and drawing the common-sense inference, the psychological lesson in Oliver's case is that putting the Cromwell together with the Alden won't be easy.

It is to Oliver's credit that he keeps looking for the unappeased "feminine" in himself—the nineteenth-century romantic potentiality that Irma has stroked and sung into consciousness—but at the age of five it is the "masculine," twentieth-century part of his personality that predominates. He likes machine toys that work perfectly, or pets that can be trained to act like machines. They can be more exact and obedient than mother or governess, and can give the boy a sense of his own material ascendancy (1.105–06).

There is nothing surprising about such egoism in a child, who quite naturally looks on all experience as food for his own peculiar development, his own exercise of power over his environment. As Nietzsche understood, the will to grow, in any young plant or animal, is the will to power: "An acorn in the ground does not strive to persevere in the state it happens to be in, but expands, absorbs surrounding elements, and transforms them into its own substance, which itself changes its form." This is the way with young things. But if one follows the biological analogy, as Nietzsche failed to do, one observes that the not-young are different: "when the oak is full grown it seems to pass to the defensive and no longer manifests the will either to perish or to grow."[13] That is to say, one task of the grown-up is to put aside the heedless expansionism of youth, and try to live in stable equilibrium with his environment. Masculine adventurism should at some point—and there is obviously no solid rule to tell when—give way to feminine rootedness, a contented sense of place and proportion. The middle-aged person settles into a quiet domesticity. The middle-aged country—what Germany ought to have recognized itself to be in 1914—stops gobbling up territory and settles down within its borders to keep shop.

To return one last time to Oliver's early childhood. He takes the first theoretical step beyond egoism toward maturity when, never questioning his instincts, he concludes, like the undergraduates relearning the obvious at the opening of *The Longest Journey*, that the world perceived through his senses, quite apart from his ideas about it, is "really there." A philosophy class might make him question it when he goes to school, but for now he believes that his bottle still exists when it isn't in his mouth; that his pony and Mrs. Murphy, like the river and the trees, are "there" though he may not be touching, seeing, hearing, or smelling them. These are by no means extraordinary discoveries, but by keeping faith with what his animal instincts believe, he in one step gains epistemological terra firma. He inoculates himself against the "artificial idiocy" of the transcendentalist—the childish solipsism of the romantic who believes that the world exists *only* insofar as he perceives it, and that it is therefore a playroom whose walls he can paint, fingerprint, or kick in as he will. Not to become—or to cease being—a transcendentalist is, for Santayana, a major philosophical achievement. Oliver's perceptions are of course relative to his own sensory equipment, but they are nonetheless "reports" of external objects, reports reliably similar to those gathered by the equipment of the other animals, human or not, who live in his neighborhood. Sure that the external world of nature—not "landscape" but stark matter—is real, and that he is a dependent part of it, Oliver will be in a position to recognize the importance of trying to come *into relation* with it.

Relation with what, in particular, and with whom? That is an exceedingly difficult question, especially for someone as singular as he is. But by never repenting his early common-sense belief in the world's independent reality, he can approach that question in terms refreshingly different from those used by other direct descendants of Wilhelm Meister, the heroes of strictly Teutonic productions like Eduard Mörike's *Maler Nolten* (1832) or Gottfried Keller's *Der grüne Heinrich* (1854–1855). As an American—it is a "complex fate," fortunately—Oliver is the beneficiary of English empiricism as well as German idealism. The "there-ness" of other things, other people, and his own interdependence with them, is never in doubt. But that is also why his ultimate estrangement from them is so damaging.

Persons and Positions: Oliver's
Philosophical Pilgrimage

Wilhelm Meister exemplifies the adventurism of the romantic, Goethean ego: the restless renouncing of one good for another, and that for another, ad infinitum. Santayana fully grants the necessity of renunciation but objects to the "godlike irresponsibility" with which Goethe and his heroes cast off their goods—particularly their lovers. Why? Because these romantic questers are guilty of a species of stupidity—or insensibility. They have failed to draw from their love affairs the Platonic conclusion Santayana thinks a mature mind can't avoid: the unsatisfactoriness of love affairs—and love is alleged to be the least unsatisfactory sort of affair—implies that the ideal happiness they promised really resides elsewhere, in a spiritual realm "beyond." The "barbarism" of Walt Whitman and Robert Browning, a derivative of Goethe's romanticism, lies in their addiction to a non-teleological series of intense, mostly sensual moments—which for Santayana means a purblind adolescent belief that one has "an infinite number of days to live through . . . with an infinity of fresh fights and new love affairs, and no end of last rides together."[14] Growing up requires that one distinguish those experiences that truly satisfy from those that don't.

Which ones *do*? Not the sensual, as in Whitman, or the psychologically passionate, as in Browning, but the intellectual, as in Dante and the Italian Platonists: "The fierce paroxysm which for [Browning] is heaven, was for them the proof that heaven cannot be found on earth, that the value of experience is not in experience itself but in the ideals which it reveals" (*Interpretations*, 139–40). Dante's development is paradigmatic. When disappointed in the flesh, as "all profound or imaginative natures" must be, he transformed the real Beatrice, a child of seven, into "a symbol for the perfect good yet unattained" (93). In doing so, Dante only retraced the grammar of emotional development delineated by Plato, who "had had successful loves, or what the world calls such, but [who] . . . could not fancy that these successes were more than provocations, more than hints of what the true good is. To have mistaken them for real happiness would have been to continue to dream" (100). Though, as we will see, Santayana isn't exactly a Platonist, he quite agrees with the Greek that amorous failure is better than success as an incentive toward the Good.

This progression from the sensually or psychologically to the intellectually or spiritually intense—from ephemeral to perdurable satisfactions—has evident affinities with Kierkegaard's aesthetic (i.e., sensual), ethical, and religious "stages on life's way," and puts Santayana in philosophical alliance with an Anglo-Catholic like T. S. Eliot, and in opposition to Lawrence, who though hardly an amoralist, as I have argued, belongs by and large to Kierkegaard's aesthetic or Santayana's barbarous stage, or to Forster, whom political events, especially in the 1930s and 1940s, had pushed into the ethical. Beyond the ethical, however, Forster could not go. The "bou-oum" of the Marabar Caves has naught to do with spirit or with the Good. It has to do with Nothing. Santayana knows about Nothing, but he isn't a caveman. Like Plato's brave prisoner who escapes the cave, he believes with Forster that the properly human thing is to behold the real world in the light of day, but further (again like Plato) to imagine a still *more real* world—that is, a morally better one.

In any event, what kind of "stuff" does Oliver display as an aesthetic stage amorist? Not much, sadly, after the pervasive chill of his mother-dominated home, but it is nonetheless interesting to see the serpent try to get out of the egg. The first object of Oliver's erotic devotion is the Jim Darnley Peter calls "Lord Jim," in affectionately jocular reference to the disgrace of his having been caught talking about, if not actually engaging in, same-sex sex while serving as midshipman on one of His Majesty's cruisers.[15] In fact, Jim is vigorously bisexual, and Oliver is alternately jealous of his relationship with Minnie the barmaid, and grateful for whatever manly hugs he gives to *him*. If Jim had to choose, he says he would "place a young friend like [Oliver] high above all the women in the world if only he dared call his soul his own and had the courage of his feelings" (2.102). But Oliver doesn't dare—or doesn't want to. His abstinence is motivated partly by fear (buggery is painful and ostracizable), partly by principle (it seems wrong because infertile, and is finally so null). The nullity is something Jim is intelligent enough to understand: "What," he asks, "is love-making [with whatever sort of partner] but a recurring decimal, always identical in form and always diminishing in value?" It can't bring on the "better world" Oliver Platonically yearns for. But Jim also understands that "it's no use trying to live on principles contrary to nature" (2.104). Lovemaking, even the same-sex sort, is part of nature, something the postpubescent simply do for pleasure without thinking, and it is childish to recoil from it. Hence it *is* Oliver's "duty" to see what he can do as a lover, if not with a man then with a woman. Considering the sorry results, which would surely detumefy the average fellow, we can't say it is altogether courage that he lacks. It is ordinary inclination. Even if he could square his fears and his principles with the come-ons of this bum or that bush, the fact is he isn't truly attracted. He is temperamentally virginal, like Hardy's Sue Bridehead, who, as Lawrence astutely remarks, *ought* to remain inviolate, since like Cassandra she has other work to perform.

Oliver's first heterosexual experiment is with his cousin Edith, who may wear a low-cut gown to show men what they may not fondle and go to church to console herself for her brother's early death, but who at least has the advantage of being less confused than Oliver about the psychology of love. His heresy is ideolatry. That is, he projects an *idea* of her: she is to play Iphigenia and lead him, Orestes, back into health and safety. She rightly declines to mix the roles of wife and sister, or lend herself to a salvationism that, as it isn't Christian, she can't comprehend. We all must live alone to some degree, she tells him. "I almost think you are one of those rare persons called to a solitary life in a special sense" (2.228). To Oliver, however, prophetic or priestly celibacy seems selfish, not to say presumptuous; therefore he turns to Jim's sister Rose, and with much the same results. He tries the Iphigenia stunt with her too, hoping she will cure the Orestesian *Weltschmerz* that ails him and show him how to spend the trust fund that is too big for him. He is so persistent and obtuse that she finally has to turn cruel: "Can't you see that I would rather die than marry you?" (2.321). What she wants is "natural, irresistible, unreasoning love," of which lust is a ground-zero form. And lust, as Oliver's encounter with the poor baronne in Paris shows, is simply not in his blood any more than it has been in his parents'.

It is perhaps right, then, for him to think of women symbolically if he thinks of them at all. Only, he should entertain the symbols in his own mind and not expect the women themselves to bother with them, or him. Let him contemplate them as irised Iphigenias or as roseate Beatrices (2.129–30), emblems of the imperishable Good.

But his contemplations will never rise to Dante's level because he isn't starting out on Goethe's. That is, one doesn't describe a persuasively symbolic Beatrice without first having truly loved her in the flesh—Dante's example, with his seven-year-old girl, showing that "truly" need only mean "feelingly." As Santayana writes in *Three Philosophical Poets*, there is such a thing as vulgar spiritualizing, a factitious *metanoia* (personal conversion), detected whenever love is facilely "extended Platonically and identified so easily with the grace of God and with revealed wisdom." We suspect in such cases

> that if the love in question had been natural and manly, it would have offered more resistance to so mystical a transformation. The poet who wishes to pass convincingly from love to philosophy (and that seems a natural progress for a poet) should accordingly be a hearty and complete lover—a lover like Goethe and his Faust—rather than like Plato and Dante.[16]

That final phrase crawfishes away from any assumption that Plato and Dante are the unsurpassable symbolists of the erotic. Santayana appears after all to want a Beatrice who died somewhat older and not as a virgin—a Gretchen glorified as in Goethe, but also systematically beatified, brought into a rationalist and absolutist ethical vision, as in Dante. A figure, in short, from a poem no one has ever written. But one gets the point about Oliver: he would be a more impressive Saint Anthony if he sometimes felt an urge to look over his shoulder at the sirens on the hillside. Yet there we are. We have to take "the third sloppy wash in the family tea-pot" (*Letters*, 305) as we find him, the product of mother-love deprivation and, more mysteriously, of genetic disinclination. His most interesting development is going to be "purely" spiritual.

He is spiritually pure in the regrettable sense of being, as a child, a culturally disinherited waif, a tabula almost rasa who is given only Irma's German songs and prayers during the week, and humdrum Unitarian uplift on Sundays. Today he would be a very recognizable kid, from an unchurched and bookless family, and a never-mention-Christmas-or-Passover public school. The Bible, for Oliver, may as well not exist, and toward the forms of imaginative literature he *has* encountered, he feels an almost Augustinian disdain. "The human world was so horrible to the human mind," he thinks, "that it could be made to look at all decent and interesting only by ignoring one half the facts, and putting a false front on the other half. Hence all that brood of fables" (1.122). His is nonetheless a case of *fructuous* disinheritance, insofar as his sense of basic decencies (telling the truth, fulfilling obligations) is fervently absolutist—to an extent that would embarrass his mother, who inculcated it into him, if she knew anything about him.

He fully expects, first, that the world will answer to the norms governing *his* conscience—there need be no congregation, no polity, behind him—and second, that other people will, like him, tell the truth, or if they don't, they will be ashamed and repent. He soon discovers that the world isn't like that. Not only will some people lie and cheat quite shamelessly; there are also perfectly acceptable alternatives to telling the flat truth, whether the commonplace one of fibbing to protect someone or something valuable, or the more unusual one of fictionalizing—telling an imaginative story—to reveal a truth that can't be got at directly. Such a story may be represented in a book; or in someone's role-playing demeanor, voice, and conversation; or in a religious institution. Since Oliver belongs to no such institution, his access to "imaginative story" must be through books (reading Plato, say) and through people like Irma, Jim, Caleb, Mario, the Vicar, and his father, who all have "stories" that contribute to Oliver's philosophical education. Behind each story is a faith, the several characters representing, in what one might oxymoronically call a supple allegory, philosophical positions—as I have said Irma represents Goethean romanticism.

Jim's position is naturalism. It may be limited, but it begins in the right place—the body's capacity for taking in food, drink, or sexual pleasure, and its ability to sail a ship or swim a race. He also looks like a gentleman, as did John Francis Russell, the second Earl Russell, after whom Santayana modeled him.[17] He has "animal faith," one of Santayana's best known phrases, signifying the quality that drives the birds to build their nests, and their fledglings to take flight into

> a hard but tolerably stable world that has bred those instincts and encouraged that faith in the [bird] race for millions of years . . . We ourselves, amid our thousand cross-purposes and perverse discussions, need that instinctive faith and pure courage for our simplest acts, those that we do well, such as throwing a missile, or making tools, or wooing a mate, or defending ourselves and our friends and families.[18]

Jim throws, makes, woos, and defends so well both because he has a good physical endowment and because he has plenty of unsentimental encouragement from his tribe. His "mother stands up for her young cub against the world," while Oliver's mother, he comes to notice, "always stands up for the world against her young cub" (1.177–78). The philosophical consequence of animal faith is a profound materialism or naturalism— the conviction that "human affairs *were* natural phenomena," just as Jim treats them, "and the whole trouble came from trying to regard them otherwise" (1.172)—or that, as Santayana says in *Persons and Places* apropos of the sporting English temper, "Man was not made to understand the world, but live in it" (*Persons*, 287).

Duty is therefore not an unconditional absolute imposed *ab extra*. It is an innative method of securing particular goods—whatever the human animal in given circumstances happens to need, and can get. Nothing could be more egotistical than to suppose, as boyish Oliver initially does, that "The most subjective of feelings, the feeling of what ought to be, [can legislate] . . . for the universe," whether the ought-to-be picture being promoted is the love of one's neighbor or "the beauty of a warrior's death" (*Three Philosophical Poets*, 181). In brief, Jim is like Nietzsche rebuking Kant (or Aristotle rebuking Plato), and is therefore a model of sanity. He not only lives in the world, as nature means for her creatures to do, but he impartially tries to understand it. Which, if he is mentally going further than nature intends, is at least in the proper *attitude* of nature. He ignores others' bullying claims about his categorical duty to God or Caesar, and just tries to satisfy his own desires—for a meal, a swim, a lover, or money, which underlies nearly everything in a society that is materialistic in the shallow sense. Which, by the way, must be why Santayana makes Oliver independently wealthy: he can then freely concentrate on less shallowly materialistic facts.

There is nothing wrong with Jim's simple, materialistic morality as long as he is sailing. The globe *is* three-fourths water, and he is "your young Triton," perfect, like Joseph Conrad's MacWhirr or Singleton, when upon the waves. But he is after all "a land animal" like the rest of us, and whenever he comes ashore to provision himself "the most vulgar seaport debauchery [can] . . . infect and destroy him" (2.87–88). Nor is it just the pimp and the publican who victimize him. He is also subject, like Herman Melville's Billy Budd, to the land's law, which penalizes acts such as homosexuality (or knocking down someone who has traduced you) that at sea are only "natural." Even if these conflicts were absent, Jim still would suffer the gradual decline of his own body, a psychosexual event that he has foreseen, and can therefore resist longer than most, but that he can't postpone indefinitely. He spends some time acting in Hollywood before being killed in the early days of the war when his ship is sunk by a U-boat.

At an early point, Jim trots out the "I could turn and live with animals" passage from Whitman's *Leaves of Grass*, which Peter, with Santayana's full endorsement, rejects as facile primitivism:

> I should have liked it well enough if he had said that he could turn and *no longer* live with the animals, they are so restless and merciless and ferocious, possessed with a mania for munching grass and gnawing bones and nosing one another, when they don't make me sick saying they are God's chosen people, doing God's work. But Walt Whitman is as superficial as Rousseau. He doesn't see that human conventions are products of nature, that morality and religion and science express or protect [not just repress and sublimate] animal passions: and that he couldn't possibly be more like an animal than by living like other men. (1.195)

What is animal and material may be the *substance* of human nature, but it isn't *all* that is real. Emotion and thought, stimulated by the body's interaction with the environment and, while doubtless having an animal–material basis, seeming at the same time separate from it, are real too. Which means that systematized emotion and thought—our moral, religious, and scientific ideas—are as integral to the world as grass, bones, and noses. Ignoring the separability of emotion and thought from the body that feels and thinks them, Jim reduces all mental phenomena to their material base and, frankly, he often hits home, as when identifying Caleb's or Hamlet's sexual repression. But a mental phenomenon, say Caleb's idea about the neglect of spirit in America, or Hamlet's about the abuse of alcohol in Denmark, isn't necessarily invalidated because the man who conceives it is embittered, or because the culture he addresses is deaf to his criticisms. People's moral imaginings will in many instances outlive those who con-structed them, and will then seem to be conventional "products of nature" just as much as are the methods of farming and fighting, and will have the similar function of protecting and improving our life in—well, the only "place" we have to live—the flesh. Science has its concepts, but what most interests Santayana are the *ideals* of the humanities, the overlapping disciplines of philosophy, religion, and (his umbrella term) poetry. Looking back on his *Interpretations*, he recalls having

> insist[ed] that Platonic ideas and the deities and dogmas of religion were *ideal* only: that is to say, they were fictions inspired by the moral imagination, and they expressed unsatis-fied demands or implicit standards *native to the human mind*. Ideals belonged to poetry, not to science or to serious hypothesis. They were better than any known or probable truth. Far from being less interested in them than if I had thought them true, I was more keenly and humanly interested, for I found them essentially poetical and beautiful, as

mere facts are not likely to be. They are acts of worship on the part of the real addressed to the good. ("Apologia," 497, my italics)

Such ideal "acts or worship" criticize things as they are—the "known or probable truth," the "mere facts"—while also projecting how things ought to be—the "better," "beautiful" world envisaged by poetry. And being "native to the human mind," they are "products of nature" that any valid philosophy must take into account. One doesn't learn about Babylonian culture just by conning cuneiform laundry lists; one also, and primarily, reads *Gilgamesh*.

If one mistake is, with Jim, to reduce moral imaginings to "mere" expressions of animal needs, another mistake is, with the mystic, to dismiss such imaginings because they are limited to particular human perspectives, which in God's eye are all equally insignificant. Santayana has identified Oliver as a mystic (*Letters*, 302), but of what sort? The answer is complicated. Santayana himself consistently backs away from what he calls absolute mysticism, the Indian writers' identification of the "final peace . . . with a longing to be merged in [the figurative sea of] primeval substance, which is an unlimited potentiality" ("Apologia," 569). On the literal sea, certainly, there are no moral, no regulative ideals at all, and for land animals like us, this suspension of moral judgment is unnatural: it renounces what is basic to our existence, namely "the *natural* attitude of welcome and repulsion in the presence of various things. . . . the essential assertion that one thing is really better than another [that is] involved in every act of every living thing" (*Interpretations*, 74, my italics). Living creatures are by nature selective and judging: that's too hot, that's too cold, this is just right. From which it follows that even sea-dwellers like fish and seaweed can't be absolute, non-judging mystics. They don't want annihilation in serene godhead; like Jim, they want the chance to live on their own as long as they comfortably can.

Peter tries to become an absolute mystic, though his attainment of "the final peace" is less through meditation than through medication. His son Oliver's Puritan conscience feels "rebuked" by the "strange spirit of holiness . . . the inscrutable, invincible preference of the mind for the infinite," on the face of his opium-soothed, comatose father. It occurs to Oliver "that life, as the world understands it, was the veritable *dope*," and "obedience to convention and custom and public opinion perhaps only . . . a cruel superstition" (1.184). At once, therefore, he becomes a sort of halfway mystic, able to detach himself, as Santayana later said, from "all the conventions . . . [represented by] his mother, the Harvard philosophers, and even the Vicar's religion" (*Letters*, 302)—but unable, and unwilling, to let evil evaporate into a universal harmony. Evil would in such case be not explained but forgotten, not cured but condoned. And the very sensibility that makes him a fully human animal, his instinct for discriminating in a given instance between what is *for him* better or worse, would then be undermined.

He will come to learn that for someone or something else, his worse will be better, his better worse. And not only this, but that all imaginative constructs, about physics, economics, communication, and divinity, as well as about moral good and evil, are relative to the people who conceive them. No system, therefore, not even in the hard sciences, can be unreservedly trusted. But all systems may be used and trusted, up to a point, as *symbols*—those of science to express our relation to physical reality, and those of poetry and religion to express our moral destiny within that reality. This reserved trust in symbols is almost always quite sufficient. To be sure, some symbols are more "conducive to human purposes or satisfactory to human demands" than others. The test—and here Santayana is "pragmatic"—lies in how well a particular symbol, like a navigational chart, gets us where we want to go:

> Our logical thoughts dominate experience only as the parallels and meridians make a checker-board of the sea. They guide our voyage without controlling the waves, which toss forever in spite of our ability to ride over them to our chosen ends. Sanity is a madness put to good uses; waking life is a dream controlled. (*Interpretations*, 14, 182)

Some of our projects in applied science may, of course, feebly control our material environment, as none of our projects in morality can claim to do. We may take seismic readings of the rock beneath our feet and find oil, or plot a course from one planetary rock to another, but our power over the universe has never been affected by calling this rock morally good or that rock morally evil.

But what about the mixed material and spiritual environment that is specifically, socially human? There, surely, our moral projects *do* exert some control—never lasting, often frail, occasionally profound, but always necessary if, like the Greeks, we are to build, on whatever acropolis, a civil refuge above the surrounding "fatal flux" of barbarism. That flux

> was not so fluid that no islands of a *relative* permanence and beauty might not be formed in it. . . . The Greeks, whose deliberate ethics was rational, never denied the vague early Gods and the environing chaos, which perhaps would return in the end: but *meantime* they built their cities bravely on the hill-tops, as we all carry on pleasantly our temporal affairs, although we know that to-morrow we die.[19]

In the human world, this rock may be designated morally good simply because it has belonged to me and my kin for generations, and that act is morally good because it preserves the rock against the assaults of other kinship groups, or of wind and rain.

Oliver's serious attention to the various moral and religious ideas that, however misguided, have helped erect cities above the flood is finally what separates him not only from Jim, the alert though not fully human animal, but also from his father Peter, the absolute though not fully human mystic. So what kind of mystic is Oliver? He is a mystic in parentheses, non-absolute. Outside parentheses, he is a moral pragmatist, which means absolute till circumstances truly force him to change—to shift his city from one hill-top to another, as his forebears did from the Old World to the New.

"In your heart you must remain a Platonist or a Christian"

As the limitations of Jim's naturalism begin to emerge, his place as tutor–companion to Oliver is taken by Mario, the chirpy Etonian whose Latin, Bacchic insouciance contrasts so strongly with his friend's Nordic, Saint Sebastian-like constraint. "Exotic, only half human, a faun or amiable demon [as against a 'cordial' Bostonian] . . . bronzed all over like a statue, . . . [like] some ancient image" (2.112), Mario is a figure who might have stepped out of a Forsterian fantasy set in Sicily or Greece, save that he is impeccably heterosexual. He hasn't suffered the mother-love deprivation that he notices at the root of Oliver's problems with women, for his own mother nursed him as an infant and caressed him as a boy. The moment he was old enough, she taught him, from *Don Giovanni*, "*Deh, vieni alla finestra*"—

> a love song for her little cockerel, but not a real love song, not serious: something to palm off out of bravado and in disguise on my valet's best girl! Do you catch that? My real love was to be still for my mother; all the rest was to be nothing but nonsense, a licentious dream, or a romp in a carnival. Because you know in that song there is really a lot of passion, but without illusion, Mephistophelian. (2.141)

So it has been: he has saved "real love" for his mother, without suffering any classic Oedipal difficulties while sleeping with other women, whom he pursues as carnival diversions. (If only Paul Morel had such luck.) It is a lusty, Don Giovannian, almost compulsive pursuit, we might think, but in fact Mario is more seduced than seducing. He can't "give it a rest" because to do so would be to forsake his idea of duty. Prima donnas simply call him to their beds, and he goes, like a Goethe or a Byron, both because it is the call of nature, and because it would be rude to say no. Not for him the chivalric Sir Gawain's problems of finding polite ways of declining.

He is mentally as well as sexually vivacious. He wittily exploits the Harvard curriculum, claiming that Barrett Wendell's daily-themes freshman course "Automatically teaches you to write good English. Indispensable training for the tabloid press, and for controlling the future thought of humanity" (2.121). In any case he wants Oliver and himself to take the same courses: "You can go to the lectures and tell me what the professor says, and I will tell you what to think of it" (2.160–61). Then there is his ribald address to Oliver's fraternity at Williams, too ripe to quote. Finally, however, one must turn churlish and acknowledge Mario's flaw. He is like the Faust whom Santayana describes in his essay on Goethe—someone splendidly absorbed in the moment, in whatever desire or cause happens to be "on," but who, with "no philosophy but this[,] has no wisdom" (*Three Philosophical Poets*, 132). Mario hasn't disciplined himself to settle on one ideal that, for passional, logical, or moral reasons, he might perceive to be *better* than others, and that doesn't have to be "on" to be valuable. We see the consequence of this heigh-ho indiscriminateness in 1914. Just as Mario has usually made love to whoever has presented herself, so he goes to war just because *it* presents itself. Soldiers don't know why they are fighting, he says, just as babies don't know why they are born, or grown-ups why they are making love. Like Jim, Mario doesn't act on anything other than animal faith, though of course he serves up the then "on" anti-Semitic, anti-Masonic, anti-parliamentary ideas of Charles Maurras to rationalize the destruction of Europe. Maurras' ideas are grovelingly Hegelian in their "animal" submission to the big battalions, the sheer power of the anti-democratic ruling classes. Santayana believes that a person owes a more-than-animal allegiance to "God or, if the phrase be preferred . . . the highest good of mankind"—an allegiance "to his family, friends, and religion, to truth and to art . . . [rather than] to the state, which for the soul of man is an historical and geographical accident" (*Egotism*, 203). In 1914, therefore, someone like Mario, who as an American is technically neutral, is in a position to bracket the state he fortuitously belongs to and consider his higher commitments. Except that he doesn't.

Santayana's attachment to "God or . . . the highest good of mankind" is obviously a kind of idealism, but what kind, exactly? We may style it a demystified Platonism: the Good is an idea we "conceive" rather than "discover." It is like the literary idea of "David Copperfield," which was first Dickens's and is now ours. Such ideas have themselves no material power to alter the world; rather, after inspiring us with notions of a better life, they leave *us* the task of altering the world accordingly. The idea of the Good that inspires Oliver, from boyhood on, descends from the Christian morality play that saw man's soul as the treasure God and Satan fought for. The play was a projection of the egotistical human imagination—hence the child's attraction to it, even if he knows nothing about Christianity—but made-up and self-aggrandizing though it is, Santayana thinks we do well to carry on *as if* such a morality play were indeed being enacted. Our position would then be only an elaboration of Lucretius': he knew Venus and Mars, like the later God and Satan, were only personifications of the material powers that with one hand produce the things we value, and with the other destroy them. But from the point of view of our particular interests, the difference between these powers is all important, and we try to be as Venusian not Martian as we can (*Three Philosophical Poets*, 27). Which is why it is after all right, in 1917 when America declared war on Germany and its Martian partners, for Oliver to go "over there." Venus favored the democracies because the democracies made life more abundant for their people. Their books, on balance, proved it. So with the Platonic myth of men's ascent out of the cave of the bad up into the light of the Good; it may be "made up" in books, but we try to look on it as a picture of the desirable.

This is what Peter is explaining in his discussion of "Jacob's ladder," a figure deriving from Dante's *Paradiso* XXII, and a passage that is crucial to understanding *The Last Puritan*. At Eton, he says in improved-Herbert Pembroke mode, "sound thrashings and gruelling races" are rungs on a ladder. To climb them is to climb the hierarchy of the school, which mirrors that of the nation. The climb is a struggle, but a boy "feels—I daresay by an illusion—that the result can't be worthless when he has paid such a price for it." The "illusion" is like believing Venus (or Mars) is on our side in the indifferent jostling of atoms. It is a

> myth . . . a picture of what the universe would be if the moral nature of man had made it. I suppose in the universe at large the moral nature of man is a minor affair . . . But [it] . . . is everything *to us* . . . Those who mistake it for an account of the universe or of history or of destiny seem to me simply mad; but like all good poetry, such [a myth]. . . marks the pitch to which moral culture has risen at some moment. (2.38)

Now, Oliver wants to *believe* in Jacob's ladder. To act "as if" he believed would seem to him a charlatan's pretense, like posing as a footballer when he really prefers rowing, or (much more seriously) like trying to reerect the stage-set his Unitarian forebears tore down after his Calvinist forebears' play was over. Perhaps history is just a succession of ladders—world-explaining hypotheses physical, mathematical, psychological, poetical—that are often incommensurable but useful one by one. Oliver doesn't like this view either, for it means the quest for truth, so-called, is just the quest for a fresh idea, which in turn will be replaced by another idea, and so on, in a perpetual unrest of errors. The only way to choose, it seems, is by lurching with eyes closed toward whichever "ladder" is nearest—mercantilism, democracy, social Darwinism, whatever— and that is something Oliver can't do.

His Puritanism, his "hereditary prejudice," lies in his demand for "some absolute and special sanction for his natural preferences," some voice from God, or pure reason, telling him that what he does feel is what he *should* feel—"as if," Santayana interjects, "any other sanction were needed for love, or were possible, except love itself." In other words, love for X or Y can't be validated by reference to some intrinsic good in X or Y. The only intrinsic good—again from the human not the cosmic perspective—is the feeling of attraction, devotion, concern, and so on that we call love. Oliver hasn't yet realized that his love (or faith and hope) must be like other animals'—a "ground-less," "arbitrary," precariously self-justifying attachment to the Good, spun like Charlotte's web out of his own bowels, and therefore peculiar to him as an organism. (Kierkegaard was right: truth is subjectivity.) Oliver must, on the one hand, acknowledge his bowels—his imagination—as the only fount love *can* have: Jim and Mario actually have gone this far. Then he must, on the other, define what the Good he loves *is*: a specifically philosophical task he alone, in this novel, feels called to perform.

The two projects are pursued simultaneously, for to define what he loves is the best way of discovering his capacity for loving. And what does he love? The inner world of moral ideas, to begin with. He *is* a Puritan. But he also loves the outer world, the world of tooth-and-claw struggle that he finds so faithfully presented in Homer. That, he is honest enough to see, is the world that moral ideas must be set *in*, though it is impossible for him to draw his moral ideas *from* that world. To do so would mean becoming a social Darwinist, for whom all virtue would reside in the sharpest teeth and claws, and the devil take the dullest. That may be nature's way, but it seems crimi-nal to him. No, "In your heart you must remain a Platonist or a Christian," he says, not because Platonism or Christianity is underwritten by nature, history, or science, but because each expresses the rebellion *against* nature, history, and science that it is "the very essence of the heart" to foment (2.246). It is Pascal without the wager—that is, without, as he thinks, the delusion.

Oliver talks about Plato and love in an essay he composes at Harvard for "Professor Santayana."[20] He argues that Plato sometimes mistakes desire, which is carnal, for love, which is spiritual—a thesis he realizes is too simple when, in 1918, he reads Plato again. The philosopher "was talking poetry about a love that is an inspiration, a divine madness; whereas I [in the Harvard essay] was talking dead prose about general benevolence, friendliness, and charity," a love full of good works but without warmth (2.323). Not that he should kindle warmth toward any particular person, for whenever he has tried that, with Rose or Edith, Jim or Mario, he has been disappointed: sex has been a let-down, as even Jim could have predicted, and the ones he has loved have been inconstant. But—an even harder prospect—he *should* kindle warmth toward the ideal, toward what may be "only an image, only a mirage, of my own aspiration," but what, detached from the real Rose or Mario in "their accidental persons," can be "truer to *my profound desire*; and the inspiration of a profound desire, fixed upon some lovely image, is what is called love" (my italics). Which leads him to conclude, epigrammatically, that therefore "the true lover's tragedy is not being jilted; it is being accepted" (2.323–24). Such a supersensual passion for the numen is what helped Dante transmute his love for the prepubescent, immanent Beatrice into love for transcendent godhead, and it might help Oliver transmute his shallow desire for a particular lover into "profound desire" for the Good. It is an imaginative vision that, the masses taking it literally and growing numbers of the intellectuals taking it figuratively, captivated two millennia of European culture.

The reasons that, in the wake of Plato's work, Christianity rather than Epicureanism emerged as the West's most persuasive myth about the Good were threefold: (a) its vivified other-world of horrors and enchantments—hell and heaven—made the moral life interesting again; (b) its ascetic discipline enabled men to love rather than fear death; and (c) its doctrines of original sin and a crucified redeemer explained the weariness of earthly existence and offered a desperate way out (see especially *Three Philosophical Poets*, 37 and *Interpretations*, 65). As the Catholic Caleb Wetherbee says in *The Last Puritan* itself, with Epicureanism or "naturalism"

> You will find yourself in an immeasurable physical or logical or psychological universe—your analysis of its substance and movement really makes little difference, for in any case your soul, and everything you love, will be a pure incident, long prepared and soon transcended.

In Christianity or "supernaturalism," Catholics like himself claim that

> A miracle . . . has occurred, both in the manger in Bethlehem and in our souls; and we have understood that [while] astronomy and biology and profane history may show the universe to be manifestly heartless, yet in reality it may be the work of a divine heart of which our heart is a distorted image. (1.205)

This is fetchingly put, but Caleb's testimony is placed in doubt, most immediately, by his unsavory appearance—the horrible grin, the humped back, the "bubbles of foam" on the mouth—which leads Jim to say: "Poor chap, he can't make love, not to any purpose; and he takes to his religion as a substitute" (1.217). This classic case of Nietzschean *ressentiment* aside, Oliver can't believe, or pretend to believe, in a "labyrinth of linked superstitions," Catholic or not. He would perhaps do better to call the superstitions "imagination," however low-wattage, but at least he is in no danger of calling them "science."

Christianity is the sort of "poem" Oliver might well understand, as the Vicar Mr. Darnley sees directly. When sermonizing on how the angel of Death "brings peace and healing and spiritual union with celestial things" to all "who have inwardly renounced the world," the Vicar notes the look of comprehension on Oliver's face (1.267). He is a son of spirit, Jim a son of nature. Nobody, the Vicar says, can be both: "Our Lord himself could not be a soldier, nor an athlete, nor a lover of women, nor a husband, nor a father: and those are the principal virtues of the natural man. We must choose what we will sacrifice. The point is to choose with true self-knowledge," and with the recognition that "sacrifice" entails tragedy:

> For just as the merely natural man ends tragically, because the spirit in him is strangled,
> so the spiritual man lives tragically, because his flesh and his pride and his hopes have
> withered early under the hot rays of revelation. (1.272)

This means, in Oliver's case, the renunciation not only of sex and politics, but of
friends and fellows. He is all alone with the Good, or with the books written by people
who have meditated thereon. It is in short the life of the celibate don who skips the
sherry hour—solitary but, given his objects of meditation, not utterly lonely. A life
rather like Santayana's.

However cut out for such a solitary existence, Oliver not unnaturally wishes he *could*
join a church, preferably the Anglican, which, the Vicar rather wishfully claims, has
preserved the poetry and banished the delusion that were compounded in early
Christianity. But thanks to his tuneless Unitarian childhood, Oliver hasn't grown
up within the imaginative idiom of Christianity, and it is too late to appropriate it
now. The Vicar is isolated as a figurative interpreter of Christianity among literal
believers—that is, as a true Anglican among, I suppose, a bunch of Methodists. But
Oliver is isolated even more strenuously, as a religious soul alien to all religious commu-
nions, and with no frame of discourse beyond that provided by science and profane
history (2.312–13).

The Spiritual Life: Standing and Waiting for a New Philosophical Poet

At one point Irma mistakes the sleeping Oliver's distorted reflection in the mirror
as an image of the crucified Christ—not Michelangelesque but Grunewaldesque,
"mediæval. . . haggard . . . so pitiful, so truly religious and deeply German" (1.241).
But she distinguishes: Christ himself "died to vindicate his knowledge that he was the
Son of God," while Oliver will simply flicker out, "young and unhappy," bringing
salvation to nobody. Why? Santayana tenders three retrospective explanations, two
of which I will treat immediately. First, in the "Preface," he reemphasizes what has
been clear in the representation of Oliver's boyhood milieu, namely his alienation from
any tradition, Christian or otherwise, that would give him a native spiritual idiom
and render his sufferings, his "modern martyrdom," significant:

> He was what the rich young man in the Gospel would have been if he had offered to sell
> his goods and to give to the poor, but then had found no cross to take up, no Jesus to
> follow, and no way of salvation to preach. (1.xv)

That is, he passionately desires to do something heroically virtuous, but he has no
"for whom" or "for what" handily affronting him. Second, Santayana echoes Irma's
concern that Oliver hasn't "the spiritual courage to be himself." The challenge looks
prima facie absurd: If there is "no Jesus to follow," why doesn't he become his own

Jesus, pursue a mission, establish a new gospel tradition, and so on? The challenge sounds extravagant—one remembers Orwell's remark, in his essay on Gandhi, that all saints are guilty till proven innocent—but America is after all a land of self-proclaimed messiahs and Santayana has invested Oliver with spiritual gifts finer than (say) Joseph Smith's. For better or worse, however, he doesn't have even Smith's originality of vision. He knows he is different from naturalists like Jim or Mario, and from super-naturalists like Caleb or the Vicar, but that is merely negative knowledge. "The trouble," Santayana says in a letter, "was that *he couldn't be exceptional, and yet be positive*" (*Letters*, 302). It is a bit like wanting to be the great American novelist but not quite knowing how. You can put sentences together very well, realize characters, and plot an action. You know you don't want to write like the naturalist Jack London or the supernaturalist Flannery O'Connor. But you have no original novelistic voice and vision of your own.

So, Oliver can't be a saint. He also can't be exemplarily commonplace—football hero, fraternity brother, banker—though at first he tries. He finally has enough courage and energy to reject that model, at least, which leaves him the role of quiet prophet, someone critically aware that a saint is certainly needed. While quiet prophets are admittedly the most sufferable kind for the rest of us, it is also true that Oliver's standing and waiting isn't very exciting. But what else would we suggest? He does manage to resist the nascent forms of forced-growth messianism his century would soon produce—the left- and right-wing totalitarianisms that were unwilling to wait for (a) an organically developed saint; and (b) the new philosophical synthesis that such a saint would instaurate.[21] And in any case we should qualify the "stand and wait" formulation not only by recalling Milton's sense of Puritan expectancy—the faith that inspiration and vocation *would* come in time—but also by noting Santayana's important distinction, derived from Aristotle's *De Anima*, between "spirit" and "animal psyche." It is Oliver's "spirit"—namely, the part of his mind that can watch himself thinking, feeling, acting—that stands and waits, while his "animal psyche"—namely, the part of his mind that pays close attention to the exigencies at hand—acts its part. Acts its part sometimes as a free agent, say when he gives money to needy friends, but oft-times as a "conscript." As he says in 1917:

> I have played all their games. I [my "psyche"] am playing their horrible game now. I am going to fight the Germans whom I like on the side of the French whom I don't like. . . . Yet in my inner man [my "spirit"] . . . how can I help denouncing all those impositions and feeling that such duties ought not to be our duties, and such blind battles ought not to be our battles? (2.326)

The spirit witnesses, in most cases sadly, how the psyche behaves, and can judge how it ought to behave better. The spirit distinguishes, for example, between the command-ments imposed by civil authority, which everyone is expected to obey, and those imposed by religious authority. The latter are "Evangelical Counsels of Perfection, like turning the other cheek, taking no thought for the morrow, or loving your enemies . . . as you love yourself." They are impossiblistic ideals, and even to try approach-ing them would bring human life to an end. And yet, Santayana insists, they are nonetheless binding "for any reflective mind, because spirit suffers and enjoys as truly in one man as in another, and is equally helpless and innocent in all." In other words, you are to love your enemy because, in spirit, he *is* yourself. The psyche's interests, however, must still be in subduing the enemy of whatever culture it happens to be part. That is how human life works: people don't commonly let their enemies kill *them*.

Where does that leave the spirit? Santayana refers to the well-known story from the *Mahabharata*, in which

> two armies face each other with drawn swords, awaiting the signal for battle. But the prince [Arjuna] commanding one of the armies has pacifist scruples, which he confesses to his spiritual mentor—a god in disguise . . . His heart will not suffer him to give the word. And then the sage [Krishna], while the armies stand spell-bound at arms, pours forth wisdom for eighteen cantos; yet the conclusion is simple enough. The tender prince must live the life appointed for him; he must fight this battle, *but with detachment*. ("Apologia," 570–71)

So with Oliver. Directed by his animal psyche, he lives his "appointed" life, marches off with the American Expeditionary Force, courts Edith and Rose, looks after his mother, bankrolls Jim and Mario, and so on—"*but with detachment*." His spirit may judge the war to be wrong, Edith glacial, Jim venal, but no matter. His animal psyche, whether praised or contemned by his spirit, plays its part to the end. This bifurcation of mind sounds nearly like a recipe for quietism, as in "Look, people have to do the jobs their culture imposes on them, and their conscience more or less has to go along." That is all right as long as the culture is benign and beneficent, as on the whole Oliver's American culture is. Still, we wonder when his spirit will feel impelled to blow the whistle on his psyche—when, that is, its conscientious objections will really change his behavior. The corrective for quietism, or what Santayana elsewhere calls "umbilical contemplation," isn't cocksure moral fanaticism. It is, as he argues in his taxing but splendid *The Idea of Christ in the Gospels* (1946) and elsewhere, a path between these extremes,[22] which an on-the-whole quietistic person like himself takes when a moral crisis forces him to act—fighting his battle with detachment.

Oliver, certainly, has been brought up to act—to treat quite a lot of moments as crises. He hasn't been brought up to be a passive player of "psychic" parts, with scripts written by the collective at large. He is supposed to have been a leader, someone who, if he were to follow the "Evangelical Counsels" of his spirit and were in Arjuna's position, might very well lead his men *away* from the battle—or would at least open peace talks. As Winston Churchill would later say, "Jaw-jaw is always better than war-war." Yet from the beginning he hasn't liked the responsibility of leadership. He would prefer the "free life" of animals, who, he is sure, don't live for others. And he is drawn to the anti-Carlylean message of his high school teacher who "whittles" down the reputations of heroes, showing that they were merely on the winning side, obeying whatever the "general will" commanded. Oliver wants to live not for but "*with* others . . . not because their ways [are] right or reasonable or beautiful or congenial, but just because those ways, here and now, were the ways of life and the actions afoot" (1.136). He just wants to fit in because, at the end of the day, everyone, even the heroic leaders, must fit in. He thinks that, properly understood, the bird at the head of the wheeling flock isn't taking some bold initiative, which it hypnotizes the others into following. Instead it is the blindest, most dependent bird of all, "pecked into taking wing before the others, and then pressed and chased and driven by a thousand hissing cries" (1.138).

This profoundly naturalistic understanding of the larger game all species play—the feeling that how we act in life has very little to do with personal choice and very much to do with the double-helixed genetic codes of our race—goes deep into the adolescent Oliver. It makes him want to shun leadership positions and, again, just fit in. Nothing could seem more irrelevant than the objections of his Puritan conscience, demanding that certain things be *re*fitted. The sensible move would be to quiet his conscience altogether, if indeed he can't reeducate it. On the other hand, the older wiser Santayana can't help envying, a little, his hero's youthful and Puritan insistence that the problem isn't his conscience, it is the world as it is. Daniel Aaron's review of *The Last Puritan* noted Oliver's affinity with the morally moping Hamlet, who knows something is rotten in the state of Denmark, and, more sympathetically, with the dike-building Faust, who in Holland tries in New Deal fashion to replace the rotten with the sound. Another spiritual link, in Santayana's special sense of "spirit," is with Shelley, who "had, and knew he had, the seeds of a far lovelier order in his own soul . . . [that might] rise at once on the ruins of this sad world, and . . . make regret for it impossible." A deluded and vain beating of wings against the cage "of this sad world," perhaps, but what a splendidly energetic protest just the same. What Shelley lacked was a philosophy sufficiently systematic (and earth-oriented) to make more than a few of the "seeds" within him sprout.[23]

What Oliver lacks—and here is the third explanation for his failure—is what frankly every other twentieth-century American of imagination has lacked, namely the genius to transform our shallowly materialist culture, our faith in gadgetry and dollars, into a profoundly materialist culture, able to accept that to God (or the universe at large) our private moral visions are of small importance. To repeat: the bird at the head of the flock may believe it is leading the way, but in fact it is following the collective, unconscious bidding of the flock itself. Oliver himself, however, though he understands this naturalistic, materialistic analysis, is Puritanically discontent with it. As Santayana tells Mario in the "Prologue": "Oliver hardly got so far as to feel at home in this absurd world: I could never convince him that reason and goodness are necessarily secondary and incidental. His absolutist conscience remained a pretender, asserting in exile its divine right to the crown" (1.11). But what if the conscience of Oliver and American culture generally were persuaded to give up its claim of "divine right"? What would a "profoundly materialist" ethics, if one were possible, look like? How would someone who acknowledges the incidentality of his idea of the Good effectually criticize a "shallowly materialist" civilization?

Dying young, Oliver never finds out. True, he has learnt firsthand how any young American with a spiritual calling, be he Bohemian poet or prep-school Platonist, either suffocates in his garret or agrees to join in the contests the would-be bloods and bankers are taking so seriously. What a relief he feels when, playing for Williams, his leg is broken by the gang-tackling Crimson Tide and he no longer has to quarterback, or pretend to enjoy it. But his criticism never matures to the positive stage, wherein he might articulate the principles of a better life, and the practical maxims about how to realize it. In short, he is part of the large brigade of twentieth-century novelistic heroes, youthful or un-, who are withering in their attacks on modern America's (or Europe's) shallow materialism, who have more than a few intuitions about how a profound materialism might be joined with a searching spiritual critique, but who are without a systematic philosophical vision, to say nothing about a rhetoric that could move others toward it.

Not to despair, though. It is immensely reassuring to share in Oliver's imaginative powers, meaning not so much his peculiar idea of "divine love," which is as unreliably fictive as the symbols—"my false Edith or my false Lord Jim"—he has projected for it, as the very *desire* that has entertained that idea and projected those symbols, and that in principle could someday fashion a more reliable fiction. *Wanting* to get there is more than half the reward. Imaginative mistakes don't matter much. Indeed, he feels, "the falser that object [of desire] is, the stronger and clearer must have been the force in me that called it forth and compelled me to worship it. It is this force in myself that matters: to this I must be true" (2.324). It is, he continues, going to be a scrupulously conscientious as well as imaginatively alert standing and waiting:

> My people first went to America as exiles into a stark wilderness to lead a life apart, purer and soberer than the carnival life of Christendom. . . . We will not now sacrifice to Baal because we seem to have failed. We will bide our time. We will lie low and dip under, until the flood has passed and wasted itself over our heads. (2.325)

For Santayana himself, Oliver's self-image is *too* scrupulously conscientious. But imaginative alertness is de rigueur: it means we keep thinking, reading, writing— rethinking, rereading, rewriting.

Only, we should do so, as Krishna advised, "*with detachment,*" or, as Santayana says in a letter, in "Epicurean contentment," which is almost synonymous with "philosophically":

> I have the Epicurean contentment, which was not far removed from asceticism; and besides I have a spiritual allegiance of my own that hardly requires faith, that is, only a humourous animal faith in nature and history, and no religious faith: and this common sense world suffices for *intellectual satisfaction*, partly in observing and understanding it, partly in dismissing it as, from the point of view of spirit, a transitory and local accident. Oliver hadn't this intellectual satisfaction, and he hadn't the Epicurean contentment. Hence the vacancy he faced when he had "overcome the world." (*Letters*, 305)

Where Santayana is busy studying and understanding the world as best he can, and then rising above and dismissing it in favor of the eternal verities—read: imaginative possibilities—that are presumably the focus of his contemplation, Oliver wants nothing less than the *presence* of the Good—the presence that would fill "the vacancy" he confronts after he has let games and friends, goods and kindred, go.

It is a case, to grant the deconstructionists their plump term, of "logocentric" paralysis. Not that there is no "unfathomable power" in the universe: the point is that it *is* unfathomable, and that Oliver can never "know" it or legislate by it. What is required, Santayana thinks, is "an unspoken and sacrificial trust" in that power—a trust amounting to calm but not self-obliterating acceptance of one's lot:

> *Worship* of this non-moral absolute Will seems to me canine and slavish, and excusable only as the sheer greatness of this universal power carries us with it dramatically, like a

storm or an earthquake which we forget to fear because we identify ourselves with it and positively enjoy it. This is a precarious aesthetic or intellectual rapture on which it would be rash and unmoral to build our religion; but *faith* and *trust* in that universal dispensation are signs of healthy life in ourselves, of intelligence and mastery; they bring, if we are reasonably plastic, a justified assurance of fellowship with reality, partly by participation and partly by understanding. ("Apologia," 508)

That seems to me a modest and comely credo, indicating, as Santayana would have it, *the* difference between the post-Christian temperaments of a Nordic Puritan like Oliver and a Latin Catholic-in-everything-but-faith like himself. The one is looking for the advent of a saint, while the other is looking—with a serene disengagement that, because it eschews "happiness," can never be popular—for the next great philosophical poet.

Such a poet would advance beyond Keats's lyric aestheticism or Whitman's liberal antinomianism into the realm of mature epic. But either the saint or the poet—it doesn't signify who comes first—would answer to the desiderata Santayana lists in the peroration to his classic book on Lucretius, Dante, and Goethe. Saint or poet would be the maker of the supreme fiction on which the myth of a happier, more organic epoch in our history might be based. His vision would be founded on the materialism of Lucretius, which knows that this palpable world is all the world there is. It would have a Goethean hunger for experience in all its forms. And it would manifest Dante's moral wisdom, now properly grounded in Lucretian science, and properly earned by Goethean erotic energy—for "the higher philosophy is not safe if the lower philosophy is wanting or is false" (*Three Philosophical Poets*, 138).

That would provide a new dispensation's idea of *Bildung* for both the individual and the wider culture. Which, from Santayana's point of view at mid-century, was a palmary reason why the liberally enlightened modern mind was so uninterested in either saint or philosophic poet, since both express what traditional religions have expressed: moral truth, sublimity, and the gods' laughter at human pretensions. The well-meaning among the liberally enlightened may, like the ancient Greeks, "hate" saints and philosophic poets because they believe the world needs mathematicians, cosmologists, and scientists. Then there is the Free Masonic sort of modern, who shuns the rigors of those hard disciplines as well as the softer ones of ethics and art, and just asks for perfectibilian nostrums and an easy life (see *Persons*, 453). Between the rationalist and the Philistine, it is therefore not surprising that, while our culture has produced some brilliant novels in the past 60 or so years, not one of them has been a *Bildungsroman* "conceptually" surpassing *The Last Puritan*. True, within this subgenre Saul Bellow's *The Adventures of Augie March* (1953) gives us an urban setting and an idiom of American English not found elsewhere. And Margaret Drabble's *Jerusalem the Golden* (1967) describes the dynamics of growing up provincial and moving to the metropolitan center in ways that are indebted to foremothers such as Charlotte Brontë, George Eliot, and Virginia Woolf and that open a window onto a female's experience sometimes obscured in the non-Jamesian novels I have treated here. But neither Bellow nor Drabble does philosophy as smartly, as sweepingly, as Santayana does, which in view of his credentials shouldn't be startling. Indeed one occasionally hears the strengths-can-be-weaknesses complaint that *The Last Puritan*'s characters, floating in the medium of Santayana's pellucid prose, are almost *too* intelligent, and that we need novels peopled by types more like ourselves. Bellow and Drabble have given us such types, certainly, and I will recur to the former at the end of my epilogue, but I for one would not want to be deprived of Santayana's stunning sport of a novel. There, as I hope I have adequately shown, he has not only made his competing world-views seem important; he has also bodied them in characters whose lives seem to throb off the page as well as on.

Epilogue

BOTTOM: *Will it please you to see the epilogue, or to hear a Bergomask dance between two of our company?*
THESEUS: *No epilogue, I pray you; for your play needs no excuse. Never excuse; for when the players are all dead, there needs none to be blamed.*

—*A Midsummer Night's Dream*, Act 5

Having no Bergomask dance to offer, and feeling that the players I have been discussing are in a manner all still alive, I tender this epilogue in an effort to sum up my priorities as a reader in general, and my findings as a reader of these novels of apprenticeship in particular. After which "The iron tongue of midnight," as Theseus proceeds to say, can toll twelve.

"The books we love are about growing up more than about being grown."[1] Thus Wright Morris has acknowledged what in one sense is a problem: How can novelists interest us in stories about "being grown," the conditions of maturity, or at least about "growing" in later stages of life, as James depicts Strether's late-in-life Gallic adventures of spirit and sense? We do need fiction to address all the cradle-to-grave stages of life. But Morris is simply acknowledging the primacy of the *Bildungsroman* in many readers' lists of the novels they love. *Copperfield* and *Sons and Lovers* probably aren't the first stories anyone reads nowadays: inveterate readers have naturally started with children's or adolescent books—*The Hobbit* or *Treasure Island*—or (for me) *The Kid from Tomkinsville, The Last Angry Man, Compulsion, Catcher in the Rye, Battle Cry,* and *Exodus,* or any book by Howard Fast or Edison Marshall. We all have to start somewhere. Once we have found the classic *Bildungsromane,* however, our ideas about fiction as such change forever. Holden Caulfield was wrong about "all that David Copperfield kind of crap." Here finally, we feel, are books that, much better than *Catcher,* help us understand what as adolescents and young adults we have been going through—*The Way of All Flesh* was the book that thus changed me at 21—and that remain among our favorites even as we discover the wider range of the family novel—*Anna Karenina, Buddenbrooks, The Rainbow*—or the novel panoramically focused on the state of a society or nation—*The Charterhouse of Parma, Cousin Bette, Vanity Fair, Bleak House, Middlemarch, War and Peace, Women in Love, The Magic Mountain.*

Reading any novel, whether its subject is an "I," an "us," a "them," or an "it," our job as readers is, first of all, to let the author speak to us, not to speak to the author. We may talk back, of course, but only after we have listened. As Virginia Woolf puts it in "How Should One Read a Book?", if we want to profit and derive pleasure from a work, we ought not to "dictate to" the author—resist or resent him, as many academic critics currently advise—but instead "Try to become him."[2] As I trust the preceding chapters have shown, I am not averse to quizzing an author, but I start by picking up his way of quizzing himself. As Yeats said, out of our quarrels with others comes rhetoric; out of our quarrels with ourselves comes poetry. If, moving beyond those intramental quarrels, we find ourselves quarreling with the author, it needn't mean divorce or even separation. After all, the quarrel might rise to the level of debate and we might *learn* something—constructively confirming differences, even changing our minds. Should we not "like" an author because he seems set against our ethnic group, gender, social class, and so on, and should we not think his criticisms of these categories are helping us understand ourselves any better than we do, then we are free to donate his book to the local library or, if we think it truly pernicious, to drop it into the recycling bin.

So, what have I learnt from the *Bildungsromane* that I have studied here? To begin with, I have learnt a little about how this or that earlier *Bildungsroman* led to a later one, less with regard to formal possibilities—self-conscious technical experiments can on occasion be fascinating, but Lawrence was right to insist that a novel's form, if it is to be "living," will emerge from the writer's struggle with his material, as against being imposed on that material—than with regard to social and intellectual history. The possibilities afforded a character by his history are, in turn, conditioned by the economic and political transformations that have occurred in a particular time and place. For a Paul Morel growing up in the colliery district in the 1890s, for example, the mental training resulting from the Education Act of 1870 is sustained by a decently financed system of lending libraries, while Oliver Alden's philosophical education in the wake of a collapsed Puritan theology is paid for by a family fortune, based in Boston real estate, which, riding the wave of comfort in this world, seems to emphasize the irrelevance, or at least the unknowability, of the next. The social-documentary value of these *Bildungsromane* is considerable, and anything one might assert about the near-term adventures of a particular tyro's spirit, mind, or body needs to be seen in the context of long-term social and economic development. (Which is to say nothing of a Braudelian *longue durée* accounting for geography, organic evolution, and climate change, the kind of perspective that hardly ever enters into the novel—*Women in Love* is a prominent exception—a genre that almost by definition concentrates on relations among people with humanly delimited memories. Yesterday or last year? Of course. A generation ago? Let's talk about it. The Pleistocene? Well, there's a museum downtown.)

The element that I have traced among these works of fiction, registering nearly 150 years of social evolution in the West—the idea of *Bildung*—began among the Weimar classicists as an expression of nostalgia for a Greek-like many-sidedness. Goethe's *Wilhelm Meister* at once paid homage to that nostalgic aspiration and soberly indicated how, under modern conditions, some of those many sides had to be renounced for the sake of excellence in one or two. Not butcher, baker, *and* candlestick maker, but just (say) baker. Not "Soldier, scholar, horseman, he," as Yeats wistfully described Robert Gregory, but just scholar—and so on. That was all right. There was quite enough reason to be enthusiastic about the prospect of an ordinary Robert or Wolfgang becoming something different than what his father had been. Let the

French Revolution complete its full cycle—from rebellious overthrow of the monarchy through gods-must-be-thirsty faction fights to imperial assertion of central control and expansionist foreign policy—the extended "moment" of transition from old régime to new signified an irreversible turn in Western history. It was crystallized for Goethe at Valmy: "From this time and place a new epoch is beginning, and you will be able to say that you were there," he told some German soldiers who on the eve of battle asked him what it was all about.[3] He went on to declare from his side of the Rhine that any tolerably circumstanced member of the Third Estate—any German burgher like any French bourgeois—now had a "right" to develop his own character. Which simply reflected the economic fact that lawyers, younger-son military officers, manufacturers, middling farmers, and even retailers had acquired a stake in the country as important as—often more important than—that of the landowning nobility. To cite Wilhelm's letter once more:

> I know not how it is in foreign countries; but in Germany, a universal, and if I may say so, personal cultivation is beyond the reach of any one except a nobleman. A burgher may acquire merit; by excessive efforts he may even educate his mind; but his personal qualities are lost, or worse than lost, let him struggle as he will. (1.319)

And there follows his determination to cultivate his own personal qualities in the theater. Goethe's plain feeling was that Germany like France could only profit from raising the ceiling for talented members of the Third Estate.

It was after all the successful English model. Since the Puritan Revolution, England had grown stronger by extending, gradually but ineluctably, the opportunity to pursue happiness to the untitled by birth and the unentitled by wealth. And the English opposition to the French Revolution, which Goethe also observed anxiously, did not in the long run dismantle the gains of her own Lockean liberalism, or prevent further gains in the nineteenth century. Naturally, England resisted French expansion, whether propelled by committee or by emperor, since it threatened, à la Louis XIV, the European balance of power. Naturally, too, a Tory ministry couldn't be fond of slogans about liberty, equality, and fraternity that jibed with the declared war aims of the recently victorious American rebels. Post-Waterloo, post-Peterloo, though, the story of nineteenth-century English political and social history is encapsulated in the titles of the two volumes that straddle the year 1830 in Elie Halévy's magisterial six-volume survey: *The Liberal Awakening* and *The Triumph of Reform*. Just as, in France, politically conservative novelists such as Balzac or Flaubert shared the convictions of liberals such as Stendhal and Benjamin Constant that at the end of the day the nation would be better off bringing forward the talents of young men and women from the provinces (or even from the Saint-Antoine), so, in England, there was a similar consensus between conservatives such as Disraeli and Trollope and liberals such as Dickens, Thackeray, George Eliot, and the Brontës with respect to the young men and women from the shires or the East End. To recall the title of another formidable historian, R. R. Palmer, in America, England, and the European continent, this *was* "the age of democratic revolution."

Politically, that is all for the better. When at mid-century we reach *David Copperfield*, which shows its youths coming of age in the years before and after the First Reform

Bill (1832), it isn't only Steerforth, it is also David, Traddles, and, however meanly, Uriah who have a chance at getting more than a rudimentary, if still very insufficient, education, and at cultivating their selfhoods (not simply being "constructed" by social and biological circumstances) in public as well as in private life. The results of their cultivating may be mixed, but we have good reason to rejoice that the tyros taking themselves so seriously aren't exclusively from the silver-fork circle of Edward Bulwer-Lytton or Harrison Ainsworth, from the squirearchical, clerical, and naval circles of Jane Austen, or (one Scott per century being all any island needs) from the high-end of the feudal and long-ago hierarchy of the Waverley novels. They come from—not *the* lower depths exactly, but the lower middle or upper working class.

If we look at a roster of English and American *Bildungshelden* from David on, we will notice that middle-middle- and upper-middle-class youths continue to have their innings too, but (sticking with the boys) they all—Pendennis, Richard Feverel, Roderick Hudson, Hyacinth Robinson, Ernest Pontifex, Rickie Elliot, Paul Morel, Stephen Dedalus, or Oliver Alden—share a *dis*advantage I have here noted repeatedly. They either don't have fathers alive or they have fathers who are tyrannical or feckless. In any case, the boys don't have fathers able to show them, with authority, the way to manhood, and in consequence they are driven now to depend on their mothers, a symbiosis finally less mutualistic than parasitic, and now to reach out to older males who might stand in for the absent, or absently present, fathers. This reaching out sometimes gets no response (Paul), sometimes half a response and more (Wilhelm and David, Rickie and Oliver), but the father-ache remains a prominent worry in the representative English and American *Bildungsromane* I have analyzed. These novels at least point to the causes of this crisis of paternity that social historians have examined in greater, quantitative detail—causes that originate in transformations in methods of production and service, which I have sketched in the Lawrence chapter and elsewhere. And insofar as the crisis continues in our own day—"Mommy, where *is* daddy?" or, later, "Mom, what *was* dad like?"—these classic *Bildungsromane* still give us something to brood (and act) on.

So far, so family-romantic. These *Bildungshelden* are, in addition, up against something more broadly cultural, which, in Santayanan phrase, we can designate as the modern, that is, post-Enlightenment, Western world's lack of philosophical coherence. The loss of fathers in the home paralleled the loss of the Father in heaven. The very revolution, liberalism, that created the possibility of self-cultivation for the common people left them bereft of the old, stable formulas for selfhood per se. Prior to the Enlightenment, in an age of what for convenience we can call Judeo-Christian humanism, the "self" typically took the form of its same-sex parent—this was the fate of eldest sons in particular—and even if it took another form, it did so according to the unwritten rules governing the behavior of members of this class or that sex, this sect or that nation. From the Enlightenment, rationalist perspective, throwing over those formulas was the whole point. They were the mind-forged manacles that Nobodaddy-haunted Blake said had to be broken. No Nobodaddy, bad-father conspiracy theory was necessary. The fact was simply that Judeo-Christian humanism, while not in principle exclusionist within the congregation of the faithful (all believers could, in their spare time, perfect their souls and make themselves worthier of God's love), had in practice been coopted by the socially powerful, a concordat between priests and kings (with the nobility in support) making the perfecting of souls, the cultivation of selfhoods, a largely leisure-time activity for the dominant classes.

The extension of the privilege of self-cultivation to the class that had, through its labor, carved out a bit of leisure for itself, was a good thing for the larger society—in as much as the old dominant classes, priests, nobles, and kings, had become complacent toward their own cultural achievements. Something fresh was wanting. This extension of power, privilege, and cultural possibility was the positive achievement of the Enlightenment-culminating French Revolution. If priests and nobles could no longer speak unanimously and authoritatively, as though acting as the monarchy's vanguard to govern the nation, then one was not supposed to feel any alarm. The middle-folks' leaders would govern, as republics or constitutional monarchies replaced the absolutism of the old régime, while in the arts—higher culture generally—the play of individual genius would be so dazzling that no one would need to bother about lack of unity, or even shared standards of judgment. In short, it was the romantic era, from the energetic on-and-on adventures of Goethe's Faust to the simply more sensualized, multi-perspectived on-and-on adventures of the dramatis personae of Browning or Whitman.

Santayana called theirs the poetry of barbarism because they lacked the organizing, morally regulated, centered intelligence that, in Dante's supernaturalist or in Lucretius' naturalist philosophies, had marked the level-headed, civilized person. Thus conceived, the problem of growing up in a romantic, barbarous era is mainly spiritual. A *Bildungsheld* has trouble knowing *who* he is because, *sub specie eternitatis*, he isn't sure what or where he is. What grounds his being, what should be his ultimate concern, what—to drop the Tillichian phrasing of my college days—is he supposed to do to enhance his sense of being alive in body and mind, to feel "planted" in the greater, live universe around him? That is Laurentian phrasing, of course, but in various ways it fits the feeling, admittedly only tacit in a character like David, in all the *Bildungshelden* I have been regarding. Because the orthodox metaphysical categories and concepts seem inadequate to the heroes' psychological and social experience of the world, they—and their authors—grope desperately for whatever serviceable categories and concepts might be available. In the heterodox Goethe and the only quasi-orthodox Dickens we see ingenious attempts to argue that the hand of the hero is cooperating with the higher hand of Providence in shaping the self and its history—though since any evidence for God's activity is merely identical with the mundane objects and events that make up the heroes' lives, only the eye of faith can discern the hidden hand's fingerprints.

My three twentieth-century novelists don't even try to dust for such fingerprints. "Seeing there's no God," as Birkin flatly states in *Women in Love*—speaking if not exactly for Lawrence, who believed in a power not ourselves for which God was as good a name as any, then for the growing number of intellectuals for whom the deity of any orthodox religion was in Nietzsche's sense "dead"—it is futile and self-deluding for any *Bildungsheld* to look around for divine sponsorship. The twentieth-century *Bildungsheld* typically learns that he is free to sponsor himself. Sponsor himself not, needless to say, in Nietzsche's superhuman sense, there being numerous immovables and inalterables that, according to Goethe's teaching in *Wilhelm Meister*, circumscribe anyone's freedom, but in the ordinary sense of having advantages and opportunities won by the liberal reforms of the Enlightenment and after. The self-sponsoring people in the West were at liberty to seek satisfactions—pursue happiness—in love and work.

Actually, we should say on the evidence of these *Bildungsromane*, they were free to pursue love more often than work. Our novelists certainly haven't been very good at depicting everyday sorts of work, no doubt because most novelists have never, from an everyman's point of view, done a lick of work in their lives. They have just written books, and what kind of work is *that*?! A lowbrow question, but it reflects the gap, sometimes masochistically celebrated in the alienated artist sort of novel, between writers and their audiences. One needn't be Tom Wolfe to lament recent novelists' lack of studious curiosity about the work other people do, a curiosity so abundant in a Balzac or a Zola, a Dreiser or an Arnold Bennett. At any rate, within the *Bildungsroman* tradition Joyce's *Portrait of the Artist* or Thackeray's *Pendennis* stands above *Copperfield* or *Sons and Lovers*, all of which shade into the *Künstlerroman*, to the extent that they particularize the process of the artist's inspiration, training, and performance.

And so to bed—and to the courtship that leads up to, and the companionship or just the getting-along that follows upon, going to bed. The *Bildungsroman* tradition has excelled in the presentment of love matters, advancing both on the excessively inward *Seelengeschichte*, the *Pilgrim's Progress* model of late-Christian pietism, and on the romantic (and often moribund) lovers-against-the-world model of, for example, the several versions of the Tristan and Isolde or the Abélard and Héloïse stories. By portraying the affective development of the hero intersubjectively—first in child-and-parents, then in lad-and-girl, and finally in young man-and-man, man-and-woman relations—the *Bildungsroman* verges on the family novel. Only, the possibility of continuing family life is in many cases aborted by the early death (Hyacinth, Rickie, and Oliver) or "derelict" condition (Paul and, arguably, Isabel) of the hero. The late-nineteenth-, early-twentieth-century hero, anyway: Wilhelm and David at least went on to marry and have children (though not necessarily in that order). The later novels—it is hardly a statistically relevant sampling, I realize—carry the symbolic suggestion that the crisis of paternity, the actual or simply felt absence of fathers in the boys' lives, leaves the latter with no paternal prompts. Not that they don't want to have intercourse—let's be real—but that they don't have much of a disciplined, acculturated tendency toward sticking around: marrying the woman and helping raise the offspring.

As Anton Chekhov said, the artist's job isn't to solve social problems but, in addition to the sine qua non of being talented, to depict them. The talented novelists studied here certainly do that job, and through the circuit of implication they lead us to consider a salutary model for coming-of-age, and by extension for any significant novel about coming-of-age, in our own era. First, be gratefully aware of liberalism's achievements from Goethe's time on, which, effectually doubling the achievement of America itself, bestowed the privilege of self-cultivation, the pursuit of happiness, upon the common people. Second, understand that children are more likely to thus cultivate and pursue if they are part of a functional family—which, au fond, is a not-so-covert preachment on behalf of sexual responsibility and marital fidelity. Such high themes aren't by themselves sufficient to make *Copperfield* or *Sons and Lovers* great in the way *Anna Karenina* and *Middlemarch* are great, but such themes are clearly part of what makes all four of those novels (plus the others I have analyzed here) important, moving, and endlessly rereadable. Third, grasp the fact that husbands, wives, and children can't live just on their love (mixed with other feelings, naturally) for one another. They must also work at something contributing to the common wealth—the theme of vocation that I have traced and that, once we get past the "portrait of the artist (or philosopher) as a young man" reflections, leaves us feeling pretty empty. What is a novelist to do? He or she might, as I have suggested, try on a bit of Dreiser or Bennett, Sinclair Lewis or John Dos Passos, if only as an antidote to the high modernist disdain for the "alienating" things people work at all day in the store, the factory, the fields, the lab, or the office. Our jobs will never become less alienating if, in fiction, we can't describe them diagnostically.

Beyond that modest call for engagement, however, I like to imagine our next great *Bildungsroman* recognizing the contributions that all kinds of workers—the machinist and the computer programmer, as well as the artist and the teacher—make to the liberal democratic society that, returning to my first point above, has all along created the conditions in which such workers can even *think* about cultivating a self and pursuing their ideas of happiness. Such a *Bildungsroman*—this is a prescription obviously based as much on a personal, Platonic ideal as on current historical conditions—would be frankly patriotic, a celebration of a political and social system that promotes the well-being of the individuated many as against the individuated (and isolated) few. What it would be patriotically committed to is a particular country, one of the Western democracies, say, but beyond that to the comity of democracies that in principle every country might one day belong to. The male- or female-centered *Bildungsroman* will doubtless have a very different "feel" in the multiracial, multiethnic literary culture that is emerging in our time. To adduce but one example, an extraordinary blend of *Bildungsroman* and family novel, Salman Rushdie's *The Moor's Last Sigh* (1995): we have a tale of an Indian hero's double-time growing up that is at once deeply (and fantastically) rooted in Catholic, Jewish, Hindu, Muslim, and other such traditions, and striving, unsuccessfully, to fly, like Stephen Dedalus, past those nets into an orthodoxy-free kingdom of tolerance.

In any case, there is more than a touch of such patriotic celebration in Goethe. His "Here or nowhere is America!" indicates that Germans have to bring about their own version of the democratic revolution lately seen in the New World. Dickens is of course nothing if not English to his fingertips, and the exhibition of *Copperfield's* stunningly variegated characters is, as I have noted, a consequence of his living in a (comparatively speaking) liberally open society. But there is no conscious defense of (a) the right-little-tight-little-island's political system—on the contrary, Dickens's conscious purpose is usually to attack its failings—or (b) its fructuous mother-of-parliaments role in the wider world. Forster is downright suspicious of anyone's unfurling the mother-of-parliaments banner. *Passage to India* shows him desiring a responsible contraction of Empire, the message having been present in the Wiltshire-centered vision of *The Longest Journey*, or the retreat from the world of "telegrams and anger" associated with business and politics in *Howards End*. We can be thankful that the rise of fascism in the 1930s concentrated Forster's mind enough to bring forth at least two cheers for democracy. Not to condescend: Lawrence never gave democracy more than half a cheer, in acknowledgment I suppose of its having provided *him* with the chance to go to school and start a career different from his collier father's, and Santayana, with other, ethico-metaphysical things to ponder, conflated his rational distrust of the *demos* (what! *their* votes determine how we are to be governed?) with an intellectual aristocrat's disdain for—no, call it removal from and therefore ignorance of—ordinary people.

Obviously, I love and *esteem* these writers. I am simply hoping that a worthy successor will move beyond them. It won't be, whatever Santayana's implicit directions, by dramatizing a new philosophical synthesis, which, he after all insisted, must first be articulated by a qualified philosopher, who from my point of view would have the daunting task of combining something like Lawrence's organic, ecological sense of the oneness of life with its almost-opposite, a qualitative utilitarianism. The worthy successor's breakthrough will occur by dramatizing an acceptance of the liberal and (yes) free-market society in which everyman can become a *Bildungsheld*, by celebrating the great varieties of life, the many possible ways of being happy within that society, and by affirming the importance of its defense.

This, following the successful defense of our open society against right-wing total-itarianism in the middle of the last century, and in the midst of what would ultimately be its successful defense against left-wing totalitarianism—respectively, World War II and what has been called World War III (the Cold War)—is what Saul Bellow nearly achieved in *Augie March*. If only it weren't in many places overwritten, its stylistic riffs unanchored, its affirmations sometimes unearned. But Bellow had the right idea. He wrote a novel that was more than what John Updike has called a "disguised diary,"[4] myopically centered on "things that have happened to me." For all my several recog-nitions that the tacit call of many classic *Bildungsromane* is that we each, emulously, write our own coming-of-age narratives, I know that anyone with a truly important narrative inside him or her won't need any such prompting. All he or she needs is time, talent, and genius. Maybe someone is writing a new and greater *Augie* at this moment. I have at any rate finished writing about these representative pre-*Augie* novels, and am ready, as the iron tongue of midnight *is* tolling twelve, to fall back again upon the hope that we also serve who only read and wait.

Notes

PROLOGUE

1. Benjamin, *Illuminations*, 86–87, 99. Hereafter cited in the text implicitly or as "Benjamin."
2. Bakhtin, "The *Bildungsroman* and Its Significance," 16–23. Throughout this book I usually say "man" in contexts where I mean "human being" for reasons similar to those discussed by Jacques Barzun, ranging from literary tradition (the obligation to write concise prose), etymology (the word's derivation from the Sanskrit *man, manu*, designating the human being as such), and the unintended exclusivity even of phrases such as "man and woman," "he or she," etc.—for one should in fairness also include teenagers and children of both sexes, which would require a lawyerly fussiness (*From Dawn to Decadence*, 82–85).
3. *Bildung* must be distinguished from *Kultur*, insofar as the latter refers, as in Herder and in later historians such as G. F. Klemm (*Allgemeine Kulturgeschichte der Menschheit*, 1843–1852), to the whole way of life of a particular people. But the terms overlap when *Kultur* refers to the "general process of intellectual, spiritual and aesthetic development," or when, as in Arnold's "culture," we are asked to think of the contents of that development, the specific canon of the best that has been thought and said. This tendency to fuse into one word the process and product of "cultivation"—a word deriving metaphorically from *cultura*, which in turn derives from *colere* (designating, most importantly here, the tending or cultivating of crops or animals)—is conspicuous not only in Arnold's *Culture and Anarchy*, but in most English usage since the mid-nineteenth century (Williams, *Keywords*, 87–93). More than *Kultur*, however, *Bildung* emphasizes the "personal" aspect of the process and, to a degree, of the product of cultivation. Hence the English equivalent, "self-cultivation."
4. As Herder bitterly wrote in June 1782 about the man who had become, after Karl August himself, the most powerful figure in Weimar: "So [Goethe] is now Permanent Privy Councillor, President of the Chamber, President of the War Office, Inspector of Works down to roadbuilding, Director of Mines, also *Directeur des plaisirs*, Court Poet, composer of pretty festivities, court operas, ballets, cabaret masques, inscriptions, works of art etc., Director of the Drawing Academy in which during the winter he delivered lectures on osteology; everywhere himself the principal actor, dancer, in short, the factotum of all Weimar" (qtd. in Craig, "Unread Giant," 105).
5. Mann, "Germany and the Germans," 59; Benjamin, 241.
6. Warshow, *The Immediate Experience*, xl–xli.
7. I think readers should let novels possess them before they attempt critically to possess the novels. Cf. Anthony Hecht's remark about the title of his *Obbligati: Essays in Criticism*, affirming "the proper role of criticism as a musical obbligato: that is, a counterpart that must constantly strive to move in strict harmony with and intellectual counterpoint to its subject, and remain always subordinate to the text upon which it presumes to comment" (vii).

8. Largely because I have some time ago published on them elsewhere, and with the usual authorial immodesty I list the relevant texts here: *Samuel Butler Revalued* (University Park: Penn State Press, 1981), primarily about *The Way of All Flesh*; "Meredith's Concept of Nature: Beyond the Ironies of *Richard Feverel*," *ELH* 47 (1980): 121–48; "Myth and Morals in *The Mill on the Floss*," *The Midwest Quarterly* 20 (1979): 332–46; "Thackeray's Pendennis: Son and Gentleman," *Nineteenth-Century Fiction* 33 (1978): 175–93. I have incorporated some more recent essays (see acknowledgments) into this book.

9. See, for instance, Elizabeth Abel, Marianne Hirsch, and Elizabeth Langland, eds., *The Voyage In: Fictions of Female Development* (Hanover, NH: University Press of New England, 1983); Susan Fraiman, *Unbecoming Women: British Women Writers and the Novel of Development* (New York: Columbia University Press, 1993); Geta LeSeur, *Ten Is the Age of Darkness: The Black Bildungsroman* (Columbia: University of Missouri Press, 1995); Annie O. Eysturoy, *Daughters of Self-Creation: The Contemporary Chicana Novel* (Albuquerque: University of New Mexico Press, 1996); Pin-Chia Feng, *The Female Bildungsroman by Toni Morrison and Maxine Hong Kingston: A Postmodern Reading* (New York: Peter Lang, 1998); Lorna Ellis, *Appearing to Diminish: Female Development and the British Bildungsroman, 1750–1850* (Lewisburg, PA: Bucknell University Press, 1999); and Patricia P. Chu, *Assimilating Asians: Gendered Strategies of Authorship in Asian America* (Durham, NC: Duke University Press, 2000).

10. See Christina Hoff Sommers, *The War Against Boys: How Misguided Feminism Is Harming Our Young Men* (New York: Simon & Schuster, 2000).

CHAPTER 1

1. Noted in George Henry Lewes's great mid-Victorian biography, still in many ways the liveliest in English, more compact than Nicholas Boyle's current, multi-volume tome. Apropos the morality of Wilhelm Meister, Lewes added Wordsworth's quip about Tam O'Shanter: " 'I pity him who cannot perceive that in all this, though there was no moral purpose, there is a moral effect.' What each reader will see in it, will depend on his insight and experience" (*The Life of Goethe*, 404–05).

2. Eliot, "The Morality of Wilhelm Meister," 146–47.

3. James, *Literary Criticism*, 947–48.

4. Great but uneven. Candor drives James to admit what many German readers have felt about the sameness and often flatness in the voices of both the narrator and many of his characters, which Thomas Carlyle's Englishing, brilliant as it is, hasn't been able to disguise. What Hermann Hesse says of the mixture of the prosaic and the poetic in Adalbert Stifter's 1857 novel, *Der Nachsommer* (*Indian Summer*)—"exactly like in a little Goethe, philistine commonplaces about art and life in a wooden language . . . [juxtaposed] to others of enchanting beauty" ("Gratitude to Goethe," 183)—can stand for similar complaints by Novalis (*Schriften*, 3.638 on), Susanne Howe (*Wilhelm Meister and His English Kinsmen*, 63), and T. J. Reed (*The Classical Centre*, 113). The "enchanting beaut[ies]" drive us ("for very pity," as James said) to discover the meaning that the arridities obscure.

5. Here and elsewhere, as with names like Aurelie and Natalie, I retain Carlyle's Anglicized forms. It keeps me consistent with quoted passages. I use Carlyle's translation, for besides being both faithful and powerfully rendered, it is the one my Anglophone exemplars relied on. Anyone wanting a twentieth-century translation can't do better than Eric A. Blackall and Victor Lange's *Wilhelm Meister's Apprenticeship* (Princeton: Princeton University Press, 1995).

6. Schiller, *Correspondence*, 1.197; hereafter cited in text as "*Correspondence*."

7. Goethe, *Wilhelm Meister's Apprenticeship*, 2.146–47; hereafter referred to implicitly.

8. Unhistorical criticism is no less salient in Europe than in England or America. W. Daniel Wilson, who teaches at Berkeley but publishes in Munich, has in *Das Goethe-Tabu* taken Goethe to task for failing to prevent the execution of a Hetty Sorel-like Weimar woman who had killed her child, or for not opposing the cashiering of the atheist Johann Gottlieb Fichte from his post at the university at Jena, or for allowing Weimar citizens to be impressed as mercenaries in the American war for independence, and so on, holding up to a public intellectual of 200 years ago the same high standards he would impose on one now. As Gordon Craig tartly notes, "Goethe's Weimar was profoundly different from Wilson's Berkeley," and a chief virtue of Mr. Boyle's new life, which he is reviewing, is its endeavor to achieve historical objectivity ("Germany's Greatest," 52).

9. Boyle, *Goethe*, 1.289. Hereafter cited in the text, by volume, implicitly or as "Boyle."

10. See Ian Watt's justly famous *Rise of the Novel* and Q. D. Leavis's less famous but equally indispensable "The Englishness of the English Novel."

11. Reed, *Classical Centre*, 106–07.

12. The Beautiful Soul is to the modern ear the preferred translation of the *Schöne Seele*, which Carlyle too Elizabethanly rendered as the "Fair Saint."

13. Humboldt had used the term *Bildung* as a botanical metaphor, which Goethe frequently if unsystematically pursued when trying to understand the trajectory of any organism's life. Reading Kant's *Critique of Judgment* had freed him from the idea that organisms—insects, plants, human beings—had any external purpose in living. Like inorganic things—rock, air, water, fire—organic creatures exist merely for themselves. What Goethe describes in essays such as "The Metamorphosis of Plants" can, as Mr. Boyle argues, be applied to the metamorphoses Wilhelm passes through: in childhood he has a sort of genetic memory of the images and ideals pictured in his grandfather's art collection, just as a seed "remembers" the glorious flower from which it sprang; and as the seed in time produces its own flower, so Wilhelm in time realizes some of the ideals depicted in the paintings, and in marrying Natalia recovers the collection itself. Further, just as a plant grows by putting out paired or alternate leaves from node to node, so Wilhelm grows through a series of encounters with paired characters—Philina and Laertes, the Melinas, Mignon and the Harper, Lothario and Natalia, or Augustin and Sperata with their story of "insufficiently differentiated development . . . who, like monocotyledons, hasten to sexual union before they have become fully formed" (2.414).

Wilhelm forms as it were his own seed at the end, when he becomes part of the Tower's new international organization that hopes to bear liberal, anti-Jacobin fruit throughout the West, and when he beholds and dedicates himself to the rearing of his biological offspring Felix. As Mr. Boyle acknowledges, however, the botanical metaphor, which is too submerged for common readers to notice, in any case finally breaks down. Schiller may epigrammatically have urged people to emulate the plant, voluntarily choosing to go through the natural process of sprouting, ripening, and decaying that the plant goes through involuntarily, but that sort of no-purpose-beyond-oneself contentment lacks the moral interest the Weimar classicists believed human life had to contain. As Kant had taught, our lives have no more natural purpose than this rock or that spider: phenomenally considered, that is, existence is without meaning and therefore the occasion for despair. Fortunately, we are able to impute a more-than-natural purpose to our lives whenever we discipline ourselves to be regulated by a moral law that transcends any individual person or culture: noumenally considered, that is, existence has a larger meaning, and is therefore an occasion for hope. So I would summarize Mr. Boyle's botany-cum-Kant treatment of Goethe's idea of organic but finally moralized *Bildung* (2.411–15). I return to Kant when speaking of Natalia.

14. Taking an expansive view of European history one can say, with Bakhtin, that the shift of emphasis from "being" to "becoming" marks the Renaissance-to-Enlightenment transition

from medieval supernaturalism to modern secularism. What Goethe does as a novelist is consonant with what he does as an amateur geologist, geographer, botanist, and so on: he focuses "chronotopically" on the connections between this point of time-space and that, the "necessary" (i.e., non-random) development from past to present, present to future. "The simple spatial contiguity (*nebeneinander*) of phenomena was profoundly alien to Goethe," Bakhtin writes, "so he saturated and imbued it with *time*, revealed emergence and development in it, and he distributed that which was contiguous in *space* in various *temporal* stages, epochs of becoming. For him contemporaneity—both in nature and in human life—is revealed as an essential multitemporality: as remnants or relics of various stages and formations of the past and as rudiments of stages in the more or less distant future" ("The *Bildungsroman* and Its Significance," 28). In short, Goethe was among the eighteenth-century investigators who made nineteenth-century evolutionary theory possible: he tried, often successfully, to *see* where "x" had come from and where it might be going. The "x" in *Wilhelm Meister* is of course primarily the hero's emerging identity.

15. The folly Wilhelm must risk is, among other things, sexual. He is never troubled by the erotic guilt that, in *The Sorrows*, makes Werther's wet dreams about Charlotte so agonizing. He does hesitate about giving in to Philina's charms, but only because he feels he should avoid women altogether after having, as he thinks, been betrayed by Mariana. But once Philina has turned up as a live succubus in his bed, he is eager for more, and would indeed get it if a real conflagration did not forestall the erotic one in his veins (see 1.358). Not that he lacks scruples. He stops short of pedophilia, being horrified at the possibility that his live succubus might have been Mignon, who indeed had been on watch that night, had her primal scene, and appeared much more womanly the next morning. And he wants to stay faithful. Aurelia's story of Lothario's perfidy makes him vow that "no woman shall receive an acknowledgment of love from my lips, to whom I cannot consecrate my life!" (1.308)—a vow that he naturally breaks during the inebriated night with Philina, but that, in spite of his frisking from her to Theresa to Natalia, he sincerely means to keep. His frisking is really a movement, as we shall see, toward the best embodiment of what his unconscious most desires, and once he reaches it, there is some reason to think he will stick.

16. Mr. Boyle points out the parallels in the *Theatrical Mission* between Wilhelm's stage ambitions, purportedly conceived in the 1750s, and Goethe's hopes for a national theater in 1778, during the Storm and Stress movement. The novelist gave his hero Shakespeare's Christian name, and made him a poet of some note who has a five-act biblical tragedy *Belshazzar* (the young Goethe had written such a drama) that is looking to be produced. Wilhelm learns what Goethe had, namely that mid-eighteenth-century Germany would be culturally unified not by the theater, which after all depended on isolated performances before small, often only courtly audiences, but by the printed book, especially the literary drama, which many people could read and which several theater companies could put on simultaneously. Goethe's disillusionment with the national theater project stemmed also from a local canker—the somewhat *louche* troupe of Giuseppe Bellomo that had begun performing at Weimar in 1784 (1.320, 365, 372, 400). By the time he turned the *Theatrical Mission* into *Wilhelm Meister*, Goethe abandoned what had amounted to an attempt at autobiographical fiction and made his hero not a playwright but a simple enthusiast (see Boyle, 2.236). No more portrait of the artist or *Kunstlerroman*: we have the portrait of a plain young burgher, mediocre (as Mann would say) in the honorable sense.

17. Eckermann, *Conversations of Goethe with Eckermann*, 132; hereafter cited in the text implicitly or as "Eckermann."

18. Lawrence, *Letters, Vol. 6*, 342.

19. See Minden, *The German Bildungsroman*, 42.

20. It is important to underscore the historical context of Goethe's plea for an integration of noble and burgherly talents, since, as we will see, someone like Franco Moretti can, in his fervor for an equality of results, dismiss these mésalliances as a mere selling out to the ruling class, and in fact regard marriage itself as a metaphor for a repressive social contract: "One either marries or, in one way or another, must leave social life: and for more than a century European consciousness will perceive the crisis of marriage as a rupture that not only divides a couple, but destroys the very roots—Anna Karenina, Emma Bovary, Effi Briest—of those sentiments that keep the individual 'alive'. For this world view a crisis, a divorce, can never be a plausible 'ending'" (*The Way of the World*, 22–23; hereafter cited in the text implicitly or as "Moretti"). But there we are: in realistic fiction, characters can do only what is historically, humanly possible.
21. Blackall, *Goethe and the Novel*, 136.
22. Lukács, *Goethe and His Age*, 56.
23. The Harper and Mignon have been placed in the background in this discussion because they contribute so little to the novel's social theme, yet as representatives of the magical, inward power of music and verse, dark energies and (in Mignon's prepubescent case) ambiguous gender, they clearly express another, nonrational, contra-Jarno side of Goethe's genius and are probably, with Philina, the book's most memorable characters—almost eclipsing the hero himself, as Micawber and Steerforth, say, almost eclipse David Copperfield.
24. Qtd. in Howe, *Wilhelm Meister and His English Kinsmen*, 65.
25. "We have defined a story as a narrative of events arranged in their time-sequence. A plot is also a narrative of events, the emphasis falling on causality. 'The king died and then the queen died' is a story. 'The king died, and then the queen died of grief' is a plot," Forster says (*Aspects of the Novel*, 86). Of course the causality Goethe is concerned with is, in Aristotelian terms, not merely efficient, it is final.
26. Mann, *The Magic Mountain*, 594.

CHAPTER 2

1. Q. D. Leavis, "The Englishness of the English Novel," 312–13.
2. Troeltsch, "The Ideas of Natural Law," 207; hereafter cited in the text implicitly or as "Troeltsch."
3. Relevant here is Dietrich Bonhoeffer's articulation of this dynamic under the yet more dangerous conditions of the Third Reich. Germans, as he noted from the prison Hitler had put him in, under suspicion of having plotted his assassination, have always been brave in obedience. "But the German has preserved his freedom—what nation has talked so passionately of freedom as we have, from Luther to the idealists?—by seeking deliverance from his own will through service to the community. Calling and freedom were two sides of the same thing. The trouble was, he did not understand his world. He forgot that submissiveness and self-sacrifice could be exploited for evil ends [e.g., by the Nazis]. Once that happened, once the exercise of the calling itself became questionable, all the ideals of the German would begin to totter. Inevitably he was convicted of a fundamental failure: he could not see that in certain circumstances free and responsible action might have to take precedence over duty and calling" (*Letters and Papers from Prison*, 137).
4. Santayana, *Character and Opinion*, 120–21.
5. In September of 2001, we learned that certain Islamic fundamentalists—turning 767s into cruise missiles to strike buildings full of people, and calling on Muslims everywhere to kill, indiscriminately, Americans and Jews—are willing to pursue the same "our way, or no way"

logic that, as Santayana lived to see, twice in the twentieth century made Germany the enemy of the democracies.

6. For a succinct account of the Reformers' views on vocation, see Mintz, *George Eliot and the Novel of Vocation*, 8–13.

7. Schiller, *On the Aesthetic Education of Man*, 43; hereafter cited in the text implicitly.

8. James, *Literary Criticism*, 947–48.

9. Carlyle and Welsh, *The Collected Letters*, 3.102.

10. Ibid., 2.434, 437.

11. Carlyle, *Reminiscences*, 241.

12. Allingham, *A Diary*, 253.

13. Carlyle himself later seems to have doubted the rightness of accent in his portrait of the *Goetheszeit*, especially when he saw an affinity between the "windy" cult of English aestheticism in the early 1850s and the implication in Goethe, as in Schiller, that if the Good is subsumed in the Beautiful, then "Art is higher than Religion" (*Two Note Books*, 158). As David DeLaura says, the idea of *Bildung* was not sufficiently moralized to remain in Carlyle's lexicon after the death of Goethe in 1832 ("Heroic Egotism," 48–49). He thereafter preferred men of action, and if before the cry was to close thy Byron and open thy Goethe, it was now close thy Goethe and open thy Cromwell, Frederick, or Abbot Samson.

14. Heine, *Selected Works*, 207.

15. Carlyle, "Goethe," 1.22. Hereafter cited in the text as "Goethe."

16. General studies of the English reception of Goethe include those by Rosemary Ashton, John Boening, Jean-Marie Carré, Patrick Crury, David DeLaura, Susanne Howe, and Richard Holt Hutton—all listed in the bibliography.

17. Qtd. in Bruford, *The German Tradition*, 42.

18. Qtd. in Howe, *Wilhelm Meister and His English Kinsmen*, 80–81.

19. In Boening, ed., *The Reception of Classical German Literature in England, 1760–1860*, 7.190.

20. Nietzsche, *Daybreak*, 111–12.

21. Mill, *Autobiography*, 151–52.

22. Qtd. in Hayek, *John Stuart Mill and Harriet Taylor*, 253–54.

23. Qtd. in Semmel, *John Stuart Mill and the Pursuit of Virtue*, 81.

24. Mill, *Later Letters*, 345–46.

25. Mill, *On Liberty*, 56.

26. See Inman, *Walter Pater's Reading*, 10–11.

27. Pater is quoting Carlyle's *mis*quotation, in "Death of Goethe," of Goethe's "*Generalbeichte*," where in the fifth stanza he says "*Und im Ganzen, Guten, Schönen / Resolut zu leben.*" It was Carlylesque to misremember *Schönen* as *Wahren*, but the translation of *Ganzen* as "indifference" is solely Pater's, and ill fits the context of Goethe's poem (see Inman, *Walter Pater's Reading*, 146–47).

28. Arnold, *Complete Prose Works*, 5.94.

29. Ibid., 10.166–67.

30. Ibid., 4.334.

31. See the essays in James Hardin's collection, *Reflection and Action: Essays on the* Bildungsroman, especially Martini, "Bildungsroman—Term and Theory," 1–25, and Jeffrey Sammons, "The Bildungsroman for Nonspecialists: An Attempt at Clarification," 26–45, plus Randolph P. Shaffner's *The Apprenticeship Novel*.

32. See Shaffner, *The Apprenticeship Novel*, 31–33.

33. Swales, *The German Bildungsroman*, 14.

34. Qtd. in ibid., 12.

35. Dilthey, *Das Erlebnis und die Dichtung*, 250.

36. Howe, *Wilhelm Meister and His English Kinsmen*, 4.
37. G. W. F. Hegel pregnantly remarks on the transformation of the knightly quester into the burgherly young man on the rise: "The contingency of external existence has been transformed into a firm and secure order of civil society and the state, so that police, law-courts, the army, political government replace the chimerical ends which the knights errant set before themselves. Thereby the knight-errantry of the heroes as they act in more modern romances is also altered. As individuals with their subjective ends of love, honour, and ambition, or with their ideals of world-reform, they stand [poetically] opposed to this substantial order and the prose of actuality which puts difficulties in their way on all sides. . . . [T]hey regard it as a misfortune that there is any family, civil society, state, laws, professional business, etc., because these substantive relations of life with their barriers cruelly oppose the ideals and the infinite rights of the heart." The young heroes accordingly try to transform the world, or to carve out some private domestic paradise—"to seek for the ideal girl, find her, win her away from her wicked relations or other discordant ties, and carry her off in defiance. But in the modern world these fights are nothing more than 'apprenticeship' [the obvious reference being to Goethe's novel], the education of the individual into the realities of the present, and thereby they acquire their true significance. For the end of such apprenticeship consists in this, that the subject sows his wild oats, builds himself with his wishes and opinions into harmony with subsisting relationships and their rationality, enters the concatenation of the world, and acquires for himself an appropriate attitude to it. However much he may have quarrelled with the world, or been pushed about in it, in most cases at last he gets his girl and some sort of position, marries her, and becomes as good a Philistine as others. The woman takes charge of household management, children arrive, the adored wife, at first unique, an angel, behaves pretty much as all other wives do; the man's profession provides work and vexations, marriage brings domestic affliction—so here we have all the headaches of the rest of married folk" (*Aesthetics*, 1.592–93). The sarcasm of this description, for all its opacities, is evident, but the modern novel's "corrective" to "the fantastic element" of early tales of knight-errantry is in the end precisely what the spirit of the age was due to bring, and is therefore welcome to all good Hegelians. The aptness of this description of the typical youth's progress will be obvious when reading most of the *Bildungsromane* on my list.
38. Howe, *Wilhelm Meister and His English Kinsmen*, 64.
39. Bruford, *German Tradition*, 30.
40. Mann, *The Magic Mountain*, 728.
41. Mr. Redfield's prize-winning book offers many learned insights into the "aesthetic ideology" of the Jena romantics, Schiller's inspired simplification of some of Kant's theories in *The Critique of Judgment*, and its pertinence to *Wilhelm Meister*, *Middlemarch*, and Flaubert's *L'Éducation sentimentale*. Mr. Redfield acknowledges large debts to the group of present and past Cornellians (Neil Hertz, Jonathan Culler, Cynthia Chase) and to J. Hillis Miller, who have fondly kept faith with Paul de Man's method of criticism, carefully separating, if I may bastardize T. S. Eliot's famous dictum, the man who suffered (and caused others to suffer) from the mind that (de)created.
42. Buckley, *Season of Youth*, 18.

CHAPTER 3

1. Hollington, "*David Copperfield* and *Wilhelm Meister*," 129.
2. Chesterton, *Chesterton on Dickens*, 332.
3. Eliot, *Selections from Letters* (to Frederic Harrison, August 15, 1866), 318.

4. Dickens, *The Personal History of David Copperfield*, xii; hereafter cited in the text implicitly.
5. Woolf, "David Copperfield," 75.
6. Mary Poovey's treatment of *Copperfield* is representative of this anti-universalist approach. Nothing about a person is accepted as "given," everything is "made" by social forces— everything including the novel—which unconsciously reproduces the "systemic class and gender inequality" of the society within which it exists (*Uneven Developments*, 123; hereafter referred to implicitly or as "Poovey"). The novelist's conscious and unconscious criticisms of that society, being inadequately Jacobin, feminist, or Chartist, never go far enough. "The concept of the individual," which for the nineteenth-century novelists like Dickens and Charlotte Brontë whom she studies "was a solution," is for Ms. Poovey "a problem": "the ego-centered subject is a historical construct" (20) that readers of a later historical moment can take apart, understand, and, when coming to themselves, their children, or their students, construct in a presumably community-centered way. This is a millenarian hope in some ways akin to Dickens's own: platitudinously, he too was against egoism. Only, he for good reasons was not a social constructionist in Ms. Poovey's sense. To put it very simply, he believed that in the process of "subject" development, nature mattered as well as nurture. "As well as" instead of "as much as," since he doesn't have a measuring-stick.

   By the way, the endnotes in this book contain most of the critical praise and combat I wish to offer my fellow critics.
7. See Leavis, "Dickens and Tolstoy," 81. While not all critics agree that David is representative— for example, Philip Collins (*Charles Dickens: David Copperfield*, 43) and Robert E. Lougy ("Remembrances of Death Past and Future," 94)—it seems evident to me that Dickens meant him to be a character that the common Victorian male reader could identify with: not a vulgarly ordinary young man, obviously, but one who, as a self-conscious autobiographer, amplifies the young man's ordinary aptitudes for observation, snobbishness, generosity, and so on. For a reading of David's psychology "within the higher ranges of normalcy," see Jerome Hamilton Buckley ("The Identity of David Copperfield," 231 and passim). A more negative account is offered by U. C. Knoepflmacher. Because David is almost always under the sheltering care of women—his mother, Peggotty, Mrs. Micawber, Aunt Betsey (sister to his father's *mother*), Dora, Agnes—he becomes "an increasingly passive and effeminate bourgeois young man" who regards women as idealized angels (or, if they are bad like Miss Murdstone or Rosa Dartle, as devils), rather than as the in-between human beings they are. When he is angry at any of the angels (his mother or Emily, for instance), he is not allowed to express it directly; he doesn't get into fights with Steerforth who has betrayed him or Heep who gives him the willies; and so he becomes increasingly wimpish, passively accepting "the female sobriquets given to him by others: Daisy, Doady, Scheherezade, Trot" ("From Outrage to Rage," 78, 82). In short, a case of failure to grow up, in contrast to the less-sheltered, manlier Pip (no woman ever shelters *him*). I don't dispute the data Mr. Knoepflmacher adduces or his interpretation of them. But I would add that, if David is at all effeminate, it is precisely because the novelist is diagnosing the crisis in absent fathers and suppressed or misdirected masculine energies found elsewhere among the *Bildungsromane* I am studying here.
8. The reliable A. D. Nuttall has noticed how, like Magwitch, Betsey is a benefactor who at first appears to be a monster, aptly enough in "the child's world of mingled fear and dependence" (*Openings*, 186). Adult fiction usually neglects the child's initial assumption that nine grown-ups out of ten are ogres, but fairy tales, Victorian children's books, and Dickens get it right.
9. Alexander Welsh quotes D. W. Winnicott's remark that "growing up means taking the parent's place. *It really does*. In the unconscious fantasy, growing up is inherently an aggressive act." David's biting of Murdstone, Mr. Welsh rightly argues, is an act of selfish aggression with which "*any* boy" in our century or Dickens's must identify: it is part of the ambition

"to pursue a career different from his father's, to enter the market place with his labor," presupposed by "the assumptions of modern [capitalist] economics." Mr. Welsh gives a "fortunate" Eriksonian, rather than a "tragic" Freudian, reading to Dickens's version of the famous plot: "There is no use experiencing an Oedipus complex unless one can leave it behind . . . . The tale of childhood that *Copperfield* tells—the weaning of the child from his mother and the biting of the hand that wards him—frees the man for labor and the punctual discharge of duties" (*From Copyright to Copperfield*, 170–71). Mr. Welsh's is the best book we have on the biographic background of *Copperfield*, *Chuzzlewit*, and *Dombey*.

10. This allusion to backbone is as good a place as any to recognize that the disciplining of David's undisciplined heart has been a theme often contested and occasionally defended since Gwendolyn B. Needham's centrist, classroom-friendly essay of 1954, "The Undisciplined Heart of David Copperfield." As Malcolm Andrews indicates, Dickens's concern for a disciplined heart and hardened head sustains an effort dating back at least to Austen's *Sense and Sensibility* and Scott's *Waverley*, and, in the dawn of his own career, to Carlyle's attempt to de-Byronize English sensibility. The early 1830s were after all the time when, according to Butler's *The Way of All Flesh*, the importance of being earnest, the *imitatio [Dr.] Arnoldi*, began to push the cultural pendulum away from dandyism and latitudinarianism generally (*Dickens and the Grown-Up Child*, 160–61). Those pre-Victorian years were, figuratively as well as literally for writers such as Dickens and Thackeray, identified with childhood—their own, and their nation's, and we can regard the comparatively earnest *David Copperfield* and *Pendennis* as would-be mature farewells to the more uncritically comic, racier productions of their early careers (see 163). This, with all our ambivalence about the costs of maturity, seems to me a "sensible" understanding of discipline: it is a process of requisite socialization that can sometimes go too far, as it does with the Murdstones and with Creakle, in which case the need is for a liberally corrective spontaneity, but that, given the inevitable conflict of desires both within David himself and between him and other people, can't be skipped altogether.

The obvious here needs to be said because of the influence, strong, for instance, in Jeremy Tambling's introduction to the new Penguin edition, of D. A. Miller's account of *David Copperfield* and other Victorian novels as illustrations of discipline *à la* Foucault, which often equates the home—with its necessary "Don't talk with your mouth full"; "Do pick up your toys"—and the prison—with its equally necessary "Time to go down to the exercise yard!"; "No weapons allowed!" (*The Novel and the Police*, 219). Such bad-boy protest rejects the notion that Dickens's characters are charming: that, Mr. Miller says, is merely a label we give these tic-ridden, "emboxed" creatures in gratitude for the illusion they offer of our own contrasting freedom (207–08). This is in addition to the trumpeted truism that identity isn't unitary, that David like everyone else isn't really "*there*" as a stable self, and that this is just as well for a hero whose profound desire since that Day of Murdstone if not before has been to live vicariously, through daydreams and ultimately through the novels he reads and writes. The same, apparently, is true of us in our novel reading: what other way is there to escape "the world's carceral oppressions" (216)? What Mr. Miller might find less dreary, one infers, would be an accouplement of David and Steerforth, or Steerforth and Emily living in Laurentian defiance of Mrs. Grundy in a villa in Italy. Frank immoralism, however, can on the evidence of Foucault's own life, to say nothing of his work, be drearier than any patch of David's.

11. Dickens, "Number-Plans," in Tambling's Penguin edition of *David Copperfield*, 822; hereafter cited in the text as "Plans."

12. House, *The Dickens World*, 132.

13. Lougy, "Remembrances of Death Past and Future," 87–92.

14. This self-in-the-mirror moment at Yarmouth is the last of half-a-dozen, beginning with little David's looking at his puffed face in the mirror after Murdstone has beaten him, when

he sees himself objectified as a creature other than his mother, who now seems to belong to Murdstone; and including his self-inspection as a mourner for his mother when at Salem House he first is told of her death, a further step in egoism, which conceives the story of her death as really the story of his own suffering, and so on. Barry Westburg's French–Freud analysis is, on careful consideration, full of insight about the autobiographer David's evolving ways of "imaging" himself, and is happily free of jargon. He draws a common sense inference from David's self-inspection at Yarmouth: he needs to stop aestheticizing other people (as images in the mirror of his own imagination, players in his life's drama) and start recognizing that they have lives of their own. "Looking-*at* rather than looking-*into* would reveal to him the banality, the emptiness of the mirror and the specular image . . . he could then look-*through* the window to others. Thus the mirror would teach that it teaches nothing: a considerable lesson." Which, however, he fails to learn and so, for Mr. Westburg, fails to grow up—being at the end of the novel a "monster-child" narcissist who still treats other people (Agnes now most of all) as screens onto which he projects his own fears and needs ("David Sees 'Himself' in the Mirror," 45–46). This seems to me too hard on David, who, yes, may fall short of sainthood when it comes to remembering the houseless etc., but who as self-centered autobiographer has if anything been most often accused of dulling himself for the sake of heightening the portraits of the vivacious people, from spear-carriers on up, who were supposed to be supporting cast.

15. Kincaid, "The Structure of *David Copperfield*," 91.

16. Simon Edwards makes the nice point that the quibble about Britannia metal versus Georgian silver means that, in David's middle-aging mind, Traddles's "*sterling* qualities" are being displaced by a radiant "collection of objects with merely *exchange* value" and so on ("*David Copperfield*: The Decomposing Self," 74). In a new-historicist mode, wherein every material and mental object connects with everything else and double entendres and puns are as common as blackberries (e.g., "Uriah Heep's name, both parts of it frankly excretory in suggestion—a paradoxical heap of piss challenging the discipline of the constipated Murdstone—hints also at a set (you-or-I) of undifferentiated, unconscious desires" [76]), Mr. Edwards is never boring, and discomfits our ideas of what counts as relevant.

17. Indicative, as Margaret F. Darby remarks, of the real power of the pen being in David's hand not Dora's ("Dora and Doady," 166). But as I think needs to be said in response to "gendered" interpretations of such situations in Victorian literature, Dickens was first of all intent on offering someone like Dora as a representative figure, brought up, in Ms. Darby's nice phrase, to "the trained incapacities of the upper class wife" (164), which echoes Dickens's working note to number 12: "Poor little Dora not bred [as against 'born'] for <the world> a working life." And in fact, the desired capablizing of such a wife came about sooner through realistic portraits such as Dora's than it would have through wishful drawings of fictive versions of George Eliot or the Brontë sisters. *They* were one-in-ten-million sorts of women, and their mute and inglorious counterparts weren't seriously going to be helped by novelists, even male ones, taking ultra-liberal attitudes (Ms. Darby seems to view the "unworthy" David as the narratorial equivalent of a Taliban spokesman); they were to be helped, as girls, by educational and work opportunities on par with what boys had, which in another century past Dickens's time they more or less would have achieved.

18. Wilson, *The World of Charles Dickens*, 216.

19. Not everyone is charmed by Steerforth the way Angus Wilson is; indeed the typical view over the last quarter century, expressed by Badri Raina for instance (*Dickens and the Dialectic of Growth*, 90), is that the young man's only attraction, if David were honest with himself, is that he is comparatively upper class—the critic adding that Heep's physical ugliness is an aesthetically prejudiced and in any event gratuitous low blow, meant to privilege the

handsome Steerforth (97). On the contrary, Dickens consistently responds to his culture's ideas of beauty and ugliness in a go-along way, only adding the sensible proviso that beautiful people (e.g., Estella in *Great Expectations*, and we remember that Murdstone is supposed to be handsome) can be spiritually twisted and physically frozen by experience that corrupts their hearts, and that unbeautiful people (Peggotty or her brother, whose skin has been roughened by work and weather) can be physically warmed and spiritually graced by experience that has enriched their hearts.

As for the ways in which an "illiberal society" has shaped Uriah Heep's 'umble demeanor, Dickens, especially in Chapter 39 (574–75) where Uriah tells David about his school-days, is no less revealing (see Hardy, "The Moral Art of Dickens: *David Copperfield*," 11, and Tambling, "Introduction," xvi–xix). Only, like most people, he has difficulty overcoming the visceral likes and dislikes he feels toward socially constructed personalities, and their innative physical and temperamental traits.

20. I would urge anyone so tempted to get buggery out of his mind, since, *pace* Oliver S. Buckton's attempt, in "'My Undisciplined Heart,'" at "declassifying homoerotic secrets" in this novel—poor David is supposed to be melancholy because he is forced to give up same-sex sex for the other kind—he as narrator never even hints at such schoolboy vice. Remember that Dickens was in this regard fortunate never go have gone to boarding school himself. This isn't to deny that he would have known that Steerforth's prototype, Byron, was bisexual or that what Robert Graves would have called pseudo-homosexual feelings (read guy-to-guy affection) obtain between Steerforth and the David he calls "Daisy." It *is* to deny that Dickens "writes into" his story a homoeroticism even as oblique as what Forster will write into *The Longest Journey*.

21. Tambling, "Introduction," xii.

22. Qtd. in ibid., xiii.

23. See Poovey, *Uneven Developments*, 115.

24. As Dickens wrote to his friend John Forster: "'Still undecided about Dora' (7th of May), 'but MUST decide to-day.' 'I have been' (Tuesday, 20th of August) 'very hard at work these three days, and have still Dora to kill. But with good luck, I may do it to-morrow'" (Forster, *Life of Dickens*, 2.101).

Death was for the Victorians what divorce was for the late twentieth century. As Michael Black writes, the haunting question of this novel is what David would do if Dora had lived, and he were left in Dickens's own domestic situation (*The Literature of Fidelity*, 101). Would he, like Dickens, separate from his wife, or would he, like an Isabel Archer, with bad-faith fidelity, stick it out? Stick it out, of course. He has accepted the unsatisfactoriness of his marriage, he tolerates and even cherishes Dora for her weaknesses, and gets help in that effort from Betsey and Agnes. He would no more throw Dora over than Betsey would throw over her dependent, Mr. Dick.

25. Slater, *Dickens and Women*, 251.

26. As Barbara Hardy correctly says, we have to grant artists the stock responses of their age ("The Moral Art of Dickens," 12), just as, I might add, we hope future generations will grant us ours. If Dickens's heart swelled at the conjunction of woman and stained-glass window, he was in his day hardly singular. Since he often associated churches, whether in village or town, with social stability, spiritual peace, and of course the Christian salvation of his soul, Arlene M. Jackson contends that, "Sharing Dickens' position, we know something David does not: he is attracted to Agnes because she emanates the warmth, security and richness of personality associated with the stained-glass window of his childhood church-going experiences" ("Agnes Wickfield and the Church Motif," 60). We don't have to be churchy ourselves to appreciate the justness of that remark, as a reminder of probable authorial intent.

27. John Carey writes: "David's obtuseness is enough to make any girl weep. For Agnes has perfectly normal instincts, in fact, and is pointing not upwards but towards the bedroom. The inadequacy lies in David, not her. . . . Readers who come away thinking Agnes a sexless saint miss the point. David sees her as that, but only because his own fear of a mature woman forces him to turn her into something untouchable" (*The Violent Effigy*, 171–72). Unfortunately, Mr. Carey's energetic formulation misses, predictably, the ethico-religious side of Agnes. But he is better than Mr. Moretti, who, as we saw in chapter 2, dismisses her (and the novel) altogether (192).

28. See Bandelin, "David Copperfield: A Third Interesting Penitent," 29—a critic acute about how David's disapproval casts Dora down so much that she simply resigns her place in the world, and about how, more subtly, David in effect sets up Steerforth—he can't in conscience take Emily to his own bed, so he "arranges" for his friend to do it for him—and then, feeling guilty, waits for time and tide to punish Steerforth for having done it. When they actually drown him and of course Ham, David irrationally feels like a murderer—two victims now in addition to Dora. Like most probings of characters' unconscious, Mr. Bandelin's seems to me deeper and darker than anything Dickens himself could have been conscious of. But then, it is really Dickens's unconscious—in a Laurentian "trust the tale" mode—that is being probed, and if the tale doesn't actually *invite* Mr. Bandelin's ethico-psychoanalytic interpretation, it does, with its abundant data-up-for-grabs, *allow* it. The same is true of (say) John O. Jordan's ethico-materialist interpretation ("The Social Sub-Text of *David Copperfield*," hereafter cited in the text implicitly or as "Jordan"). I am trying to stick with an interpretation that the novel's data seem expressly to invite.

29. Kincaid, *Dickens and the Rhetoric of Laughter*, 181.

30. As Humphry House points out, Dickens "never meant Micawber to be a Chestertonian saint who 'never ought to succeed,' whose 'kingdom is not of this world.' . . . The moral of Micawber rather is that even in a man as fantastically improvident and as gay about it as he, there is a secret possibility of success. This moral is plainly more trite than Chesterton's; but its triteness was peculiarly topical" (*The Dickens World*, 85). In any case, David suffers a significant loss when Micawber and the Peggotty group emigrate, for, as I argue, they represent forces with which neither his middle-class sense of self nor his wife Agnes can live without embarrassment. The best treatments of this uneasy aspect of the novel's ending are in Robin Gilmour, "Memory in *David Copperfield*," passim; Jordan, 85–89; and Malcolm Andrews, *Dickens and the Grown-Up Child*, 170.

31. Quite aside from the biographical knowledge that as a boy Dickens would have seen plenty of degrading sexual activity in the streets of London—David mentions how "ashamed" he was to have become such a "knowing" little chap, a remark his author might have made of himself—and that he (Dickens) thereafter tended to connect promiscuity with the wild, and dirty, lower depths of society (see Ackroyd, *Dickens*, 89–90), we might still judge that Emily is rather severely punished. She both loses Steerforth and isn't allowed, afterward, to marry even one of the reformed convicts she would encounter in the back of beyond. There, in Australia, Martha may marry as she pleases, but Emily, who hasn't fallen more than a ledge below respectability, must spend the rest of her life in an open-air convent.

32. The Peggottys' uncle–niece, the Wickfields' father–daughter, and the Strongs' husband–wife relationships have, not surprisingly, seethed with possibilities for dysfunction-hunting caseworkers whose actual credentials read "English professor." Still, while eschewing the more pointless of their diagnoses, there is no reason to deny that, beneath the surface of many of Dickens's homely relationships, energies are stifled and spirits unhappy. Representative studies of morbidity in *Copperfield* are by Brian Crick (" 'Mr. Peggotty's Dream Come True' ") and Philip Weinstein ("Mr. Peggotty and Little Em'ly"), who don't

approve of Mr. Peggotty's horny hand on the rescued Emily's shoulder. Well, Dickens's mythically virtuous figures, "a going to seek" whatever sheep or coin may be lost, have hormones like the rest of us, and I don't believe a fair-minded jury of readers will convict Mr. Peggotty of sexual harassment. His impulses are well in check.

33. For a different, exclusively political interpretation of Ham, Mr. Peggotty, and all the other sub-middle-class characters, see Jordan. One can willingly applaud an attempt, in the spirit of E. P. Thompson, to disclose the repressed social implications of a novel most critics have considered exclusively domestic. But Mr. Jordan's determination to see *Copperfield* as a deluded "Whig history of class relations, narrated by a middle-class subject" (79), is such that David, in a sexual transfer meant to prove him Steerforth's social equal, is said to "give" Emily to the Byronic youth in exchange for Rosa Dartle (69–70); or that the grins on the faces of Mr. Peggotty and Ham merely cover up "their class resentment and anger" (74); or that Heep is a "scapegoat . . . victim of the ruling class, just as his Biblical namesake, Uriah, was for King David" (79). Ms. Poovey acknowledges her debt to Mr. Jordan's essay, and with her too I think a resistant reading puts us in an insupportably extreme opposition to the novel's express intentions. We need, for example, to take seriously the narrator David's distinctions between the unconscious wrongdoings of his younger self (letting slip the reference to Mr. Mell's mother's indigence, or introducing the seducer Steerforth into the Emily's life) and the conscious wrongdoings of Uriah. True, they are both fatherless, poor boys and later self-made men, but they aren't mere doubles of one another (117–21). Uriah's blackmail, forgery, and theft aren't simply illegal; they are, within the community of sensibilities implied by this novel, immoral, and since he undertakes these acts deliberately, they are punishable. We may feel, as Dickens certainly felt, that the society that allowed the rise of David and disallowed that of Uriah should do more to open up educational and therefore social and economic opportunities to poor children generally. But it is a too-common mistake to construe chapter 61 ("I am shown Two Interesting Penitents"—namely Uriah and Littimer) as an indictment of inequality of opportunity, when it is palpably an indictment of these "model prisoners' " stubborn persistence in a this-is-*your*-fault self-pity that would make even a truly equal-opportunity system unworkable.

Mr. Jordan and Ms. Poovey nonetheless ought to be read by everyone interested in this novel, for like any good critic who combs through a text asking a single insistent question, they draw attention to epithets and speeches others have overlooked, and challenge us to see them not just with David's eyes, nor finally with Marx's, but with our own.

34. See, for instance, J. Hillis Miller, *Charles Dickens*, 155–59.

Chapter 4

1. Comic not tragic. The tone, as F. R. Leavis insisted in a once-famous exchange with Marius Bewley, is "extraordinarily high-spirited," and while the grown-ups' adulteries obviously bring "pathos" into Maisie's life, there is no sense of portentous evil such as we get in *The Turn of the Screw*. "It is no more the pathos of innocence assailed or surrounded by *evil*," Leavis writes, "than the distinctive pathos of the early part of *David Copperfield* is that" (*Anna Karenina*, 80). I would add only that the tonal difference between *Maisie* and *Turn* is, where assailed children are concerned, like that between *Copperfield* and *Bleak House*.

Comedy, it should go without saying, is quite as serious in its moral and psychological insights as tragedy, which is why—to cite another most eminent mid-century critic—Edmund Wilson was not denigrating *Maisie* when he called it, along with the other late novels, "a sort of ruminative poem which gives us not really a direct account of the internal workings of [James's] characters, but rather [his] reflective feelings, the flow of images set off in his mind, as he peeps not impolitely inside them." In short, James is not a "deep" psychologist—not (I would claim) in the way Lawrence is, or Kafka—but "his sense of life" is nonetheless "often profound and sure" (*Triple Thinkers*, 126). Exactly.

2. I find myself echoing J. Hillis Miller, who puns that Maisie is often "'amazed' . . . as a wondering spectator" (*Versions of Pygmalion*, 53). The child all a-wonder at adult goings-on wasn't, of course, a merely English fictive type. F. O. Matthiessen long ago pointed to Nathaniel Hawthorne's *The Scarlet Letter*, where Pearl gazes, knows, and drops gnomic sayings (see *American Renaissance*, 279).

3. James, *What Maisie Knew*, 13; hereafter cited in the text implicitly.

4. Thus Diane Johnson in her introduction to the Modern Library edition: *What Maisie Knew* "seems wonderfully modern today because of our familiarity with its central situation: the remarriage of divorcing spouses, and the ongoing custody battle in which a child is used as a pawn by her two warring parents." Ms. Johnson grants that what today is "practically a commonplace of life" seemed to James "extreme, even fanciful," but she shares none of his dismayed outrage at what such divorces do to children ("Introduction," xi).

5. As James writes in the "Preface" to the novel, "Small children have many more perceptions than they have terms to translate them; their vision is at any moment much richer, their apprehension even constantly stronger, than their prompt, their at all producible, vocabulary. Amusing therefore as it might at the first blush have seemed to restrict myself in this case to the terms as well as to the experience, it became at once plain that such an attempt would fail. Maisie's terms accordingly play their part—since her simpler conclusions quite depend on them; but our own commentary constantly attends and amplifies" (x). In short, *What Maisie Knew* is a rather different project than *The Adventures of Huckleberry Finn*. Maisie hasn't Huck's richness of regional dialect, nor does James have quite the same ironical intentions Twain does: what the latter is willing to leave confused and analphabetic in his hero's heart, the former pushes toward articulation in his heroine's head.

6. Many critics write "Countess" in quotation marks, on the forgivable assumption that Beale is lying: "Oh yes, my dear, but it isn't an English title. . . . No, nor French either. It's American" (177). Doesn't that make it plain that she is a mulatto South American countess, a titled descendant of someone like Miss Swartz in *Vanity Fair*? There were, e.g., countesses in Brazil before 1889. On the other hand, James in the "Preface" (xii) refers to the woman as Mrs. Cuddon, the name Mrs. Beale thinks correct, but he may be misremembering, for he has made Beale say, "My dear child, my wife's a damned fool! . . . she doesn't really know anything about anything" (178). A small point, but I am sticking with South American countess.

7. For Mr. Miller, Maisie's "spasm" is part sexual, "a paroxysm of sexual desire [for Sir Claude] and loss" (*Versions of Pygmalion*, 37; cited implicitly throughout this note), and part epistemological, a feeling of falling "into a bottomless chasm" (39)—the chasm opened, for this deconstructionist, by "the incommensurability between ascertainable meaning and historical effect" (77). He is referring to the inevitable "interval" between words and the things, acts, feelings, and ideas they are supposed to identify and convey. *Maisie* is a ripe text for deconstructive analysis, since James's awareness of the discrepancy between his heroine's childish language and his (or his narrator's) own suggests indeed that some of what she thinks and feels will remain unexpressed and ergo unknown. From this it is only a backward half step to declare the unknowability of everything, especially ethical universals. What is "universal"—the word is James's in the "Preface" (xii)—for Mr. Miller is precisely that unknowability. This epistemological blank entails an incommensurability between any act of expression (whether Maisie's, the narrator's, James's, or the reader's), on the one hand, and "any straightforward ethical action that will 'do good' in the social and political world, on

the other. Maisie, like James's other signal protagonists [Isabel, Strether, Maggie, Milly], ultimately renounces participation in the social round. She withdraws in order to protect her moral and imaginative deal [*sic!*—he means 'ideal'], which cannot be made materially operative in the real world. This harsh law would presumably hold in any conceivable society. The fact that Maisie's bliss is bale for others is not a contingent historical fact. It is, according to James, a universal law of human life" (79). In short, Maisie's purity is a consequence both of her refusal to participate in, or even referee, the crisscross sexual games the grown-ups play, and of her withdrawal into a nonpractical, nonpolitical, and therefore oddly nonethical realm of meditative being. James had reasons to be skeptical about language, thought, and action, but, as I argue, he wasn't as beaten as this clever pyrrhonistic account would suggest.

8. Apropos of the possibility of incest, Julie Rivkin presents it as at best a subject of ambivalent concern. "Viewed in terms of the structure of the oedipal family," she writes, the propriety of Maisie's implicit suggestion that she and Sir Claude become lovers is as "perfectly undecidable—both proper and improper"—as his own suggestion that she become part of an adulterous *ménage* with himself and Mrs. Beale. "To speak [Maisie's] desire as an 'older' woman, rather than as a daughter, is to compromise herself as daughter, to remove him from his paternal position, and to neutralize the meaning 'incest' which the oedipal family frame would have assigned her desire. Because her desire is spoken from a position already outside the family relation, it is both incestuous and not incestuous at once, undecidably, a confirmation of the oedipal scheme and an abandonment of its logic."

Translation and commentary: The solution is to break with the Oedipal family, which Maisie would do by transforming Sir Claude from stepfather into boyfriend and, we presume, finally into husband. No more incest, no more adultery—but (wouldn't you know!) yet another basis, should she bear him a child, for oedipal family romance and the recrudescence of incestuous and adulterous impulses. Maisie's absconding with Mrs. Wix is not, *pace* Ms. Rivkin, the meaning of her uniqueness—"renouncing the family," "ceas[ing] to be the agent of other characters' projects of representation" (*False Positions*, 158–59). Maisie is again accepting Mrs. Wix as her surrogate mother, and she will in all probability one day leave her to marry somebody who isn't Sir Claude.

9. James, *Literary Criticism*, 1229.

10. Ibid., 1230.

11. Homosocial, homosexual, "family-man," "grandmother": there is more than a little gender confusion in Sir Claude's mind, not least because, as he explains, in his culture "there *are* no family-women—hanged if there are! None of them want any children—hanged if they do!" (61). He himself wants children, if only to provide a male heir to his baronetcy, and if Ida is too busy playing billiards to care for children (to say nothing of conceiving them), then he feels compelled to care for his stepdaughter himself, and to look out for another woman who might provide him a son. He is no Henry VIII, however, for whatever woman he is with, including Mrs. Wix, he is the one who is supine. John Carlos Rowe picks up his name's homophonic suggestion: "as if he has been *clawed* by the Furies" (*The Other Henry James*, 128).

12. James, *The Portrait of a Lady*, 1.22–23; hereafter cited in the text implicitly. I prefer the metaphoric fullness of the New York Edition (1908), which more than just rhetorically is a very different book from the one James published in 1881. Among the several treatments of the two versions, the best is Nina Baym's "Revision and Thematic Change," which maintains that the Isabel of 1908 is much more inward, less socially conscious than the Isabel of 1881, and that accordingly her comfort lies not in imitating the truly independent Henrietta but in simply seeing and knowing aright. The practical problem for readers remains, however: they can take in only one *Portrait* at a time, just as they can look at, say,

only one of Constable's several versions of *The Leaping Horse* at a time. Spatial constraints in any event dictate that I address myself to the 1908 version alone.

13. The Kantian influence on New England philosophy was central, and James's father, Henry James, Sr., was sharply critical of its solipsistic proclivities—its sinking of "the finite" and "the relative" under the weight of "the Infinite" and "the Absolute," and accordingly its "rabid glorification of our natural Egotism" (qtd. in Taylor, *Henry James and the Father Question*, 128). This exactly anticipates Santayana's uneasiness with transcendentalism, not least in its American, Emersonian guise. In any case, James the novelist exposes, through the characterization of Isabel Archer, the fallibility of the transcendentalist "approach to knowledge through intuition and feeling, the assumption of a benevolent universe, the highly self-conscious dedication to the spontaneous realisation of the self," and so on. Mr. Taylor adds that the chapter "Brook Farm and Concord" in *Hawthorne* (1879), which James was writing in the early stages of contemplating *Portrait*, offers us an Emersonian key to the puzzle of Isabel's self-regard.

14. These direct, "Trollopean" pleas for patience and sympathy not only ensure that we won't miss the tenderness in James's irony toward Isabel; they bespeak his love, in her figure, for his cousin, Minny Temple, who died at 24, nearly a decade before he began to write Isabel's story, and who has been the object of biographical speculation that needn't divert us here. Richard Poirier has made the important point: James's love for his character precedes, and is indeed the condition for, his knowledge of her. If, remembering Hippolyte Taine's famous dictum, "Balzac *aime sa Valérie*," the courtesan careerist of *Cousine Bette*, so James *aime sa Isabel*—and works to induce us to love her too (*Comic Sense*, 208–09).

15. Joel Porte discusses Isabel's acculturation within the Arnoldian, Paterian tradition I have outlined in chapter 2. He makes the correct general point that Isabel comes to Europe thinking she will cultivate her garden-self like a connoisseur (Osmond, for instance) picking up impressions—wanting "to see, but not to feel," as Ralph notes (1.213)—and she learns that, as Arnold and Pater had understood, feeling is in fact required, if her garden-self is to achieve moral beauty. Which is to say, she learns that suffering is required, not to sharpen self-pity, an emotion belonging to childhood, but to connect her little garden-self with the equivalent garden-selves that constitute the race (see Porte, "Introduction," 15–17, 22–24).

16. And who, as Ms. Baym rightly notes, was decidedly a feminist paragon in the 1881 version—not "loud, overbearing, and obnoxious," the clichéd "tough, efficient career girl," but "pretty, decorous, and ladylike," and a "highly talented and thoroughly professional" journalist to boot. The Isabel of either version lacks the stuff of Henrietta, whose marriage to Bantling "is presented as a happy event"—happy because they don't depend on marriage "to give life meaning" ("Revision and Thematic Change," 86). The problem, as I point out, is that Isabel lacks her friend's vocational inspiration—indeed that her access of fortune removes the "get a job" imperative from her life—and that she therefore, like most women of her class and era, *does* rather count on marriage to give her life meaning.

17. Dorothea Krook appreciated this motive better than most of James's critics, of her time (the 1950s and 1960s) and since. Isabel's apparent coldness or hardness has nothing to do with "frigidity" and everything to do with protecting herself till she finds the "right person," i.e., a man who can help her develop her mind and whom she can also serve (see *Ordeal of Consciousness*, 366–67). The burden of Krook's argument is that Isabel's believing that Osmond is the right person is a tragic, not merely foolish, error. That is, she is no ditsy victim but a moral agent responsible for her choices, subtly tainted by the aestheticism so unsubtly dominant in Osmond's character.

　　Mr. Poirier finds tragedy too, but only in the second half. The first has been a theatrical entertainment that turns out to be deceit: "life is only a masked ball into which a Cinderella invariably wanders who must stay after midnight and do the cleaning up"

(*Comic Sense*, 230). True, but Isabel's clean-up job is no temporary position, it is "for the rest of her life" (2.196). In which case it isn't comic role-playing—Mr. Poirier in 1960 was evidently reacting against the "organization man" stiffnesses of the 1950s—but a commitment to vocation and community that will keep her spiritually alive.

That was not quite the conclusion of another 1960s critique, one of the best ever written on this novel, Charles Feidelson's "The Moment of *The Portrait of a Lady*," which bracingly celebrates Isabel's "embattled consciousness" but alas neglects what to James was correlatively interesting, her conscience—the faculty that in *Maisie* is more often called "moral sense." I would tender the same criticism of what is otherwise the best recent book on James, Millicent Bell's *Meaning in Henry James*, which grants the romantically self-creating Isabel less achieved moral wisdom at the close—less understanding of "the discrepancy between reality and her theories" (91–92)—than, to me, the text indicates. But this is a quibble that the body of my discussion works through.

18. James, *Complete Notebooks*, 13–14.
19. We may reasonably recoil from Osmond's crooning: "My dear girl, I can't tell you how life seems to stretch there before us—what a long summer afternoon awaits us. It's the latter half of an Italian day—with a golden haze, and the shadows just lengthening, and that divine delicacy in the light, the air, the landscape, which I have loved all my life and which you love to-day" (2.81) and so on—but the novel in some measure does achieve James's intention, which was to make the *vie de dilettante*, in the honorable sense of amateur of the arts (Osmond's drawings, Madame Merle's piano), as attractive to Isabel as Maisie will find the *vie de bohème*. Such lives are sweet, but one has to watch out.
20. James, *Complete Notebooks*, 14.
21. An implicit corollary is that, in persuading his father to bequeath half his patrimony to Isabel, Ralph has grievously misassessed the chances of Isabel's falling prey to a fortune hunter—indeed, that it is nearly always a mistake to gift an *un*prepared receptacle any huge sum of money, for the simple reason that he or she will surely waste, mismanage, or be robbed of it. A *Bildungsheld* such as Santayana's Oliver Alden, who is born to financial independence, as we will see, is badgered by the needy often enough, but he manages all right because he has grown up with a sense of noblesse oblige. He is the exception that proves the rule illustrated by Steerforth, who regards inherited wealth as a license to prey on boys like David and girls like Emily. The characters in these novels who fare best in their relations to money are those compelled to earn it, as David does.
22. Among the many passages pertinent to the theme of connoisseurship is this, registering Osmond's conception of himself: "If an anonymous drawing on a museum wall had been conscious and watchful it might have known this peculiar pleasure of being at last and all of a sudden identified—as from the hand of a great master—by the so high and so unnoticed fact of style. His 'style' was what the girl had discovered with a little help; and now, beside herself enjoying it, she should publish it to the world without his having any of the trouble. She should do the thing *for* him, and he would not have waited in vain" (2.12). And this one suggesting Isabel's matching conception of herself: "she had put away her mourning and she walked in no small shimmering splendour. She only felt older—ever so much, and as if she were 'worth more' for it, like some curious piece in an antiquary's collection" (2.42). Both Isabel and Osmond are collectors, but while he is often content to regard himself as a specimen, she regards herself as a *self*—and with greater intensity as her suffering increases.
23. "Sin" is a word James didn't blench from, and for reasons a Catholic such as Graham Greene was in a position to understand: the good and evil of human nature generally was inside the artist—either pole helping him grasp the other. In Greene's words: "For to render the highest justice to corruption you must retain your innocence: you have to be conscious

all the time within yourself of treachery to something valuable. If Peter Quint [from *The Turn of the Screw*] is to be rooted in you, so must the child his ghost corrupts: if Osmond, Isabel Archer too" (*Collected Essays*, 28).

This, as Mr. Taylor has suggested, is one reason James preferred "the power of blackness" in Hawthorne to, say, the pungency of *mal* in Baudelaire. The American writer understood evil to reside within himself, as it does within all human beings; the French writer obsessed about a nastiness external to himself, an offense not to his moral sense but to his "olfactories" (see *Henry James and the Father Question*, 129, citing James, *Literary Criticism*, 155–56).

24. Tony Tanner's "The Fearful Self" remains the standard essay on the Kantian difference between regarding oneself and others as objects (means) and as subjects (ends).

25. The only true European we get to know in the novel is Lord Warburton, who, as F. W. Dupee finely said at the dawn of modern James studies, has a self so identified with "his inherited functions as head of the family, landlord, and member of the House of Lords" that the Americanized Europeans, and even the mere travelers Caspar and Henrietta who have perfectly decent jobs and families back home, seem by contrast to be bizarrely "*self*-seek[ing]" (*Henry James*, 122). Not that we should conflate all Europeans with Lord Warburton or all Americans with these expatriates. European *Bildungshelden* such as Wilhelm, David, or Paul Morel, inasmuch as they leave their class of origin, are akin to these self-seeking, self-defining Americans abroad, just as stay-at-home Americans can, in this or that Rutland (unfortunately named town), accustom themselves to the same honorable *ruts* Lord Warburton is so bored with at moated Lockleigh.

26. Bell, *Meaning in Henry James*, 98.

27. Joel Porte connects Isabel's melancholy brooding over Roman ruins with Virgil's *Sunt lachrimae rerum*: "they weep here / For how the world goes," per Robert Fitzgerald's translation (Virgil, *Aeneid*, 20). When following the poignant scene of Ralph's death Isabel sees the ghost of Gardencourt, we know that, morally at least, she has grown up. No more fluttering for what Mr. Porte calls "a Gothic frisson—a private thrill at seeing crumbling castles and predictable ghosts" (24). Deflating Horace Walpole's *The Castle of Otranto* or Ann Radcliffe's *The Mysteries of Udolpho* is no mere joke, as it tends to be in Austen's *Northanger Abbey*.

28. Cf. Bell, *Meaning in Henry James*, 121. The critic aptly suggests that such an investment of Isabel's money would not duplicate "Ralph's fatal endowment" of her, for instead of making Pansy a target for adventurers it would enable her to marry the man she has already committed herself to.

29. A notebook entry suggests an idea that is submerged in the novel itself: Madame Merle springs on Isabel the news that Ralph "induced" his father to leave her a fortune because she "wishes [Isabel] to make a *coup de tête*, to leave Osmond, so that she may be away from Pansy" (James, *Complete Notebooks*, 15). That is, the birth mother is jealous of the stepmother, who, given the former's designs on the girl, has a moral obligation to stand fast. Mid-century critics' language turned needfully austere round this subject, from Dorothy Van Ghent's transformation of freedom to enjoy life "into the freedom of personal renunciation and inexhaustible responsibility" (*The English Novel*, 261), to Richard P. Blackmur's *basso-profundo* dourness about the heroine's "conceit [having] turned to a suicidal obstinacy" under pressure from the "force of marriage—not love but marriage," to Krook's insistence that Isabel's dutiful return to Rome means "enduring, simply *enduring*, her life" with her husband (*Ordeal of Consciousness*, 360).

Recent critics have mostly eschewed such austerities—take, for instance, Alfred Habegger, who remarks that "For the American girl to become a lady means the suffocation of her heart's desire, a final acceptance of an absurd set of constraints" (*Gender, Fantasy, and Realism*, 69)—and have consequently had difficulty understanding James on his own terms. Readers too eager to say, from their own current perspective, what makes for real manliness or womanliness, scarcely allow the novelist to do his or her own social history and critique. Mr. Habegger isn't *that* eager, but after noting, e.g., James's account of Isabel's maternal impulses, he dismisses her rejection of Caspar as a symptom of conventional "Victorian" sexlessness—quite as he dismisses the New York Edition's revision of the "*prick*" Caspar's kiss as "absurdly melodramatic, maybe even hysterical," a sign of James's "exaggerated fear of [male] aggression," particularly in its robber–baron American form (78). James's fear is only marginally relevant if at all. The dramatic point is that, after being rebuffed so often by Isabel, Caspar has been driven to playing it rough, and that she, like the majority of "ladies" in more epochs than her own, insists that he back off. It isn't, to be anachronistic myself, a cry of "date rape"—she doesn't reach for her lawyer. It is a perfectly capable act of self-defense.

CHAPTER 5

1. Orwell, " 'Such, Such Were the Joys,' " 334.
2. Erikson, *Childhood and Society*, 79.
3. Forster, *The Longest Journey*, 4, 8; hereafter cited in the text implicitly.
4. Forster, *Howards End*, 105.
5. Cavaliero, *A Reading of E. M. Forster*, 79.
6. Conjectures about Forster's familiarity with Moore's ideas have been complicated by S. P. Rosenbaum, who regards *The Longest Journey* as "an imaginative interpretation and extension" of Moore's anti-Berkeleyan paper, "The Refutation of Idealism," which appeared in *Mind* (October 1903). But as P. N. Furbank rejoins, it seems clear on Mr. Rosenbaum's own evidence that Forster never actually read either Moore's book or his paper. Not only is Forster's own testimony about his very oblique familiarity with Moore's ideas unequivocal (see Rosenbaum, "*The Longest Journey*: E. M. Forster's Refutation of Idealism," 33, 287, n. 4), but Mr. Furbank rightly "suspect[s] that Moore's rather 'scholastic' and arithmetical way of talking of 'organic unities' . . . would have repelled [Forster] had he encountered it. All one can find about Berkeleyan idealism in Forster, surely, is what any educated person of this century or the previous one knew: that is to say the idea summed up in the famous limerick about the tree in the Quad. Forster in this sense was philosophically naïve, though only in this sense." The limerick goes:

    > There once was a man who said God
    > Must find it exceedingly odd,
    >> If he finds that this tree
    >> Continues to be
    > When there's no-one about in the Quad.

    See Furbank, "The Philosophy of E. M. Forster," 45, 50, n. 13.
7. Forster, "Looking Back," 58.
8. Russell, *Autobiography*, 86.
9. At Nassenheide, Germany, in the spring of 1905, "Elizabeth" (Countess von Arnim, later Countess Russell) lent Forster a copy of Butler's *Erewhon* (Furbank, *Forster*, 1:130). He had already, in February, been reading *The Way of All Flesh* and recording his reaction in his diary: "so clever it is at describing character, so bad at making people: the scheme so immense, the effect so unreal because he is resolutely unconventional" (Heine, "Introduction," xlviii; hereafter cited in the text as "Elizabeth Heine"). What did impress him were Butler's witty inversions and his iconoclastic ideas, which, as he remembered of *Erewhon* in 1944, were "a little farther down . . . [the] particular path" he himself was walking (*Two Cheers* 222; hereafter cited in the text as *Two Cheers*).

10. Forster, *Marianne Thornton*, 265.

11. The notion that the school is the world in miniature goes back at least to Sir Thomas Booby, who in Henry Fielding's *Joseph Andrews* (III.v) is quoted as saying that "great Schools are little Societies, where a Boy of any Observation may see in Epitome what he will afterwards find in the World at large"—a position Parson Adams strongly denounces in favor of a "purer" upbringing at home. Compare Forster's review of commencement addresses in 1933, in which he notices how insufferably often speakers summon boys from "the world in miniature" into a still more distorted "world which, as far as my own notions go, has very little connexion with reality, a world where everyone is either managing or being managed, and where the British Empire has been appointed to the post of general manager." He himself would like to reassure boys that "There's a better time coming" ("Breaking Up," 119), when presumably they will be able to cultivate their post-imperial gardens. First, however, would have to come an empire-destroying war, which would leave a lot of ash on those gardens.

12. See Forster's introduction to William Golding's novel (ix–xiii): his enthusiasm has something to do with the latter's realistically dark assessment of *undeveloped* human nature.

13. Forster, "Aspect of a Novel," lxix–lxx.

14. When Forster said that *The Longest Journey* "is the only one of my books that has come upon me without my knowledge" ("Aspect of a Novel," lxvi), he was thinking particularly of the character of Stephen, whose club-footed "original" he had met and shared a pipe with in 1904. It was an experience of Scholar-Gipsy-like reciprocation that he later recalled in the early 1920s for the Bloomsbury Memoir Club. There had been no sexual contact, just pleasant talk about nothing: "I had planned the book before I took that walk to Figsbury Rings; its meagre theme (a man learns he has an illegitimate brother) and its meagre moral (we oughtn't to like one person specially) had both been noted. Then the emotion welled up, spoiling it as a novel but giving it its quality. . . . Although vague and stagy, [Stephen] is the only character who exists for me outside his book, and restores to the world of experience more than he took from it" ("Memoirs," 305–06). It is striking that Forster should have transferred the shepherd's club foot to Rickie, perhaps expressing a desire that the one should have the other's "inherited" homosexual temperament. Striking, too, is a similarity between this shepherd and the Millais-like image of Christ that Forster prefers to the churchy one: "Suppose I could think of Christ not as an evangelical shop walker, but as the young carpenter who would smoke a pipe with me in his off time and be most frightfully kind. 'A man shall be a hiding place in a tempest' would suddenly mean something" (qtd. in Furbank, *Forster*, 1:163). Furbank's two-volume life is standard.

15. Ever since W. H. Beveridge's doubts about this "blend of pagan god and modern hooligan" (qtd. in Elizabeth Heine, lviii), opinions about Stephen have been predominantly negative, though a few have praised him, notably Peter Burra ("The Novels of E. M. Forster," 30) and P. J. M. Scott, who aptly notes that one's judgment of such a character depends to some degree on "one's own experience of our species" (*E. M. Forster*, 101). In an unpublished essay, "Three Countries," Forster himself conceded that Stephen "can be boorish and a bore" (qtd. in Colmer, *E. M. Forster*, 69), and to James McConkey he admitted that "I never showed (except perhaps through his talk with Ansell) that he [Stephen] could understand Rickie, and scarcely that he could be fond of him. So that, in the end chapter, he lies as a somewhat empty hulk on that hillside. Who cares what he thinks, or doesn't think of?" (Forster, *Selected Letters*, 2:267). A major difficulty, we can now see, is that Forster discarded large portions of manuscript centering on Stephen—not just the "Panic" chapter that he mentions in his introduction, but much of the "talk with Ansell," which might have helped make him a more articulate presence. As Ms. Heine remarks,

the lingering memory of these passages probably heightened Stephen's importance for Forster, who in 1964, near the end of his life, revisiting the Ring with William Golding, could write: "I exclaimed several times that the area was marvelous, and large—larger than I recalled. I was filled with thankfulness and security and glad that I had given myself so much back. . . . I shall lie in Stephen's arms instead of his child. How I wish that book hadn't faults! But they do not destroy it, and the gleam, the greatness, the grass remain. I don't want any other coffin" (qtd. in Elizabeth Heine, lxi, xlii).

16. See Tony Brown, "E. M. Forster's *Parsifal*," and Robert K. Martin, "The Paterian Mode in Forster's Fiction." Judith Herz very finely summarizes the "operatic" (specifically Wagnerian) techniques, early noticed by Benjamin Britten ("Some Notes on Forster and Music," 82): the rhythmic alternation between unlyrical recitative and aria- or ensemble-like big comic or emotionally tense scenes. For some late-Victorian and Edwardian homosexuals, enthusiasm for Wagner was "a lightly coded affirmation of sexual preference" (141), and for Ms. Herz the correspondences of plot and character between *Parsifal* and *Journey*, reinforced by the latter's "music," especially its "Love, the Beloved Republic" arias, tell a "sexually disruptive . . . queer story" ("'This is the End of Parsival,'" 141, 149). She demurs, however, against the assumption of critics such as Nicola Beauman (*Morgan*, 180) that Forster "hated" his own sexual tendency, though surely it is too much to claim "there is no evidence" for such hatred; and she fruitfully suggests that his "making Ansell Jewish was in part an anti-Wagner move" ("'This is the End of Parsival,'" 142, 148), as are the skeptical questionings his deflatingly plain prose brings to his poetical passages, which I find almost embarrassing to quote in isolation, however beautiful they are in context.

17. Forster, *Abinger Harvest*, 176; hereafter cited in the text as *Abinger Harvest*.

18. Trilling, *E. M. Forster*, 56. In one sense Trilling is right: as Richard Jenkyns has convincingly shown, Greek motifs were by Forster's time the tired properties of a legion of then popular but now forgotten writers. There is a nice irony in Agnes's common-sense criticism of the artificiality of Rickie's stories mixed with her belief that his themes are original. "Forster returns to this motif later," Mr. Jenkyns says, "when Rickie is dead and Mr. Pembroke is proposing to issue his stories posthumously under the title *Pan Pipes*. Wonham asks, more shrewdly perhaps than he realizes, 'Are you sure "Pan Pipes" haven't been used up already?' And here there is a further irony still: Pan's pipes are 'used up' because Greek religion is used up" (*The Victorians and Ancient Greece*, 191). In this last sentence, however, the irony may be on the critic: Forster's endeavor is to find a renewed validity in "Greek religion," which means doing something subtler and more complex in *The Longest Journey* than he (or Rickie) had done in "Other Kingdom."

19. Forster, *A Passage to India*, 282.

20. In a series of astringent essays since *The Cave and the Mountain*, Wilfred Stone has addressed Forster's capacities for "connecting" on the personal and the national level, and he finds a record spotty at best. See his "'Overleaping Class,'" 404, "Profit and Loss," 76–77, and "Subversive Individualism," 32.

21. Bonnie Blumenthal Finkelstein too has caught here an echo of Shaw's Jack Tanner, who in *Man and Superman* (1903) puts up a stouter fight against *his* "emissary of Nature," Ann Whitefield, than Rickie does against Agnes. Ms. Finkelstein also notices the nickname, Ricky-Ticky-Tavy, which Ann gives Octavius, the artist-figure who like Rickie is shy of the Life Force (*Forster's Women*, 43–44). The coincidence, which is probably all it is, points up what may be a hard-wired difference between the untutored impulse toward promiscuity in males and the untutored impulse in females toward keeping the impregnator around to help feed and care for the offspring. See Robert Wright's *The Moral Animal*, which is a subtle yet accessible application of Darwinism to philosophical anthropology, and which gives many nuances to the generalization I have just offered.

22. In addition to Ms. Herz's aforementioned essay on Wagnerian elements in this novel, see her "The Double Nature of Forster's Vision," which concentrates on homosexual allegory in the platonic Dickinsonian vein, wherein the "invert" temperament is more important than the "invert" experience (259–61).

23. For Lawrence's complicated counsel and Forster's response, see Furbank, *E. M. Forster*, 2:10–11, 124. The canceled "Prologue" to *Women in Love* is a crucial text for understanding Lawrence's attitude toward homosexuality, and since he is the subject of the following chapter, I address that attitude here. Four years before the opening action, Birkin has during a mountaineering trip with two male friends fallen in love with Gerald, and Gerald (unconsciously) with him: "each would die for the other" (*Women in Love*, 500; cited implicitly to the end of this note). At the same time, Birkin's feelings are clearly bisexual, as he is drawn to intellectual women like Hermione and mere sex-pots like Pussum, who very roughly parallel the Miriam and Clara we see in *Sons and Lovers*. He gets no erotic satisfaction from either sort of woman, and therefore still finds himself attracted—it is a pattern salient in Forster's life—to "ruddy, well-nourished fellows" (like Stephen Wonham) who aren't very bright but who take care of "his delicate health more gently than a woman would . . . . He wanted to caress them," but doesn't dare. After a while, however, these friendships fade, and he looks back on the fellows "as [having been] tedious" to talk to (512). David-like, Birkin knows "that is was [not] well for him to feel this keen desire" for these Viking or Mediterranean Jonathans, and so he suppresses it, but (again) he can't uncreate a feeling, any more "than he can prevent his body from feeling heat and cold." So he goes on, waiting for the day when his compass will change, "when the beauty of men should not be so acutely attractive to him, when the beauty of woman should move him instead" (514). Ursula Brangwen, it should be clear, is in the plot destined to "move him" in the whole, profound way that Hermione or the Pussum figures haven't, while his friendship with Gerald evolves, as he hopes, into a *Blutbrüderschaft* (198) based not on buggery but on conversation and wrestling.

In a letter to Russell (February 12, 1915) Lawrence had this to say about Forster: "why can't he act? Why can't he take a woman and fight clear to his own basic, primal being?" It is because Forster is caught up in "the love for humanity—the desire to work for humanity." Heterosexuality or homosexuality: for "the ordinary Englishman of the educated class" the sex act is mere onanism, and "a man of strong soul [like Forster] has too much honour for the other body—man or woman—to use it as a means of masterbation [*sic*]. So he remains neutral, inactive. That is Forster" (*Letters*, 2.284–85).

24. Forster, *Albergo Empedocle*, 142.

25. Forster conceives his story in terms of "Greek Drama, where [as Ansell reflects] the actors know so little and the spectators so much," adding, behind Ansell's back, that he (Ansell) is also an actor playing his unconscious part (236–37). Such hints seem to put the novel into a tragic mode, though its conclusion is obviously comic. The point is that we should distinguish our attitude from Aunt Emily's, which is comic in a bad sense: having forgotten what people are really like, she just stands apart and laughs at everything and everybody.

26. See Forster, *Passage to India*, 264.

27. Just how important this white-bread, civilized posture became to English writers in the 1930s is evident in Christopher Isherwood's *Down There on a Visit* (1962), where he recalls that *his* representative Englishman was not Chamberlain but Forster, "the anti-heroic hero": "While the others tell their followers to be ready to die, he advises us to live as if we were immortal. And he really does this himself, although he is as anxious and afraid as any of us, and never for an instant pretends not to be" (qtd. in Furbank, *Forster*, 2:229).

28. See Forster, *A Room with a View*, 49.
29. Ansell's mandala introduces a leitmotif of circles within squares that many readers have noticed: the most important circles are Rickie's dell at Cambridge, which he would mark with a sign saying "This way to Heaven" (20), and Cadbury Rings, at the center of which stands a tree of knowledge. When Stephen is seen leaning against the tree like a heroic, Blakean Satan, he is unwittingly presenting Rickie with the keys to the kingdom. See, e.g., Barbara Rosecrance, *Forster's Narrative Vision*, 59, and Richard Martin, *The Love that Failed*, 94. For an exhaustive list of the recurrences of the motif, see Elizabeth Heine, xi.
30. It is Frederick C. Crews who, uncharacteristically, has most seriously failed to read it thus. First, he says Rickie must "beware of the 'bankruptcy' that follows from overestimating the worth and permanence of the people he loves," when Forster's idea is that he must learn "the true discipline of [such] a bankruptcy"—which suggests that there is at first some point in loving not wisely but too well. Second, he says Rickie's greatest weakness is "an inherent tendency to view his experience symbolically rather than realistically" (*E. M. Forster*, 53, 58). No, viewing the world symbolically should *enable* him to get at its "core" reality—if only he will deploy the right symbols.
31. See Forster, "Memoirs," 303–04, and "E. M. Forster on His Life," 11.
32. Forster, "A Conversation," 55.
33. Stone, *Cave and Mountain*, 213.
34. Cf. Brian May, *The Modernist as Pragmatist*, 49. Connecting Rickie's Oedipal limp, for which, in a cancelled passage, he is said to "hate" his father, to what Forster believed to be his own congenital homosexuality, Ms. Heine maintains that the novelist, thus disguised, was able to express his own bitterness against "his paternal heredity" (xxi). Forster was after all only two years old when his father died, but his resentment lasted a lifetime, not least because his condition precluded his having children. Even Ellis was morally severe about the question: "Sometimes, indeed, the tendency to sexual inversion in eccentric and neurotic families seems merely to be Nature's merciful method of winding up a concern which, from her point of view, has ceased to be profitable" (xxiii). That is why it must be the sexually unambiguous Stephen whose seed will perpetuate the race.

Chapter 6

1. Lawrence, "Foreword," 469–70; hereafter cited in the text implicitly or as "Foreword."
2. A fact often occluded by the followers of Kate Millett, who associate Lawrence with male supremacism. Misandric commentators on Lawrence, academic and popular, have been legion in the years since Millett and Norman Mailer fought it out in the early 1970s—see her *Sexual Politics* and his *The Prisoner of Sex*—but there have also been some valuable nonpartisan assessments of the novelist's ideas about femininity and feminism. See, for instance, Judith Arcana's "I Remember Mama," which correctly insists that Lawrence doesn't simple-mindedly blame the mother; Hilary Simpson's *D. H. Lawrence and Feminism*, which treats Lawrence's female characters in the context of early-twentieth-century England, with its Suffragist movement; and Janice H. Harris's "Lawrence and the Edwardian Feminists," which brings its title nouns into illuminating dialogue.
3. See Robert Bly, *The Sibling Society*, 119–20. Many reviewers have dismissed Mr. Bly with a shrug, pitying or otherwise, but this book, like his *Iron John* (1990), contains two parts pay dirt for one part sludge—a better ratio than most academic publications can offer.
4. Lawrence, *Sons and Lovers*, 323; hereafter cited in the text implicitly.

5. Miles, *God, a Biography*, 253.

6. Qtd. in Frieda Lawrence, "*Not I, but the Wind . . . ,*" 74.

7. Lawrence, *Phoenix*, 133–40; hereafter cited in the text implicitly or as *Phoenix*.

8. Spender, *The Struggle of the Modern*, 96.

9. Lawrence, *Phoenix II*, 597–601; hereafter cited in the text implicitly or as *Phoenix II*.

10. I have never seen an attempt to identify this "new one." It is obviously not Lawrence himself, since his name wasn't yet legion. Among contemporary candidates, Forster is a possibility, but Lawrence didn't know enough about him in January 1913 to call him a new Oedipus. Tracking down this or other biographical information is made relatively easy in Lawrence studies by the fine indexes to the Cambridge edition of the letters, the three-volume Cambridge biography by John Worthen, Mark Kinkead-Weekes, and David Ellis (1991–1998), or the one-volume biography by Jeffrey Meyers (1990), which is the source to start with.

11. Lawrence, *Complete Poems*, 490–91.

12. F. Scott Fitzgerald put the perdurable dilemma with beautiful simplicity: "The present was the thing—work to do and someone to love. But not to love too much, for he knew the injury that a father can do to a daughter or a mother to a son by attaching them too closely: afterward, out in the world, the child would seek in the marriage partner the same blind tenderness and, failing probably to find it, turn against love and life." This from "Babylon Revisited" (*Short Stories*, 628).

13. See R. P. Draper, *D. H. Lawrence: The Critical Heritage*, 67.

14. Larkin, *Collected Poems*, 180. Respecting this famous line, Larkin told an interviewer in 1979 that he was worried the *Oxford Dictionary of Quotations* would "lumber" him with it: "I wouldn't want it thought that I didn't like my parents. I did like them. But at the same time they were rather awkward people and not very good at being happy. And these things rub off. Anyway, they didn't put that line in. Chicken, I suppose" (*Required Writing*, 48).

15. See Van Ghent, *The English Novel*, 296–315.

16. Lawrence, *Psychoanalysis and the Unconscious*, 9.

17. Lawrence, *Fantasia of the Unconscious*, 159–60. The reference to "the girl"'s life being creamed sounds out of place, since most of Lawrence's analysis in these studies of the unconscious is devoted to sons. In passing, however, he does forward some fruitful remarks about the Electral problem that a daughter's relationship with her father can generate, parallel to a son's Oedipal problem generated by his relationship with his mother. The stories in *The Rainbow* of Anna and Ursula and their fathers (Tom is Anna's stepfather, of course) could be the source of the later theoretical remarks.

18. Judith Farr describes the trope's derivation from the Grimms' "Briar Rose" as well as from Perrault, and its reworkings by Tennyson and the Pre-Raphaelites, whose poems and paintings Lawrence would have known. Throughout the novel Mrs. Morel is "asleep," imprisoned in a bad marriage and waiting for a son-knight to waken and rescue her ("D. H. Lawrence's Mother as Sleeping Beauty," 204). Also asleep is Clara, toward whom Paul can more directly play the prince.

19. Michael Black notes an allusion to John 12.24: "Except a corn of wheat fall into the ground and die, it abideth alone: but if it die, it bringeth forth much fruit"—adding that "this is not a temptation to suicide, it is, as in the Gospel, a demand for a rebirth" (*D. H. Lawrence*, 83). Fair enough, though since in the context of Lawrence's paragraph the emphasis is on Paul's *not* dying, one must, as often in the Gospel, understand the dying metaphorically. Paul has to die to the life of overdependence on his mother, and be reborn into a life now of detached independence, now of mutualistic interdependence.

20. Lawrence, *Letters*, 1.477.

CHAPTER 7

1. Mumford, "The Genteel Tradition at Bay," 27.

2. The primary source for Oliver was Edward Bayley, whom Santayana knew in his youth: "A dumb inglorious Milton who was not a prig, an Emerson with warm blood, who was not proud or oracular or cosmographical, and never thought himself the centre of the universe. Young Bayley was my first, perhaps my fundamental, model for *The Last Puritan*" (*Persons and Places*, 178; hereafter cited in the text implicitly or as *Persons.*). See also the likeness to (a) the finely sensitive but more assimilable Cameron Forbes, typical of the "grandsons" of the great merchants, the as it were third-generation Buddenbrooks, whom Santayana taught at Harvard (347–48); and (b) Lawrence Butler, whose indecisive falling-between-two-stools and "vegetative" "petering out" seemed to Santayana suggestive of the befogged Nordic as against the sunny Mediterranean consciousness (383). The young Bayley, Forbes, and Butler were his friends, but friends soon lost after graduation, leaving Santayana, who had been cut off from potential friends closer to his own age by diversities of "race, country, religion, and career," still lonely and socially "somnambulistic" (351–52).

3. Santayana wrote in 1928 of how his novel, then in draft, had come to be about "the sentimental education of a young American of the best type, who convinces himself that it is morally wrong to be a Puritan, yet can't get rid of the congenital curse, and is a failure in consequence. It is like the maladaptation of Henry Adams, only concentrated in the first years of youth: for my hero dies young, being too good for this world. He is an infinitely clearer-headed and nobler person than Henry Adams, but equally ineffectual" (qtd. in John McCormick, *George Santayana*, 329; hereafter cited in the text as "McCormick.") Reviewing the novel, Conrad Aiken saw the Adams connection for himself, calling it "the perfect companion-piece" to *The Education* ("*The Last Puritan*," 37).

4. Peter Conn does a competent job of placing *The Last Puritan* in its 1930s context. Reviewers favored it because it avoided the fashionable ways of dealing with the hardships of the Depression: escapist novels such as Hervey Allen's *Anthony Adverse* (1933), Pearl Buck's *The Good Earth* (1932), or Margaret Mitchell's *Gone With the Wind* (1936), which sold 50,000 copies a day, or left-wing engagement novels such as Albert Halper's *Union Square* (1933), Clara Weatherwax's *Marching! Marching!* (1935), or Robert Cantwell's *Land of Plenty* (1934). *The Last Puritan* seemed timely as a continuation of American writers' critique of Puritanism, from Brooks Adams to Randolph Bourne to H. L. Mencken et al., which in the 1920s focused on its sexual repressiveness and in the 1930s on its "capitalist-acquisitive values": "As prosperity had ratified those values, so bankruptcy [in 1929] challenged them, and the Puritan became a commonplace emblem of failed arrogance and the harm that a narrowly conceived sense of duty can inflict" (Conn, "Paternity and Patriarchy," 276).

5. Wilson, *Europe Without Baedeker*, 51.

6. English democratic pluralism had more in common with Santayana's idea of America than most critics have realized. A careful reading of his *Character and Opinion in the United States*, essays such as "Americanism," and his acerbically funny poem, "Young Sammy's First Wild Oats" (1900), reveals that what offended his soul was the intellectual ambience of Brahmin Boston ("a nice place with very nice people in it; but . . . a moral and intellectual nursery, always busy applying first principles to trifles" [*Persons*, 49]), and especially Cambridge, which among other things regarded America as an "exceptional" country. No, it was an ordinary country, going through stages of economic, social, and political development like others before, whereas the New England, Puritanic exceptionalists were—well, "eccentric and self-banished from the great human caravan" (86). In this vein Santayana had written Van Wyck Brooks in 1929: "I . . . think that art, etc., has a better soil in the ferocious 100% America than in the Intelligentsia of New York. It is veneer, rouge, aestheticism, art

museums, new theatres, etc. that make America impotent. The good things are football, kindness, and jazz bands" (Santayana, *Letters*, 157; hereafter cited in the text as *Letters*). He could therefore only rejoice that the United States came in on the side of the democratic powers in 1917 and again at the end of 1941, though by then he was a very old, very disengaged man.

7. Santayana himself linked *The Last Puritan* less with the ordinary Book-of-the-Month-Club selection than with "something like Wilhelm Meister or Don Quixote, if I may modestly place myself in good company." Mr. McCormick, who has written the best biography of Santayana, nonetheless sees the work as a *roman à thèse*, like Walter Pater's *Marius the Epicurean*, rather than as an *Erziehungsroman* or *Bildungsroman*, insofar as Santayana is supposed to deny "the possibility of *Erziehung* or *Bildung*, conceptions that assume a chameleon changeability at the center of the human psyche making for drama, for domination of experience, no matter what its derivation or direction." And he quotes Santayana's own account of Oliver: "while not an ordinary boy, he must be a boy at first, and grow older step by step, while remaining the same person. *I don't believe in development of character* [McCormick's emphasis]; the *character* is always the same; but there is a progress from innocent to mature ways of giving that character expression" (McCormick, 327–28). But Santayana is simply maintaining his belief in a core of selfhood, not his disbelief in the unfolding of that self—its movement through different critical stages in a temporal medium, and according to a certain logic of philosophical alternatives and consequences. That is what this chapter is about.

8. And it is what makes his independent income an ironic blessing. Santayana no doubt grants it to him because, after his own mother's death in 1912, he himself had one, and because, as an early form of MacArthur Fellowship, it allows his hero to think out philosophical problems undistracted by pecuniary necessities. But the income also cuts Oliver off from other people, exacerbating a tendency to withdrawal that is already there psychologically. He and Santayana nonetheless try to use their money charitably, and as a way of connecting with people. Santayana's Sturgis-derived resources were considerable: he was worth $600,000 in 1945 (that is nearly $6,000,000 in today's money), and was able to gift the needy but not very grateful Russell with £500 in 1937. The gift was anonymous, but Russell did know who had given it (see McCormick, 373, and Ronald William Clark, *The Life of Bertrand Russell*, 456).

9. Santayana, "Why I am not a Marxist," 78–79.

10. Santayana evidently learnt a great deal from his father's traditionalism in art (he was an amateur painter) and agnosticism in religion, and he often quoted his phrases. See McCormick, 109 and passim. But the determinative fact of his young life was this separation from his father and the ensuing feeling that he never really belonged to the city of Boston, the "Great Merchant" Sturgis family (to which his mother was connected through her first marriage), America, and indeed the world itself. Significantly, he called the world his "host," upon which he was somehow a parasite, an outsider, though more "inside" than an immigrant Midwesterner like Thorstein Veblen ever was (see Daniel Aaron, "A Postscript," 225–26). Along with a feeling of alienation, naturally, went one of tragedy, which was most unAmerican. Oliver's contemporaries at Harvard achieved so little, Santayana thought, because they never really understood that life ends in death, that there is no personal God to give meaning to either the one or the other, and that the joke of the cosmos is on us (see letter to Henry Ward Abbott, January 16, 1887, *Letters*, 14–15). The joke was played on him, he too harshly felt, almost from the moment of fertilization—this sperm from that father: "That fact that he was my father, whose character and destiny were strikingly represented, with variations, in my own, called up a lurid image of what my life in the world was likely to be: solitary, obscure, trivial, and wasted" (*Persons*, 424).

11. The public-spirited side of Harriet is very unlike Santayana's own mother, who deliciously told the president of the Roxbury Plato Club, who wondered what she did with herself: "In winter I try to keep warm, and in summer I try to keep cool"—to which Santayana adds that "Diogenes could not have sent the President of the Plato Club more curtly about her business" (*Persons*, 32). But she and Harriet are similarly distant from and dominant over their sons, concerned that their education should produce a conventional "*persona fina*," "virtuous and enlightened," rather than that it should widen their interests or pleasures and clear their way "to important actions or interesting friendships" (*Persons*, 33). Just ten months before his death in 1952, Santayana told Bruno Lind that "The relation between Peter and his wife was *emotionally* based on that between my father and mother, but *historically* the two cases are contraries. He had money in the novel; she had it in real life, what little there was of it. But my father, if he had been very rich and yet independent of the world . . . would have lived much as Peter did, and would have behaved towards me as Peter did to Oliver" (qtd. in William G. Holzberger, "The Significance of the Subtitle," 243). As he said in *Realms of Being*, "We sometimes find that the mother we love is not the mother we should have liked" (qtd. in McCormick, 16).

12. Santayana, *The Last Puritan*, 1.112; hereafter cited in the text implicitly.

13. Santayana, *Egotism in German Philosophy*, 215; hereafter cited in the text implicitly or as *Egotism*.

14. Santayana, *Interpretations of Poetry and Religion*, 144–45; hereafter cited in the text implicitly or as *Interpretations*.

15. Homosexuality must be part of what Santayana referred to when, in a letter, he spoke of "the dangerous sides of the book—and it has more than one such—[which] seem to have been overlooked or timidly ignored by the critics." He was disappointed that nobody noticed, for prior to publication he had praised fiction as "the only living art," wherein "now it seems possible to print what in earlier days we hardly ventured to whisper" (*Letters*, 309, 207). To pursue this subsidiary subject:

    Santayana said in 1929 that "I suppose Housman was really what people nowadays call 'homosexual' . . . I think I must have been that way in my Harvard days—although I was unconscious of it at the time." He would hardly have remained unconscious had he been at the other Cambridge, especially at King's College among the Apostolic "buggers," as Lytton Strachey and his friends called themselves. The young Forster was in this sense on the Apostolic periphery. In America, Santayana continued, "our prejudices against it ['Paiderastia'] are so strong that it hardly comes under the possibilities for us. What shall we do?" Certainly he never married, though at Harvard there was considerable pressure to do so: President Eliot's "doubts and fears about a man so abnormal as Dr. Santayana" clearly had to do as much with his mysterious celibacy as with his contemplative detachment, brilliant eyes, and military cape (qtd. in McCormick, 51, 71, 97).

    In any event, I concur with H. T. Kirby-Smith (*A Philosophical Novelist*, 129) that W. H. Auden, reviewing *My Host the World* in 1952, and other critics since have been impertinent in criticizing Santayana for treating homosexuality (or for that matter heterosexuality) as a "distraction to the healthy psyche." His fondness for his male colleagues and students at Harvard or for Jim's original, the handsome charming predatory Frank Russell, whom he all but worshipped with an ardor like that of Copperfield for the similarly Byronic Steerforth, was quite as innocently clueless, with regard to sexual expression, as was the relationship between Tennyson and Arthur Hallam. His sexless celibacy, in good part the result of what Mr. Kirby-Smith calls the emotional "emasculation" he suffered during his bicontinental, broken-home childhood, was central to his character, and I would say he made the best of it. All the more credit is due him, given the early twentieth century's culture of obligatory heterosexuality and the later twentieth century's culture of obligatory "follow your promptings" sexuality of any sort. Cf. Joseph Epstein ("George Santayana," 326) and Irving Singer (*George Santayana*, 59), both of whom rightly object to Mr. McCormick's too-positive insistence that Santayana was knowingly gay. He was first and last interested not in sex but in intimate though cool friendship, based, as in Aristotle, on "the pursuit of common ideals" (*Reason in Society*, qtd. in Singer 60). And he roundly disapproved of Oscar Browning's openly pederastic comportment at King's as unsuitable "for a teacher of youth," which the authorities ought to have suppressed but didn't (*Persons*, 435).

Readers can profit from Ross Posnock's excellent essay about "genteel androgyny" in Santayana, Henry James, and Howard Sturgis, this last being one model for Mario (see *Persons*, 359–60). Though I think Mr. Posnock describes a younger Santayana more aware of his own sexual inclinations than the record seems to indicate, he has valuable insights into the philosopher's pro- "fop," pro-feminine protests against the red-blood masculinists of the day, and he nicely differentiates the ways in which these three authors acted on their indeterminate sexual feelings: "Sturgis's flamboyant effeminacy, Santayana's fastidious, immaculate asexuality, and James's passionate sublimations represent three efforts to mitigate both the nervous repressions of the genteel and the aridity of pragmatic Americanism" (Genteel Androgyny, 61–62). Unfortunately, the "asexuality" that Santayana viewed as an ascetic renunciation, to be only mildly regretted, and that freed him to concentrate on reading, thinking, and writing, Mr. Posnock views as a kind of crucifixion—something a genteel, homophobic Boston society coerced him into (67–68). That is not altogether the way Santayana remembered things, but it is certainly evident that he felt suffocated in the Puritan capital, and for reasons that were sometimes indefinable. His castrating mother, for instance. But Mr. Posnock tends to blame her too exclusively for her son's inability to trust his own body's impulses or to get close to other people (71–72, 79). His case is like Oliver's in this regard, and some of the "blame," if we must point a finger, must be shared by his absent father. As we have seen with Lawrence, a little dandling, a little wrestling, a little handiworking with the father can help a boy find ways to discover and exercise his masculine energies, and get past androgynous indecisions.

Finally, there is Robert Dawidoff's piece on Santayana's critique of the "genteel tradition," which underscores the degree to which his sense of being out of the sexual mainstream increased his critical distance from the political, philosophical, business, literary, even sartorial mainstream (*The Genteel Tradition and the Sacred Rage*, 153–58). One does notice, however, the reluctance of most critics, including Mr. Dawidoff, to grant Santayana's own Platonic logic—his feeling (which he makes Oliver share) that renunciation of sex is the natural next step for a young person who has discovered the hollowness of that kind of love, be it gay or straight. Of course it is true that, this side of renunciation, a feeling of sexual otherness will compel a person to understand and criticize the wider society he or she lives in, but that is also true of several sorts of otherness—in Santayana's case, being a Spaniard among New Englanders, a raised Catholic among Protestants, a Boston Latin graduate at Harvard among alumni of St. Paul's and Groton, and so on.

Less ample on Santayana, but of considerable interest for his Cambridge milieu, is Kim Townsend's *Manhood at Harvard* (see especially 138–49).

16. Santayana, *Three Philosophical Poets*, 88; hereafter cited in the text implicitly or as *Three Philosophical Poets*.

17. Frank Russell was Bertrand's older brother, and three years younger than Santayana. Russell had been sent down from Oxford for committing buggery with Lionel Johnson, and when his housemaid's sister brought a breach-of-promise suit years later, he was threatened with exposure of his other homosexual escapades. In a letter, Santayana described Russell as "the ablest man, all round, that I have ever met. . . . He isn't good, that is he is completely selfish and rather cruel. . . . But then both practically and intellectually

he is really brilliant" (qtd. in McCormick, 67). Russell seems in fact to have treated Santayana with boorish contempt, but the latter bore all with an unattractive mixture of snobbery and self-abasement: "I am quite willing to stand anything, however outrageous, that comes from a certain quality" (68; see also 61–62, 77–78, 122). There are things in every author's life that one would rather not know.

18. Santayana, "Apologia Pro Mente Sua," 581; hereafter cited in the text implicitly or as "Apologia."

19. Santayana, "A Brief History of My Opinions," xvi.

20. Actually based on an essay by one of Santayana's pupils at Cambridge University (see *Persons*, 394).

21. In the "Prologue" Santayana qualifies what I am noting here—Oliver's resistance to Marxism as well as fascism. Since Catholicism and the monk's life were impossible to a skeptic and Nordic like him—as a Catholic one forgets life is a mission and thinks it a picnic, Santayana says, and how Oliver hated picnics!—if he had lived he would have become a communist, "capable of imposing no matter what regimen on us by force" (1.9). He would have liked the Bolshies' Puritanic scorn of compromise. Well, Marxism did indeed become the religion of more than a few intellectuals after the 1917 *Revolution*, but one should remember that Santayana wasn't one of them. As he writes in *Persons and Places*, "I love Tory England and honour conservative Spain, but not with any dogmatic or prescriptive passion. If any community can become and wishes to become communistic or democratic or anarchical I wish it joy from the bottom of my heart. I have only two qualms in this case: whether such ideals are realisable, and whether those who pursue them fancy them to be exclusively and universally right: an illusion pregnant with injustice, oppression, and war" (227). Which is presumably why he told Edmund Wilson, who visited him in the convent at Rome after World War II, that the United States was called, not by Manifest Destiny but "in the natural course of things," to oppose Russian totalitarianism: "not to do so was to make '*il gran rifiuto*'" (Wilson, *Europe Without Baedeker*, 45).

22. Cf. Levinson, "Pragmatic Naturalism and the Spiritual Life," 83.

23. This, and the fact that he was morally unintelligent. He couldn't understand why logic didn't produce love, or understand evil even when he did it himself. If, Santayana goes on, Shelley had read Spinoza he would have seen that nothing is evil in itself. "Evil is an inevitable aspect which things put on when they are struggling to preserve themselves in the same habitat, in which there is not room or matter enough for them to prosper equally side by side." It is all very well to ask cancer-microbes to be reasonable, but they can't listen to reason. They go on propagating unless exterminated utterly. "And fundamentally men are subject to the same fatality exactly; they cannot listen to reason unless they are reasonable; and it is unreasonable to expect that, being animals, they should be reasonable exclusively. . . . [T]hey are not more capable of sacrificing themselves to what does not interest them than the cancer-microbes are of sacrificing themselves to men" ("Shelley," 241–42). This entire essay, a study of a kind of English romantic Puritan, repays careful reading.

EPILOGUE

1. Morris, *About Fiction*, 61.
2. Woolf, "How Should One Read a Book?" 259.
3. Goethe, *Campaign in France*, 652.
4. Updike, *Hugging the Shore*, 777.

Bibliography

Aaron, Daniel. "A Postscript to *The Last Puritan*." 1936. In Price and Leitz, 223–31.

Ackroyd, Peter. *Dickens*. New York: HarperCollins, 1990.

Aiken, Conrad. "*The Last Puritan*." 1936. In Price and Leitz, 37–38.

Allingham, William. *William Allingham: A Diary*. Ed. Helen Allingham and D. Radford. London: Macmillan, 1907.

Andrews, Malcolm. *Dickens and the Grown-Up Child*. Iowa City: University of Iowa Press, 1994.

apRoberts, Ruth. *Arnold and God*. Berkeley: University of California Press, 1983.

Arcana, Judith. "I Remember Mama: Mother-Blaming in *Sons and Lovers* Criticism." *The D. H. Lawrence Review* 21 (1989): 137–51.

Ariès, Philippe. *Centuries of Childhood: A Social History of Family Life*. Trans. Robert Baldick. New York: Knopf, 1962.

———.*The Hour of Our Death*. Trans. Helen Weaver. New York: Knopf, 1981.

Arnold, Matthew. *The Complete Prose Works of Matthew Arnold*. Ed. R. H. Super. 11 vols. Ann Arbor: University of Michigan Press, 1960–1977.

Ashton, Rosemary. *The German Idea: Four English Writers and the Reception of German Thought, 1800–1860*. Cambridge: Cambridge University Press, 1980.

Bakhtin, M. M. "The *Bildungsroman* and Its Significance in the History of Realism (Toward a Historical Typology of the Novel)." In *Speech Acts and Other Late Essays*. Trans. Vern W. McGee. Ed. Caryl Emerson and Michael Holquist. Austin: University of Texas Press, 1986. 10–59.

Bandelin, Carl. "*David Copperfield*: A Third Interesting Penitent." 1976. In Bloom, 21–30.

Barzun, Jacques. *From Dawn to Decadence: 500 Years of Western Cultural Life, 1500 to the Present*. New York: HarperCollins, 2000.

Baym, Nina. "Revision and Thematic Change in *The Portrait of a Lady*." 1976. In *Henry James's Portrait of a Lady*. Ed. Harold Bloom. New York: Chelsea, 1987. 71–86.

Beauman, Nicola. *Morgan, a Biography*. London: Hodder & Stoughton, 1993.

Beddow, Michael. *The Fiction of Humanity: Studies in the Bildungsroman from Wieland to Thomas Mann*. Cambridge: Cambridge University Press, 1982.

Bell, Millicent. *Meaning in Henry James*. Cambridge: Harvard University Press, 1991.

Bell, Rudolph M. *Holy Anorexia*. Chicago: University of Chicago Press, 1985.

Benjamin, Walter. "The Storyteller." 1936. In *Illuminations*. Trans. Harry Zohn. New York: Schocken, 1969. 83–109.

Black, Michael. *D. H. Lawrence, Sons and Lovers*. Cambridge: Cambridge University Press, 1992.

———. *The Literature of Fidelity*. London: Chatto and Windus, 1975.

Blackall, Eric A. *Goethe and the Novel*. Ithaca, NY: Cornell University Press, 1976.

Blackmur, Richard P. *Studies in Henry James*. New York: New Directions, 1983.

Bloom, Harold, ed. *David Copperfield*. Major Literary Characters Series. New York: Chelsea, 1992.

Bly, Robert. *Iron John: A Book about Men*. Reading, MA: Addison-Wesley, 1990.

———. *The Sibling Society*. New York: Addison-Wesley, 1996.

Boening, John, ed. *The Reception of Classical German Literature in England, 1760–1860: A Documentary History from Contemporary Periodicals.* 10 vols. New York: Garland, 1977.

Bonhoeffer, Dietrich. *Letters and Papers from Prison.* 1953. Trans. Eberhard Bethge. London: Fontana, 1959.

Boyle, Nicholas. *Goethe: The Poet and the Age. Vol. 1: The Poetry of Desire (1749–1790).* Oxford: Clarendon, 1991.

———. *Goethe: The Poet and the Age. Vol. 2: Revolution and Renunciation (1790–1803).* Oxford: Clarendon, 2000.

Britten, Benjamin. "Some Notes on Forster and Music." 1969. In Stallybrass, 81–86.

Brown, Tony. "E. M. Forster's *Parsifal*: A Reading of *The Longest Journey.*" *Journal of European Studies* 12 (1982): 30–54.

Bruford, W. H. *The German Tradition of Self-Cultivation: Bildung from Humboldt to Thomas Mann.* Cambridge: Cambridge University Press, 1975.

Buckley, Jerome Hamilton. "The Identity of David Copperfield." In *Victorian Literature and Society: Essays Presented to Richard D. Altick.* Ed. James R. Kincaid and Albert J. Kuhn. Columbus: Ohio State University Press, 1984. 225–39.

———. *Season of Youth: The* Bildungsroman *from Dickens to Golding.* Cambridge: Harvard University Press, 1974.

Buckton, Oliver S. " 'My Undisciplined Heart': Declassifying Homoerotic Secrets in *David Copperfield.*" *ELH* 64 (1997): 189–222.

Burra, Peter. "The Novels of E. M. Forster." 1934. In Bradbury, 21–33.

Carey, John. *The Violent Effigy: A Study of Dickens' Imagination.* London: Faber, 1973.

Carlyle, Thomas. "Goethe." 1827. In *Wilhelm Meister's Apprenticeship and Travels,* by Wolfgang von Goethe. Trans. Thomas Carlyle. Vols. 22–23 of the Centennial Memorial Edition. Boston: Dana Estes, n.d. 22.13–33.

———. *Two Note Books of Thomas Carlyle.* Ed. Charles Eliot Norton. New York: Grolier Club, 1892.

———. *Reminiscences.* Ed. Charles Eliot Norton. London: Dent-Everyman, 1932.

Carlyle, Thomas and Jane Welsh. *The Collected Letters of Thomas and Jane Welsh Carlyle.* Ed. Charles Richard Sanders and Kenneth J. Fielding. 31 vols. to date. Durham, NC: Duke University Press, 1970–.

Carré, Jean-Marie. *Bibliographie de Goethe en Angleterre.* Paris: Plon-Nourrit, 1920.

Cavaliero, Glen. *A Reading of E. M. Forster.* London: Macmillan, 1979.

Chesterton, G. K. *Chesterton on Dickens.* Vol. 15 of *The Collected Works of G. K. Chesterton.* Ed. Alzina Stone Dale. San Francisco: Ignatius Press, 1989.

Clark, Ronald William. *The Life of Bertrand Russell.* New York: Knopf, 1976.

Collins, Philip. *Charles Dickens:* David Copperfield. Studies in English Literature 67. London: Edward Arnold, 1977.

Colmer, John. *E. M. Forster: The Personal Voice.* London: Routledge and Kegan Paul, 1975.

Conn, Peter. "Paternity and Patriarchy: *The Last Puritan* and the 1930s." 1991. In Price and Leitz, 272–89.

Craig, Gordon A. "The Unread Giant." Review of *Goethe: The Poet and the Age, Vol. I,* by Nicholas Boyle. *Atlantic Monthly* (April 1991): 102–05.

———. "Germany's Greatest." Review of *Goethe: The Poet and the Age, Vol. II,* by Nicholas Boyle; *Das Goethe-Tabu,* by W. Daniel Wilson, and other books. *New York Review of Books* (April 13, 2000): 52–57.

Crews, Frederick C. *E. M. Forster: The Perils of Humanism.* Princeton: Princeton University Press, 1962.

Crick, Brian. " 'Mr. Peggotty's Dream Come True': Fathers and Husbands, Wives and Daughters." *University of Toronto Quarterly* 54 (1984): 38–55.

Crury, Patrick. "The Victorian Goethe Critics: Notions of Greatness and Development." *Victorian Institute Journal* 13 (1985): 31–58.

Darby, Margaret F. "Dora and Doady." *Dickens Studies Annual* 22 (1993): 155–69.

Das, G. K. and Beer, John, eds. *E. M. Forster: A Human Exploration: Centenary Essays.* New York: New York University Press, 1979.

Dawidoff, Robert. *The Genteel Tradition and the Sacred Rage: High Culture vs. Democracy in Adams, James, and Santayana.* Chapel Hill: University of North Carolina Press, 1992.

De Quincey, Thomas. "Goethe as Reflected in His Novel of 'Wilhelm Meister.' " 1824. In Vol. 6 of *The Works of Thomas De Quincey.* Boston: Houghton Mifflin, 1877. 443–83.

DeLaura, David J. "Heroic Egotism: Goethe and the Fortunes of *Bildung* in Victorian England." In *Johann Wolfgang von Goethe: One Hundred and Fifty Years of Continuing Vitality.* Ed. Ulrich Goebel and Wolodymyr T. Zyla. Lubbock: Texas Tech Press, 1984. 41–60.

Dickens, Charles. *The Personal History of David Copperfield.* 1849–1850. New Oxford Illustrated Dickens. London: Oxford University Press, 1948.

———. "Number-Plans." In Jeremy Tambling, ed., *David Copperfield.* By Charles Dickens. London: Penguin, 1996. 814–55.

Dilthey, Wilhelm. *Das Erlebnis und die Dichtung: Lessing, Goethe, Novalis, Hölderlin.* 1913. Göttingen: Vandenhoeck and Ruprecht, 1921.

Draper, R. P., ed. *D. H. Lawrence: The Critical Heritage.* London: Routledge, 1970.

Dupee, F. W. *Henry James.* New York: Sloane, 1951.

Eckermann, Johann Peter. *Conversations of Goethe with Eckermann.* 1836–1848. Trans. John Oxenford. 1850. London: Dunne, 1901.

Edel, Leon. *Henry James, a Life.* New York: Harper & Row, 1985.

Edwards, Simon. "*David Copperfield:* The Decomposing Self." 1985. In *David Copperfield and Hard Times.* Ed. John Peck. New York: St. Martin's, 1995. 58–80.

Eigner, Edwin M. "*David Copperfield* and the Benevolent Spirit." *Dickens Studies Annual* 14 (1985): 1–15.

Eliot, George. "The Morality of Wilhelm Meister." 1855. In *Essays of George Eliot.* Ed. Thomas Pinney. New York: Columbia University Press, 1963. 143–47.

———. *Selections from George Eliot's Letters.* Ed. Gordon S. Haight. New Haven: Yale University Press, 1985.

Ellis, David. *D.H. Lawrence: Dying Game, 1922–1930.* Cambridge: Cambridge University Press, 1998.

Epstein, Joseph. "George Santayana and the Consolations of Philosophy." 1987. In *Partial Payments.* New York: Norton, 1989. 320–45.

Erikson, Erik H. *Childhood and Society.* 2d. edition. New York: Norton, 1963.

Farr, Judith. "D. H. Lawrence's Mother as Sleeping Beauty: The 'Still Queen' of His Poems and Fictions." *Modern Fiction Studies* 36 (1990): 195–209.

Feidelson, Charles. "The Moment of *The Portrait of a Lady.*" 1968. In *The Portrait of a Lady.* By Henry James. Ed. Robert D. Bamberg. New York: Norton, 1975. 741–51.

Finkelstein, Bonnie Blumenthal. *Forster's Women: Eternal Differences.* New York: Columbia University Press, 1975.

Fitzgerald, F. Scott. *The Short Stories of F. Scott Fitzgerald: A New Collection.* Ed. Matthew J. Bruccoli. New York: Scribner's, 1989.

Forster, E. M. *Abinger Harvest.* New York: Harcourt, 1936.

———. *Aspects of the Novel.* New York: Harcourt, 1927.

———. "Breaking Up." *The Spectator* (July 28, 1933): 119.

———. "Aspect of a Novel." 1960. Rpt. as "Author's Introduction" in Elizabeth Heine, lxvi–lxx.

———. *Albergo Empedocle and Other Writings.* Ed. George H. Thomson. New York: Liveright, 1971.

Forster, E. M. "A Conversation with E. M. Forster." With Angus Wilson. *Encounter* (November 1957): 52–57.

———. "E. M. Forster on His Life and His Books: An Interview Recorded for Television." With David Jones. *Listener* (January 1, 1959): 11–12.

———. *Goldsworthy Lowes Dickinson*. New York: Harcourt, 1934.

———. *Howards End*. 1910. New York: Knopf, 1954.

———. Introduction. *The Lord of the Flies*. By William Golding. New York: Coward-McCann, 1962. ix–xiii.

———. *The Longest Journey*. 1907. New York: Vintage, 1962.

———. "Looking Back." *The Cambridge Review* (October 22, 1960): 58.

———. *Marianne Thornton: A Domestic Biography 1797–1887*. New York: Harcourt, 1956.

———. "Memoirs" (written in the early 1920s to be read before the Bloomsbury Memoir Club). In Elizabeth Heine, 293–306.

———. "The Old School." 1934. In Elizabeth Heine, 290–92.

———. *A Passage to India*. New York: Harcourt, 1924.

———. *A Room with a View*. 1908. New York: Knopf, 1923.

———. *Selected Letters of E. M. Forster, Vol. 2: 1921–1970*. Ed. Mary Lago and P. N. Furbank. Cambridge: Harvard University Press, 1985.

———. *Two Cheers for Democracy*. New York: Harcourt, 1951.

Forster, John. *The Life of Charles Dickens*. 1872–1874. 2 vols. London: Chapman and Hall, 1908.

Furbank, P. N. *E. M. Forster: A Life*. 2 vols. New York: Harcourt, 1977–1978.

———. "The Philosophy of E. M. Forster." 1982. In Herz and Martin, 37–51.

Gay, Peter. "The 'Legless Angel' of *David Copperfield*: There's More to Her Than Victorian Piety." *New York Times Book Review* (January 22, 1995): 22.

Gilmour, Robin. "Memory in *David Copperfield*." *The Dickensian* 71 (1975): 30–42.

Goethe, Johann Wolfgang von. *Campaign in France 1792. Seige of Mainz*. 1793. Trans. Thomas P. Saine. Ed. Thomas P. Saine and Jeffrey L. Sammons. In Vol. 5 of *Goethe's Collected Works*. 12 vols. Princeton: Princeton University Press, 1994. 618–776.

———. *Wilhelm Meister's Apprenticeship and Travels*. 1795–1796; 1829. Trans. Thomas Carlyle. 1824. Vols. 22–23 of the Centennial Memorial Edition. Boston: Dana Estes, n.d. (Cited treating Vol. 22 as Vol. 1, and Vol. 23 as Vol. 2.)

———. *Wilhelm Meister's Apprenticeship*. 1795–1796. Trans. Eric A. Blackall and Victor Lange. 1989. Princeton: Princeton University Press, 1995.

Greene, Graham. *Collected Essays*. 1969. New York: Viking, 1983.

Habegger, Alfred. *Gender, Fantasy, and Realism in American Literature: The Rise of American Literary Realism in W. D. Howells and Henry James*. New York: Columbia University Press, 1982.

Hardin, James, ed. *Reflection and Action: Essays on the* Bildungsroman. Columbia: University of South Carolina Press, 1991.

Hardy, Barbara. "The Moral Art of Dickens: *David Copperfield*." 1970. In *Charles Dickens's David Copperfield: Modern Critical Interpretations*. Ed. Harold Bloom. New York: Chelsea House, 1987. 9–19.

Harris, Janice H. "Lawrence and the Edwardian Feminists." In *The Challenge of D. H. Lawrence*. Ed. Michael Squires and Keith Cushman. Madison: University of Wisconsin Press, 1990. 62–76.

Hayek, F. A. *John Stuart Mill and Harriet Taylor: Their Correspondence and Subsequent Marriage*. Chicago: University of Chicago Press, 1951.

Hecht, Anthony. *Obbligati: Essays in Criticism*. New York: Atheneum, 1986.

Hegel, G. W. F. *Aesthetics: Lectures on Fine Art*. 1832. Trans. T. M. Knox. 2 vols. Oxford: Clarendon, 1975.

Heine, Elizabeth. Introduction and notes to *The Longest Journey*. By E. M. Forster. London: Arnold, 1984. vii–lxv.

Heine, Heinrich. *Heinrich Heine: Selected Works*. Trans. and ed. Helen M. Mustard. New York: Random, 1973.

Herz, Judith Scherer and Martin, Robert K., eds. *E. M. Forster: Centenary Revaluations*. Toronto: University of Toronto Press, 1982.

Herz, Judith Scherer. "The Double Nature of Forster's Fiction: *Room with a View* and *The Longest Journey*." *English Literature in Transition* 21 (1978): 254–65.

———. " 'This is the End of Parsival': The Orphic and the Operatic in *The Longest Journey*." 1997. In Martin and Piggford, 137–50.

Hesse, Hermann. "Gratitude to Goethe." In *My Belief: Essays on Life and Art*. Trans. Denver Lindley. Ed. Theodore Ziolkowski. New York: Farrar, Straus and Giroux, 1974.

Hollington, Michael. "*David Copperfield* and *Wilhelm Meister*: A Preliminary *Rapprochement*." *Q/W/E/R/T/Y: arts, literatures & civilisations du monde anglophone* 6 (1996): 129–38.

Holzberger, William G. "The Significance of the Subtitle of Santayana's Novel *The Last Puritan: A Memoir in the Form of a Novel*." 1991. In Price and Leitz, 232–55.

House, Humphry. *The Dickens World*. 2d. edition. London: Oxford University Press, 1942.

Howe, Susanne. *Wilhelm Meister and His English Kinsmen: Apprentices to Life*. New York: Columbia University Press, 1930.

Hutton, Richard Holt. "Goethe and His Influence." 1855. In *Literary Essays*. New York: Macmillan, 1871.

Inman, Billie Andrew. *Walter Pater's Reading: A Bibliography of His Library Borrowings and Literary References, 1858–1873*. New York: Garland, 1981.

Isherwood, Christopher. *Down There on a Visit*. New York: Simon and Schuster, 1961.

Jackson, Arlene M. "Agnes Wickfield and the Church Motif in *David Copperfield*." *Dickens Studies Annual* 9 (1980): 53–65.

James, Henry. *The Portrait of a Lady*. 1881. Vols. 3–4 of *The Novels and Tales of Henry James*. New York Edition. New York: Scribner's, 1908. (Cited treating this edition's Vol. 3 as *Portrait's* Vol. 1, and Vol. 4 as Vol. 2.)

———. *What Maisie Knew*. 1897. Vol. 11 of *The Novels and Tales of Henry James*. New York Edition. New York: Scribner's, 1908.

———. *The Complete Notebooks of Henry James*. Ed. Leon Edel and Lyall H. Powers. New York: Oxford University Press, 1987.

———. *Literary Criticism: French Writers, Other European Writers, The Prefaces to the New York Edition*. New York: Library of America, 1984.

Jeffrey, Francis. "Wilhelm Meister's Apprenticeship." 1824. In *Contributions to the Edinburgh Review*. Vol. 1. London: Longman's, 1844. 257–301.

Jenkyns, Richard. *The Victorians and Ancient Greece*. Cambridge: Harvard University Press, 1980.

Johnson, Diane. "Introduction." *What Maisie Knew*. By Henry James. New York: Modern Library, 2002. xi–xviii.

Jordan, John O. "The Social Sub-Text of *David Copperfield*." *Dickens Studies Annual* 14 (1985): 61–92.

Kaplan, Fred. *Dickens, a Biography*. New York: Morrow, 1988.

Kincaid, James. "The Structure of *David Copperfield*." *Dickens Studies* 2 (1966): 74–95.

———. *Dickens and the Rhetoric of Laughter*. Oxford: Clarendon, 1971.

Kinkead-Weekes, Mark. *D.H. Lawrence: Triumph to Exile, 1912–1922*. Cambridge: Cambridge University Press, 1996.

Kirby-Smith, H. T. *A Philosophical Novelist: George Santayana and* The Last Puritan. Carbondale: Southern Illinois University Press, 1997.

Knoepflmacher, U. C. "From Outrage to Rage: Dickens's Bruised Femininity." *Dickens and Other Victorians: Essays in Honor of Philip Collins*. Ed. Joanne Shattock. New York: St. Martin's, 1988. 75–96.

Krook, Dorothea. *The Ordeal of Consciousness in Henry James*. Cambridge: Cambridge University Press, 1962.

Larkin, Philip. *Collected Poems*. Ed. Anthony Thwaite. New York: Farrar, Straus, and Giroux, 1989.

———. *Required Writing: Miscellaneous Pieces, 1955–1982*. New York: Farrar, Straus, and Giroux, 1984.

Lawrence, D. H. *The Complete Poems of D. H. Lawrence*. Ed. Vivian de Sola Pinto and F. Warren Roberts. New York: Viking, 1971.

———. *Fantasia of the Unconscious*. 1922. In *Psychoanalysis and the Unconscious and Fantasia of the Unconscious*. Intro. Philip Rieff. New York: Viking, 1960. 53–225.

———. "Foreword." 1913. In *Sons and Lovers*. Cambridge Edition. Ed. Helen and Carol Baron. London: Penguin, 1994. 467–73.

———. *The Letters of D. H. Lawrence, Vol. 1, September 1901-May 1913*. Ed. James T. Boulton. Cambridge: Cambridge University Press, 1979.

———. *The Letters of D. H. Lawrence, Vol. 2, June 1913-October 1916*. Ed. George J. Zytaruk and James T. Boulton. Cambridge: Cambridge University Press, 1981.

———. *The Letters of D. H. Lawrence, Vol. 6, March 1927–November 1928*. Ed. James T. Boulton, Margaret H. Boulton, with Gerald M. Lacy. Cambridge: Cambridge University Press, 1991.

———. *Phoenix: The Posthumous Papers of D. H. Lawrence*. Ed. Edward D. McDonald. New York: Viking, 1936.

———. *Phoenix II: Uncollected, Unpublished, and Other Prose Works by D. H. Lawrence*. Ed. F. Warren Roberts and Harry T. Moore. New York: Viking, 1970.

———. *Psychoanalysis and the Unconscious*. 1921. In *Psychoanalysis and the Unconscious and Fantasia of the Unconscious*. Intro. Philip Rieff. New York: Viking, 1960. 3–49.

———. *Sons and Lovers*. 1913. Cambridge Edition. Ed. Helen and Carl Baron. 1992. London: Penguin, 1994.

———. *Women in Love*. 1920. Cambridge Edition. Ed. David Farmer, Lindeth Vasey, and John Worthen. Intro. and notes by Mark Kinkead-Weekes. 1987. London: Penguin, 1995.

Lawrence, Frieda von Richthofen. "*Not I, but the Wind . . .*" New York: Viking, 1934.

Leavis, F. R. *Anna Karenina and Other Essays*. 1967. New York: Simon and Schuster, 1969.

Leavis, Q. D. "Dickens and Tolstoy: The Case for a Serious View of *David Copperfield*." In *Dickens the Novelist* (with F. R. Leavis). New York: Pantheon, 1970. 34–117.

———. "The Englishness of the English novel." In *Collected Essays, Volume One: The Englishness of the English Novel*. Ed. G. Singh. Cambridge: Cambridge University Press, 1983. 303–27.

Levinson, Henry Samuel. "Pragmatic Naturalism and the Spiritual Life." *Raritan* 10 (1990): 70–86.

Lewes, George Henry. *The Life of Goethe*. 1864. New York: Ungar, 1965.

Lougy, Robert E. "Remembrances of Death Past and Future: A Reading of *David Copperfield*." *Dickens Studies Annual* 6 (1977): 72–101.

Lukács, Georg. *Essays on Thomas Mann*. Trans. Stanley Mitchell. New York: Grosset and Dunlap, 1965.

———. *Goethe and His Age*. 1947. Trans. Robert Anchor. London: Merlin, 1968.

Mailer, Norman. *The Prisoner of Sex*. Boston: Little, Brown, 1971.

Mann, Thomas. "Germany and the Germans." In *Thomas Mann's Addresses Delivered at the Library of Congress*. 1945. Washington: Library of Congress, 1963. 47–66.

———. *The Magic Mountain*. 1924. Trans. H.-T. Lowe-Porter. New York: Knopf, 1968.

Martin, Richard. *The Love that Failed: Ideal and Reality in the Writings of E. M. Forster*. The Hague: Mouton, 1974.

Martin, Robert K. "The Paterian Mode in Forster's Fiction: *The Longest Journey* to *Pharos and Pharillon*." 1982. In Herz and Martin, 99–112.

Martin, Robert K. and George Piggford, eds. *Queer Forster*. Chicago: University of Chicago Press, 1997.

Martini, Fritz. *"Bildungsroman*—Term and Theory." Trans. Claire Baldwin and James Hardin. 1991. In Hardin, 1–25.

Matthiessen, F. O. *American Renaissance: Art and Expression in the Age of Emerson and Whitman*. New York: Oxford University Press, 1941.

May, Brian. *The Modernist as Pragmatist: E. M. Forster and the Fate of Liberalism*. Columbia: University of Missouri Press, 1997.

McConkey, James. "Two Anonymous Writers, E. M. Forster and Anton Chekhov." 1979. In Das and Beer, 231–44.

McCormick, John. *George Santayana, a Biography*. New York: Knopf, 1987.

Meyers, Jeffrey. *D. H. Lawrence, a Biography*. New York: Knopf, 1990.

Miles, Jack. *God, a Biography*. New York: Random, 1995.

Mill, John Stuart. *Autobiography*. 1873. Ed. Jack Stillinger. Boston: Houghton Mifflin, 1969.

———. *The Later Letters of John Stuart Mill, 1849–73*. Ed. Francis E. Mineka and Dwight N. Lindley. Toronto: University of Toronto Press, 1972.

———. *The Letters of John Stuart Mill*. Ed. Hugh S. R. Elliot. 2 vols. London: Longman's, 1910.

———. *On Liberty*. 1859. Ed. David Spitz. New York: Norton, 1975.

Miller, D. A. *The Novel and the Police*. Berkeley: University of California Press, 1988.

Miller, J. Hillis. *Charles Dickens: The World of His Novels*. 1958. Bloomington: Indiana University Press, 1969.

———. *Versions of Pygmalion*. Cambridge: Harvard University Press, 1990.

Millett, Kate. *Sexual Politics*. Garden City, NY: Doubleday, 1970.

Minden, Michael. *The German Bildungsroman: Incest and Inheritance*. Cambridge: Cambridge University Press, 1997.

Mintz, Alan. *George Eliot and the Novel of Vocation*. Cambridge: Harvard University Press, 1978.

Moretti, Franco. *The Way of the World: The Bildungsroman in European Culture*. London: New Left [Verso], 1987.

Morris, Wright. *About Fiction: Reverent Reflections on the Nature of Fiction with Irreverent Observations on Writers, Readers, and Other Abuses*. New York: Harper & Row, 1975.

Mumford, Lewis. "The Genteel Tradition at Bay." 1931. In Price and Leitz, 27.

Needham, Gwendolyn B. "The Undisciplined Heart of David Copperfield." *Nineteenth-Century Fiction* 9 (1954): 81–107.

Nietzsche, Friedrich. *Daybreak: Thoughts on the Prejudices of Morality*. 1881. Trans. R. J. Hollingdale. Cambridge: Cambridge University Press, 1982.

Novalis [Friedrich von Hardenberg]. *Schriften*. 2d. edition. Vol. 3. Ed. Paul Kluckhohn and Richard Samuel. Stuttgart: Kohlhammer, 1960.

Nuttall, A. D. *Openings: Narrative Beginnings from the Epic to the Novel*. Oxford: Clarendon, 1992.

Orwell, George. " 'Such, Such Were the Joys.' " In *In Front of Your Nose, 1945–1950*. Vol. 4 of *The Collected Essays, Journalism and Letters of George Orwell*. Ed. Sonia Orwell and Ian Angus. New York: Harcourt, 1968. 330–69.

Pater, Walter. *The Renaissance: Studies in Art and Poetry*. 1893. Ed. Donald L. Hill. Berkeley: University of California Press, 1980.

Poirier, Richard. *The Comic Sense of Henry James: A Study of the Early Novels*. New York: Oxford University Press, 1960.

Poovey, Mary. *Uneven Developments: The Ideological Work of Gender in Mid-Victorian England*. Chicago: University of Chicago Press, 1988.

Porte, Joel. "Introduction." *New Essays on* The Portrait of a Lady. Ed. Joel Porte. Cambridge: Cambridge University Press, 1990. 1–31.

Posnock, Ross. "Genteel Androgyny: Santayana, Henry James, Howard Sturgis." *Raritan* 10 (1991): 58–84.

Price, Kenneth M. and Robert C. Leitz, III, eds. *Critical Essays on George Santayana*. Boston: G. K. Hall, 1991.

Raina, Badri. *Dickens and the Dialectic of Growth*. Madison: University of Wisconsin Press, 1986.

Redfield, Marc. *Phantom Formations: Aesthetic Ideology and the* Bildungsroman. Ithaca, NY: Cornell University Press, 1996.

Reed, T. J. *The Classical Centre: Goethe and Weimar 1775–1832*. New York: Barnes and Noble, 1980.

Rivkin, Julie. *False Positions: The Representational Logics of Henry James's Fiction*. Stanford: Stanford University Press, 1996.

Roberts, David. *The Indirections of Desire: Hamlet and Goethe's "Wilhelm Meister."* Heidelberg: Carl Winter, 1980.

Rosecrance, Barbara. *Forster's Narrative Vision*. Ithaca, NY: Cornell University Press, 1982.

Rosenbaum, S. P. *"The Longest Journey:* E. M. Forster's Refutation of Idealism." 1979. In Das and Beer, 32–54.

Rowe, John Carlos. *The Other Henry James*. Durham, NC: Duke University Press, 1998.

Russell, Bertrand. *The Autobiography of Bertrand Russell, 1872–1914*. New York: Bantam, 1968.

Sammons, Jeffrey L. "The Bildungsroman for Nonspecialists: An Attempt at Clarification." 1991. In Hardin, 26–45.

Santayana, George. "Apologia Pro Mente Sua: A Rejoinder." In *The Philosophy of George Santayana*. Ed. Paul Arthur Schilpp. Evanston: Northwestern University Press, 1940. 497–605.

———. "A Brief History of My Opinions." 1930. In Vol. 2 of *The Works of George Santayana*. Triton Edition. 15 vols. New York: Scribner's, 1936–1940. vii–xxvii.

———. *Egotism in German Philosophy*. 1915. In Vol. 6 of the Triton Edition. 145–249.

———. "English Liberty in America." 1920. *Character and Opinion in the United States*. In Vol. 8 of the Triton Edition. 108–30.

———. *Interpretations of Poetry and Religion*. 1900. In Vol. 2 of the Triton Edition. 3–201.

———. *The Last Puritan: A Memoir in the Form of a Novel*. 1936. Vols. 11 and 12 of the Triton Edition. (Cited treating this edition's Vol. 11 as *Last Puritan's* Vol. 1, and Vol. 12 as Vol. 2.)

———. *The Letters of George Santayana*. Ed. Daniel Cory. New York: Scribner's, 1955.

———. "Shelley." 1913. In Vol. 2 of the Triton Edition. 227–52.

———. *Three Philosophical Poets*. 1910. In Vol. 6 of the Triton Edition. 3–142.

———. "Why I am not a Marxist." *Modern Monthly* 9 (April 1935): 77–79.

Schiller, Friedrich. *Correspondence between Schiller and Goethe*. Trans. L. Dora Schmitz. 2 vols. London, 1877.

———. *On the Aesthetic Education of Man: In a Series of Letters*. 1793. Ed. and Trans. Elizabeth M. Wilkinson and L. A. Willoughby. Oxford: Clarendon, 1967.

Scott, P. J. M. *E. M. Forster: Our Permanent Contemporary*. New York: Barnes and Noble, 1984.

Semmel, Bernard. *John Stuart Mill and the Pursuit of Virtue*. New Haven: Yale University Press, 1984.

Shaffner, Randolph P. *The Apprenticeship Novel: A Study of the "Bildungsroman" as a Regulative Type in Western Literature with a Focus on Three Classic Representatives by Goethe, Maugham, and Mann*. New York: Peter Lang, 1984.

Simpson, Hilary. *D. H. Lawrence and Feminism*. DeKalb: Northern Illinois University Press, 1982.

Singer, Irving. *George Santayana, Literary Philosopher*. New Haven: Yale University Press, 2000.

Slater, Michael. *Dickens and Women*. London: Dent, 1983.

Spender, Stephen. *The Struggle of the Modern*. 1963. Berkeley: University of California Press, 1965.

Stallybrass, Oliver, ed. *Aspects of E. M. Forster: Essays and Recollections Written for His Ninetieth Birthday January 1, 1969*. London: Edward Arnold, 1969.

Stewart, Garrett. "Mr. Micawber's Novel." 1974. In Charles Dickens, *David Copperfield*. Ed. Jerome H. Buckley. New York: Norton, 1990. 836–42.

Stone, Wilfred. *The Cave and the Mountain: A Study of E. M. Forster*. Stanford: Stanford University Press, 1966.

———. "E. M. Forster's Subversive Individualism." 1982. In Herz and Martin, 15–36.

———. "Forster on Profit and Loss." 1979. In Das and Beer, 69–78.

———. " 'Overleaping Class': Forster's Problem in Connection." *Modern Language Quarterly* 39 (1978): 386–404.

Swales, Martin. *The German Bildungsroman from Wieland to Hesse.* Princeton: Princeton University Press, 1978.

Tambling, Jeremy. "Introduction." *David Copperfield.* By Charles Dickens. London: Penguin, 1996. vii–xxii.

Tanner, Tony. "The Fearful Self: Henry James's *The Portrait of a Lady.*" 1965. In *Henry James: Modern Judgments.* Ed. Tony Tanner. London: Macmillan, 1969. 143–59.

Taylor, Andrew. *Henry James and the Father Question.* Cambridge: Cambridge University Press, 2002.

Townsend, Kim. *Manhood at Harvard: William James and Others.* New York: Norton, 1996.

Trilling, Lionel. *E. M. Forster.* New York: New Directions, 1943.

Troeltsch, Ernst. "The Ideas of Natural Law and Humanity in World Politics." 1922. Trans. Ernest Barker. In *Natural Law and the Theory of Society.* By Otto Gierke. Cambridge: Cambridge University Press, 1950. 201–22.

Updike, John. *Hugging the Shore: Essays and Criticism.* New York: Knopf, 1983.

Van Ghent, Dorothy. *The English Novel: Form and Function.* 1953. New York: Harper-Perennial, 1967.

Virgil. *The Aeneid.* Trans. Robert Fitzgerald. New York: Knopf-Everyman, 1992.

Warshow, Robert. *The Immediate Experience: Movies, Comics, Theatre and Other Aspects of Popular Culture.* 1962. Enlarged edition. Cambridge: Harvard University Press, 2001.

Watt, Ian. *The Rise of the Novel: Studies in Defoe, Richardson and Fielding.* Berkeley: University of California Press, 1957.

Weinstein, Philip. "Mr. Peggotty and Little Em'ly: Misassessed Altruism?" 1984. In Bloom, 83–88.

Welsh, Alexander. *From Copyright to Copperfield: The Identity of Dickens.* Cambridge: Harvard University Press, 1987.

Westburg, Barry. "David Sees 'Himself' in the Mirror." 1977. In Bloom, 31–46.

Williams, Raymond. *Keywords: A Vocabulary of Culture and Society.* New York: Oxford University Press, 1983.

Wilson, Angus. *The World of Charles Dickens.* London: Penguin, 1972.

Wilson, Edmund. *Europe without Baedeker: Sketches among the Ruins of Italy, Greece and England, Together with Notes from a European Diary, 1963–1964.* 1947. New York: Farrar, Straus, and Giroux, 1966.

———. *The Triple Thinkers: Twelve Essays on Literary Subjects.* 1938. Rev. and enlarged edition. New York: Oxford University Press, 1948.

Wilson, W. Daniel. *Goethe-Tabu: Protest und Menschenrechte im klassischen Weimar.* Munich: Verlag, 1999.

Woolf, Virginia. "David Copperfield." 1925. In *The Moment and Other Essays.* New York: Harcourt, 1948. 75–80.

———. "How Should One Read a Book?" 1926. In *The Second Common Reader.* Ed. and Introduction by Andrew McNeillie. New York: Harcourt, 1986. 258–70.

Worthen, John. *D.H. Lawrence: The Early Years, 1885–1912.* Cambridge: Cambridge University Press, 1991.

Wright, Robert. *The Moral Animal: Evolutionary Psychology and Everyday Life.* New York: Random, 1994.

Index

In sub-headings, connectives such as "and," "in," and "of" are usually implicit.